Storm Constantine's
'Wraeththu Mythos'

Presents

Breeding Discontent

Wendy Darling & Bridgette M Parker

IMMANION
PRESS

Stafford, England

Storm Constantine's Wraeththu Mythos: Breeding Discontent
By Wendy Darling and Bridgette M Parker
© 2003

Cover by Eirian (http://eirian.net)
Art Direction and Typesetting by Gabriel Strange
Editor: Storm Constantine

Set in Souvenir

First edition, Immanion Press, 2003

0 9 8 7 6 5 4 3 2 1

1st Immanion Press Edition
http://www.immanionpress.wox.org/
info@immanionpress.wox.org

ISBN 0-9545-0362-7

Printed in the UK

Storm Constantine's Wraeththu Mythos

Breeding Discontent

Also in the Wraeththu Mythos

The Wraeththu Chronicles
The Enchantments of Flesh and Spirit (2003)
The Bewitchments of Love and Hate (2003)
The Fulfilments of Fate and Desire

The Wraeththu Histories:
The Wraiths of Will and Pleasure

Coming Soon

The Wraeththu Chronicles
The Fulfilments of Fate and Desire (2003)

The Wraeththu Histories:
The Wraiths of Will and Pleasure (UK Edition)
The Shades of Time and Memory (UK Edition)

Other Products
Wraeththu from Enchantment to Fulfilment

Joint Acknowledgments

We both would like to offer our undying thanks to Storm Constantine for not only embracing and publishing this book, but the way she has inspired and assisted both of us to change our lives. Through her books and stories, her example, her friendship and her lessons in writing and editing, both of us have been guided onto paths we didn't expect to ever find. We would also like to point out what an outstanding example Storm is as an author open and friendly with not just fans, but fan-fiction writers. She allows everyone to share, knowing the creative energy will expand and feed us all without dying itself.

Tremendous thanks also goes out to the fan-fiction community that nurtured us and then egged us on as we wrote what turned out to be an epic. While our co-workers and families were sometimes saying, "What are you doing, all this writing?" the online fans were simply clamoring for more. Their feedback and enthusiasm endowed this story with strength and also gave us the confidence and dedication to go through the labor of editing it for publication. It is our hope that original fans of the online story will enjoy this version even more than the original.

Other thanks start with Gabriel Strange and Lydia Wood of Immanion Press, who've both worked hard to support the publication of this book, taking care of actual production and marketing. Eirian, creator of this book's sexy cover, has also put in a lot of time, going so far as to read the manuscript and then doing revisions as us picky authors fussed over hair and jewelry.

We would also like to thank Mischa Laurent, known as the "father of Wraeththu fan fiction," who created the 'Forever' web site to host Wraeththu fan fiction (and weekly chats) and also started the "Pinkboard," where authors could post works in progress and enjoy feedback from readers and fellow writers. Mischa's spirit of generosity as well as extreme good humor made Forever a very homey place.

Acknowledgments from Wendy Darling

Naturally of all the people I need to thank for the success of this novel, my collaborator Bridgette Parker is at the top of the list. Without Bridgette, her friendship, and her talents for writing, not only would this book never have come into being, but I would have been a lot more miserable.

Two other Wraeththu fans also deserve my thanks: Addie Fielding, an online friend who first introduced me to Wraeththu; and Kris Dotto, whose feedback on the story and late night YIM chats with me fed my mind.

On a more familial note, I of course must offer thanks to my family, especially my Mom and Dad, Richard and Hannah Darling, for putting up with all my creative outbursts (literally) as a child and the way they allowed me to develop my own interests and outlets instead of ever telling me what to do.

On a related note, I'd like to thank my dear friend Caleb Racicot for "allowing" me to write even though he thought possibly there were better (and healthier) things I could be doing with my time.

Also thanks to 'Outwriters', a writers' group here in Atlanta (part of 'Outworlders', a queer sf/fantasy/horror group) that's helped me hone my writing and who provided valuable feedback on the opening chapter.

Finally, thanks to Susanna Farina, who is bonded to me in soul to the point I don't mind how many thousands of miles away she is or that she already has a partner.

Acknowledgments from Bridgette Parker

In addition to the wonderful people we've acknowledged together, my deepest thanks go to my wonderful husband, Paul Parker, who patiently allowed me hours of time monopolizing our Internet connection and never failed to treat my writing as important "work" even before publication became an issue. And although he's yet to read my work, he was always responsive when I talked about what he termed the "hermaphrodite baby factory." Paul has never failed to exhibit faith in my ability to become a successful published writer; in fact he's carried enough faith for the both of us.

Thanks and appreciation also go out to my family and friends who showed so much enthusiasm, patience, and open-mindedness when I told them about this book and then endeavored to explain it to them! In fact, I personally dedicate this book to my parents, Donald and Roxanne Morvant. Mama and Daddy have always encouraged my interest in writing and this story in particular has reminded me of how lucky I am to have grown up with two loving and deeply devoted parents. So much of what I am, I can trace back to these two individuals.

Last but never least is my wonderful co-author, Wendy Darling. I will never cease to be amazed by the way that the magic of online fan fiction brought together two completely different young women who found themselves to be kindred spirits. Wendy has unrelenting patience, staggering talent and creativity, and unimaginable stores of energy. In addition to being an acclaimed online writer and editor, she is truly central to the very heart and soul of the Wraeththu fandom. Thank you, Wendy.

Introduction

By Storm Constantine

This novel began life in the world of fan-fiction, a vast phenomenon especially prevalent on the Internet, in which writers create new stories and characters set in existing worlds; fantasy or science fiction worlds being among the most popular. I wrote the first Wraeththu trilogy back in the 80s, and am currently working on a new one, but for many years I was unaware of the creative impulses Wraeththu had inspired in others. This book is one of the best examples of what good writers can do with a previously created mythos, in that the story becomes "shared world," rather than simple fan-fiction. It is "part of canon," which means it fits well with the novels and stories I have written myself, and actually extends them without compromising existing work.

There have been many fan-fiction stories involving the Wraeththu, to be found on various web sites, and when I was told where to find them, I realized that a lot of them were very good indeed. "Breeding Discontent" was the first to leap out at me. Once I started Immanion Press, I wanted to publish some of the fan-fiction, and "Breeding Discontent" was the obvious first candidate. I was impressed with the authors' feel for the world of Wraeththu, even though they had come at it from a different viewpoint to my own.

I spoke to Wendy and Bridgette about the whole creative process, and we decided the best introduction for this book would be a kind of interview between us, to show readers how the ideas developed and the writing process worked.

So, the first question has to be: *How did you two meet?*

Wendy told me, "Notably, up through the completion of the manuscript, Bridgette and I have never actually 'met' except via email, bulletin boards and online chat. We've never even talked on the phone. Once I sent flowers to her home in Texas (and she sent me flowers back) so I know she does exist, but... He he.

"Seriously, Bridgette and I first encountered one another as part of an online 'fandom,' where both of us were reading and writing fan fiction. Over the course of some months we went beyond simply commenting on one another's writing and on to mutual editing instead. From there we turned into 'online pals.' When we both got into Wraeththu, our mutual fan fiction interests, editing and online friendship continued, which is how *Breeding Discontent* eventually came to be."

Bridgette adds, "I also have to give my online friendship with Wendy credit for introducing me to Storm's writing. Wendy, and other members of the fan-fiction community, recommended Wraeththu to me. As soon as I finished the original trilogy, Wendy and I eagerly shared our thoughts by emailing discussion questions back and forth and *Breeding Discontent* soon followed."

I think it's interesting the way the ideas for the story developed between you. One thing that fascinates some readers is the idea of hermaphroditic beings reproducing amongst themselves. This was obviously a fascination you shared. Can you tell us more about how this developed into a full-length story?

Wendy: "Bridgette and I had already spent a lot of time developing Wraeththu fan fiction stories on our own, when one day, exchanging email, we discovered we had both come up with similar, related ideas. Mine started off as some Wraeththu hara discovering a har who'd been forced into becoming a harling-maker. I pictured them finding him locked up in a cabin somewhere with all these harlings, which are Wraeththu children. He'd been chained up there, and his Varr masters (a warlike Wraeththu tribe) had made him keep producing harlings, then had abandoned him, at some point after their war with the Gelaming tribe. I hadn't really thought too much beyond that, except it was something tragic, dramatic and, as usual for me, having to do with pearls, Wraeththu procreation."

Bridgette: "And my idea was to follow the life of a har who'd been indoctrinated with a 'gender role' via the Varrs designation of 'progenitors.' A big inspiration in all this was the various degrees in which girls are conditioned in human societies past and present, as far as being pretty, being encouraged to like 'girly' things, decorating themselves, wearing makeup, etc."

Wendy: "After exchanging our ideas, it seemed like there was a common thread of soume (more feminine) hara being brainwashed and exploited by the Varrs, and once we had that, we began *Breeding Discontent*."

It's not always an easy process collaborating on a book. How did you go about it?

Wendy: "Well, the truth is, it's rather hard to come up with a simple answer. It was definitely a lot more work than it probably would have been for one person. Imagine if you had more than one brain! One thing I do think needs to be made clear is that we didn't write this novel like a role-playing game, with one of us 'playing' Lisia and the other writing the present-day scenes. Instead, it's the product of two writers working together extremely closely, developing all chapters together. It's true that for certain sections of the story one of us would write the bulk of an initial draft, but after that we each added our own bits onto the other's work. In Lisia's diary, we are *both* Lisia and, similarly, the present day scenes are the product of us merging our visions. This collaboration involved hundreds of emails, versions of chapters and scenes going back and forth, and lots of online chatting. And that was just for the first draft!"

Bridgette: "I agree most parts of the book are a complete collaboration. For example, Wendy might email me a five-page chapter and I'd email it back to her expanded to ten pages. Writing together might have been more work, but I definitely think the result was worth the effort."

You worked really hard and quickly on the rewrite of the novel, to make it more suitable for professional publication. How long did the book take to write from start to finish?
Wendy: "The original draft of the story was written, and posted to the Internet, over the course of about six months, during late 2001 and the winter and spring of 2002. It was originally posted to the 'Pinkboard,' which is for Wraeththu fan fiction in progress. Later the whole story was posted to my fan fiction web site, Procreation. The story is no longer online. Once we'd begun work on the final version, rewriting and editing took about four months."

Every writer is always asked how much of themselves appears in a story. Would you say that Breeding Discontent *has shades of the autobiographical?*

Wendy: "There's a lot of both of us in the story, both in terms of specific incidents and recurring themes. For example, Bridgette and I both like to talk about dreams, especially ones that seem symbolic, and in the story there are several dreams. The dream in which Lisia imagines he's ouana (male-aspected) with another hostling was actually based on some very

11

strange, confusing dreams I had during a time when I was struggling with gender and sexuality issues.

"There are also some sections of the story that are there simply because one or the other of us really wanted to explore the concept. I was very interested in writing about a harling undergoing feybraiha (the coming of age rite) and I was also keen to write about hosting (Wraeththu pregnancy) and pearl delivery. While I didn't write all the final scenes on those topics, it was an interest of mine, and in the initial draft I know I pushed some of those topics."

Bridgette: "When this question was asked, Wendy reminded me of a detail I'd forgotten. I based the scene where the facility director talks Lisia out of quitting is based on an incident from my girlhood when a teacher talked me out of my desire to delay my Confirmation. In fact, while I recall Wendy as being the first person to suggest setting the facility in an old convent, I definitely used imagery and experiences from my own Catholic school past. And while I've always have considered Lisia to have a personality all his own, he and I definitely share the trait of having started out life as a bit of a goody-two-shoes and becoming more cynical with the passage of time."

Do you think that Breeding Discontent has a message for its readers?

Wendy: "A lot of the story deals with the effects and remedies of brainwashing and exploitation. We wanted to show Wraeththu who were not learning from the mistakes of humanity but repeating those mistakes.
"We also liked the idea of showing an atrocity or 'war crime' that was not something blatant, like a concentration camp or a pile of bodies, but something that was the product of a more controlled, 'genteel' plan. It's a more *subtle* form of violence and oppression. Lisia is never physically beaten and his upbringing is filled with caring. He is well educated in some regards, he's allowed to be happy, but there is an underlying cruelty in all of it. He lives in a place with pretty gardens, learns to sing and dance and write poetry, is taught all this nice stuff, but in the end he's treated like a breeding stock animal... and he really doesn't even know it."

Bridgette: "I definitely agree with Wendy about the subtlety. We were both determined to create a contrast to the sort of overt 'evil' described so well in Fulminir in *The Bewitchments of Love and Hate*. By that same token, the indoctrination of the 'Lilies' creates an interesting reflection of human society, as we mentioned before. And while there is nothing at all intrinsically wrong with gender identification, I also wanted to explore the institutionalized discrimination that often goes hand in hand with a strict observance of gender roles. A hermaphroditic har provides an ideal protagonist for this because of the innate equality that comes from the absolute removal of physical gender.

"When we embarked on the rewrite of our fan-fiction draft for Immanion Press, the opportunity to explore more political issues evolved as well. This is interesting since Wendy and I have notably different political views. I suppose that readers could come away with a message about the autonomy of conquered nations – but I think that the book has a very moderate, common sense sort of stance."

For some readers, fan-fiction will be something new. Can you expand a little about its world, and how you feel about it?
Wendy: "Although I've always written a lot, if it hadn't been for finding fan fiction a few years ago, I'm not sure when or if I would ever have really started to write fiction, either short stories or novels like this. (I had written a ton of essays, reports, autobiographical stuff, poetry, but never fiction really.)

"Taking part in online fan fiction communities allowed me to follow my impulse and develop my writing, as I explored parts of books and fictional worlds that I'd always wanted to explore. In some cases, this was strongly discouraged by the originators of the books and worlds in question, but thankfully I eventually found Wraeththu, where I found as much freedom as I could ever want.

"As Bridgette and I worked on the original draft of this story and posted it online, we got heaps of feedback from members of the Wraeththu fan fiction community. It was a delight and a special pleasure (not enjoyed by regular novelists) to get 'instant feedback' on each chapter as we posted. It was not only flattering to find them enjoying it, but also a chance for us to gauge if readers reacted to the material as we expected. I remember one instance where, in the original draft, we managed to get a lot of readers very angry with one of the characters and because of this, we ended up making him a 'good guy' by the end. Some readers' feedback eventually made its way into sequels to this story, since there were things we couldn't cover, such as what happened to certain characters after the end."

Bridgette: "I'd like to add that writing fan-fiction and participating in the feedback process has done more to teach me the craft of writing fiction than any class or textbook.

"Also, the fan-fiction community has often been my introduction to new authors or movies and television shows, which have inspired me to seek out the original works. Many opponents of fan-fiction fear that amateur works take away from the rights and income of the copyright holders, but in many cases the opposite is true."

Speaking of things that are new, and online fandom, do you have any recommendations for those who are new to the world of Wraeththu and might want to have some background information before reading this novel?

Wendy: "Well, I'm glad you asked that because I'm a webmaster for several such sites and fans of even more. For a general reference to Wraeththu (which will really help people out, especially with the biology and basic stuff) I'd strongly recommend Trish's creation, 'The Wraeththu Companion', http://www.metrogirl.com/wcompanion/. Of course there's your site, http://www.stormconstantine.com, as well, which will connect people with just about anything else out there related to Wraeththu or your other writings and interests."

You have written a great many Wraeththu stories, but you also have original works in progress too. What are your plans for the future?

Wendy: "Now that I actually work as an editor for Immanion Press, and have explored as a writer what initially inspired me to create Wraeththu stories, I will concentrate mainly on material based in worlds of my own invention. In fact, I have the beginnings of fantasy novel already completed, just put on the back burner while I've been working on *Breeding Discontent*. But I will never disrespect fan fiction. In fact, if anybody ever wants to write fan fiction based upon my work, that's OK with me. What a hypocrite I'd be otherwise!"

Bridgette: "Once I'm done with *Breeding Discontent*, I'm looking forward to being able to catch up on my reading. Specifically, I have several fan-fiction friends who've been left without a "beta reader" (fan-fiction editor) while I've concentrated on the book. I'm looking forward to possible opportunities to further the Wraeththu Mythos, and I'm also feeling inspired to work on some completely original stories as well."

'Forever' fan-fiction web site: http://www.angelfire.com/ca6/forever/

If you would like to be notified of future Immanion Press publications as they are released, please join our mailing list:

Or write to:
Immanion Press
8 Rowley Grove
Stafford ST17 9BJ
England

Or via E-mail:
info@immanionpress.wox.org

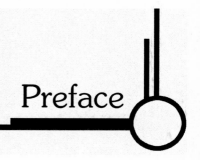

Preface

I really don't know how much longer I can keep this up. Nobody is ever going to come for us! The fall harvest is coming in and it's true we have food now, but for how much longer? Winter comes fast and I don't know how to make the food last. For the harlings, especially the oldest, I act strong and brave and full of hope, but I don't feel it inside anymore. Did I ever feel it? I think part of me always expected that we were all going to die, but I just couldn't think about it then. I wonder if one day, a long time from now, hara will find this diary, even if it's too late to find us. I wonder what they'll think of it – probably that I've been a fool.

Chapter One

The Gelaming army had ceased to be greatly surprised by anything they encountered. Lost, slightly backward Wraeththu tribes, hidden weapons depots, pockets of human refugees, and gruesome reminders of Varrish oppression were found throughout this part of Megalithica. Many of these discoveries had already been catalogued and put on the list of matters to be resolved by the new Parsic administration. Still, if this was a Varr military installation, it was apparently going to be a bit different from any they'd investigated so far.

"Look at this, General," Captain Paran Nemish urged, gesturing to the right. Coming down the path from the mountains, they'd entered a small forested valley. They hadn't known precisely what to expect — reconnaissance had only noted a large structure, no other details given — but even so, they found themselves rather puzzled at the sight before them.

"Flowerbeds," General Ashmael Aldebaran remarked. Edged by a border of fruit trees, heavy with ripening fruit, the beds stretched out for several acres. "I notice they're not in the best of care." Some of the plantings were wilted, obviously not having been properly watered or nurtured. A few were overcome with weeds.

"It makes sense," Paran said as they passed around the bend and toward what they presumed would be the entrance to the driveway. "Off in the back woods like this, I wouldn't be surprised if they're still ignorant of the change in Megalithica. Probably they have other priorities besides tending their flowers — like defending themselves from the onslaught of 'terrible, bloodthirsty Gelaming.'"

Ashmael nodded with a small, grim smile at Paran's little jest. This location was extremely isolated, the nearest town a good 50 miles distant and that only a small trading village. When the village hara had been questioned about any sort of military installation in the mountains to the north, they hadn't had the slightest idea. This was confirmed when Listener Edrei Faraliesse executed a brief mind scan, at Ashmael's request. Their thoughts revealed that, yes, occasionally Varr soldiers had come through the area and there had been some limited trading, but locals had always assumed the soldiers were simply passing through. However, earlier-gathered intelligence from Fulminir, the now-defunct seat of power, indicated to the Gelaming that the Varr military had, at one time, sent a great deal of supplies to an unspecified location in this general vicinity.

Ashmael's scouting group had ridden up through the mountains not knowing what to expect. They'd left behind an entire troop of hara, camped several miles back in the wilderness awaiting orders. Now, however, Ashmael began to wonder whether he would have any orders to issue. What type of military installation planted flowerbeds in the wilderness? From what Ashmael had observed, most Varr encampments had been ensconced in old human buildings, with the surrounding areas blighted by neglect and warfare. None of their institutions had been adorned with landscaping; only the private estates of the wealthiest and most secure Varr leaders had ever possessed such frivolities.

A metal gate that stretched across a long, gravel driveway marked the entrance to this mysterious compound. The plantings just beyond appeared better tended than those noted earlier. Flowering bushes and colorful blossoms bobbed in the high breeze of the late summer afternoon. On the right stood a sign post with a surprising message: "WELCOME & ATTENTION: No Weapons Beyond This Point."

Nearly every har in the small group began murmuring comments regarding the unexpected notice. "What on earth is that about? Any ideas, tiahaar?" asked Paran, turning to their commander.

"We'll find out shortly, I'm sure," the general answered, frowning. There was no order to dispense with their weapons, which, Gelaming or no, they possessed in plenty, ready for any eventuality. The sign was presumably a remnant of former authority. Since liberating Megalithica several months earlier, the Gelaming had remained consensually to police the territory, though it was technically governed by the native leadership they had placed in power. If the tenants of this particular bastion were still blissfully unaware of the change in circumstances, Ashmael was not about to deliver the message unarmed.

The general ordered one of his soldiers to dismount and open the gate. The hinges squealed in protest: Clearly they had not been oiled recently or put to much use.

As the group passed through, a dozen Gelaming warriors and their otherworldly horses, *sedim*, Ashmael issued an order to halt. He called out to Edrei, their Listener, trained to gather information from the ethers. What could he sense, up beyond the hedges? Surely that was where they would find the reported structure. Was it populated?

Edrei acknowledged the order and let his eyes go blank as psychically he scanned the area. A ripple of emotion — surprise? — flitted across his face as he put his finely honed senses to use. Always valuable in investigations of this sort, Edrei was rarely in error.

"It's harlings, General," he announced finally, his gaze snapping into focus.

"Harlings?" Ashmael asked, intrigued. "How many?" Harlings on a military installation surrounded by flowers and with a sign warning against weapons — this situation grew more interesting all the time.

"I can't tell you exactly, General," Edrei explained apologetically, "but I'm getting the impression it's more than a few — I'd say... maybe as many as a hundred."

"A *hundred?*" Now this was something for which Ashmael had not been prepared. "We're outnumbered by harlings!" He chuckled, mildly amused by the notion, if not yet ready to dismiss the need for caution. "Do you think they're any threat?"

Edrei shrugged. "I... I don't think so. I mean, they're not... Well, they're certainly not hostile. They're just harlings."

Ashmael prompted his *sedu* to move a little way up the drive. "A hundred harlings," he mused. "Perhaps the Varrs are even more advanced in that regard than we thought. And what of adults, tiahaar? Any sense of hara?"

Edrei shook his head. "No, tiahaar, I didn't catch that, but that doesn't mean they're not there. I would assume they *must* be there — they wouldn't have left that many harlings unprotected, even if they *are* Varrs. They could possibly be shielding themselves."

"That seems reasonable to assume," Ashmael remarked. "Let's go in." He turned to regard his hara briefly before moving forward. "Remain alert."

With that, the group proceeded up the drive, following the curve up the rise, where a thick line of hedges cut off any glimpse of what lay beyond. Flowerbeds continued along the sides of the drive, these plants clearly the recipients of more attention than those further out on the periphery. Snapdragons bobbed their heads as the soldiers passed, while clusters of daisies stood at attention.

Finally they made it beyond the hedges and gained a view of their mysterious destination. It was a large structure of dark brick, two floors, and had the appearance of an old-fashioned human institution.

"Looks like an old school," Ashmael remarked. "Or maybe even a convent or monastery." He nodded, confident in his observations

"Certainly a religious institution; I see a cross on the roof." When these words yielded no response, Ashmael checked the faces of his companions. "You do know about human religions, don't you?"

"I'm sorry, but not really, General," Corporal Karan admitted. The youngest of the group, he was a pure-born Wraeththu. Unlike the rest who had been metamorphosed by Wraeththu blood from men into physically and psychically gifted hermaphrodites, Karan had never been human or lived during a time when human ways still dominated. Ducking his head in embarrassment, he continued, "I know what crosses were about but I'm not sure—"

"It's really rather sad," Ashmael interrupted. "An example of humanity's obsessive separation of the two genders and fear of sexual freedom. There was a huge emphasis on chastity. A convent was a place where humans, specifically women called nuns, lived in isolation from society."

"But why would they do that?" the corporal asked. "Did somehar — men, I would guess — force them to?"

"Not really," Ashmael replied, feeling impatient at having to offer the clarification. "Men had their own isolated sects in monasteries. The isolation was part of their religious system; their lives were to be devoted to worship and study, and sexuality was to be left out of that. In any case, this is generally the sort of building they used to live in and obviously such a large structure in the middle of nowhere would have to have some very specific purpose."

"We appreciate your insight, General," Paran said.

"Being ancient does have its advantages," Ashmael conceded with a wry smile.

As they continued up the drive, however, all thoughts of the building or human religious practices vanished, replaced with a spectacle Edrei's scan had predicted, but for which the army party was not quite prepared: harlings, in great abundance.

The soldiers brought their *sedim* to a halt as before them more than fifty harlings looked over across the yard. It was clear to Ashmael that the children represented a range of ages, some as young as three, but there appeared to also be some young hara, certainly not far past their feybraiha, the time of Wraeththu maturation, which usually begins between the ages seven and eight.

Ashmael's sharp mind quickly began cataloging the harlings, just as he would any other group of unknown hara he encountered on a mission. The harlings wore stunned expressions, their bodies suddenly frozen amid their tasks. Ashmael took note of their toil-dirtied appearance and the way their clothing hung loosely on their thin bodies. It was suddenly easy to realize what harlings might be doing on a Varr military compound; as slave labor Wraeththu children would be much hardier than sickly, desperate humans.

. Clearly, the older harlings were running the show, overseeing domestic chores like washing and hanging clothes and linen, while the younger ones appeared to be busy with plantings, as they sat on the ground amid dozens of small flowerpots and trowels. In one corner of the yard, a group was tending to a vegetable garden. They now stood staring, baskets of beans and squash hanging from their arms.

Ashmael urged his *sedu* onward and then halted at the edge of the yard, where the long entryway ended, and dismounted. The others followed suit and as they did, the harlings broke from their gawking freeze and began to rush forward, their shocked faces suddenly breaking into broad smiles.

"Oh, tiahaara, we're so glad you're here!" cried a fair-skinned one, reddish-blond hair hanging long, almost to his waist. Despite being dirty from work, it was obvious that the dress he was wearing, a loose-fitting silken robe, was quite an elegant garment, embroidered with colored beads all around the neckline. The clothing was strange indeed, quite incongruous with the strenuous work that was taking place in the yard. Ashmael noted the dainty jewelry hanging from the harling's ears and of course the long hair. Unlike most Wraeththu tribes, members of Varr society had mostly denied the feminine aspects of their natures, except for a select few assigned traditionally female roles. If this harling had long hair, Ashmael presumed, he had no doubt been picked out as a future "progenitor."

It was difficult to ascertain his age; he could have been an older harling or a young har. He was taller than the others and seemed to take the lead. The other harlings stood behind him, also smiling; the younger ones nudged one another, whispering among themselves excitedly. Ashmael observed them closely as he sought to evaluate the situation and form a proper course of action. They were certainly not hostile; in fact the harlings' manner was clearly friendly and welcoming. The group also harbored great curiosity, staring eagerly at the soldiers and their *sedim*. But they were also shy, smiling but casting their glances downward when any of the Gelaming tried to make eye contact.

The harlings were apparently relieved to have visitors and seemed intent on making a favorable impression on Ashmael and his hara, strangers or no. Ashmael noted that most of them, particularly the older ones, were turned out similarly with long hair and elaborate, feminine manners of dress. These almost-hara were a self-conscious bunch as well, nervously smoothing sweat-dampened tresses and furiously brushing at the garden grime smudging their once-elegant garments. Again Ashmael turned an analytical eye to the scene — why would these harlings be so adorned if they were merely military slaves? What other purposes did they serve?

The tall one, who seemed lost in thought amid what had become an awkward silence, shook himself slightly as if suddenly remembering a forgotten protocol. He swept into an overly graceful sort of bow and asked, "How may we be of service to you, tiahaara?" The smile never left his face.

Ashmael cleared his throat. "Hello," he began. It was difficult to know exactly what to say to such an audience; he had never seen so many harlings together, in Megalithica or anywhere else.

All the young ones said hello in return in singsong unison, many also offering respectful bows.

"I am General Ashmael Aldebaran. My colleagues and I will be visiting here. Do you have any stables for our horses?" He addressed his question to the apparent leader of this odd group.

"Oh, of course, tiahaar!" the tall harling purred. He approached the Gelaming leader slowly with a gait that was unmistakably, disconcertingly sensual. As he drew closer, Ashmael noted that despite his height and demeanor, the harling's bare arms were hairless as a newborn's. While clearly the oldest, this redhead hadn't even begun feybraiha, and yet seemed to be offering a come on! *Does he approach all visitors this way?* Ashmael wondered silently.

"There are stables in the rear," the harling continued, gesturing to where two of his companions eagerly waved and beckoned, indicating the stables were back around the corner of the building. Ashmael glanced at his soldiers and signaled for of a few of them to follow. Once the *sedim* were gone, six Gelaming remained. They were still surrounded by smiling, nearly giddy harlings.

The tall harling took another step closer to Ashmael. "We used to have horses of our own and lots of visitors," he said, "but now they're all gone... so the stables are empty."

"I see," Ashmael murmured, processing this additional information and wondering what sort of visitors the harlings were accustomed to.

"My name is Pansea, by the way," the harling offered brightly, before continuing on with his chatter. "We used to have a mule but two weeks ago, we had to kill it for food."

Ashmael glanced at Paran, who merely shrugged. In the meantime the harling added, "Our hostling said we needed the meat."

Pansea twisted a lock of his hair and cast his eyes downward in a move Ashmael was suddenly convinced was calculated.

So there is at least one adult in residence.

A slight frown suddenly erased Pansea's smile. "And, I'm afraid we still don't have much to offer in the way of refreshments, tiahaar. At one time we would have had trays and trays of delicacies for you and your hara, but as you can see," he gestured humbly around, "we weren't expecting visitors." He paused for a moment before smiling brightly and continuing rapidly, "But we have some really lovely, delicious fruit," he gestured toward the harlings with heavily-laden baskets, "and fresh vegetable stew tonight."

"We have our own provisions," Ashmael interjected, hoping to steer the conversation back to more important issues.

But the harling was too quick, "Ah, I see," he answered, a dark flicker crossing his face for just an instant. "How very fortunate. In the meantime, I must see to getting you settled. I'm afraid we no longer have hot running water, but we can start heating some right away."

"Hot water?" Ashmael was growing more and more confused — and impatient.

"For bathing," the harling answered, as if it were obvious.

"Bathing?" Ashmael frowned. This harling's rambling was not heading in the direction the general wanted.

"Oh, I meant no offense, General Aldebaran!" Pansea suddenly appeared quite flustered. "It's just always been the custom, a nice hot bath with attendants before aruna. I suppose we can still do the massages and entertainment." He frowned again and continued in a very apologetic tone, "I assume that you, as the leader of this group, will be the one." He held out his hand gracefully, "Shall we get started, then?"

Ashmael flinched away from the harling's touch. "No!" For several moments after, he simply stared open mouthed. Wraeththu were very open about sexual matters, but this was most unsettling. A smaller harling had even jumped up and down and announced, "I can sing for you while you're waiting for the hot water!" Some of the other soldiers, who had remained quiet until now, whispered disapproving comments regarding the insinuations. Pansea began to look confused.

A myriad of questions fought for dominance in Ashmael's mind. Surprisingly, the one that won out was, "How old are you?"

"Probably late in my sixth year, maybe even seventh," Pansea said, his willowy stature puffing up with obvious pride.

"You aren't sure?" Ashmael asked. He didn't wait for an answer. "You said that your hostling was here. I must speak with him."

"Oh, I'm sorry, tiahaar," Pansea apologized, bowing slightly. "I should of course alert our hostling to your arrival." He summoned two smaller harlings. "Go find Lis! Tell him we have visitors at last! Everything's going to be okay!" The harlings scampered over to the building and went in the main door. "Lis will be so happy you're here!" Pansea exclaimed. "There haven't been any soldiers in such a long time!"

Ashmael was still feeling perplexed, questions swarming left and right. Who was this hostling? Whoever he was, he couldn't be the only har in residence. Otherwise, who could be caring for all these harlings? And where had the harlings come from? They couldn't have sprung up out of the ground like the flowers.

Ashmael's thoughts went to the soldiers Pansea had just mentioned. Was this some sort of Varr musenda staffed by harlings? Ashmael didn't even think such things possible, but after the atrocities they'd discovered at Fulminir, the rotting heart of the Varr empire, he'd come to expect just about anything, including the prostitution of harlings.

He decided to get some information from Pansea while it seemed free for the taking. "I'll be happy to meet with this Lis you speak of. But first I have some questions. And, I must make it clear, whatever purpose has brought soldiers here in the past, that is not why *we* are here. Understand?"

"Yes, tiahaar," Pansea replied, deferentially.

"Thank you," Ashmael said. "First, tell me, your hostling is Lis?"

"Lis is *our* hostling," Pansea corrected. "His whole name is Lisia. We call him Lis." Pansea paused, obviously uneasy. "So, you're not here for aruna."

Ashmael shook his head slowly. He was used to interrogating Varrs, but not Varr children. "No," he answered. "I must speak to whoever is in charge of this facility."

A quick succession of emotions flitted across Pansea's face. "Oh, are you here to take away more of the little ones?"

Ashmael looked down at the assembled harlings. He certainly hadn't planned on returning to camp with a group of harlings, but suddenly he realized that he might be forced to do just that if this place was half as evil as he suspected.

"There are some outside right now if you want to view them." Pansea gestured toward the far side of the building, in the opposite direction from where the soldiers had taken the *sedim*.

"There are *more* of you?" Ashmael asked.

"Well, of course," Pansea answered. "Shall I show you?"

Ashmael nodded, and he and his company followed Pansea as he walked across the broad lawn. Harlings scurried out of the way but hung close about the soldiers' knees. Ashmael continued his questions. "And this Lisia — he hosted some of you?"

"Yes, some of us at least," Pansea agreed. "I don't know which, though — nohar does. There were many different hostlings. Many hostlings and also teachers and helpers and assistants and, of course, the administrators. Now there's only Lis."

Just as they reached back of the building, the soldiers who'd gone to the stables joined up with them. Along with Ashmael and his group, they stood stunned when they saw what was inside large fenced pens at the side of the yard: more harlings.

There had been plenty of them running about outside, but not like these. Most of these harlings were much younger, all under two years old. With an unsettling collective awareness, they stood still, gazing upon the soldiers as if with one eye. At first they did not speak or call out.

There were also some older harlings in the pens, but certainly none older than five. Similar in dress to the ones in the yard, these harlings appeared pleasantly surprised by the arrival of newcomers, but were quickly distracted in their efforts to calm the little harlings, who all at once decided to rush forward inside the pen and offer a rousing "Hello!"

Ashmael stepped back from the fence. Watching the older harlings herd the younger ones into a less crowded configuration, he was reminded of old illustrations of shepherds with sheep. And the harlings seemed little more than that. They were grubby and thin, their faces and arms tanned from the sun. Most were clothed only in long shirts, once brightly colored but now faded and worn.

Some of them didn't have any shirts at all, and it was when some of these harlings turned around that the Gelaming saw the tattoos: strings of characters etched into their flesh in dark ink

"Oh, no..." Paran groaned. "General, I think I know what this might be." Ashmael suspected he'd had the same thought but he didn't interrupt. "Maybe this was a Varr 'farm' and that's why the harlings are branded. Maybe this is where they were growing harlings to take and use for food," Paran shook his head grimly. He and many of the others had been at Fulminir and were all too aware of certain Varrs' occasionally depraved dining habits.

"Hush, Paran," Ashmael warned softly. "I concur with your assessment but I don't want to cause a panic; there are tender ears here."

"And my ears as well!" cut in an angry voice from behind.

Startled, Ashmael wheeled around to face the har who was, without a doubt, the aforementioned hostling, or at least *a* hostling. Ashmael still didn't quite understand what Pansea had been trying to explain to him about that, but as he'd expected of a Varr hostling, this har clearly favored the feminine aspect of his nature. He was striking, with golden-bronzed skin and waist-length hair the color of caramel, and an unusual yellow forelock that framed his face on one side. Like the harlings, he was clothed in elaborate but dingy skirts.

"How *dare* you!" the har challenged in a fierce whisper. "I overheard your remarks and I must say, you have a lot of gall. I've never heard a more insulting, and altogether vile and disgusting, insinuation before in my entire life! Who *are* you? And what are you doing with the harlings?"

"You must be Lisia," Ashmael said dryly.

Lisia did not reply but instead stood imperiously awaiting an answer to his question, with one hand on his hip, the other hand extended to clasp the hand of a young harling. Clinging to his skirts were three more — none more than six months old, or so Ashmael guessed. In the meantime the penned harlings once again rushed forward, this time crying "Lis," waving and jumping up and down to get his attention.

Ashmael straightened up and, turning away from the distracting scene, prepared for an official interaction. "Tiahaar, I am General Ashmael Aldebaran of the Gelaming army, and a member of the Hegemony in Immanion."

"Ah, I should have known; you certainly don't look like Varr soldiers. So have you won? Is that what gives you license to stomp in here—" Lisia broke off as if seeing the Gelaming clearly for the first time, "And you bring weapons! What kind of vicious barbarians are you? What exactly do you mean to do here, hmm?" He leaned past Ashmael and eyed the various soldiers. "Conquer a bunch of defenseless harlings and plant your Gelaming flag in their playpen? Are you planning to annex our gardens? Confiscate what little we have left?"

The har was livid, but Ashmael suspected that his blustering outrage was a cover for defeat and resignation — resignation to a fate he plainly misunderstood.

In the meantime, Lisia's accusations had garnered startled whispers from the audience of harlings. Ashmael glanced round to see Pansea, who until then had been stationed faithfully at his side, suddenly back away. "Weapons?" Pansea mouthed silently, staring at the soldiers as if they'd all suddenly grown horns and fangs. "I didn't even know… I didn't even think… I *never* thought you were *Gelaming* soldiers!" He looked over to Lisia apologetically. "I swear, Lis, I thought they were just strange Varrs. They didn't look how I thought they would — and now they're going to kill us!"

"I assure you, all of you," Ashmael replied firmly, trying to hide his exasperation as he gestured around, "we have no intentions of stealing your land or your supplies — or killing you. Our presence in this country is peaceful."

The hostling's expression was dismissive; he clearly wasn't buying Ashmael's assurances for a minute. "And yet you are armed. Weapons have never had a place here — they are forbidden! Didn't you read the signs? Are you even capable of reading?"

"We saw the sign," Ashmael replied flatly, refusing to rise to the bait, despite ample provocation.

"And you came in anyway!" Lisia commented. "I guess being the conquering army, you do what you like."

Ashmael repressed the urge to sigh in frustration. He could see they certainly weren't racking up any points with this har and the hostling's hostile attitude would only serve to hinder his interrogation. "Tiahaar, we are soldiers and approached this facility thinking it was a military installation. We had no way of knowing what awaited us beyond your gates. Surely, you understand that I can't expect my hara to enter an unknown situation unarmed!"

Lisia suddenly swooped down to grab the shirt of one of the tiny harlings who had detached himself and was intent on scurrying off. Lisia's voice was therefore muffled as he replied, "Well, hopefully you can see now that your hara have nothing to fear here." He smiled briefly at the would-be runaway, who was now latched on to his leg, shyly hiding his face from the strangers. "Unless you're afraid of getting hugged to death by affectionate little harlings."

As if on cue, another harling, a creature with white-blond hair sticking out in every direction, laughed loudly. Chortling happily, he proceeded to hide his face behind the flowery cloth of Lisia's skirt before popping up again and squealing in laughter.

Ashmael glanced round and caught two of his hara making faces and wiggling their fingers at the playful harling. Upon noticing the general's attention, the soldiers straightened and erased the smiles from their faces. Gritting his teeth, Ashmael decided to refocus on their mission before the situation grew even more out of hand.

"We are not here to bring harm of any kind, tiahaar. We have information linking this facility to the Varr military, which you are correct in surmising has been defeated and deposed. My hara and I are here to investigate and document this place."

For a moment the hostling looked disappointed. "I can give you the information you seek," he said, sounding resigned, "but first I need to go back inside. I have to take care of these harlings. Please follow me and do not, I ask you, disrupt my charges any further. In fact, I'd prefer if you and your hara kept away from them altogether."

"That would be rather difficult, seeing as they're everywhere," Ashmael countered, following Lisia away from the pens.

When they had reached the front of the building, Lisia turned his attention to Pansea and his companions. "I will speak to you and the other Lilies about this later." Then gesturing to the entire group, "Now go back to what you were doing and stop this gawking. All of you!" He eyed the assemblage of nervous youngsters and they reluctantly began to retreat to their various stations around the yard.

Lisia, apparently confident that matters were tended outside, turned toward the building's entrance. Ashmael observed the graceful manner in which the hostling avoided stumbling on any of the little ones still clinging to his legs and led the way through the main doors.

With the electricity, not surprisingly, non-functioning, the interior of the building was dim, lit only with what natural light filtered through the exterior windows. Lisia led his visitors through a series of hallways, most of them decorated with colorful artwork and pencil drawings. Beyond closed doors, Ashmael detected the high-pitched voices of yet more harlings, apparently engaged in supervised lessons of some kind. Several of the rooms had doors which opened at the top, allowing a window to the interior. Glancing into a few, Ashmael observed brightly colored rooms with juvenile furnishings and accessories. Small groups of similarly aged harlings, invariably guided by older ones, were engaged in activities like singing, drawing, or basic lessons.

As they were walking, Ashmael summoned one of his hara and quietly instructed him and five others to explore the remainder of the building. No matter how free of threat the place appeared, they needed to be certain of its security; for all of Lisia's adamant assurances, it was possible it was all a set-up for an enemy ambush.

The group stopped at an open door situated at the end of a hall. Lisia turned to address the Gelaming, "I need to see to these harlings first. Then I'll answer your questions."

Ashmael was growing impatient with the entire situation. Before he could protest, Paran spoke up. "Surely there is some other har who can meet with us. The harling outside said that you were the only adult, but I don't think he understood our questions. When will the administrators of this place return? I believe they should be the ones to answer our questions, since you obviously have other priorities."

Lisia made a rough sound that might have been a short laugh but for its bitterness. He did not turn to regard his visitors as he began speaking but instead entered the room, where two of the small harlings were immediately swept up into the arms of two older ones. Four other harlings shared one of the two beds in the room, all of them curled up asleep under one large knitted blanket.

"The administrators are long gone," Lisia said, straining to keep anger out of his voice. "I *am* the only har here. And I apologize for being so rude, tiahaara, but you're correct about my priorities. Answering questions for Gelaming soldiers is really not my area of expertise. I simply must care for these young ones. If you can't be bothered with me, then please feel free to search for the administrators somewhere out there," he gestured vaguely to the surrounding wilderness. "They left some time ago and I assure you that there is nothing left here that can be of any interest to you."

Edrei the Listener spoke up. "If you truly are here alone with all these harlings, then it seems obvious that you are in need of some assistance, and that certainly is our concern." He paused. "Or rather, it's the concern of those we represent. Why don't you just let these capable helpers of yours see to the younger harlings and then we can sort this all out."

Ashmael observed that the two helpers, again feminized, one dark skinned and one very fair, were practically full-grown hara. Both attendants were visibly intrigued by the presence of the soldiers but they tended dutifully to the harlings, speaking to them softly before placing them side-by-side on the other bed. Noticing their beautiful but weary faces and the patches of red skin on their faces and arms, Ashmael deduced that they were both suffering through feybraiha, which unlike human adolescence descended upon harlings between the ages of six and eight and brought about all the physical changes of puberty in the space of a few weeks. The result, while blessedly shorter than the years of hormonal upheaval experienced by humans, was something like a sickness.

Lisia scooped up the blond harling clinging to his leg and reached over to hand him to one of the helpers. Ashmael noticed for the first time how gaunt and thin the hostling was. Perhaps his earlier fierce indignation had drawn attention away from his person, but now that he had calmed somewhat, Ashmael could see the way Lisia's wrist bones stuck out, beyond the cuffs of his long-sleeved blouse, the way his cheeks were slightly sunken. He might have been taking care of the harlings, but he'd been skimping on himself.

Ashmael had a feeling that sympathy might be a means of moving the investigation forward. "Don't worry, tiahaar. We have every intention of helping you."

One of Lisia's soft brown eyebrows arched questioningly at Ashmael's words. He turned quickly to hand the last harling to a helper and appeared to be considering the general's comments. Lisia motioned for the Gelaming to follow him and led them down the hall from the harling nursery into an empty classroom with larger tables and chairs. The walls were painted in shades of pink. He gestured towards the chairs. Ashmael nodded to his hara and they quietly seated themselves, content to observe, gather information and await the general's orders. Ashmael himself remained standing. Lisia leaned against the front of the instructor's desk and crossed his arms. "Help us how exactly?" His tone and body language screamed mistrust.

31

Ashmael raised his hands in a placating gesture. "Let me reassure you, tiahaar, we aren't here to make war. We are here foremost to gather information, but part of our mission is to bring peace to all former Varr territories, to right any wrongs, to help everyhar get back to their lives."

Ashmael had deliberately chosen not to mention the new name for the Varr tribe; introducing the change so soon might lead them off track. He was therefore annoyed to note the way Lisia's expression twisted.

"Get back to their lives?" he exploded. "Get back to— Oh, and how do *we* do that here? The war, the final battle or whatever happened that you beat us — it changed all our lives. Nothing's been the same. Are you proposing to reopen the facility, then?" Lisia did not relax in the slightest. In fact he appeared to become even more wary.

Ashmael paused for a moment to consider the most diplomatic response to offer the distrustful, beleaguered har. *To hell with diplomacy!* He assumed a more commanding posture. "That remains to be seen, but I sincerely doubt it. The Gelaming are not in the habit of subsidizing facilities that run off the hard labor of half-starved harlings."

."Oh, they're not?" Lisia sneered.

Ashmael thought Lisia had been livid before, but now anger was emanating from the hostling like heat waves. Lisia even stepped forward from the desk, his hands clenched into fists; for a moment Ashmael thought Lisia might be foolish enough to try assaulting him. But the attack was purely one of words. "You think that I *want* the harlings doing all the work? Do you think I *enjoy* living like this? You don't know *anything!*"

Lisia gestured broadly to the room around him and, by extension, the entire facility. "This was a happy place once. We were taken care of; the harlings never had to work except to learn. I certainly wasn't used to this lifestyle of working and worrying every single moment of every day. There was plenty of staff to do the chores, cook the food, care for the little ones, teach them. We had supplies; I didn't lie awake at night wondering how I was going to feed these helpless harlings come winter. I never had to stop and wonder just how little food could be rationed to growing harlings before they starved. Do you think any of this misery is intentional? That's absurd. We're in this state because of *you!* Everything was fine before you started your stupid war. We were fine, but you made everything change. *You* caused this!"

Lisia looked like he was prepared to continue with his tirade but he was interrupted by the door softly creaking open. "What?" he shouted, past all patience.

"We— we finished outside. I just wanted to see what's going on with the Gelaming soldiers. Are they staying? Are we supposed to do anything for them?" stammered a wide-eyed Pansea. The harling appeared almost ready to flee, but for the moment he stood his ground in the half-opened doorway.

Lisia, flushed with anger, seemed suddenly embarrassed by his outburst.

His demeanor softened immediately and he approached the door. "I'm sorry that I shouted at you," he said. "No, I don't want you to do anything for these soldiers. In fact, I don't want you or any of the others to go near them at all. I want you to tell this to everyhar. No talking to strange hara, even soldiers. Understood?"

Pansea became a little bolder and stepped forward into the room. Several other older harlings stood behind him. He gave the soldiers his full attention for a few moments — although he'd abandoned his ostentatious flirtations — and appeared to be processing what the hostling had told him. "Why? Lis, we all just heard you yelling and you seem really upset. What's happening?"

Lisia put a comforting hand on the harling's arm. "Nothing for you to concern yourself with, Pansea. They say that they're here to help us, but they don't seem to know our ways or the rules, and until I'm sure that they do, I don't want them interacting with anyhar but me. Can you understand that?"

Pansea nodded and the other harlings behind him murmured agreement.

"Good. Now I know there's still plenty to do. Some of you relieve the Lilies in charge of class four and the rest help the Lilies in the kitchen."

Once Pansea and his companions had gone, Ashmael took advantage of the moment. "I can assign some of my hara to help you in the kitchen and to undertake whatever other work needs to be done until we can find a more permanent solution to your situation. There's no reason why you and the harlings should have to continue working as you have." Ashmael neglected to mention that he did not intend to be a part of the permanent solution. Already he was calculating whether he could wrap up this interview in time to sleep back home in Immanion. He cast a glance a Paran; his captain could coordinate whatever actions were necessary and soon this bizarre encounter would be nothing more than a good anecdote for the general to share at the next Hegemony meeting.

"Thank you," Lisia offered slowly and uneasily, clearly still angry but perhaps working toward hope that he might find help. "I hope you have some food supplies you can bring to us here. That and some help in getting some things fixed."

"Yes, yes, tiahaar," Ashmael assured impatiently.

Apparently encouraged, Lisia began pacing and counting off items on his fingers. "We're very low on all the staples. I need flour, yeast, salt, sugar, cooking oil. And meat, fresh meat, would be lovely, but what we really need are supplies that will keep for a long time — smoked or cured would be good. And I can't remember the last time we had dairy goods — milk, eggs, cheese. Do you think you could get us some livestock? I'm sure we could learn how to work with them. And seeds for next year's vegetables. Oh, and soap — lots and lots of soap, all kinds of soap—" He looked up at Ashmael suddenly, "Shouldn't you be writing all this down?"

"Don't worry, I have a good memory," Ashmael replied dryly.

Lisia again quirked an eyebrow at Ashmael's words. "We'll see," he said. "In the meantime, I'd appreciate it if you could get started right away on the repairs. We have no training in these matters and we've been without electricity and hot water for months. Plus, the sewage system has backed up behind the building and I've no clue how to fix it. I had to give up trying for fear of making it worse and instead we just made that part of the yard off limits, but—"

"Lis! Lis!" an agitated high voice shrieked. A flustered harling with dark brown hair burst into the room; Ashmael recognized him as one of the "shepherds" who had been working in the pens outside. "Lis, a harling just ate a bug!"

Lisia took on a slightly mortified expression for a few moments. "How charming," he murmured, then snapped quickly, "But he's all right? He didn't get sick or choke on it or anything, right?"

"No, he seems to be okay," the harling answered, twisting his hands. "I tried to take it out of his mouth, but..." he paused to grimace, "...he swallowed it before I could. He said he was hungry! I didn't know what to do."

"Well, there's nothing *to* do," Lisia replied. "Just calm down and try to watch the little ones a little more closely, hmm. I know you're all feeling distracted, but we must all be responsible, remember."

The harling blushed and nodded.

"Now, don't worry about it too much, dear, these things happen." Lisia put his hand on the harling's cheek reassuringly. "If he gets a little sick, we'll clean him up and if not then he just got a little extra dinner, like he said."

The harling smiled shyly and thus reassured, Lisia sent him on his way before turning back to the Gelaming.

"By Ag, can't you lock that door?" Ashmael groused. "We'll never get anywhere with these constant interruptions!"

Lisia looked at him sternly. "No, tiahaar, this door doesn't lock — we've done away with all the locks. There's always a crisis of some magnitude with little ones, they need to come get you," he said, as if trying to dismiss the embarrassing incident. "Now where was I? Oh yes, the water system. It needs—"

"Certainly," the general interrupted. "We will see that all your basic utilities are restored. You realize that I'll need to bring in additional hara for this?"

Lisia nodded, his expression grim. "Just as long as they understand that this facility is not open for business. I need you and your hara to be crystal clear on that, tiahaar. None of the harlings have completed feybraiha yet, much less received any proper training. I am the only hostling here and I haven't hosted in more than four months." The last sentence was uttered with an air of significance Ashmael couldn't fathom.

Here it was again, thought Ashmael. What on earth had been going on at this facility? Flowers? Crowds of harlings, all ages, some kept in pens? The fact that Varr soldiers had apparently been frequent visitors at one time? Just as he was about to put forth his question rather bluntly, Edrei spoke up.

"So... You haven't hosted in... more than four months," he began, groping diplomatically for answers. "So you would normally be hosting by now?"

Lisia stared blankly for a moment and then came back, voice confident but exasperated, "Yes, of course I would be! How absurd of you to ask! There's been time for a hosting and a half, almost two hostings if you do them especially close together!"

"Back up, back up," Ashmael enjoined. "You... you normally have pearls... one after the other?"

"Of course I do! I'm a hostling!"

From the way Lisia made this statement, Ashmael could tell they were obviously working from very different assumptions. Although the gestational period for Wraeththu reproduction was short, only about two months, Ashmael couldn't imagine anyhar wanting to go through that crucible more than once, much less within months.

"I understand that," Ashmael returned smoothly, despite waning patience. "Now as for your own, how many of these harlings are yours?"

Lisia's green eyes flickered — obviously this was a touchy subject. He covered the look quickly. "Mine? I have no idea. Altogether I've had 24 but many of them have already been selected and—"

"Wait!" Paran interrupted. "Did you just say you've delivered *24* pearls?"

This was a record beyond anything the Gelaming had ever encountered. Ashmael had once met a hostling who'd birthed eight and he had found that number astounding, almost beyond belief.

"Yes, I did say that," Lisia affirmed. "I've been very productive."

"Yes, so it... seems. 24." To Ashmael, the number was incredible, so much so he had a fleeting urge to try and contact one of the newspapers in Immanion. But then he strongly suspected the hostling was lying.

"Now tell me, tiahaar, what was your position here, before you took over care for these harlings?"

"I was a hostling *obviously!*" Lisia replied with great vehemence.

"Obviously, yes, Lisia, but—"

"But nothing — Ashmael — was it? But nothing."

"A professional hostling?" Ashmael asked, rhetorically. "But 24 is so many! How old are you?" It was difficult to gauge ages for hara. Lisia could have been 20; he could have been 50. Because he seemed casteless, Ashmael had assumed Lisia was young, probably a pure-born, but that was impossible if he'd had so many pearls.

"I'm 14, maybe 15 by now," the hostling replied.

Ashmael was intensely skeptical of Lisia's truthfulness in the matter. "And you were how old when you started?"

"About nine."

For a few moments Ashmael stared in disbelief, but immediately he began to work out the math. Lisia had been hosting for six years. "Tiahaar, are you telling us the truth?"

Lisia exhaled out through his nose and clenched his fists as his sides. "Yes, of course I am. What, are you jealous that your own hostlings were never so successful?"

Ashmael had an impulse to offer a rather undiplomatic reply to this taunt but before he could, Edrei stepped into the exchange. "No, tiahaar, we are not jealous. Not at all. In fact we've never heard of such a thing — a har beginning to host so young and then producing pearls almost continuously. You mustn't have had many breaks. It's — it's unheard of."

Lisia shrugged. "Well, we'd been told your ways were different." He pronounced the last word with thinly veiled disdain.

"But why produce so many harlings?" Ashmael ventured. He wondered if Paran had been correct and this was indeed a Varr "farm."

"To further increase the Varr race, of course!" Lisia replied incredulously. Then, as if it was the most obvious thing in the world: "This *is* a breeding facility."

"A breeding facility. I... see." Suddenly all the clues made perfect sense, though the fact that the Varrs had accomplished such a feat was certainly astounding. Glancing behind him, he noted his companions' faces registered similar reactions.

Deciding it was time for some strategizing, Ashmael addressed Lisia. "Tiahaar, I'd like a short conference in private with my staff."

Lisia breathed out loudly through his nose and crossed his arms over his chest. "Well, since I don't seem to have any authority or weapons to keep you from doing whatever you want and ordering everyhar about, you can certainly do that." He turned and headed for the door only to stop in his tracks. "Just remember to send those supplies and help, General."

As soon as the hostling had closed the door behind him, everyhar was up in arms. "I can't believe it!" Paran cried. "*24!* How is that possible? Varrs could never have managed something like that!"

Another har agreed, arguing that Lisia had to be lying, perhaps covering up for some other project. Several hara were looking more sick than outraged.

"How could they *do* that?" Ashmael heard one ask in a slightly horrified voice.

Corporal Karan, the pure-born who had earlier asked about convents, just kept shaking his head. "My hostling told me what it was like for him to deliver a pearl. How could anyhar do that more than once?"

"Somehow I doubt the hara involved had much choice in the matter," Ashmael said loudly.

"You believe the hostling is telling the truth, then?" Paran asked.

Ashmael nodded. "I think he could be. It would explain the harlings and certainly Lisia looks the part of a Varrish hostling." Ashmael paced over to the window and gazed thoughtfully out the window. Groups of harlings were still working outside, tending the gardens and washing clothes. "I wonder how they did it."

"I wonder *if* they did it." Paran had come to stand beside the general. "The Varrs were never great achievers in the realm of caste magic and I hardly think they managed to put together an entire breeding facility filled with Ulani-level hara."

"True enough," said Edrei, "but that's assuming they used a method we're familiar with."

"What do you mean?" Ashmael turned away from the window. "Is there some other method we're not aware of? Hara can't make pearls simply by going at it like rabbits!"

"Maybe, tiahaar, but that's what we have to find out." Edrei was sitting on the edge of a desk, his face wearing the reasonable expression he always used when patiently convincing his commander to change his mind. "They *did* do it, I'm sure of it, caste training or no. Lisia is no high caste har, but I am certain he was telling the truth. He produced 24 pearls *somehow*."

"Interesting," Ashmael remarked. "As I said before, perhaps this is an area in which the Varrs were far more advanced than we thought, more advanced than other tribes."

Paran nodded. "There might be something to gain from this, then."

"Yes..." Ashmael crossed the room, hands clasped behind his back. "Knowledge of procreation. Hosting, pearl-bearing... Our healers in Immanion have barely scratched the surface on all this!"

Ashmael stopped his pacing as the door opened; the hara he'd sent to scout the building had returned. He looked to the har in charge expectantly. "Report?"

"It's amazing, General," Corporal Branad began. "This place is huge, a giant dormitory, kitchen, dining hall and everything. There are a lot of harlings here now, but it's obvious there were quite a few more at one time, plus a much larger staff."

Ashmael glanced briefly at Edrei. "Good, so Lisia was telling the truth."

"The truth about what?" Branad asked. "Did I miss something?

Ashmael offered him and the others a short summary of Lisia's explanation.

"That must be what the records are," the soldier said.

Paran stepped forward. "Records? What sort of records?"

"That's the thing," said Branad. "We can't tell because they're all encoded. But looking at them, it did seem like some of them could be medical. There was obviously a lot of personal information and lots of charts with dates."

Ashmael fingered his chin in thought. "I see more and more potential. A treasure trove of information, if we can get at it. It could be a key that would explain so much — areas we still haven't explored."

"I wonder if they kept genetic records?" Branad asked. "If they did, I wonder what it would show about these harlings. They do seem unusual, don't they?"

"If you mean unusually soume, then yes," Paran agreed.

"No, not just that," Ashmael said. "You saw those harlings in the pens. They're not the same as other harlings."

Edrei got off his perch on the desk top. "How do we really know that? Do any of us really have such great familiarity with harlings?"

There was a pause as they considered the question. Although they had the requisite knowledge, the Gelaming were not great breeders. They preferred to keep their relationships elevated, above such intense, exclusive unions as would result in pearls. Soldiers in particular had little experience with harlings.

It was Ashmael who finally replied. "We don't have the knowledge, Edrei, but maybe this is an opportunity to get it." Before the others could ask "How?" Ashmael elaborated. "We could make a study of this entire situation — how they did it, the records, the harlings, even Lisia. This could be priceless knowledge, allowing us to make a leap ahead."

Paran nodded, then frowned. "I see your point, General, but how do you propose we do that? Set up a station here and conduct a research study?"

"Hardly," Ashmael chuckled. "You think I want us to stay here, at this monstrous place in the middle of nowhere? Certainly not. No, I see another approach. We need to take care of the immediate problems here, just as I promised the hostling. And we need to check the harlings, make sure they're in decent health. Then we get them — and all the records — and we high-tail it out of here."

Paran grunted in agreement. "That does seem like a feasible plan. Now just where do we take them? Immanion?"

Ashmael grinned. "That's for you to work out. Immanion might be best, but perhaps they could be taken elsewhere on the continent, somewhere like Imbrilim. In any case, you'll be making the decisions. I'm heading back home tonight." Ashmael was relieved the conversation had reached such a satisfactory conclusion.

"I understand, General," said Paran. "I will handle this."

Edrei, who had not spoken in some time, looked concerned. "But can we really be making these decisions about the harlings? *Should* we be?"

"What, you want to just leave them all here?" Paran questioned.

"No, not necessarily, but before we go making decisions, we *do* need to consider where we are. This is Megalithica and we are not the only authority. In fact, technically we are not the authority at all. This is a matter for the Parasiel."

"Lord Swift." For a moment, Ashmael's sense of relief flickered as he saw a possible obstacle to their plan, but then he shrugged it off. "Well, it's not as if they're any powerhouse and certainly they'll trust us to handle this matter. We can bring them in and ask their opinion, but I wouldn't say it's their decision. We found them based on our intelligence gathering, after all."

Ashmael turned to a soldier on his right. "Sergeant Tarkan, I'd like you to be ready for otherlane travel to Galhea later tonight, to deliver a message. You may return back to camp, where I'll find you later."

"Yes, General." The young soldier headed toward the door. "I will await your orders."

"Fine."

The soldier opened the door and headed off.

"I'll stay around for a few hours today, do some hands-on investigating, have a look at those records and probably write a report," Ashmael announced, "but after that, I'm leaving Captain Paran in charge of the dirty work — with Parsic approval, of course."

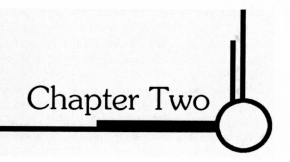

Chapter Two

Swift Parasiel sighed contentedly and lifted his head from where it rested on his chesnari Seel's shoulder. He took another sip of the chilled glass of sheh in his hand. As he did so, he glanced over to the large windows of the second floor room where the family was gathered. A soft breeze rustled the pale green curtains, which were parted to reveal an abundance of stars shining in the clear black sky above the tall, gently swaying cedars.

Galhea, newly installed as the capital city for the recently reborn Parsic tribe, was a quickly expanding town and most important Wraeththu settlement on the vast continent of Megalithica. But unlike the old human cities, Galhea was unburdened by messy problems such as industrial pollution. Like their more warlike predecessors, the Varrs, the Parsics were an agricultural society. The area's inhabitants were all farmers, soldiers, and hara who traded goods and services with these groups. The resulting community was almost eerily idyllic, and nowhere was this more evident than within the walls and grounds of *We Dwell In Forever*, Swift's seat of power and family home. To Swift, however, the timeless grandeur of the old human mansion was simply home.

"You've been quiet," Cobweb, Swift's hostling, commented to his son. The room had grown silent except for the occasional noise from the two harlings busying themselves on the soft carpet. Cobweb pulled on the elegant clasp that pinned his long hair above his neck and stretched languorously as dark tresses cascaded down his back.

Swift made a small dismissive gesture. "Just relaxing, enjoying the peace and calm while I can." He leaned forward to get a better look at his hostling, who was relaxing in an adjacent wingchair. "I'm sorry I've been such dismal company. Honestly, I'm exhausted. Every time I close my eyes I see field reports or trade analysis statistics."

Seel Griselming squeezed his chesnari's hand supportively. "I know how you feel. But I promise, things will lighten up once we've completed the reorganization and hara settle down into the new Parsic way of life."

"I know," Swift replied, turning to answer Seel's concern with a patient smile. In truth the burden of administrating an efficient and just government was a task that seemed wearying and endless to the young har, but he put on an optimistic face for his beautiful and more experienced Gelaming chesnari. At ten years of age, Swift was fully adult, but still young, even by Wraeththu standards. Second generation hara were very rarely found in high leadership positions. It was, however, the idealism of youth that helped him face the burdens of defying his heritage to help bring victory to the Gelaming and instill sweeping changes among his tribe.

"I was just thinking," Swift said, turning back to Cobweb, "that the sky is feeling very promising tonight — there's some sort of expectant quality. I get the impression that the night sounds could tell me secrets if I listen closely enough."

Swift couldn't help but grin at the preposterous sound of his own words and his hostling gave him a wistful smile in return. It was an odd little exchange that spoke volumes between hostling and son. "I sound just like Cobweb," Swift thought to himself. Terzian, Swift's father, had been a fearsome Varr general, and as master of Galhea and its surrounding lands, was second only to the infamous Ponclast. Although Terzian had tolerated Cobweb's powerful mysticism, he would have been displeased to hear this sort of talk bantered so freely under his roof. Things had changed so much in the short time since his death.

In a quick mindtouch Cobweb merely commented, *You're finding your balance, my son.*

Swift nodded to the silent statement. When he'd grown up and been forced to confront the harsh reality of life outside of *Forever*, he'd discarded Cobweb's mystical teachings and sayings as childish, only to discover that magic and mysticism were, in fact, a very real part of that outside world and a part of himself as well.

As if reading his companions' thoughts, Seel threaded his fingers with Swift's and mused, "Hmm, maybe you sense something important is about to happen." He paused to bring Swift's hand up to his mouth for a quick kiss before continuing, "Then again, we've been buried in paperwork for planning the future of Parasiel so it's only natural that you'd have a sense of anticipation." Seel shrugged. "Either way, maybe we should meditate on it before we go to sleep; it could be the ethers will have some answers for us."

Cobweb hid a smile in his glass before grumbling, "I don't see why you must bury yourself in reports and papers all day. Don't you have a staff for those things?"

Swift rolled his eyes. "Yes, I have staff. I've got staff coming out of my ears, it seems! But I have to make big decisions and I need to be well informed in order to do that." He grinned again and nudged Seel. "And since Seel's my number one advisor, he needs to know even more than I do."

Seel smiled back and then stretched and stifled a yawn with his hand. "Or at least know enough to convince the Hegemony that we've got everything under control."

"I'll drink to that," Swift chimed in facetiously, raising his glass for another sip. If there was one thing the three of them agreed upon it was that Megalithica required Immanion's support and even assistance — but *not* its interference. After several years of leading the Saltrock community, Seel was fond of declaring that governments couldn't really control societies and that societies should control governments. This was not a philosophy commonly embraced by the Hegemony, which tended to take a very paternal view of the Megalithicans, so recently liberated from years of Varrish oppression.

Shifting slightly in his position on the couch with Swift, Seel stretched sleepily and continued, "Things are just a bit overwhelming for us right now with all these end-of-season reports coming in at the same time. I think that we should consider staggering the deadlines next time, don't you think, Swift?"

Swift didn't answer, having become distracted by a sudden altercation between the two harlings. Four-year-old Tyson had been quietly engrossed in creating a schematic diagram of one of the large weaving machines used in Galhea's largest mill; the assignment had been given to him by his tutors. Meanwhile, Azriel had been occupied with a drawing of his own design; Swift judged it was a map of *Forever*'s own grounds. However, the ten-month-old harling's attention seemed to have shifted suddenly to Tyson's work, resulting in a sudden plaintive exchange of "Azriel, what do you mean? The drawing's perfect!"

"No, that doesn't look right."

"How would you know — you haven't even been to the mill."

"Here, let me show you, I'll draw it."

"Not on my homework, you won't, just mind your own business!" and finally, "Swiiift!"

Swift could tell his half-brother was feeling especially beleaguered, not only from the way he'd expanded his name into three syllables, but from that fact that he'd bothered to address him at all. As the offspring of Terzian and his second consort, the enigmatic interloper Cal, Tyson's young life had been a flashpoint of intrigue and instability from his very birth. Now Terzian was dead and Cal was missing, presumably imprisoned by the Gelaming for past crimes. But Tyson had inherited his hostling's appearance and the fierce willfulness of both his parents. As such, he was very much a living ghost, mostly silent and an often-unsettling reminder of the volatile past.

Just as Swift was about to tell Azriel to leave Tyson alone, Azriel suddenly reached to grab hold of one of Tyson's graphite pencils. With little patience and more than a bit of annoyance, Tyson blocked Azriel from his work area, and when Azriel only tried to worm around him, promptly shoved Azriel off his feet and flat on his back.

"TYSON!" Cobweb sternly admonished.

Swift stifled the desire to groan aloud as he anticipated the inevitable altercation to follow. Seel lurched forward in his seat.

Tyson looked just as startled by Azriel's tumble as the adults did. "I didn't mean to!" he said quickly to Cobweb, his frowning adoptive hostling.

Dazed for only a few moments, Azriel merely scrambled to his feet and retaliated for the assault by diving into Tyson and sinking his teeth into his upper arm.

"Ow! Stop it, you little shit!" Tyson yelled, smacking Azriel resoundingly in the face. This resulted in a furious tangle of screaming, kicking and hair pulling, and it took all three hara several moments to pull the snarling and red-faced harlings apart.

"Damn it, Tyson, can you try to manage a little self control—" Seel snapped before Swift quieted him with a calming touch. Meanwhile, well knowing his best ally, Azriel hugged his hostling's legs and gazed up at him with large, "innocent" eyes. Seel picked him up, which Swift judged was for the best, as it would keep him from Tyson's drawing.

"I just didn't want him to ruin my assignment," Tyson said in defense. "Swift, you know he always does; he messes up all my stuff."

"That's no excuse," Seel cut in. "It's a homework assignment and Azriel was just trying to help you. And perhaps if you had listened to him, he wouldn't have ever tried to mark it up."

"I don't want to see that again," Cobweb added. "That got well out of hand."

Seel turned to Cobweb angrily. "Maybe if somehar would—" Azriel took the opportunity to stick his tongue out at Tyson from over Seel's shoulder while the older harling glared daggers at him in return.

"Both of you have behaved badly and I think both of you should go to bed right now," Swift interjected. Mentally he projected to his hostling and his chesnari, *Don't you two start! Where do you think they're getting this from?* Tyson opened his mouth to protest but Swift added, "It's way past your bedtimes, anyway." He glanced towards Cobweb for backup since it was not truly his place to order Tyson to his room.

"Ty, go," Cobweb ordered stiffly, and with little pause the harling stomped off to his room. Swift moved closer to Seel, where Azriel was perched conveniently at eye level. "Azriel Parasiel, we do *not* bite!" he said sternly. Azriel tried to hide his face in Seel's neck. "Azriel—" Swift prompted warningly.

Before he could continue Cobweb pried the harling from Seel's arms. "I'll take Az up and get him ready for bed," he said to Swift. "I'll make sure he and Ty make up."

"Nooo," Azriel wailed stubbornly as they moved towards the door, but Cobweb only half-smiled, seemingly bemused with his highharling's attempted manipulations.

"Swift—" Seel started.

"Don't, please," Swift muttered, sitting heavily on the couch. "I swear I might as well be in battle as be in my own home." Seel remained silent and picked up a report from the stack that had lain neglected on the couch. He sat and began reading while Swift finished his now-warm sheh.

Edrei Faraliesse was having a difficult time eating. Field rations had never been a particular favorite of his, but his present lack of appetite was more a symptom of distraction than dislike for the food. All around the bleakly furnished dining room, wide-eyed harlings stole furtive glances at him from above their half-filled soup bowls. Dutifully following Lisia's instructions, these older harlings kept as much distance as they could from the handful of Gelaming eating their rations at one of the well-worn tables at the back of the room.

Edrei marveled at how polite and impeccably mannered these Varrish children were. Many of them were eating only after having first helped to prepare and serve food to the younger ones. Harlings who had already eaten dutifully cleared bowls and organized younger groups to return to the dormitory rooms. Edrei gathered that for weeks on end, many of these older harlings had literally been working at some task or another from the moment they woke until the moment they went to bed at night. Perhaps they were simply too weary to make much noise; despite the fact that well over fifty harlings filled the room, it seemed eerily quiet — on the physical plane at any rate. Edrei couldn't help but tune into their thoughts:

What do they want from us?
Will they bring more hostlings here?
Look at the meat they have — I'm so sick of this stupid soup!
Will the little ones go into the Gelaming army now?

He doesn't look like a soldier at all — he's too pretty, like a hostling!

Will they still let us be hostlings or will they make us slaves like tiahaar Sennaflur said?

They seem kind of nice.

Are those guns? Pansea said that Lis called them weapons.

"Hey."

Edrei had sensed his chesnari's presence, but being so intent on the myriad of thoughts floating on the ethers, he jumped when Paran laid a hand on his shoulder. Paran chuckled and began running his fingers through the feather-light locks of Edrei's pale blond hair.

"Don't," Edrei said softly, ducking away from the touch. He glanced behind him, seeing that the rest of their party had entered with Paran. He nodded in greeting to them.

"Why not?" Paran asked, annoyance clear in his voice.

"We're working," Edrei replied. "How'd it go? Where's the general?"

"The grounds are secure and we didn't find any more files. He's finishing up that report and then as soon as he hands it to Tarkan, he's off to the otherlanes. He said he wanted to make it to the Hegemony meeting tomorrow, but secretly I think all these harlings just drive him nuts." Paran paused to smile at his own jest. "And we're not really working right now," he continued, leaning forward to kiss the top of Edrei's head. "We're not on alert and we're having supper break."

Still, Edrei remained tense and uncomfortable. Picking up on this, Paran propped a foot on a simple metal chair and leaned in next to Edrei's face. "Shit, Edrei, the general doesn't care about us and neither does anyhar else, because it's not like I don't share you with them all the time anyway! What's your problem tonight?"

"Shhh! Don't say that in front of the harlings," Edrei whispered.

Paran laughed. "Yeah, because this lot would really be traumatized by the thought of soldiers having aruna! By Ag, it would be good for them. Let them see healthy Wraeththu behavior for a change!"

"Not that," Edrei whispered with a grin. "Don't say, 'shit.' These harlings are all very proper and you'll start them on crude habits."

Edrei munched a piece of dried fruit as Paran rolled his eyes, though smiling all the same at the scolding. After a moment, Paran's brow creased in confusion as his eyes searched the room, obviously looking for somehar. "Where's Branad?"

"Oh, we decided that until we manage to round up hara from the neighboring village to take over some of the harlingcare, he would be assigned to help with those really young ones," Edrei explained. "Would you like me to call him back?"

"No, Ashmael said to help where needed, at least until those Parsic volunteers get here."

Edrei nodded. "It's a good assignment for him. You know Branad told me he's been thinking about hosting, someday at least. This will be good practice."

"Hopefully the little creatures will scare the... will scare him and then we won't have to lose a good har!"

"Shame on you, Paran. You know we still have a lot to learn."

"If you say so," Paran grumbled as he reached over to steal a piece of dried meat from Edrei's plate. "Is that har Lisia with him? I need to talk to him to work out the immediate assignments."

"No, Lisia's helping in the kitchen."

Paran sauntered into the kitchen, which apparently had finished serving soup for the night since Lisia was the only har still there. The soldier was already weary and watching Lisia hard at work just made him feel more tired. Waiting for an acknowledgement, he rubbed a hand over his face and through his closely cropped dark blond hair, then cleared his throat when the busy hostling failed to look up from the basin of steaming water.

Lisia looked over to him. "Can I help you?" he asked in a voice that evinced more annoyance than enthusiasm.

"General Aldebaran is leaving soon and as his captain he's put me in charge."

Lisia made no reply.

"I thought you should know."

Lisia glanced up again and then furtively tried to push back a lock of damp hair that had fallen in his face. "Thank you for informing me, tiahaar," he said flatly.

Paran got the distinct impression that he was being dismissed. Bristling slightly, he continued, "My hara and I will be staying on the grounds at least for tonight. I know that you don't like us around the harlings, but the only efficient way of helping you is to be close at hand. I need you to find accommodations for us in the building, and then I'd like to ascertain what you think should be our first priorities in getting the harlings cared for."

Lisia drew his lips together in a tight line, wiped a stack of bowls with a grimy towel and then plunged them into the hot water. "I believe there's room for your hara in the staff/administrator wing if you're willing to share rooms. Those rooms are the best we have. They're up on the top floor with the administrator's office – you know where you were going through all those files?"

"Yes, that will do perfectly."

Lisia nodded. "As soon as I'm done here I'll get you settled into your rooms and then I'll write out a list for you of everything that needs to be done around here and then you can coordinate your hara with my senior harlings. They'll be able to show them everything."

"Excellent," Paran replied. He eyed the tall stack of bowls and, taking into account the numerous dishes steadily accumulating beyond the serving counter, he frowned. *This could take all night!* "Tiahaar, let me have some of my hara help you here." He stepped forward and noticed for the first time how lividly red the hostling's hands were. The water must have been boiled on the stove and it was still nearly scalding hot. "By Ag, that water's hot. Should you really be doing that?"

"We don't have any soap left. This is the best way to get them clean."

Paran grimaced at the thought. Hating the idea of eating off dishes and utensils washed without soap, he suddenly regretted that the troop had no supplies immediately on hand. And the scented bath soaps most of their hara carried in their packs probably wouldn't be very practical on soup bowls. He would have to remember to order some tomorrow. "Well, I think you've done enough. I'll get somehar to take over and we can get started on the rooms."

"I can do it," Lisia snapped. "I've been doing it for weeks."

Paran frowned. He was nothing if not a practical har. If this hostling was too emotional and too stubborn to accept help, then he was of no use whatsoever. Even more irritating was Paran's suspicion that the har was making him wait just to be petulant and difficult. He stepped forward, pulled Lisia's hands out of the water and dragged him away from the sink. "I said somehar else will do it." He wanted to say more but held his tongue.

Lisia seemed to be holding his tongue as well but his glare spoke volumes to Paran. "Very well, tiahaar," the hostling said. "I'll show you to your rooms."

Swift had begun scribbling notes in the margin of a field report, while Seel continued to compare statistics from numerous different sheets of paper. Both were half-reclining on opposite ends on the couch with bare feet propped together in the middle. Just as he was about to instigate some diversionary tactics with his foot, Swift was surprised to see Cobweb return. He had expected his hostling would retire for the night after seeing to the harlings.

"Is everything alright with Az?" Swift asked.

"Of course," Cobweb replied. He held up a sealed envelope and approached the couch. "But I intercepted Morro out in the hall. A Gelaming messenger just arrived with this."

Though both hara reached for it, Cobweb handed the message to Swift, who noted General Aldebaran's seal with a frown. "Oh great," he grumbled morosely as he opened it, "I wonder what sort of glad tidings the general has for us this time."

"What is it?" Seel asked, gesturing to the papers with concern. "Not another uprising?" Cobweb, who returned to his favorite chair, looked on with open curiosity as well.

Scanning the papers quickly, Swift shook his head and after a few moments announced, "No, nothing violent. Ashmael has just uncovered yet another wonderful legacy that we now have to clean up. This time it's even more creative than usual — I'm almost impressed. It's a breeding facility for harlings! They found it in the wooded mountains of the northwest."

"A breeding facility?" Seel asked. "You mean a *Varr* breeding facility?"

"I'm surprised too," Cobweb muttered. "I never thought they'd manage it."

"You *knew* about this?" Swift accused.

Cobweb shrugged. "Terzian mentioned it once, years ago, but I didn't think it was actually functioning. Was it really successful?"

"Seems so," Swift replied, looking through the papers. "This one had 182 harlings. The really tragic thing is that after Fulminir fell the project was ordered abandoned and almost all the hara simply left, leaving the harlings behind. By the time the Gelaming found it, there was only one adult, a hostling, still left at the place."

"What? With all those harlings?" Seel asked incredulously.

"By Ag, the poor har," Cobweb murmured.

"I'll read to you from Ashmael's report," Swift said. He pulled himself into a upright position on the couch, tucking his feet beneath him, and pushed his hair behind his ears.

> *Following military intelligence from confiscated supply records, I led a troop of hara out to the Northwest region in search of a secret military installation. Preliminary reconnaissance indicated a large structure in the wilderness, although local hara knew nothing of any military activity in the area.*
>
> *My scout group found the reported building, which housed a total of 182 harlings, the majority under three years of age. When we arrived, overall conditions at the facility were deplorable: After the administration and staff fled, the harlings had attempted to keep the facility running by themselves. All are malnourished, the younger ones are greatly under-socialized, and the older*

*ones have been psychologically conditioned to act like...
how shall I describe it? Harling princesses — not quite
kanenes but close. We found only one adult har, a
ferociously maternal hostling. Most of the information
I've gathered derives from him, though he is a somewhat
hostile witness.*

*Fortunately, the Varrs who administered the facility
appear to have been quite meticulous in their record
keeping and there are file cabinets full of documents.
Most of these documents are encoded, however, and it
is taking us time to decipher them.*

*According to the hostling, Lisia, the facility opened
about fifteen years ago. Lisia, a pure-born of unknown
origin, was among the first group of harlings brought
here, we would guess stolen from their parents.
Gradually more harlings were added. All were trained to
think of themselves as progenitors only. The masculine
side of their natures was completely suppressed and all
those trained as hostlings were morbidly feminized. The
hostlings were also extremely sheltered and kept in
political and social ignorance. Lisia and the harlings have
never left the grounds and have almost no knowledge of
common Wraeththu society or origins.*

*We are still only in the beginning stages of
understanding the matter, but from what Lisia has told
us, it seems that caste training in the facility centered
exclusively on aruna and pearl conception. Instructors
worked with the selected hostlings after their feybraiha,
training them to open the cauldron of creation at will,
resulting in frequent pearl conception.*

*Selected hara of the Varr military were brought in to
mate with the hostlings and the resulting production was
of staggering volume. Lisia claims to have delivered 24
pearls in only six years and indicates that this was close
to average among the hostlings.*

"No!" exclaimed Seel and Cobweb at exactly the same moment. Both
had instinctively clutched their abdomens, undoubtedly because they
remembered quite vividly what pearl delivery was like.

"That's impossible!" Seel said, now rubbing his stomach and
frowning in disbelief. "Isn't it?"

"Well, I'm afraid that's what it says," Swift said grimly. He held out
the document. "See, Ashmael actually underlined it: *24.*"

Cobweb groaned, leaning back in the wing chair. "In six years, you said? That would make four a year, maybe more some years!" Cobweb had pulled down a lock of hair from each side of his head, and was now tugging on them uncomfortably. "He must have been hosting almost the entire time!"

"I can't imagine it," Seel murmured. "To be kept like that, like a brood mare, like—"

"An animal," Swift supplied. "I know. But wait, it gets worse... more animalistic. Let me carry on.

> *All harlings born in the facility were separated from their hostlings, who were prevented from knowing which pearls were their own. Harlings, like the hostlings, were each tattooed with individual codes so they could be identified, tracked, and associated in records. After the age of three, most harlings (except a few who were retained to become hostlings) were shipped to a separate facility where they were allegedly trained to become members of the Varr military. They were not even given names.*

Cobweb shook his head sadly. "I always think I've heard the worst about what used to go on in the Varrish world but... there's always something else."

Swift gave his companions a sympathetic glance before continuing.

> *It is of grave concern that the surprise discovery of this training facility represents a significant gap in our military intelligence. I am having my hara search this location for any evidence that might lead to the identification of similar facilities elsewhere. I have already requested additional resources from the Hegemony for this purpose. In my opinion, should this facility continue to function unchecked it could pose a high security risk to the new Parsic governing structure. But there is a significant possibility that if such establishments existed, they have since been dismantled and destroyed by the remnants of the Varr military. Regardless, it is imperative that we investigate immediately all possibilities surrounding this project.*
>
> *According to the hostling here, supplies and staffing for the project had been in decline due to Varrish concentration on the war effort. Around four months ago, the administration of the breeding facility received*

orders to destroy all evidence of the project, presumably including the living Wraeththu evidence.

Swift broke off. "They were going to—" He put the papers down for a moment, staring at his companions. "They were going to—"

"Slaughter them," Seel quietly finished for him. "Remember, Swift, remember—"

"Fulminir. Yes, Seel, I remember," Swift sighed. "Still... harlings." He drew one hand over his eyes. Despite the gruesome reports he'd already been given in the Gelaming camp, nothing had prepared Swift for the level of depravity he'd witnessed when he'd accompanied them into the defeated Varr stronghold. Frozen in time by the Gelaming's powerful magic, Swift himself saw scenes that he never would have believed otherwise — poverty, torture, murder and even cannibalism. He would always be haunted by the sins of his tribe. He lowered his hand and once again picked up the papers.

> *Instead of complying with this imperative, the staff informed the hostlings of the situation and fled with them and a small number of harlings. A handful of hostlings volunteered to remain behind with the majority of the harlings, but all except Lisia eventually left in search of help. Presumably these other volunteer hara became lost in the wilderness and perished.*
>
> *To alleviate the immediate crisis, I have assigned my hara to provide temporary services to the harlings we discovered, and we are also in the process of recruiting hara from the nearest village to provide harlingcare. However, I stress that this is only a temporary arrangement, for we hope that very soon, working with your administration, we can move these harlings out of here and possibly south to Imbrilim. From that point there are several possibilities we see for studying and/or rehabilitating them. However, this is not a decision we can make entirely on our own because this is after all a Parsic domestic problem and your hara must have some input.*

"Ash has also added a personal note to me."

> *Swift: I do think that in addition to sending up some of your hara to assist, you should visit this site personally, since it's possible you may discover evidence of more facilities elsewhere in Megalithica. Also, I should point out that Lisia, the resident hostling, is protesting*

*vehemently against the dissolution of the institution and
demands to speak to the highest possible authority on
the matter.*

The three hara sat in stunned silence for several moments. Swift folded
up the papers. "Needless to say, we'll be going to the facility tomorrow,
first thing in the morning. The reports will just have to wait. I must see
this place for myself and make sure that all resources are available for
getting these harlings properly cared for."

"Is it really necessary for you to leave tomorrow?" Cobweb asked. "It
seems you're away half the time. How can the Gelaming expect you to
lead if you're never in Galhea?"

"Cobweb, how can I lead if I don't know anything about my own
hara? I don't like being away from home either, but it's necessary.
Besides, this is something I want to do. An injustice of this magnitude — I
need to be involved, to see to it personally that things will be set right."

Cobweb frowned but said nothing more.

"Actually, I agree with Cobweb," Seel said softly. Swift quirked an
eyebrow in surprise. "We definitely need to send some hara out there
right away to relieve Ash's troops, but you can't just drop everything and
run off every time a crisis develops. You can still go out there and
investigate, make decisions, but we really ought to see to the end-of-
season reports first."

Swift's expression was troubled as he bent to retrieve his shoes from
the floor. "Well, I suppose I can wait a day or so before going out there."
After putting on his shoes, he began gathering papers. "I'm going to get
that aid dispatched and then I'm going to bed." Wearily he left the room
without another word.

"I can't believe you did that!" Edrei said, his arms folded firmly across his
chest. The bright, light of morning filtered through parted velvet drapes
in the well-appointed bedroom that had once belonged to this facility's
head administrator.

"It's evidence, Edrei!" Paran countered, waving the pilfered notebook
between them. "Besides, I did try very hard to wake him first. And he
did leave it lying right out in the open." He paused as he appreciatively
watched his chesnari pull on a shirt. "It's already eight o'clock and that
har was just dead to the world. You know that's what he gets for
sleeping in like that."

"He's exhausted!" Edrei shook his head. "He was swaying on his feet
last night. You should let the poor har sleep. It's probably the first time
he's been able to 'sleep in' since they abandoned him here."

"I was trying to be considerate. I thought he'd want to supervise
before we started interacting with his precious harlings. He was so

protective about our being around them yesterday. I can't understand how he could sleep so easily today."

Edrei sighed. "Well, regardless, we don't need him. You've got the list of chores." He paused in thought. "Why don't we find that harling, Pansea? Lisia seemed to put him in charge of a lot of things. We can check in with him until Lisia wakes up."

Edrei had no problem locating the strawberry-blond harling. Paran's body language made clear that he thought they were wasting their efforts, but he was willing to trust in Edrei's instincts for diplomacy since this wasn't really a time for military strategy. For his part Pansea seemed ready to flee when the two Gelaming hara approached him. Even after Edrei patiently explained the situation, the harling was hesitant.

"By Ag, kid, we don't bite!" Paran blurted, throwing up his hands in exasperation.

"I know, tiahaara, and I apologize for being difficult," Pansea said. He blushed and stared at the floor, wringing his hands together. "It's just that Lis said not to associate with you and until he tells me otherwise, I can't."

"But we're in charge now, not Lisia," Paran replied.

Pansea looked up, his eyes wide. Clearly the harling was frightened.

Paran's eyes narrowed suspiciously. "Look, are you afraid of Lisia? He can't punish you for talking to us."

"Oh no, Lisia would never hit me, or any of us. I don't even think he can since he's a hostling." Pansea shrugged. "Besides he burned all the paddles and things long ago – oh, but not to break the rules, it was because he had to make a fire to keep Rosea warm." Pansea shook his head sadly and then looked at the hara with watery eyes. "Poor Rosea. He was one of the hostlings who stayed with us, but he got very, very sick. He was cold right in the middle of summer." Suddenly the harling's face took on a panic-stricken expression. "You said that you couldn't wake Lis up! He's not sick is he? Because Rosea -- he *died*!" Pansea said the word as if it were a terrible secret.

Edrei was now the one to crouch before the terrified harling. "No, no," he said placing a reassuring arm on Pansea's shoulder. "I'm certain Lisia is just extremely tired. He's been working hard, after all. And even if he were somehow sick, our healers could fix him up — no problem."

Pansea breathed a sigh of relief, but his expression was still troubled. Concerned, Edrei probed the youngster's thoughts: *I think I should help them, but Lis was so serious about staying away. I've worked so hard to make Lis proud of me and be a good example. I don't want to disappoint Lis by being bad again – not after all that he's has done for us.*

But if Lis is sick from working so hard, maybe helping them is for the best. I just don't know if I can trust them; hara always lie to us.

He just doesn't know whether to trust us, Edrei projected to his chesnari.

As if in reply, Paran pulled a folded sheet of paper from his pocket and handed it to Pansea. "When I was talking to Lisia last night, he told me that I should get my hara together with the senior harlings to help out. See, he even wrote out a list of things for us to do. He must have just been too tired to tell you himself."

Pansea studied the note; his eyes glanced back and forth from the paper to the hara, a serious expression of contemplation on his fair face.

"You can trust us, Pansea," Edrei added. Using the psychic ability common amongst hara with the proper training, he projected trust toward the timid harling. "I know the Varrs told you horrible things about us, but those were lies. And why should you believe them when they went and left you here like this to fend for yourselves?"

Pansea stared at the floor again, and replied thoughtfully, "Well, I suppose somehar ought to take over for Lis until he wakes up."

"Of course," Paran agreed. "He wants you to help us."

"Well, I suppose the first thing we should do is get some hara to help with breakfast. We picked the fruit yesterday, but we only washed it, and it needs to be cut up. It gets all brown and yucky if you cut it up too far ahead of time. We can do it ourselves, but it will be faster with more hara to help and then we would have more time for..."

He talks a lot, Edrei projected as Pansea continued to chatter enthusiastically about chores.

No shit, Paran silently replied.

He talks more than Lisia and I think he has a decent amount of information about this facility.

Paran smiled broadly at Edrei and winked. *I knew I was with you for more than your gorgeous body!* He interrupted Pansea's chatter: "Yes, yes, it's clear you know exactly how to help us." He smiled charmingly and continued, "It's obvious why Lisia likes to put you in charge even though you're not the oldest. In fact, how would you like to be my official assistant?"

The harling looked up, excitement and pride shining from his face. "Okay, tiahaar — I mean Captain!"

Forever was still in darkness when Swift awoke.

He'd been having a dream, not quite a nightmare, but a dream of strange visions and uneasy panic. In the dream Seel had been hosting a pearl. It wasn't Azriel, but another pearl. Only it wasn't just one, it was many. Pearls kept piling up in the bed, and then another would come.

There was never any birth; Swift would only see Seel and know he was hosting and then see the pearls. Swift was alarmed and kept worrying about how they would care for all the harlings, but Seel was strangely calm.

Swift was glad to be back in wakeful reality even though he knew he had a long and possibly unpleasant day ahead of him. The sun was already rising. Aware that Seel would be eager to get a start on the day's work, Swift snuggled against his chesnari and sought his lips. Sharing breath was the best way to wake up, in his opinion.

Seeming to share that attitude, Seel smiled for a few moments before returning Swift's kiss with ardor. It was many moments later before the beautiful tawny-haired Gelaming opened his eyes. "Is anything wrong, Swift?" he asked.

Swift shook his head, surprised to realize that he'd conveyed any unease. "It's just a bad dream that I had. Nothing important."

"Tell me." Swift did so, prompting a grin and a quick kiss from Seel when he was done. "I promise you, love, you never, *ever* have to worry about *that* dream coming true!"

Swift frowned and sank back against his pillow. "You know, I think that maybe I had that dream because subconsciously Ashmael's report made me think about the way that we had Azriel. I don't mean to say that it was in any way the same as that Varrish breeding project, but Seel," here he paused, reluctant to ask the question, "do you resent that the Gelaming basically ordered you to bear a pearl for me?"

Seel rolled onto his side to face Swift as he spoke. "You know I did, but not as much once I got to know you and love you." Swift smiled at the words, but deep down he felt a faint twinge in his heart for the manipulations that Lord Thiede, the secret Aghama and force behind the mighty Gelaming, had used to create the ruling house of Parasiel.

"And, of course, I do care for Azriel very deeply," Seel continued. "More than I thought I could before he hatched." He reached over and squeezed Swift's hand affectionately. "I guess if I resent anything, it's that Thiede might take him away from us to suit some grand political purpose. It doesn't seem fair at all, especially when I look at Azriel and see how helpless and vulnerable he is. I just want to protect him."

Swift threaded his fingers with Seel's. "Azriel will never be helpless. Even if we can't always protect him, he'll be strong because he comes from a strong family. Besides," he laughed, "judging from last night, he's already a fierce warrior."

Seel frowned. "That was only self defense."

"It was not!" Swift laughed again, shaking his head. "Azriel has got you so wrapped around his finger. You know it's a first generation thing. You let Azriel get away with too much because you keep thinking that he's younger than he really is. And Az knows that in some sort of instinctive way. You really have to get rid of that human time frame, especially when you help me evaluate all those harlings in a few days."

Leaning forward suddenly, Seel pulled Swift into his arms and covered his mouth with his own. Surprised but pleased, Swift closed his eyes and leaned into the embrace as their souls intermingled in the sharing of breath.

When they finally pulled apart, Seel smiled and ran his hand through Swift's dark hair. "I'm not going with you," he said quietly.

Swift frowned, "What do you mean? Why not?"

"I think that I should stay here to make sure the regular work doesn't get out of hand. I hate to admit it, but I don't think we're going to be able to travel together much anymore – at least not while things are so busy. Besides, you don't really need me to go with you. You've become a strong leader, Swift. You can make all the decisions on your own; you don't really need my advice." Seel grinned as he continued, "Not that it will stop me from giving it to you."

Swift closed his eyes for a few moments as disappointment in their upcoming separation vied with elation at Seel's confidence in him. "Well, you certainly make a good argument, and if my advisor says I don't need his advice, I guess I should listen," he said after a few moments. "Just promise not to spoil Az too much while I'm gone."

"Not likely! You're the one who spoils him, the way you let him run wild all day."

Swift grinned and, pushing Seel back into the mattress, positioned himself on top of him, grinding their hips together seductively. "Well, that's just the way pure-borns are supposed to be. They run wild and then learn how to seduce older hara with their supposed youth and innocence." He leaned down and bit Seel's lower lip playfully.

"I knew he was getting that biting thing from you."

Swift grinned before launching a second attack. *Let's be late for work.*

Tarkan arrived with a second message just as the entire family was finishing up supper together. Wanting to disrupt as little as possible, Swift excused himself and tended to the matter quickly. When he returned he held a simple black book that was about as thick as his thumb.

"You're going to read to me?" Azriel asked excitedly as his father walked in. Swift went over and hugged his harling close, savoring what he knew was a fleeting moment. "No, precious, this is for your hostling and me."

He turned to Seel and held up the book. "This is the journal of that hostling, Lisia. The bad news is that it looks like I might have to leave for that breeding facility as early as tomorrow, if you can take care of my schedule for me."

"A breeding facility? What kind of breeding does it do?" Tyson asked.

Cobweb cast an annoyed look at Swift for being so indiscreet. They'd agreed that the harlings shouldn't be as sheltered from the outside world as Swift had been during his childhood, but secret harling breeding facilities was too sordid a topic for dinnertime discussions.

"That's none of your concern, Tyson, but official business of the Parasiel," Cobweb said firmly. "Would you please take Az to play with you in his room while we hara discuss this?"

Tyson looked up at his adopted hostling with stunned betrayal. "That's not fair!" he declared passionately. "Why should I have to leave? I just asked a question. It's not my fault it's some stupid secret." Cobweb merely cast Tyson a look, which told the red-faced harling that his protests were falling on deaf ears.

"Ty, I know it's frustrating but," here Swift mouthed the words silently, "I don't want Az to hear." Aloud he continued, "I'd really appreciate it if you'd take care of Az for me. I think Yarrow made some of your favorite cookies for dessert. Why don't you and Az go help yourself in the kitchen?"

"I want cookies too!" Azriel shouted happily.

With Tyson somewhat placated by Swift's demeanor, and the promise of cookies, the harlings left and Swift continued. "Ashmael has put Captain Nemish in charge of the breeding facility. Paran acquired this journal from Lisia, who is apparently being rather uncooperative. In the meantime they also seem to have found some leads on locating other similar facilities scattered around Megalithica and are making progress with the records they found. Obviously, this needs to be investigated right away and to move things along I plan to saddle up Afnina and leave first thing in the morning." He looked down at the journal ruefully. "It looks like I'm going to have a great deal of reading to do tonight."

Chapter Three

My name is Lisia. This is my diary. Tiahaar Illanex gave it to me today as a special present for doing so well in our writing lessons. He said that he had found this nice extra big writing book in the box with our regular notebooks and he had saved it to give to somehar. I was the first harling who he thought deserved it, because I write so well. I'm glad I can write because I don't draw very well. A lot of the other Lilies spend time drawing pictures but I don't like to because I'm not very good. Now I can write in this diary instead.

Before today I didn't really know what a diary is or why I would want to make one, but tiahaar Illanex explained it. He said some things he had already said in our lessons, like the reason we learn to write is because writing down things is important. He then said some things get made into books for lots of hara to read and sometimes just one har writes something down to explain to another har.

I asked tiahaar Illanex why Lilies like me need to learn writing since we are all going to be hostlings and hostlings don't need to write anything. He said that hostlings need to be smart in order to make smart harlings and so that's why we need to learn and write. I think I must have made a grumpy face because then he said that writing makes you smarter and he said that sometimes writing down what you're thinking can make you feel better if you're sad. Finally he said that was called a diary and I understood more.

I'm sad now because I tried to draw a pretty flower and it doesn't look right. I think the diary makes me feel better but I'm not really sure. It's hard to tell.

Today I want to write down some things about myself. That first entry was boring because it didn't say anything except that this is a diary. Now I want to put some things in this book so later when I'm older, I can remember. After all, tiahaar Illanex and the other teachers have said we won't be harlings for very long because we grow so fast, so I should hurry to write down my memories before I'm a har.

First of all, I want to say that I'm a Lily of the Valley. All my friends are Lilies too. A Lily is a special harling because when we grow up, we will all be beautiful hostlings. I've been a Lily as long as I can remember and I am so glad. It's a very beautiful and important thing.

Tiahaar Nordica talked about it in a lesson. He told us all the Lilies of the Valley were picked out like beautiful flowers and brought here especially. It was funny at first when he said that because I almost pictured somehar going through a field picking out flowers that later turned into harlings by magic. But then I realized that's silly because the teachers always say that harlings come from pearls. I wasn't the only one confused though, because Hyacinth then asked if we all came from a field. Tiahaar Nordica seemed to think that was a stupid question because he laughed, but not like it was something funny. He told us we had all been picked out but not from fields of flowers.

It's strange. Until the other day, when I wrote about the Lilies and how we were picked out, I never thought very much about where we come from. Then after that lesson, I started wondering about it over and over. There aren't any hostlings here so we must come from somewhere else. I asked a few other Lilies about it, but nohar knew so we were all wondering. Then Calla said that we probably all came from a place just like this one, where hostlings are making harlings. We were probably moved here when we were small because we would have more room to grow and learn, since the other place was probably crowded from all the other harlings. Calla is very smart and all of us agreed, because he's probably right.

That reminds me. Today we got to find out where our names come from. Some of us have very easy names like Hyacinth, which is a flower we grow in the garden, and then Rosea, which sounds so much like rose. Some of us have names that you can't tell though. I didn't know how wonderful my name was until today. My name comes from lisianthus, a very pretty flower that comes in all different colors, like pink and purple and white. I was so excited when tiahaar Illanex showed me a picture in the flower book he brought. I'm so glad that my name means something so pretty. I wish we had some in our garden here. I would go to look at them all the time.

Tiahaar Illanex had taken some books from the upstairs library and every Lily got to find out about his name. Only Lily harlings have names, they told us. Calla is named after calla lily, which is perfect since of course we're all Lilies. Coral got to see a picture of some coral, which is a special kind of rock that's only found in the ocean. Seagrass found out his name comes from the ocean too, since seagrass is a kind of beautiful, long grass that grows underwater, almost like it's in a meadow. None of us have ever seen a real ocean, but the pictures in the book were very pretty.

Coral had an idea today and I can't believe none of us ever thought of it before. We each have a pencil for practicing lessons and drawing and writing, but yesterday Coral was given a pen as a reward for doing all of his sums right. A pen uses ink and it can't be rubbed off if you make a mistake. But ink is prettier than old gray pencils. Coral's pen writes in ink that is dark blue.

Today after supper, Calla asked Coral what he was doing really loud and that made us all look. Coral had taken off his doll's dress and started drawing on his back. Coral said that he was giving his doll a code so he would be a Lily like us. I said that I didn't think he should do that since Altec, who is our watcher when we are not in lessons, is always telling us that we're not allowed to mark on anything except for the paper that our teachers give us.

But Calla said that the dolls belong to us and not to anyhar else, so we should be able to do whatever we want with them. I think Calla is right, and so did everyhar else, so we all asked if we could use Coral's pen for our dolls too. At first Coral wanted to be selfish and not share, but we asked really, really nice and finally he did.

I'm a little sad with my code. I tried to draw a fancy shape to go with Petunia's numbers, but the ink wouldn't do what I wanted on the cloth and it made sort of a splotch instead. Seagrass did a very silly thing and ended up crying when Calla told him why. He wrote the exact same code on his doll that he has himself! But of course no two Lilies have the exact same numbers and marks, even if they're almost exactly the same like Rosea and Spirea's are. Rosea was very fancy with his doll. He made a very nice straight code set on the back and he even drew in fingers and toes because our dolls are very simple and don't have any. He was about to start drawing a ouana-lim too, but Coral got mad and took his pen back because he said we would use up all his ink.

I feel sad today. When we were playing after lunch Hyacinth took Petunia and cut off most of his hair with scissors. He did it even though I told him not to and he made my doll all ugly. I was very mad so I told tiahaar

Nordica, who was our teacher for today. Tiahaar Nordica was angrier than I thought he'd be and he took Hyacinth to the front of the room and hit him with the paddle over and over. Hyacinth cried a lot and I felt sorry that I told on him.

I'm still angry about it because we each only have one doll, and mine is ruined, but still, instead of paddling him I think would have been fairer if I got to cut the hair off of his doll. That would be very fair. And then maybe I could have his cookies at snack time since he was so mean. Well, maybe he didn't try to be mean. I think maybe he didn't believe me that the hair wouldn't grow back. Hyacinth isn't that smart. I wish that tiahaar Nordica hadn't hit him and made him cry. I know I shouldn't think that because that's what hara are supposed to do to harlings who are bad. I hope I am never bad.

Tonight I'm all excited because I decided my doll isn't really ruined. When Hyacinth cut off the hair I was mad because Petunia had always had long hair like me and I thought that was the only way he could be. I didn't even want to play with him any more.

I guess I was just being silly, though, because tonight at dinner, I was looking at the teachers and administrators, who were at a table together, and realized that none of them have long hair. Not one of them! Just because they don't have long hair doesn't mean they are ugly though. Some of them are really wonderful to look at, handsome is what you call it, and they wear their hair different ways, like spiked up or so short it's almost shaved on the sides.

Anyway, I suddenly realized that maybe Petunia doesn't have to be a Lily like me. He can be a regular harling who would grow up to be a regular har like the teachers. Because of this, I decided to change his name. I didn't want him to be named like a Lily so instead I've named him Eagle. I love to watch the eagles that fly over the gardens sometimes.

Today was so much fun that I just had to write down about it. When we woke up this morning it was very cold and Spirea yelled for us to go and look out the window. It was so beautiful. During the night it has snowed and it was still snowing in the morning. Everything was white and sparkly in the sun. Later on, when we were in class after breakfast, tiahaar Illanex noticed how we were all looking out the windows at the snow and he smiled and said he had a big surprise for us. There was a great big box next to his desk that had our coats and gloves in it. We almost never wear clothes like that because when it gets cold, we just stay inside. But today tiahaar Illanex said that we could go outside and learn about what makes the snow.

Snow is such a weird thing. It falls just like rain but it's not wet until it melts. We ran around outside and had fun playing with the snow. Me and a bunch of the others kept trying to see a single snowflake because they are supposed to be very beautiful, like flowers but with straight lines and holes in them and each one is supposed to be different. But the snowflakes were too small for us to see. They just looked like fuzzy dots.

Because it's a new year, today we had new lessons and we're learning new things now. We are having singing lessons this year. I like singing a lot. It's more fun to me than drawing and I'm a much better singer than I am an artist. Tiahaar Carthall is our teacher now and tiahaar Illanex is teaching the Lilies who are a year younger than us. I'll miss him because he was nice, but I like tiahaar Carthall too. Tiahaar Carthall gives us pretty ribbons when we are very good and very smart. If we're bad or don't learn the lessons we'll have to give ribbons back. And we get to pick out the color we want. I got an orange ribbon today because I remembered to say "please" and "thank you" without being reminded. I want to get lots of ribbons.

Today was halfway through the year and tiahaar Carthall told us that from now on all the Lilies in my age group will start spending every other day helping the hara who take care of the very small harlings. We won't all go on the same day, half will be in lessons and half will help the hara and then on the next day the two halves will switch. I'm so excited about this! I just love little harlings. They are so sweet and they always seem to like me. We have to be very, very good when we help with the little harlings, though. Tiahaar Carthall said that the hara would watch us very carefully and that they would paddle us if we were careless or mean to the little harlings. I'm not too worried about it though because I would never let anything bad happen to a little harling.

I learned something very surprising today. The big house where we live used to have a bunch of hostlings here a long time ago. But they weren't called hostlings then, they were called Sisters.

We found out about the Sisters by accident last night after dinner when we were having fun. I was doing hide and seek with Spirea and Calla and Coral. Coral was the finder and Calla and I went to hide under a bed, but it wasn't either of our own beds because that's where Coral would always look first. So we were under the bed and it wasn't that dark because we had to leave the lights on.

We were lying there only a few seconds when Calla poked me with his elbow and whispered that he saw something was written on the wood. It looked familiar and I think I remember seeing it on other things before but I couldn't read what it said then. But now we knew how to read it and it said "Property of the Sisters of the Sacred Heart." Calla and I didn't know what that meant. We'd never heard of "Sisters" before. We had never heard "Sacred Heart" before either but that sounded very nice and very important.

But the words would mean that the bed belonged to these Sisters and that seemed strange because the beds belong to us and we all belong to the Varr tribe. I wondered if Sisters were like another tribe, but then why would the bed belong to them? Coral ended up finding us because we were whispering, but then we didn't want to play anymore anyway because the Sisters thing was much more exciting.

We all were talking about what we thought the Sisters were and Spirea said we should look to see if all the beds said the same thing, so we looked under all the beds in our room and they did. Calla said we should go check the beds in the younger harlings' rooms too but I didn't think that was a good idea. The younger harlings would want to play with us then and they make too much noise and the administrators would notice and be grumpy about us getting under the beds because we weren't supposed to play on the floor because that was dirty. No Lily should do dirty things. So then Calla said that we should check the dressers and we pulled one away from the wall a little and it said the same thing.

Then today I couldn't believe what happened. During lessons, Calla raised his hand and asked tiahaar Carthall what Sisters are. And I was so scared that he'd get mad because he'd know we were looking under the furniture where it's all dirty. I tried to give Calla a look so he'd be quiet, but he wouldn't look at me. Anyway, tiahaar Carthall asked where Calla heard that word and Calla said that he saw it on furniture in our room. Tiahaar Carthall didn't ask where on the furniture that the words were written and he got quiet like he had to think hard about what the word meant. I guess he couldn't remember at first, but then he said that Sisters is another word for hostlings but that it was a very, very old word and nohar uses it anymore and we shouldn't say it either. So then Calla asked why our beds belonged to these old Sisters. Tiahaar Carthall said that they used to live here a long time ago and that the writing was left over from then. He said that it was so long ago that all the old Sisters were probably dead.

I decided today I am really happy to be a Lily. I decided that because today was a day when I got to take care of the little harlings. I do that every other day, of course, but today was special because I suddenly realized that I am going to make wonderful little harlings. Of course I know that's what hostlings do but that's so amazing! I was reading a story to a group of some of them who are about three and they were all listening to me and smiling and laughing. These harlings are all so sweet. I wonder if they're so nice because they're Lilies too, only they're too small to know they've been picked yet. I wonder what the harlings I make will be like. I can't wait to meet them and play with them like I do with these little ones. I feel very special to know that I've been picked to make something so wonderful. Lilies are very important.

I am using my diary to write down something that I think might be a little bit bad. But the reason hara write things down is because they are important and we think that this is something very important even though we're not sure yet. Let me get to what happened.

Today tiahaar Carthall told us that we were having a new group of very small harlings coming to stay here. A little group usually comes about once a year, but sometimes we get one or two new harlings at a time. Anyway, tiahaar Carthall told us that because we were getting to have so many Lilies here, we are also getting more staff and teachers and other hara to help take care of us all. These new hara will need a place to stay, so instead of having lessons we were given the special job to get rooms ready for them.

Calla and I were cleaning up a small sleeping room. Even though this is a sleeping room there was a little desk like the teachers all have. We were wiping the desk with rags because it had gotten dusty just by sitting there. We noticed that even the insides of the drawers were dirty so we took them all out to wipe them. When Calla pulled out one of the drawers a piece of paper fell down way in the back. I didn't think much of it until he picked it up and called me over to read it to me. I wanted to take it to tiahaar Carthall right away and ask him what it meant. Calla said okay but that the teacher probably would just take it away and not tell us anything important. We decided to copy the letter into my diary first. This is what is says:

> *Dear Sister Margaret,*
>
> *I sympathize deeply with your concern for the children. I would give my life to ensure the safety of your order and its precious charges. Unfortunately there is very little that I can do. The depraved gangs have already ransacked our churches and stolen anything they perceive of as monetarily valuable. The few remaining parishioners live in fear, fiercely guarding their wives and children and rarely leave the scant protection of their own homes. The police are helpless against the growing*

threat. I have included a check, but I fear it would prove worthless even if you were able to find a use for it.

We must have faith in our Heavenly Father, Sister. The Lord truly works in mysterious ways and though you fear, I believe that you and the children may be blessed by your very isolation. The Wraeththu are prone to wallow in their own wake of destruction. They will remain in the more populated areas where there are supplies to steal and boys to corrupt. I can't imagine them traveling all the way to the country and certainly they would have no use for a modest convent and a school for orphan girls.

Stay strong, Sister. I will continue to pray for you all every day and night and I encourage you to do the same. Pray that the Lord will preserve us and protect us from this evil. And pray for us trapped in the towns and cities, and pray for the many innocents dead at the hands of the Wraeththu. But remember, too, to pray for the souls of the corrupted that they will turn away from their demonic cult and find mercy in Christ Jesus.

At the bottom it says *Sincerely, Monsignor Peter Ardolino.*

Tiahaar Illanex told me that sometimes a diary is for writing secrets in but until now, I didn't really have any. Now I do have a secret because nohar knows that I copied the paper into this diary. Actually Calla knows too, but it's still a secret.

I'm glad Calla thought of writing this because when we showed the letter to tiahaar Carthall he told us that we must not tell any of the other Lilies about the letter and he took it and tore it up into little pieces.

There are still lots of things I don't understand about the letter, because there were lots of words in it that I don't know. But maybe I'll learn what they mean when I get older and have more lessons. Calla had been very scared when we first read it and I really was scared too because there was the word "evil" and "dead" on it. Even worse, it seemed to be saying that Wraeththu are evil and maybe that maybe hara died because of them. Wraeththu is another name for hara. The Sister and the har who wrote the letter seemed scared of them. Why were the Wraeththu evil?

When we asked tiahaar Carthall about it he just said that Wraeththu who live here are not evil, which, of course, we knew already. He also said that the letter was written a long, long time ago and that nothing bad like that would happen again. Calla tried to ask him more but he sent us to our rooms and told us that we would be punished if we told any of the Lilies anything about it. Maybe there were evil hara here before, in olden times, but not now.

Calla and I talked about what to do about the note. At first he wanted to tell the others but I made him promise not to because I don't want to be in trouble.

I'm feeling so sad today. I hate the way I look. I wish I was beautiful like hostlings are supposed to be. I have stupid hair that's not even all one color. Maybe if it was two colors mixed up better it would be pretty, but I've just got the one yellow part and it's just on one side. Maybe if at least it was on both sides it wouldn't look so stupid. A lot of the other Lilies call me Stripe because of my hair and I don't like it one bit. The rest of my hair is just plain brown. I wish it was all yellow and maybe curly like Coral's. And I wish I had pretty long eyelashes and blue eyes like Calla. At least I'm prettier than Hyacinth.

It's important to be pretty to be a hostling. Tiahaar Carthall said that if we don't grow up to be pretty enough we won't get to be hostlings at all, we'll have be regular hara instead. I remember tiahaar Illanex had told us a story about an ugly duckling that grew up into a beautiful swan. It was supposed to make harlings who aren't that pretty feel better. Of course I know that I'm going to grow up to be a har not a swan so the story doesn't really matter. But, I hope that I really do get prettier when I get bigger. At least I still have more ribbons than even the prettiest Lilies.

This year's lessons are all very different from what we were learning before. This year we are finally learning about how we will make the harlings once we are old enough to be hostlings. Our teacher this year is tiahaar Neydish and so far he told us that when we get big enough we'll make the harlings inside our bodies and to do that requires another har, one who is not a hostling.

Of course I knew that we would make the harlings and that used to worry me a bit because making a harling seems impossible and I was afraid I wouldn't be smart enough to learn how to do it. But he said that we don't actually have to make the harling ourselves. It will grow inside us, inside a pearl, all by itself. It happens automatically, just like we don't have to do anything to make ourselves grow, it just happens on its own. He said it's like magic. But before we learn about the details of having pearls, we have to learn about our bodies and what's inside us and how it works. It's called biology. I think these lessons will be very interesting.

Other than biology, all our lessons are entertainment and art to make us better hostlings who are interesting to the other hara who will help us make the harling pearls. And this year we don't all have to do the same things. I will still have singing but I don't have to do drawing anymore at all. We'll also have dancing and lessons all about how to makes ourselves more beautiful. I wonder, will the beauty lessons help me fix my hair? I hope so.

I can't believe what happened today. I am so shocked I feel almost sick. I feel really bad. I already wrote in this diary before about Hyacinth, how he's not as smart or pretty as the other harlings. I'm really sorry I wrote that because something bad has happened.

It was today right after lunch that tiahaar Neydish said instead of starting class like normal, the head administrator tiahaar Upsari was going to come talk to us. I could tell it was going to be an important talk since it was the head administrator, but I never guessed what he would say. He came into the classroom where we all were and he told us that the administrators are starting to make some decisions about us becoming hostlings. That sounded normal but then he continued talking and explained that what they were deciding on is which Lilies are going to be hostlings, since not all of us might be good ones.

The administrators and teachers had already told us this a few times before, but as soon as he said that, every Lily in the room was upset, wondering what the administrators were deciding and if they had already made the decision. Well, as it turns out, they had. Tiahaar Neydish told us that after observing all of us, in our classes and at lunch and everywhere, they had found one Lily who was not going to be a hostling. It was Hyacinth.

Hyacinth wasn't in the room, but instead with the other group taking care of harlings. Tiahaar Upsari said they hadn't told him yet. I felt like a giant rock had just hit my stomach. At the same time, I was angry. Seagrass is a good friend of Hyacinth and although he tried to be polite, he spoke up and asked, "What's wrong with Hyacinth? He's a good Lily, he always does what we're supposed to—" But tiahaar Upsari interrupted and said that they all know Hyacinth is a good harling but he is just not good enough to be a hostling. Anyway, he said, Hyacinth will still live with us, only he will work in the kitchen.

I am still upset about Hyacinth, especially since today, after two days of sleeping in our same sleeping room, he now has to sleep somewhere else, over with the staff hara. The administrators changed their minds. Tiahaar Upsari said it was because Hyacinth was not a Lily and therefore should not be living with Lilies anymore. Besides, he said, Hyacinth was upsetting all of us. I suppose that is true because for two nights and most of the day, he was crying and crying. But still, I think it's just horrible. Now that Hyacinth is working in the kitchen, he doesn't have any more lessons and doesn't get to play, just do chores like take care of garbage and wash dishes and help the cooks, all dirty things no Lily would ever do. I know hostlings are supposed to be special and beautiful, but Hyacinth wasn't so bad at all. I really hope I am good enough because if somehow they told me I wasn't, I could never stop crying.

Today tiahaar Neydish used the big blackboard and did drawings of the internal organs inside our bodies that will make the pearls and hold them while they grow inside us. It was just a simple drawing and the inside parts didn't look at all like I thought that they would. It didn't look any more special than any other organs. That really seemed strange to me since the pictures of the ouana-lims that grown up hara have are kind of pretty like flowers and he had always said that in aruna the ouana hara would be like bees and they would fertilize the flowers that grow inside our bodies. So I asked, "If we're the flowers by being soume, how come it's the ouana-lims that look like flowers? How come they're prettier?" Tiahaar Neydish had to think about it for a while and then he said, "That's just the way it is."

Of course, that's always what hara tell us when they really don't know the answer to something. Then he erased the drawing from the board and told us each to take out a sheet of paper and write down the steps of conception and pearl-hosting. He went out of the room and put Spirea in charge to make sure nohar cheated. When he came back, he had tiahaar Sennaflur come with him. After we passed up our papers, tiahaar Sennaflur said that he had an answer to the question that I'd asked.

He said while the ouana-lims may look like flowers, the more important flower is hidden inside our bodies. He said that the part deep inside of us is like a flower that is still in the bud and we will learn how to make it bloom into a very, very beautiful flower and this is what will make a pearl, just like flowers make seeds. I already understood this pretty much, though I hadn't thought about pearls being like seeds before, so I asked why the flower would be hidden away where we can't see it and how do they know what it looks like and that it's pretty. After all, what good is a flower if you can't see it or even smell it?

Tiahaar Sennaflur said that the flowers inside of us aren't flowers to see, but flowers to feel. He said that as pretty as a flower is to look at, this is what it will feel like when we learn how to open up the flowers inside of us. He then said that it's even more wonderful than just seeing a flower. What tiahaar Sennaflur said makes sense to me and it's very exciting.

I wonder why tiahaar Neydish didn't know the answer before. He always seemed so smart about everything else, but now I think maybe he just knows the answers that are written down already for him. Really I think he must be pretty dumb not to know something so obvious. I can't wait to be able to open my flower. I wonder what it feels like.

Chapter Four

The thick grass was still damp with morning dew when Swift and Tarkan touched down in the open fields at the eastern edge of the breeding facility. Despite the remote location, the journey from Galhea had taken little time, thanks to use of *sedim*, which had the ability to eclipse the normal boundaries of space and time by traveling with their riders via the otherlanes. Unfamiliar with the area, Swift had asked Tarkan to stay the night at *Forever* and join him in his journey the following morning; this way Tarkan's *sedu* could psychically direct Afnina to their destination.

Swift patted Afnina's neck appreciatively as he appraised his new surroundings. His eyes first focused on the large, neatly symmetrical brick building. He frowned; it reminded him of a smaller but similar old human building in Galhea that the Varrs had used as a prison. This was a much more inviting establishment, however, with an abundance of flowers and shrubbery framing not only the building but also the several walkways and outer buildings around it. Skirting the area were green expanses of open grass and large, organized gardens. Harlings, watched over by adult hara, were out in an open area further to the side, but none were in the immediate vicinity.

In the distance, a high, rusted metal link fence, topped with barbed wire, separated the facility from the thick conifer forest beyond. Heavily wooded mountains bordered the land on two sides. Swift inhaled deeply as he and Afnina followed Tarkan and his mount to the stables. The fresh, clean scent of pine, marigolds and other growing things dominated the air, yet Swift nonetheless seemed to detect a faint, lingering whiff of foulness. Perhaps it was because he knew what had happened there.

He'd had enough time – staying up late into the night and waking early that morning – to go through a good chunk of the hostling Lisia's journal, and what he'd read had both moved and shocked him. He was still astounded that such an immense undertaking as the facility could have taken place for years amid such secrecy.

Swift observed a small group of Gelaming and Parsic soldiers gathering before the building's main entrance. Apparently, they had sensed his arrival from the otherlanes. He dismounted from his *sedu*, leaving Tarkan to take Afnina to the stables, and strode over towards them. "Greetings, Captain Nemish," Swift called out. The tall har gave a curt bow and stood at respectful attention, although Swift could sense his ever-present air of superiority

Swift focused on his own hara, responding in kind to their salutes. "Captain Totral," he addressed his highest-ranking Parsic officer, "have your relief efforts progressed according to plan?"

"Yes, tiahaar Swift," Captain Hyriit Totral replied. "All my hara are assigned to various tasks. Repairs on the utilities are nearly complete; we're merely waiting on a fuel source for the power generator, and that should arrive any time now. Continuing on from what the Gelaming have already begun, we're using hara from the nearest village to handle most of the harlingcare. Until yesterday they had no idea there were any harlings here, but now they're eager to help clean up this mess in their backyard."

Swift nodded. It made sense to use locals rather than career soldiers. "And the surplus food rations? They've been distributed?"

"Yes, tiahaar, and we have high hopes for using the road that the Gelaming uncovered; delivery should proceed much faster than we'd originally anticipated."

Paran took this as a cue. "The uncovering of the road is yet another example of the importance of having a Listener in every unit. We were quite surprised at how thoroughly the Varrs had it hidden, but our Listener Edrei Faraliesse managed to sense the visual distortion." Paran cast a glance at the other soldiers gathered around. "Tiahaar, might I pull you away from your hara for a briefing on the security aspects of our findings?"

"Certainly, tiahaar Nemish." Having worked closely with General Aldebaran's elite ever since he had agreed to join forces with the Gelaming, Swift was already very familiar with Paran, and his know-it-all attitude came as no surprise. He turned to Hyriit. "I'll meet with you again this afternoon, tiahaar. Please carry on with your assignments until then."

As the Parsic soldiers left, Paran also dismissed the Gelaming hara. Once he and Swift were alone, Swift asked, "Have you set up a headquarters where we can review the files and discuss your findings?"

"I have, but it's a bit crowded at the moment with hara up there transcribing and decoding. With your permission, we can speak out here." He gestured to a few empty benches circling a large tree trunk several yards away. "I'll be brief at any rate."

Swift nodded his agreement, but wasted no time. He asked his first question as they were still walking. "What have you uncovered regarding the existence of additional facilities?"

"Not much more," Paran replied, grimacing slightly. "Questioning of Lisia and the harlings revealed that they all believe in the existence of other facilities for both breeding and military training, but they had no knowledge of the location, or even number, of these sites. However, in going through the files, we found a few references of 'transfers to Facility 2 and Facility 3.'"

"Transfers of what?"

"Harlings, it would seem, but there were also references to transfer of personnel among the facilities."

"Any names of those involved?"

"No, most hara were referred to by the codes tattooed on their backs. However, I'm hoping that the decoding will reveal more details. About that and other things."

"Perhaps we'll find locations as well," Swift said, wondering what the captain might have meant by "other things," but choosing to let that pass in light of more important questions. "Have the Gelaming begun an organized search? If so, I'd prefer to coordinate those efforts myself, since my hara have better knowledge of the land and Varr practices."

"Yes, tiahaar, we had planned on your involvement. In fact, I believe that General Aldebaran is arranging authorization for those efforts from Immanion and I expect to receive more details any time now."

Swift nodded. "Please alert me as soon as you hear from Ashmael. Locating any other facilities is my top priority, aside from seeing to the welfare of the victims here. Please accept my gratitude for the work you and your hara have done."

Paran responded with a short but courteous nod. "This certainly isn't the type of duty that I was expecting to undertake, but we've managed it well. We've brought in the troop healer to begin looking over the harlings. And since the arrival of your hara and the local volunteers we've been able to reassign most of our non-essential troops back to their regular patrols."

"Still," Swift replied, "I imagine that you're personally eager to be moving along as soon as possible."

"Well, I admit I would like to get out of this place sooner rather than later, but I expect my involvement will continue once we leave. This project may last several months, perhaps even years."

"Project? You mean these harlings?"

Paran shrugged dismissively. "Well, yes, but they're hardly the main point of it."

Swift felt his hackles rise. "Aren't they? I mean, we do have close to 200 harlings here in need of immediate assistance, don't we? Unless I read the general's report incorrectly."

"No, no, you didn't, it's just that since then we've discovered there's really more to this whole business than we first imagined."

Paran rose from the bench and began to pace. Swift watched him with a growing sense of unease. "In fact, based on our discoveries, General Aldebaran has already captured the interest of the Hegemony, who are now eager for Gelaming involvement. Messages have already been sent to Imbrilim in preparation and experts will be sent down."

"Well, I thank you for informing me of all this, tiahaar," Swift replied slowly, his voice like ice. "Although seeing as I am governor over these lands it would seem that *you* should be waiting on *me* to inform you of *my* decisions in this matter, rather than the other way around. You haven't even explained your reasons to me, but have simply made a decision — without me. This is a 'Parsic domestic problem,' is it not?"

The captain barely blinked. "I apologize for any offense, tiahaar, but I assure you, when you get all the facts, and meet the harlings, you'll agree we're making the right decision."

"We shall see," Swift said curtly. He could already feel his heels digging in for a fight. "In the meantime, there is somehar I would like to meet with even more than the harlings. Unless you have anything else crucial to share, I think I should speak to the hostling. Where is he?"

Paran glanced towards the building. "He's inside, very likely sleeping. He's been doing a lot of that."

"Is he sick?"

"No — exhausted." Paran frowned. "Been through a lot these past months. Resentful of us. Suspicious. Lisia tried to keep watch over our activities and maintain some control over the situation, but the day after the general sent out his report to you, he collapsed." A slightly mischievous grin appeared on Paran's face. "That's how I got to pilfer his journal. He was dead to world in his room and there it was. Too much of a temptation. Don't think he would have given that up willingly, do you?"

"Probably not," Swift conceded. "Has he noticed it's missing?"

"If he has, he hasn't mentioned it. I'm just relieved he's asleep so much."

Swift was surprised by the comment and regarded Paran skeptically.

Paran's expression became defensive. "You should see the way that creature baits me! He's like some caricature of a nagging human female at times. They're all brainwashed here. Drooping around like flowers in the rain. No doubt they think displays of physical fragility and weakness make them more appealing."

Suddenly, there came a voice from behind – a strong, indignant voice. Lisia. "I overheard that, Captain Nemish! And I take the gravest possible exception!"

Paran turned, his manner casual, as if by that point he were used to such interruptions and attacks. "My, my, Lisia, eavesdropping again? I should put a bell on you!"

Swift turned as well, facing Lisia for the first time. After reading so much of the hostling's journal, he was surprised by what he saw. Although Lisia certainly was feminized, his overall looks were nothing terribly extraordinary. This har had not been picked for his duty because of any great beauty, but plucked out of a normal childhood simply because he had been available, a sacrifice to the Varr war machine. He had become what he had through training and had kept his position through his ability to produce many, many pearls. This was not to say he wasn't lovely, with his sun-kissed hair and golden skin. But Swift had been half expecting him to resemble a painted, scantily clad kanene, like he'd seen in the prostitution trade uncovered in Fulminir.

While Swift made his assessment, Lisia continued his eruption of fury and impatience. "Captain, if I didn't *eavesdrop*, I'd never know what's going on, because nohar ever *tells* me anything." He stood his ground before the captain, hands on hips, glowering. "And as for my 'weakness,'" he continued, "if I'd been weak, I wouldn't *be* here, now would I? Do you think it was *easy* to deliver all those pearls, tiahaar? *You've* never done it!"

Paran was chuckling softly under his breath; if Lisia noticed it, he gave no sign.

"Do you think it required no strength for me to oversee this entire facility *by myself*? Ha! So much for your understanding – of lack thereof – of the meaning of 'weakness.'"

Finally satisfied, Lisia turned his eyes to Swift, who unlike the soldiers, was not in military gear and whose hair was shoulder-length. "So, Captain, who is this?"

"This, Tiahaar Lisia, is Lord Swift Parasiel, Governor of Megalithica — the 'higher authority' you requested." Paran bowed slightly and gestured to Swift.

Lisia, appearing mollified and a tad embarrassed, straightened his wrap-around blouse. "Oh. Please excuse me, Lord Swift. I've petitioned the captain over matters here and he'd told me you'd be coming but—"

"It's quite all right," Swift interrupted, wanting to smooth matters over and get off to a good start. "I understand that you've been under a great deal of stress. Care to take a walk with me?"

Lisia stood, listening and at the same time blatantly inspecting the newly introduced Governor of Megalithica. "Walk with you?" he asked, clearly perplexed.

"Yes," Swift replied, "I've only just arrived, and I thought you'd be the perfect har to give me a tour of this place. Besides, it would give us a chance to discuss matters privately. Tiahaar Nemish, would you let us be?"

"Certainly, tiahaar," said Paran. "I'll be inside getting an update on the file decoding." Paran headed towards the building and disappeared through the main door.

Swift turned to Lisia. "So, can we talk?"

"Yes, tiahaar Swift," Lisia replied, taking a cue and dropping the more formal title of "Lord." Once again he straightened his blouse, which he wore with an ankle-length skirt. Both garments were dyed a striking orange and were made of a finely textured silk.

Swift began to walk towards the yard where the harlings were playing. "How are you feeling now?" Swift asked. "Captain Nemish tells me you're exhausted."

Lisia shot Swift a sideways glance that seemed to say, "The captain can stuff it!" but instead of voicing such a thought, managed a slightly more polite turn of phrase. "All things considered, I'm doing rather well. Your Gelaming friends have 'graciously' been carrying out my requests and even, imagine, allowing me to stay here, in my own home."

The hostling's hostile tone was unmistakable, but for the moment Swift chose to ignore it, remaining silent. He would counter Lisia's assumptions about Parsic policy at a later time. At this point they'd reached another set of benches beneath the shade of a large, graceful aspen. In a neighboring field, a group of harlings was gathered for some outdoor activity or game.

Lisia eyed them, then paused to brush off dust before settling onto a bench. "Yesterday I was finally able to have my clothes properly washed. It's good to wear something beautiful again." Lisia smiled, eyes returning to the harlings, and to Swift it seemed his sudden shift in tone was an attempt at currying favor. Suddenly, however, Lisia's expression changed to one of puzzlement, even surprise. "What are they doing?"

The harlings, all about four or five years old, had formed into two parallel lines of five harlings each. A village har stood off to the side, apparently having organized this game. Within a few moments, a harling from one side was aiming a large ball at the other group. Nohar on the other side attempted to catch the ball, but instead dodged out of its path.

"What on earth does that har think he's doing?" Lisia exclaimed, clearly outraged. "They're going to try and hit each other!"

"Yes, it seems so," Swift replied, turning to the hostling, who was staring with an expression of horror on his face.

"But those aren't soldier harlings," Lisia fumed. "They shouldn't be throwing things or doing anything violent."

Swift observed as a harling with long brown hair awkwardly aimed a ball and threw it at the opposing side. The ball did hit somehar but in the process the brunette lost his balance, falling to the ground in an ungainly heap. "Well, perhaps the har isn't teaching them violence," Swift suggested, "but skills they might not have learned here before — like the value of quick reflexes, agility... and coordination." He smirked as another harling in the game was hit in the middle of the chest, having completely failed to avoid being hit.

Swift returned his gaze to Lisia, and could see the hostling was still tired and not altogether focused. Watching the harlings break what had apparently once been facility rules wasn't helping. "I'm sorry, tiahaar, perhaps there are too many distractions out here," he said gently. "You could show me around inside."

"Umm, sure," Lisia said. He got to his feet and gracefully smoothed out his skirt. "I'm sorry for getting so wrapped up in that game, I've just never seen something like that. Look at the way they're aiming at one another! They could get hurt!"

"Oh no, they'll be fine," Swift said.

As if on cue, yet another harling was hit and fell to the ground. Lisia jumped, startled, and was clearly about to rush over but, before he could, the harling looked over to him as if sensing the hostling's distress and called out, "I'm OK, Lis! Don't worry, this is fun!" He was grinning broadly.

Lisia smiled back tentatively and waved, then followed Swift back to the building. He sighed. "I just don't understand this. Any of this."

Swift nodded silently and followed Lisia through the front door. As they passed down the halls of the building, Lisia pointed out classrooms that were filled with harlings, working on crafts and singing. Lisia explained that all were under the supervision of adult hara.

"It appears you've managed to keep things running pretty smoothly," Swift said. "I'm surprised to see lessons in progress."

"We tried to keep regular lessons going, even after the teachers all left," Lisia said, "but it's been hard, obviously."

"Some hara in your position might not have bothered."

Lisia, who'd momentarily paused to look through a window into one of the classrooms, straightened up and continued walking. "For now I've decided that the harlings should just concentrate on fun activities in class. Keep a routine going. Everyhar is so distracted by the soldiers and new faces that they wouldn't really learn much anyway, at least not until things have been… resolved."

At the end of the hall they came to a room which was apparently a kind of nursery, or such as could exist for rapidly growing harlings. Through the door, Swift observed a number of small harlings sleeping snuggled together on two beds. A Parsic volunteer stationed inside smiled and waved, then said something Swift couldn't quite catch.

Just as he was about to follow Lisia into the room, suddenly two small harlings appeared from nowhere and almost bumped into him. "Lis! We missed you, we missed you!" Each of them put their arms around Lisia's legs.

Lisia's expression glowed with pleasure as bent and rubbed the harlings' heads affectionately. "I haven't been gone that long, you two! Isn't tiahaar Ilita treating you well?" he asked, casting the har a sidelong glance. It was not lost on Swift that the har in question had short hair and a decidedly ouana aspect.

"Oh, no, he's good!" defended the smaller of the two. "We just are so bored in this room." He looked at Lisia hopefully. "Could we come with you, wherever you're going?"

Lisia sighed and looked to Swift. "I'm sorry about this, tiahaar."

"It's quite all right," Swift said. "I don't see why they can't come with us while we talk, as long as they aren't a nuisance."

"They won't be." Lisia squatted down before the two harlings. "Okay, you can come with me, but you have to behave and not be too loud. And, Two, we're going upstairs, so come here." He opened his arms and Two stepped forward and allowed Lisia to pick him up.

Swift wondered at the name and why the harling was being carried, but couldn't ask a question before Lisia spoke. "All right then, let's go. Ilita, I'll see they return back here when they've satisfied their need for freedom." The har nodded and watched Lisia back out of the room. Swift got out of the way and was about to follow the hostling down the hall when he felt something tugging on his pants legs. It was the second harling. "Can you carry me, too?" he asked.

"You're old for that, aren't you?" Swift asked. The harling appeared to be about five months old.

"Yes," he admitted, "but until the new hara came, we were left alone a lot. Everyhar was too busy. We didn't get picked up much."

Swift's heart, which until that moment had been for the most part all business, instantly thawed. He bent over and picked the harling up. "What's your name?"

"Five."

Swift suddenly realized that these harlings had numbers rather than names. Lisia was standing a short distance down the hall watching him. "I think we're all set, tiahaar," he said. "Sorry for the delay."

"You know, tiahaar, you don't have to be taking care of these harlings," Lisia commented as he led the way down the hall. "That's my job. I'm a hostling."

Swift kept on walking, gripping Five just a little more securely. "No, you're a har and so am I. Besides, I know perfectly well how to handle harlings. I have a son myself, by my consort."

Lisia did not reply except to nod silently and gesture with his head to a set of double doors, which he pushed inward, revealing a stairway. As the hostling began to climb up the steps, carrying the harling, Swift noticed the effort he was putting into appearing strong. And yet the har was clearly still weak and underweight.

At the top of the stairs, they entered a lounge, a common area for what Swift assumed had been the hostlings' living quarters. Lisia walked to the far side of the room and put Two down on a large sofa covered in a worn knitted blanket. Swift let Five down and the harling went to join his friend. "Now you two can play some games over here, but don't be too loud," Lisia instructed. Two and Five nodded in unison and immediately began to whisper, as if conspiring together in sharing some harling secret.

Satisfied his charges were well in hand, Lisia took a seat in what was obviously a comfortable, if well-worn, chair. Swift sat opposite on a small sofa. "I'm impressed by your understanding of harlings," the hostling said.

Swift couldn't help but be warmed slightly by what he took to be a profound compliment, considering the source. "Well, I'm no expert. But, Seel — that's my chesnari — he's always saying that pure-borns must have more natural hostling instincts." Swift chuckled. "He keeps insisting that I should do any future hosting."

"You can't do that!" Lisia exclaimed, horrified.

"Why not?" Swift asked, already anticipating what the hostling would say. In addition to knowing the background of this particular har, Swift was quite accustomed to confronting the "old fashioned" ideas that had been promoted by the Varrs.

"Because you're not a— you're a..." Lisia struggled to explain himself. "Well, I'm just confused because I know you're not a hostling, since you say you have a consort... but you're not even soume!"

Swift shook his head. "No, I don't suppose you would think I am. But neither is Seel, my consort. We're *hara*, not soume *or* ouana. We're *both*. Surely you've observed the soldiers and other hara and how they behave. They avoid designating fixed procreation roles. You should realize that every har with the proper caste ability can sire or host a pearl. A har doesn't have to be designated as a hostling to enjoy caring for a harling. And hostlings are free to pursue whatever activities they desire in addition to bearing pearls."

"Yes, Paran has explained his Gelaming philosophy to me more than once, tiahaar, and it's very... interesting. But—" Lisia closed his mouth and frowned.

"But?" Swift prompted.

"But you're Governor of Megalithica!"

Swift couldn't help but laugh, a healthy relief for the tension he'd felt in the moments before. "Well, that's a good point. Believe me, we don't plan on making any pearls in the near future. Certainly we would wait a few years, until Azriel's older and I have more time." He shrugged, unconcerned. "I'm not sure what we'll ultimately decide, but I like the idea of hosting one day. It seems very natural to me, as it does to many hara."

Lisia continued to look a little perplexed, different emotions playing across his features. Swift sighed. It seemed clear that Lisia was not ready to accept this new way of thinking, and that did not bode well. "You still think it's wrong?" Swift asked.

"No," Lisia replied quickly. He paused, clearly struggling to find the right words. "It's just, I thought... I didn't expect... Well, I was under the impression that you were a Varr like me and the administrators."

"I see," Swift replied. "Well, the answer to that is yes and no. I was raised in that tribe, but it no longer exists. The philosophies and traditions of the Varr tribe have been abolished and I am establishing a new tribe in its place, the Parasiel. That is my tribe, and it is yours as well, tiahaar."

"How can you do that?" Lisia asked in genuine bewilderment. "How did you get all the Varrs to just change their minds overnight? I don't understand how you could just change hara from one thing to another."

Swift couldn't help but give Lisia a grim smile. "Well, in a way it was done just overnight and in another way, it's still going on right now. But, I can explain more about how the Varrs were defeated later – that's not important. To answer your question, you must understand that many Varrs weren't very happy with the way things were. Nohar really enjoys fighting all the time and making war and that is much of what the Varrs were all about. So, many hara were willing to accept the new Parsic philosophy and leave warfare behind. As for those who weren't — well, most of them respected my authority anyway."

"Why? Honestly, you don't seem like the sort of har to lead the Varrs!" Reconsidering his harsh declaration, Lisia immediately amended, "Not that I intended any offense, tiahaar. It's just that you don't strike me as a soldier and soldiers are the power behind a tribe, aren't they?"

"Power is the power behind a tribe, Lisia, and power comes from within oneself and from unity among hara. And, you are right that I was never truly a Varr soldier, but I am the rightful heir to rule Megalithica. My father, Terzian, was a great general and respected leader. Therefore, those who were loyal to the old regime are willing to accept me as governor."

Lisia's eyes widened in surprise as if to say, *You are General Terzian's son?* But he shook his head as if to dismiss that thought and said, "Well, I understand, you became ruler because you are Terzian's heir." But confusion once again returned to his eyes.

"You still have questions," Swift prompted.

"Oh, it's just that I assumed that Ponclast's son would have been the rightful ruler," Lisia replied. "And, I take it that Terzian is dead — I'm sorry for your loss."

The comments were unexpected and Swift felt a brief pang of grief. He also mentally squirmed at the casual knowledge this extremely isolated har seemingly had of his father and Ponclast but opted to ignore those implications for now.

"Ponclast's son is dead," Swift answered, gazing levelly at the hostling. "He was executed by his own father and by mine."

"Ponclast killed his own son! His heir!" Utter shock registered on Lisia's face. He was clearly at a loss for any further words.

"I'm afraid so," Swift said. "That was a large part of what made me realize that I would prefer to stand with the Gelaming rather than with Ponclast." For a moment, bitter memories rose up, but Swift quickly banished them, needing to focus on the here and now. "Tiahaar, I know that you..." He stopped himself, realizing that he'd almost mentioned having read the hostling's secret journal. "Well, I didn't come here to talk about myself and my family. I came here to set things right at this facility. To do that I'd like to hear from you about what happened. I came to see the harlings, see the facility, and hear your opinions. This is a unique situation and I want to grasp it completely before coming to any decision."

"I'm grateful, tiahaar," Lisia said earnestly. "It seems to me I can trust you to listen. Ever since the Gelaming arrived, everything has been topsy-turvy and nohar seems to be listening to me."

"I'll listen to you," Swift said.

An outsider certainly wouldn't have picked Captain Paran Nemish as the assigned leader of a troop of elite Gelaming warriors. Always a no-nonsense type of har, his preferred garments were more modest than the usual Gelaming attire, and although his appearance did not fail to impress, he did not appear particularly commanding at this moment.

Paran was hunched over a large desk, which was strewn with partially decoded papers. Ilhenny, their resident code expert, was taking a much needed break and although he'd never admit it, Paran was wishing he could do the same.

A knock sounded on the door.

"Enter," Paran replied. He straightened up briefly but allowed himself to relax when he saw Edrei enter the room.

"Still no luck?" Edrei said, his expression infused with both sympathy and disappointment.

"Not really," Paran replied. "It's not that Ilhenny can't decipher it — it's pretty basic Varrish coding — but so far it seems like the damn files just don't say anything that important. I think they must have destroyed the good stuff."

"Or else they never kept material evidence to begin with," Edrei mused. "Remember how hard it was to find this place."

Paran grunted in affirmation and slumped back in his chair, which he tilted backward. "I really hope we find it, or else this has been some wasted effort. Anyhow, did you have anything to report?"

Edrei shook his head. "No, not really. I'm not sensing anything from the harlings." He sighed slightly. "Not anything useful to us, anyway."

Paran straightened up and motioned for Edrei to come closer. "I'm sorry; this place is hard on you, isn't it?"

Edrei sat near him on the edge of the desk and shrugged. "I'm trained to handle it and we've been to worse places. I'm just frustrated. I can sense the injustices done here and I feel the harlings' lingering memories of hurt and fear, but I feel like there's nothing else for me to discover. I want to be doing something useful!" He paused for a moment, frowning. "I should be out there searching for the other facilities or just hustling us over to Imbrilim right now — we're useless here!"

Paran reached over and squeezed Edrei's hand reassuringly. He knew that as the acting commanding officer he ought to discourage the Listener's criticism of their orders, but he didn't. He told himself it wasn't because of their relationship. After all, blind obedience and flawless discipline really weren't much a part of Wraeththu nature, even in the opinion of a dedicated soldier like Paran.

The day seemed to pass quickly as Swift questioned Lisia on various aspects of the breeding facility. Although it was obvious that some of the administrative details and motivations were unknown to him, Lisia was clearly answering the questions as best he could.

Swift found himself impressed with the bold manner in which Lisia responded to the interview. He had expected the hostling to be meek and reticent. Instead the har was extremely self-assured and although his manners were flawlessly polite, Lisia did not attempt to hide the fact that describing these details was a mundane experience for him, and one that he had already performed for the Gelaming. In fact, Swift got the impression more than once that he was being humored by the carefully poised hostling.

"You think my questions are foolish, don't you?" he asked, mildly amused.

"Oh, of course not, tiahaar," Lisia answered.

Swift gave him a look that showed he didn't believe his protests.

"Well, I must admit that I don't understand how and why you don't know any of this," Lisia conceded with a soft smile. "The Gelaming are from across the sea, so I can understand their ignorance of our ways, but you're Terzian's son. I think you must be testing me to see how I'll answer. There's no way that you were never taught about these things."

"But Lisia," Swift explained, "you must understand that this facility was a closely guarded secret. You were lied to about Varr customs. As far as I know this breeding project was merely an experiment. Certainly it was not part of our normal way of life."

"I understand that, Lord Swift," the hostling answered, his voice tightening just slightly. "I've been told how we were deceived. Still, I thought that surely *you* would know these things, from your father or from taking over the leadership."

"I see your point but, no, I was never told about this place or this project," Swift said. "And, we did not interrogate any of the high-ranking military warriors who we defeated." He paused for a moment, reflecting on the folly of that course of action. At the time Fulminir fell, he'd been willing enough to trust Thiede's judgment: Ponclast and the last of his hara had simply been deposited into Gebaddon, the psychically contained forest that the Gelaming had created in southern Megalithica in lieu of a prison or maintaining any continued contact. However, over the past months he'd suggested that a party venture into Gebaddon, for just that purpose, only to be assured by Thiede that such interaction was impossible.

Quickly, Swift dismissed that line of thought and returned his focus to Lisia. "As for my father, he was captured shortly after my feybraiha, and there was never an opportunity for him to share this sort of information with me, assuming that he even would have done."

"I hadn't realized." Lisia's smile was apologetic. You seem older than you obviously are." He considered for a moment before continuing. "But I find it odd that you were kept in such ignorance. In my experience, harlings begin training for their future roles from about the age of three." He sighed wistfully. "I suppose things are just very different for heirs."

The wording caught Swift's attention. It was not the first time Lisia had made a reference to 'heirs.' "So you *were* aware that some hara had families... if they were important enough? Didn't that make you feel resentful?"

"Oh no, tiahaar. As we understood it, hara worthy enough were honored with property and wealth and authority. They required assistance in wielding their power and carrying out their duties and so the only way to get hara worthy of the honor was to make them — heirs. Plus the heirs would obviously inherit the property." Lisia sighed again and frowned. "Honestly, the reality is much more confusing to me. I don't understand how just any hara can be allowed to make pearls whenever they please. Harlings are a big responsibility. What if the hara who make them don't know how to care or provide for them properly?" Lisia shook his head gravely. "It doesn't make any sense to me."

Swift was carefully formulating a response when they were interrupted. For nearly two hours, both the young harlings had kept completely to themselves, whispering and playing games. Then, about a half an hour earlier, both harlings had fallen asleep, snuggled up on the sofa amidst the cushions. Suddenly, however, one of them awoke and, hopping off the sofa, darted across the room.

"Five, get back here this instant!" Lisia commanded sharply.

The harling turned immediately to Lisia and squawked just as indignantly, "But I don't want to stay here anymore!" He hedged toward the door. "Two is asleep, having a bad dream about... well, you know. It makes me sad. I want my other lings. I'm going to the nursery right now!"

"Well, not with that tone of voice!" Lisia replied in a manner that reminded Swift vaguely of his childhood tutor, Moswell. "That is impolite. Five, you ask nicely and I will take you to the nursery." Lisia was then interrupted by a loud yawn. "There, you see, you woke up your ling." Five seemed unconcerned. He skipped eagerly to the other harling and began talking excitedly, his desire to make an escape having suddenly vanished.

Swift was astounded and turned to Lisia in surprise. "I didn't think they were properly socialized to talk to hara. He's very bright and speaks perfectly well." His brow. "What's a 'ling' — short for harling?"

"Well, of course they're socialized and talk. Did Paran tell you they don't?" Lisia shook his head in frustration. "That har simply doesn't understand *anything* about harlings. He probably thinks the harlings are stupid because they say 'lings' but actually 'ling' is simply one of the many words the youngest group made up. It's caught on all over the facility. It means harling of the same age group. There are lots of other words, but honestly I haven't had time to learn many of them."

"That's fascinating," Swift replied. "It's like they've formed a small-scale harish tribe."

Lisia chuckled. "Yes, I suppose you could say that. Anyway, just another example of how there's so much to learn from observing harlings. In fact, I didn't mention it to you talking just now, but the language ability was a large part of how the administrators separated the future hostlings from the future soldiers and workers. The theory was that the harlings who made more attempts at communication without being prompted were more soume and the ones more prone to action and mechanical work..." Here, Lisia simply shrugged.

"You can't tell me that the harlings acted that differently at that age," Swift said skeptically. The idea was unsettling.

"Well, we hostlings weren't really allowed to work with the very small harlings so I can't truly say, but from what I've seen since then, most harlings tend to act all the same. It is true, however, that a few do show tendencies from the beginning, and communication, assertiveness, empathy, and problem-solving are all factors that usually indicate pretty definitely which ones want to be soume and which want to be ouana."

"But clearly most of the harlings created here were chosen for the military and not for hosting," Swift mused. And then, grumbling under his breath, he said, "When in doubt, strengthen the army." He glanced up at Lisia to see if he'd heard or reacted to the comment. The hostling was gazing off into the distance, obviously sad.

The somber silence was broken by the older harling, whose hair was a riot of messy brown ringlets. "I need to *go*," he said, very urgently.

"OK, I'll take you," Lisia said pleasantly, sadness wiped clean from his face. He got up and the harling followed him across the room. Swift was startled to notice that the child struggled to get up from the soft sofa. He also walked awkwardly, with a limp. "Do you need me to help you?" Lisia asked him as he opened a door. The harling shook his head vigorously as they moved beyond the open doorway, where Swift could see a hallway with two rows of identical doors on either side, apparently the hostlings' rooms. Lisia led the harling further down to where the bathroom must be.

"Lisia, what's wrong with him?" Swift asked as soon as they returned.

Lisia looked pained. "It was a terrible accident — before we were very organized in caring for the harlings. It took us by surprise when Two suddenly learned to walk and he got away from us and tried to climb up a set of shelves. The whole thing came down on him and he was badly hurt." Lisia looked positively ill as he thought about the incident. "We weren't sure if he would make it. We had no doctor, hardly any medicines and what we had, we didn't know how to use. The Gelaming healer said that his hip healed in the wrong position and that's why he limps. He said that it would take much more than a field medic to fix it."

Swift gave Two a sympathetic look. Noticing the attention, Two nodded solemnly and said, "It hurt a lot. There was blood." At that his ling hugged him supportively.

"We came to embrace the concept of pens around that time too," Lisia went on, the vaguely haunted expression still on his face until it hardened suddenly into indignation. "Your Gelaming friends think it's cruel beyond measure and they've already torn them down, but believe me, it was far kinder to keep them fenced in a small area than to watch helplessly as they hurt themselves or wandered off into the wilderness. I couldn't expect my older harlings to keep track of them all scattered about."

Swift nodded as the logic of the situation became clear. "Yes, I see," he said. "Lisia, there is one thing that puzzles me, though. It's obvious that you care for the harlings very much. You've even taken the habit of referring to them as 'my' harlings. So why haven't you given names to any of the small ones? Surely, they should be known by something other than the breeding codes you were telling me about before?"

Lisia returned Swift's nod. "Oh, I've been very tempted to give them names, especially since, as you pointed out, I have come to consider them all to be my own in a way. These smallest harlings were named One through Ten simply because we didn't know what was going to happen, if the Varrs should come back." Lisia paused to smile at the two harlings, who were once again seated on the sofa. "But the older harlings and I discussed it early on, in one of our idea meetings, and we decided to uphold the old policy to an extent."

Lisia returned to his chair. "You know, normally none of the harlings had names unless they were chosen to stay on as hostlings. At that point, the chosen were given the opportunity to select a name for themselves." Lisia paused again, smiling slightly in reminiscence before continuing. "Well, within reason, anyway. Of course there won't be any more selections, but we've decided that when each harling gets to be about three years old, there will be a celebration and at that time he will choose his own name."

While Lisia had been speaking, they'd been joined quietly by an older harling with long reddish blond hair. He politely waited for Lisia to finish before speaking. "Excuse me, Lis, but Captain Nemish asked me to bring Lord Swift to him." The harling looked at Swift with obvious curiosity, but did nothing to acknowledge him directly.

Lisia made a face, which was half amused and half annoyed. "Tiahaar, may I present to you Pansea. He's one of my most reliable harlings and your Gelaming captain has commandeered him away from me." Turning to the harling he continued, "Pansea, this is Lord Swift, governor of all Megalithica. He's here to help us."

Pansea smiled broadly and swept into a very graceful bow. "It's a tremendous honor to meet you, Lord Swift. Please consider me at your service."

Swift noted how surpassingly poised the harling was and couldn't help but smile at his fawning behavior. In Swift's experience, most harlings of that age were completely self-absorbed. "Thank you, Pansea. Just remember, I'm only a har, so call me tiahaar. Not Lord." He winked so the harling wouldn't feel corrected.

"Pansea, could you please take Two and Five back down to the nursery for me?" Lisia asked.

"What about..."

"Don't worry, Captain Nemish can wait for a few minutes."

"Yes, please, Pansea," Swift chimed in. "I'd like to finish my conversation with Lisia. Assuming he didn't indicate that I was needed urgently, the captain can wait."

"OK, then I'll be right back." Turning to the small harlings Pansea beamed and said quickly, "Let's go downstairs. Two, I can carry you if it's too hard." The curly-haired harling shook his head, indicating he would try the stairs on his own. "Like hostling, like harling," Swift thought, as they left the room. He turned to Lisia. "They're very strong. Pansea especially — so helpful and responsible."

"He's had to be," Lisia replied, looking meaningfully into the governor's eyes. "All the trained harlings have had to work very hard and they're extremely dedicated to caring for the younger ones."

Swift took this in and, as impressed as he was by the selflessness of the harlings, vowed silently that this way of life would be forever changed. He stood up and brushed off his pants in preparation for leaving. "Tiahaar Lisia, exactly what kind of future would you like for the harlings who were raised here?" He hated to fling such an important question at Lisia right before he left to see Paran. He felt certain that the hostling had not yet had the time or energy even to consider their future, but he wanted him to begin thinking about it. However, the green-eyed har answered Swift's inquiry with surprising confidence.

"Well, first of all, I want an end put to this nonsense about my harlings being sent to that Imbrilim place or anywhere else!" Lisia declared vehemently. "Of course they may want to leave on their own when they're older and that's fine. I don't want them limited or consigned to a particular role in life like I was. But this talk I've heard of moving and then some new school, living with other families, Gelaming or Parasiel... I don't like it. It's all too sudden! For now we need to be together. I want them to have their friends around them as they adjust to all these changes."

Lisia walked over to the window, gazing at the bright late summer sky. "As for the future, I've thought about it, especially while I was lying in bed, so worn out after the Gelaming first arrived. And I've decided I definitely want them to learn as much as they can about life outside of the facility — not just basic lessons but real information about what the world is really like." He turned back to Swift and continued in a resolved tone, "And I want them to learn about the past too — so that they can understand what happened here and how things should have been instead."

Having read the har's diary, Swift wasn't surprised that Lisia would be in favor of change, but he was nevertheless impressed with the extent to which he had formulated plans for the harlings' future. Swift wondered briefly what plans Lisia had for his own future.

Lisia turned around and was now half-sitting on the windowsill with his arms crossed, eyes downcast. "I'd like to stay here and have this be our school. Of course, we'll need teachers, new staff and supplies to help me run things and take care of everyhar properly. I'm not sure how to get that except through you or the Gelaming." The hostling paused briefly. "I suppose we'll have to offer something in trade for the assistance," he continued softly. "I considered going back to making pearls, but honestly I don't want to do that and I don't want that for my harlings either." He looked up at Swift again, an expression almost of pleading on his face, "Many of us have other skills though, so maybe—"

"Oh Lisia," Swift interrupted, "you needn't worry about that. It's our responsibility — the new Parsic government's — to see to it that each and every one of you is provided with everything you need, be that supplies, staff, teachers, healers, guidance in the outside world or whatever else. You don't have to worry about the cost or having to pay us back." He paused, searching the hostling's eyes as he continued, "Of course, you realize this place will not be reopened as a breeding facility. That's just not something that—"

"Certainly," Lisia answered, nodding. "I'm glad we're in agreement on that. No, I'd like this facility to remain as a home where I can raise my harlings, and where they can learn. Certainly, many of the older ones are going to want to be hostlings as they've been raised to aspire to that, but I want them to make their own choices. I want them to learn the skills they need, so that they can choose to do other things with their lives instead, if that's what they want."

Lisia paused in thought, playing with a strand of his hair. "Maybe someday we could even move into the outside world, so that they'd have exposure to additional role models — but not too soon. I don't want to throw too many changes at them all at once." He gazed at Swift with a hopeful expression.

Swift nodded in understanding and Lisia quickly continued. "And I'd like for them to have access to proper 'caste training'; the Gelaming have told me that all hara can learn to use special powers if they have the proper training that focuses on spiritual matters instead of just aruna. I'd like my harlings to learn that. I want them to be strong so that nohar will ever be able to force them to do anything that they don't want to do."

"And what if their choice is to leave here?" Swift asked gently.

Lisia's face fell slightly and he took a deep breath as if resigned. "Well, assuming that it's in their best interest or that they're old enough to choose for themselves, then I'll have to let them go. It'll be hard since we've become so close these past months. But, I suppose I'll just have to get used to losing them; that was always a fact of life here in the past."

Lisia was silent for several moments before continuing, "Of course it will be even harder now. In the past, once we hostlings came of age, we were never allowed to spend time with the small harlings. They never had any one particular caregiver. Nohar formed close attachments," Lisia interlocked his fingers and gestured at Swift. "Not until after a harling was chosen to stay on at the facility... though even they were sometimes taken away if they didn't live up to the expectations." The hostling shook his head. "Things have changed since the administrators left. We've all become like a family now. I don't think I could survive these harlings being taken away from me like my pearls were. And," he added firmly, "I don't think it would be good for the harlings either."

Swift wanted to reassure Lisia, but he felt it was too soon to make promises and anything else seemed trite and superficial. The silence was just becoming awkward when Pansea returned from his errand to the nursery.

"So, are you and Lord... I mean *tiahaar* Swift done talking?" Pansea asked.

Lisia glanced at the Parsic governor, who nodded. "I suppose. Shall I prepare a room for you while you meet with the captain? I assume you'll be staying for a few days."

"Yes, I want to get a feel for the situation here. Whatever accommodations have been made for the officers will suit me just fine."

Lisia twirled a strand of his hair thoughtfully. "I'm afraid all of the administrators' quarters have been assigned to the Gelaming, so I'll have to arrange for somehar to move to one of the old hostling quarters. They're along this hall." He pointed to the hallway Swift had observed earlier.

"Actually staying up here with you will be fine , tiahaar," Swift replied, smiling. He liked the idea of being in one of the hostling's rooms.

He felt it would somehow draw him even closer to understanding what the hara here had felt and thought, as if he could somehow absorb their essence from the rooms they'd left behind and use it to help in making his decisions.

"So, how are you getting along with the Gelaming?" Swift asked Pansea, as they neared the first landing. It was interesting to have the opportunity to observe one of the older harlings.

"Oh, we get along very well, tiahaar Swift," Pansea replied carefully. "The Gelaming are very helpful hara."

Swift sensed a hesitation in the harling's voice. "Yes, they are very helpful, but I suppose it must be frightening to have all these strangers here."

As they paused on the landing, Pansea turned to him and shook his head. "It's not that — there were always strangers when the soldiers would come. It's just... never mind. I'm sorry, tiahaar, I shouldn't say anything."

"If something is troubling you, I really need to know Pansea," Swift replied patiently "otherwise I can't fix it."

Pansea's eyebrows furrowed as he frowned. "All right then, it's the fact that however helpful they are, they're the enemy — and they're talking about making us all move away from here and get changed! Are they really going to do that?" Pansea bit back on tears that had risen along with his apparently pent up hysteria. "It's like they've captured us. Who knows what will happen once we move. We might not ever be together again and—"

"Oh Pansea," Swift broke in. "It was the captain who told you all these things, wasn't it?"

"Yes, I heard him telling his soldiers," Pansea replied. "He said that some hara in a Hege... Hege-something had said it. And my friend Delphin said that he heard them say something about 'deprogramming' us and studying our 'genetic patterns.' What does that mean?"

Swift stepped back and looked into the harling's uncertain eyes. "I'm going to be honest with you, Pansea. I don't know yet what will happen to all of you. Nothing has been decided. You might go to live in Imbrilim and you might stay here. Or, maybe some of you will go to different places. I don't know. But, I do promise that you won't ever be prevented from communicating with each other. You'll still be able to talk to your friends, even if you end up far apart."

"But the Gelaming act like we're going to go with them to this Imbrilim place and we don't want to go to live with *them*!" Pansea said. "They think we're..." he paused searching for the right word, "They think that there's something wrong with us harlings! Especially the lings who are my age and almost ready to be hostlings. They want to change us to be like they are, but I'm happy the way I am. I don't want to change."

Swift clasped Pansea's trembling hands. He certainly empathized with this young har, remembering how it felt to be coming of age with all the emotional torment it entailed, while the outside world seemed to be collapsing around you. "Nohar is going to force you to change, Pansea. You are who you are and nohar can take that away from you. But, you must understand that your future *has* changed." He softened his tone. "You are not going to be a hostling — at least not in the way you were told. You need to learn about what the world is really like beyond these walls and then you must decide what you want to do with your life."

"Does that mean I'll have to be a soldier or some sort of *worker*?" Pansea asked.

Swift couldn't help but smile. "I daresay that whatever occupation you choose, you'll never have to work as hard as you have here taking care of the smaller harlings. It might seem daunting now, but you'll be surprised at how many exciting options will be open to you." Swift squeezed the harling's hands reassuringly. "And if you do decide to have pearls, they will be yours. You won't have to give them away. You'll take care of them until they grow up."

Pansea fell silent, obviously deep in thought. Taking that as an indication that the harling was sufficiently reassured, Swift suggested that they proceed in finding Paran.

"He'll be in the head administrator's office," Pansea said, turning towards the last section of steps. "I'll show you where it is."

Chapter Five

I haven't been writing so much lately, since I've been so busy with things this spring. There have been lots of changes in our routine this year. We don't have as many classroom lessons as we did before and we're not helping with the small harlings as often either, because the harlings in the groups just below us are doing that more and more.

One thing that we have been doing instead of our regular lessons and activities is planting flowers around the grounds. I have to admit that I wasn't at all happy about that idea at first. Our teachers have always taught us that proper hostlings shouldn't be dirty and now, right when we are almost old enough, they start telling us to plant flowers in the dirt! And the others were even grumpier about it than I was. I didn't really want to say anything, of course, but luckily Calla brought it up first.

But tiahaar Sennaflur explained that planting the flowers was another lesson for us to get ready for hosting. He said that delivering a pearl, and even aruna, can be messy. So in some circumstances it is necessary for a proper hostling to get dirty in order to create life. It's the same way with planting flowers in the dirt. Of course Coral and Calla were saying we'd have understood that lesson perfectly well without actually having to practice getting dirty, but we all did what we were told.

And I have to admit it really isn't bad. I actually like working in the garden a lot. The weather is beautiful this time of year and it's nice to be outside. Plus, I get a lot of satisfaction from nurturing the little seeds into plants and deciding on creative patterns to plant them in. And then, when the flowers are mature, we cut them and make gorgeous arrangements that are placed all throughout the building for everyhar to enjoy. And even better than all of that, when we're working outside, we don't usually have teachers, or administrators, or any staff with us. In fact, I think one of the reasons they are having us do this is because they are much too busy with the younger harlings to spend time with us anymore.

It makes me feel very grown up to be left to work on my own. Plus, it gives us all a chance to talk and visit with each other a lot more than we could before. We talk a lot while we're working on the flowers. Mostly we talk about feybraiha and what we think that will be like. We all seem to feel pretty much the same way, which is that we are nervous about changing, especially because the teachers all say we might not feel very well when it starts. But even so, we're all very, very excited about becoming grown-up hara and actually practicing aruna instead of just hearing about it in class.

I thought I had pretty much learned all the main things about aruna and making pearls or, well, everything I can know before my feybraiha, but today tiahaar Neydish showed us something I had never even guessed at.

It started out when he was having us talk about the differences between hostlings and other hara, the ouana hara. He used the chalkboard, and on one side he put notes about hostlings and on the other side, ouana hara. He told us to just call out whatever we thought and wrote it all down — so by hostlings we had "pretty," "neat," that they can sing, dance, tell stories, are good with harlings, and then by ouana hara we said "strong," "handsome," that they can protect hara, and so on.

Well, we had a pretty good list going and tiahaar Neydish was busy writing down in the ouana hara list when he suddenly stopped and said, "You know, I just realized you're missing something very important from this list. Actually several things!" Right away we all kind of scrunched down in our seats, feeling like we'd failed and missed something obvious, but then we tried to guess what it might be. We called out some other things but the tiahaar just shook his head. Finally he said, "Well, I can give you a hint: The adult ouana hara you'll meet will have some physical differences too." Oh, did we laugh then, because of course they're different, otherwise they wouldn't be ouana hara! But it turns out the tiahaar wasn't talking about that at all. Instead he got this serious look and he said, "You don't really know what I'm talking about. It's something you just have to see."

He put down the chalk then and stood up right at the front of the room and then, to everyhar's surprise, began taking his shirt off! We all looked at one another, confused, but at the same time staring at tiahaar Neydish. He had his shirt off and we saw what he was talking about. He wasn't like any har I'd ever seen, though now that I think about it, I guess really I hadn't ever seen anyhar with his shirt off, except for harlings. Instead of having just a smooth chest with tiny little rose-marks on, he had these two funny round, dark circles on it, right where the chest muscles are. Up close (he had us all get up and look) we saw the circles were made out of his actual skin and had little fleshy points on them and a tiny bit of hair, like light fur. It was the weirdest thing!

After we had all seen this up close, tiahaar Neydish had us all sit down and explained it. He said the circles are called "nipples." We have them too, but in harlings they're hardly more than blemishes. Apparently, when hara grow up, the little marks turn into these nipple things, but ouana hara tend to have darker, bigger ones. We wanted to know what they were for, and tiahaar Neydish explained that it feels good when nipples are touched. It's part of aruna. He also said it was a good thing he had remembered to tell us that because otherwise when we had our first arunas with ouana hara, we might have been really surprised!

We said thank you and thought the lesson was done but it wasn't. "Something else you will see on the ouana hara is this," tiahaar Neydish said. He held out his arm, and on the forearm, he showed off a big, long white scar I'd somehow never noticed on him before. I didn't like to look at it; it was ugly and it scared me to think about how he had got it.

"What happened?" everyhar asked.

He explained that once hara grow up and become ouana, most also have a special ceremony where they are cut on the arm, as a sign of strength. Once again, I am very glad I am a Lily, because I could never have somehar cut me on the arm!

Today was so exciting. Spirea didn't come out with us to the gardens. None of us knew the reason why, so we went looking for him. He wasn't in his room either and then we saw tiahaar Tolea in the hallway. He had been looking for us to tell us that Spirea has started his feybraiha! Spirea had gone to tiahaar Laran in the infirmary first thing in the morning because he'd noticed the changes. Tiahaar Laran said that because Spirea is now becoming a har, he will not be staying in our room with us anymore, and it turns out that we will each get our own rooms once we start our feybraiha, because we will officially become hostlings-in-training!

One thing that's kind of sad, though, is that we won't be able to see Spirea until his feybraiha is over, because he needs peace and quiet to go through his changes properly. I have to admit that I hope he is finished with it soon, so that he can tell us all about it.

Well, it's been two whole weeks and Spirea still isn't done with his feybraiha yet. I'm not really that surprised, because tiahaar Laran came and spoke to us all about feybraiha, and he said that it would be many weeks before Spirea was all finished. He said that even he didn't know exactly how long the changes would take, because it is different for each harling.

And now Calla has started his feybraiha too! He woke us up early this morning and said that he had an achy feeling in his abdomen and he was all sweaty. We all went to tell tiahaar Tolea together, but then he wanted to talk to Calla alone and we were sent away to work in the garden. That was frustrating, because we ended up not getting to say goodbye before they moved Calla out into his own room. Coral was very upset. I guess I should feel sad that I won't be seeing Calla for a long while, but mainly I'm just excited, because I know it will be my turn soon.

I can't believe this! It's so unfair. I wasn't even surprised when Coral started his feybraiha a few days after Calla, and I was even glad for him. But today I heard that Aster has started. Aster! He's not even in our group; he's supposed to a whole year younger than us. Tiahaar Tolea said that we just need to be patient, because sometimes feybraiha comes early for some harlings and late for others.

I must admit that I was starting to worry that I might never start changing and that I wouldn't get to be a hostling after all, but tiahaar Tolea promises that it will happen to each of us. I know he's right but I'm getting so tired of waiting and something else is worrying me. What if I end up being the very last one in our group to change? That would be so embarrassing. And lonely, too, because I could end up in our big room all by myself, just waiting.

It finally happened! I'm going through one of the most exciting, important times of my whole entire life! Feybraiha!

The funny thing is that, despite all that our teachers and doctors have taught us harlings about feybraiha, and how much I really had been looking forward to it, when it finally came (stupid me!) I didn't notice it right away. I'm glad tiahaar Tolea noticed, because otherwise it might have happened a lot later and then maybe I would have felt even stupider.

It all started yesterday during the afternoon lesson — or that's when tiahaar Tolea noticed anyway. We've started having classes every day in the afternoon because it's getting too hot to work in the gardens. I was getting a little bit bored with class and just hoping it would be over soon. I really feel like things are getting boring. We've gone over everything so much and plus now some harlings are missing with their feybraiha. Anyway, I was really hot and started daydreaming about maybe taking a nice bath after class or at night or something. I felt all sweaty and uncomfortable, but I thought it was the room that was hot.

Finally the lesson was over and tiahaar Tolea told us we could all go. I was so relieved I stood up really fast. Before I could leave, though, tiahaar Tolea called out my name. When I turned around, he gestured for me to come over to him. I didn't know whether to be worried, since I thought maybe tiahaar Tolea knew I hadn't been paying attention.

So tiahaar Tolea said he wanted to talk to me, which was obvious. Then he asked me how I was feeling. I was surprised he asked me that, but I told him how I'd been feeling really hot. He then asked if I was itchy. I started to tell him no, but then I noticed that right at that moment I was scratching myself in an itchy spot between my hip and my groin, so then I told him I was.

After that tiahaar Tolea sent me to tiahaar Laran, one of the main doctors. As soon as he told me to go and see the doctor, I realized what was happening. I just couldn't stop smiling; I was so excited.

I gave tiahaar Laran a note that tiahaar Tolea had written for him, but I told him that knew this had to be about my feybraiha. He said that I was right and that he wanted to do an examination. I had to take off all my clothes and lie on the table. Tiahaar Laran stood by a counter on the side of the room preparing some sort of notebook. While I was still undressing, which felt good in a way since I was so hot, he asked me how I was feeling. I told him the same thing I'd told tiahaar Tolea, that I was hot and itchy, but I also said how I was sweaty and feeling sort of bored, a little tired.

Finally, I was all undressed and the doctor came over to look at me as I was lying on the table. It felt strange to be totally naked with somehar looking at me like that, but at the same time I knew he was just doing his job. He walked around the table a couple of times and wrote some notes in his notebook. He touched my arms, which he had me raise up a couple of times. He also had me lie on my side and even had me roll over onto my stomach for a little bit.

After that, he told me to sit up with my legs over the edge of the table. I did just what he said. Honestly, I didn't know what he would do next, so anything would have surprised me. Still, I jumped a little bit when he said he was going to touch me. He noticed that and asked me if it would bother me. I said no, I was just surprised, sort of jumpy. That's when he reached out and touched me — right on my ouana-lim!

This was the last thing I had expected! Except for a few times, when we'd talked about it in lessons or a couple of other times, I'd never really been interested in that part of my body, but I know that it's supposed to change during feybraiha so I got extra curious about it.

Tiahaar Laran was trying to be very gentle with me, I could tell. He didn't pull or pinch or do anything rough with it, but he just held it in his fingers and raised it up to look at the underside. Then, with his other hand, he felt around a little bit in the area below that, which is the soume-lam. I felt a little strange when he did that, because I couldn't see and his hands were a little cold.

He was looking at me for maybe a minute, then asked me if I'd noticed any changes in my ouana-lim. I told him I didn't pay any attention to it, though I must admit that I've been checking it just about every day to see if it has started to grow or anything that might signal feybraiha. Tiahaar Laran said I should really look at it closely. Well, what could I do but look?

And, it *did* look different. It must have happened so fast! It hadn't looked that way when I had my bath last night. First of all, the beautiful flower you *can* see had changed color. It wasn't a very, very bright color like in the pictures we'd been shown, but it was a light orange color, like an orange blush. It was very subtle color, but definitely different, and I knew it had to be something that had changed. I also saw, looking at myself, that some hair was growing on the shaft, fine hair almost like thin fur. And the whole organ was bigger than I remembered it being.

I won't say what happened in the rest of the examination because this journal entry is getting pretty long and I'm tired. The doctor told me it's normal to be tired during feybraiha. He told me all about it. He looked at me some more and showed me other signs, how there was a bit of hair in my armpits and some areas of rash starting on my arms and legs. Then he told me lots more things about feybraiha that they hadn't told us before. I didn't realize how many little small signs there are, so I guess maybe it's not my fault that I didn't notice the changes right away.

And, of course, there's the other very exciting thing that has happened because of this. I have my own room! That happened this evening. Tiahaar Tolea took care of it while I was with tiahaar Laran. I am so happy!

They moved all my things into my new room. I have a nice bed and even new sheets and blankets. The sheets have roses on them and so of course I love them. I also have a dresser for my clothes and another dresser that's empty, because I don't know what to put in it yet and I don't have a lot of things. I also have a big mirror, which is good because I need to start paying more attention to how I look. Soon, I'll need to start entertaining the hara who will come here, and I need to look good to make them want to have pearls with me.

I almost can't believe this is finally happening. I have my own room and the bed I sleep in is the one where I'm going to conceive my pearls. I hope it doesn't take me too long to learn how. Tiahaar Laran mentioned to me yesterday that special trainers had just been hired to teach us all the special skills of conceiving and I'm happy because I want to learn how to do it the best I can, as soon as I'm ready.

But oh, well. I'm really tired suddenly, even though I haven't done much at all today. I have no lessons and I can't go out and do anything — no work in the garden, no playing with the little ones, no visiting with any of my friends. I'm kind of disappointed about that because I thought I'd at least be able to see the others who've started their feybraiha, but instead I have to stay in my room. I think I may really miss my friends, but the administrators said they don't want me to see anyhar because they said that staying away from other hara and harlings will make it more exciting when I see them again finally. I think they're trying to make me really excited about my first aruna, but they don't have to do that, I'm excited already. Maybe they just want me to be by myself to keep me from being embarrassed. They said I might sweat a lot or feel sick. So far I feel OK, just tired and a little itchy in spots. I hope it all happens quickly.

The first week of my feybraiha really hasn't been so bad. Mostly I've just been hot and itchy and had a few headaches. But even though I normally sleep very well, last night I woke up for no reason at all and just couldn't go back to sleep. It's like I couldn't turn my mind off to go to sleep. I keep thinking about what I'll look like when my feybraiha is done and what aruna will be like and wondering how difficult it will be to learn to make pearls and how much longer until I make my first one. There's just so much on my mind it seems impossible to sleep. But at the same time, I feel awfully tired. It's a good thing I don't have to worry about lessons anymore; I don't think I'd ever be able to pay attention.

I feel so horrible. It's been two weeks that I've been stuck in this room with my feybraiha, but it feels like I've been here forever. I hate it! For the past three nights, I've hardly been able to sleep, I'm so hot and itchy. I've had a headache for two days. During the day I feel sleepy. Sometimes I feel OK, but less and less. Right now I feel OK except that my insides hurt. I know this is good, since the doctor says it's my soume-lam that's hurting, and it only hurts because it's stretching and growing in order to make pearls, but really it doesn't feel good at all. I thought I could take my mind off it by writing, but just now I wrote about it, so I guess that didn't work. I'll write again later.

I had the weirdest dream just now. I can't remember it perfectly because it was so strange — like it would jump from one thing to another very fast. It didn't seem very real, but the feeling it has left with me is very real.

I dreamt I was outside planting flowers in the garden, even though it was nighttime. And while I was out there I realized that I shouldn't be able to see what I was doing because it was dark, but then I thought well maybe it's a full moon and that's why I can see.

So, I looked up in the sky to see if it was a full moon and it was. There was a great big, beautiful full moon shining huge in the sky. The moon looked so big that it felt kind of scary — like it was beautiful, but it just wasn't right. So I decided to look at the stars instead and as I was concentrating on the stars they became brighter and brighter and the sky was just full of them. And then I got this thought in my head that each of those stars represented a pearl, and that if I was lucky I would have many, many pearls like that. But then I got that funny kind of scary feeling again, like even though it was beautiful, it just wasn't the way that things are supposed to be.

And then all of a sudden in my dream I realized that I already had a pearl growing inside of me. This really startled me and I wondered how it had gotten there. I started to panic that maybe the pearl wouldn't grow right, because I hadn't even learned how to have aruna yet, so the pearl couldn't possibly be the way it's supposed to.

Next thing I knew in the dream, I was suddenly back up in my room, but I wasn't able to sleep. In my dream I was lying in bed trying to sleep, but I was too worried about this pearl. So then I got this idea that if I went back to my old harling room, the pearl that wasn't supposed to be there would just go away. I know that doesn't make any sense (it doesn't make sense that I could possibly have a pearl without aruna either), but in the dream I was just so sure it would work, it made perfect sense.

So, I went back to our old group bedroom and I saw that all of our stuff was in there but none of the harlings were left. I guess all the rest of them had finally started their feybraihas too. So I sat down on my old bed and I was starting to cry, because I just didn't know what to do. And I got this strange feeling like it wasn't a pearl inside me but a tiny harling and it felt very, very strange and I knew it had happened that way because I hadn't learned the aruna.

Then this tall beautiful har came to into the room. He was unlike any other har that I had ever seen and I realized that he must be one of the Sister hostlings that used to live here. He didn't tell me that's who he was, but I knew it must be, because he didn't look like any of the hara who work here and so he must be a hostling. He came and stood at the foot of my bed and told me that it would all be okay and that he was there to look after me and then he told me to go to sleep.

And then I woke up! It was such a bizarre dream. I don't know whether to feel happy or scared about it. I wish it were morning already, because I know I won't be able to go back to sleep.

Just when I thought feybraiha had got to the very worst, something even more horrible has happened! This has to be the most embarrassing, horrible time in my whole life. At first it was OK and I was excited, but now I'm just so confused.

Here's what happened. Last night I couldn't sleep — of course not! I still have headaches at night and get all hot and sweaty. I guess I must have fallen asleep finally, though, because it turns out I overslept. Normally Svona, who's been my servant since I got moved to this room, comes in at mid-morning to give me a late breakfast and then a bath. Usually I've already been awake for a while and have dressed myself, but this morning when he came in, I was still sleeping. Svona shook me a little to wake me up and called me "sleepyhead" but he's been pretty nice to me overall.

Anyway, this is when the horrible thing happened. Svona had woken me up and told me to get up to go take a bath, so I got up out of bed. Because I'd been so hot, I was just wearing my light cotton nightgown, and that was really bad because as soon as I stood up, I knew that something had happened in my sleep and my ouana-lim was sticking out in front, stiff as a pole!

I must have made some noise and I know I just froze for a second, horrified. Why was it doing that? I was just about to force it down with my hands when Svona looked and me and suddenly said, "Oh, growing, eh?" What a horrible thing to say! I was so mad at him but I was also more embarrassed than I think I've ever been. I don't want anyhar looking at my ouana-lim like that, not even through my nightgown!

I know I must have gotten all red in the face and looked really angry, because Svona immediately apologized and said not to worry, that it was normal. I couldn't really believe Svona though. Why was my ouana-lim... so big like that? From everything I've ever been taught, I know I'm not ever meant to use it and besides, it was just the most embarrassing thing. It also took about ten minutes for it to get down to normal size — the more I wanted it to go down, the more it stuck out, until finally I just had to sit and wait. Svona was nice and let me wait so I wouldn't have to go out into the hall like that.

After my bath, Svona made breakfast for me and then left me to eat by myself. About fifteen minutes later, tiahaar Laran came in. He comes to see me every day, asks me how I slept, how I'm feeling. He says he doesn't want things to be too difficult for me since I'm special and will be hosting pearls later. He wants everything to be very nice and comfortable.

Anyway, this morning he came in and asked me the usual questions and I answered him. I hadn't mentioned about the horrible thing that happened but as it turns out, I didn't need to because Svona had told him. I guess that's OK because tiahaar Laran is taking care of me, but I was surprised. So tiahaar Laran told me he had heard that I'd woken up "very, very ouana." I told him that was true and that I was really upset about it.

He told me not to worry, but just like when Svona told me that, I couldn't help it. I told him I knew that my ouana-lim would grow and change color during feybraiha, but I didn't understand why I had woken up like that, since that was like exercise for something it would never be doing, since I'm going to be a hostling I won't be needing it. Tiahaar Laran didn't really give an answer, just said again that I shouldn't worry. He did say one thing that made me feel a little better, which is that no matter what, when I have aruna, it will disappear and I'll be soume. My soume-lam are growing just as much as my ouana-lim, he told me, but they're hidden inside. I'm so glad because for a little bit I was scared that maybe I couldn't be a hostling if I had that problem.

My feybraiha is almost over and I'm feeling much better. I also feel like I've learned a lot. There are so many things I've found out that I just didn't know before because it's hard to explain in words. I also think a lot of things are just secrets that nohar told us, but I hope that more and more I will learn all the secrets.

You know something occurred to me today that I probably should have thought about a long time ago. I wonder if Hyacinth has had his feybraiha. And I wonder if he's getting his own room and special sheets like we are. I get the feeling that he's not. It makes me really sad to think about. I hadn't thought about it in a long time but I really miss him.

Last night something bad happened, something really, really bad. For the first time, I got in pretty bad trouble and actually a whole bunch of us did. I try so hard to be good, but now some of the administrators are really mad. I can understand why they're mad, since it was our fault and we were stupid, but I don't like it that the administrators think I'm a bad because I'm not. It was just an accident!

Anyway, what happened was that after having to be all alone in our rooms for a few weeks, six of us were allowed to have dinner together. It was the first time I'd seen any of them that whole time. I wasn't the only one who looked different. The other five all had changed. It was Calla, Coral, Seagrass, Spirea and Rosea. Their skin looked different and their hair was shinier. I noticed that Calla's shoulders seemed to have gotten wider. During dinner, I was looking at all of them and I worry about saying it, but I was even wondering about their ouana-lims and their soume-lam, if theirs had grown as much as mine and how they felt. I know I didn't like it when Svona looked at me, but by the time dinner was over, it was all I could think about.

As it turns out, I wasn't the only one who was having thoughts like that. After dinner, we all went into Coral's room. He had a bed that was a little bigger than mine and also had two chairs instead of just one, so it was a good place for all of us to sit. We were told we could stay up and talk for an hour or so. Well, at first we just talked. Since we were completely alone, we started to talk about feybraiha. Everyhar talked about what we went through. Some of us had had worse headaches. Seagrass had had some scary nightmares. Calla, silly thing, said his *stomach* had hurt him really bad — we had to tell him not to be stupid, since it was his soume-lam that hurt. I don't know how he didn't know that since it was in our lessons a million times.

After that, we all started talking about our aruna parts. All of us had talked with the doctors. I was still embarrassed, but I even told my story about waking up "very, very ouana." I told them what tiahaar Laran had said, how it didn't matter and I shouldn't worry because I would be soume when I needed to be. As soon as I told that story, Coral started laughing. The same thing had happened to him — and in fact, it was happening again!

I feel wicked writing this, but I don't think anyhar will read this (nohar has before, this journal is private), so I will tell what happened next. Coral was talking and then said something like, "It's happening again!" The next thing the rest of us knew, Coral had raised up his skirt and pulled down his underclothes and we were looking right at his ouana-lim, which was sticking out just like mine had! Coral has always been pretty wild, which matches his curly hair, but that shocked me. At the same time, I looked at it pretty carefully. I had been thinking about it and now I was getting the secret wish I'd had at dinner. It was a lot like mine only instead of being dark orange and gold, it was turquoise blue with a bit of purple. It was very pretty, really like a flower.

We all stared at it and didn't even talk, just looked. Then Spirea pulled down his pants and showed his (green and light blue), which wasn't all stiffened up like Coral's but still — then there were two! Rosea was next, and then Seagrass. Seagrass had a flower that was a beautiful bronze, and Rosea's was both mostly red. Looking at all of them, it seemed funny that I'd been embarrassed since we all had them. I took mine out and showed it as well. Spirea made a joke about how it wasn't striped like my hair, but it was a nice joke, not mean, because he also said it was pretty.

Finally all five of us were sitting there with our ouana-lims showing — all of us but Calla. We were all sort of waiting suddenly and then Coral said, "Hey, are you going to show us yours?" I thought maybe Calla didn't want to and would be mad, but instead he just smiled and stood up from where he was sitting. He told Coral to lie on the bed. Spirea and I got up so Coral could do that and then Calla walked over. Calla was smiling as he pulled off his skirt completely and pulled off his underclothes. Underneath he had become completely soume!

Calla was right at the edge of the bed and crawled on top of Coral and started talking about how he was feeling ready and how he hoped we could all have aruna soon. Coral was lying there and I noticed that his organ got a lot bigger while Calla was talking. I guessed that for Calla to be soume his whole body had to have been getting ready for aruna. You can't just walk around soume, you have to be aroused, or at least I think so. The look on his face was something else as well — he looked so different, very... lustful, I will have to call it. When I saw that look in his eyes and the way he was wriggling over Coral, and how Coral was looking, I started to feel scared. We had just been curious, but now things were serious and what if something happened? They couldn't just have aruna!

I think it's good, just the best luck ever, that right at that moment the door opened, because even though at the beginning it was fun to be showing each other like that, things had gotten out of control and I swear, I think those two would have done a very bad thing, which they both knew and we all know they shouldn't do. Two administrators came in just to check on us and there we were, half-naked, and the hara got so angry with us! They ran over to Calla and pulled him off the bed and they slapped him and Coral both. We were all so ashamed we didn't even talk or fight or make excuses. They made us all get dressed and go into our rooms immediately and I was happy to go. I never like to get in trouble and this time it was the worst, because we had all been doing something wicked and I knew it.

This morning, we all got brought together for a special meeting. Four administrators put us all in a room and told us we'd been very, very bad. They asked us if we understood what our purpose was and how important we were to the future of Varr society. Of course we all said we did, but then they told us they thought maybe we didn't, because otherwise we wouldn't have done what we had done. We're going to be hostlings and that's our purpose. If we do stupid things like getting naked and comparing our ouana-lims or — and here they spoke right to Coral and Calla — thinking about having aruna with each other, or being ouana, which was forbidden and unnatural for hostlings, which is obvious and we all know that, then whoever did it will be in big trouble.

They said if we did that we wouldn't be allowed to be hostlings! All of us got so scared then, because that's all any of us want. I almost started to cry and I had to hug myself to make myself stop. I have wanted that so much and I am almost ready after waiting so long. I swear I won't ever do anything except what I'm allowed to do, because I just want so bad to have pearls!

I am so happy and I have to write everything down so I can remember it forever. Last night I had my first aruna. It's such an important step for me, not just because they say it is, but because of how I feel. I feel so different now, like I'm another person. Before, I think I doubted a little bit that it could be so good but it really was good and I am so happy because I know that from now on, I'll have my training and I will have a chance to do it a lot.

Yesterday was a really special day. For breakfast I got my favorite breakfast food — toasted bread with sweet blackberry jam. I also got a glass of water with some rose syrup and sugar in it. Then I got a bath that was extra special because Svona actually gave me a massage. When we got back to my room, there was a surprise for me. Tiahaar Laran was there with two administrators and they had a special dress for me, a lovely white one with crimson ribbons running down the front and around the bottom. They said it was a dress I could keep for training and afterwards but that really it was a reward for (except for that one horrible mistake) being so good all during my feybraiha, even though it was hard. They said it was also a reward for being a good Varr. I'm glad I got a reward like that — better than all the ribbons and jewelry I'd ever been given for my lessons!

All afternoon I didn't do much, but then Svona came in with a whole new set of blankets and sheets for my bed, so much more beautiful than before and the sheets were purple *silk*! I couldn't believe it, but Svona said it was another gift. I could keep my other blankets and sheets from before, he said, but for my first aruna and for other special times, there was the silk. After the bed was made, Svona went to the kitchen and brought back a light dinner. He said I shouldn't eat too much. I had some barley soup with crackers and some roasted vegetables. I also got a glass of wine, my very first, which Svona said I could have since I am now a full-grown har and because it would relax me for aruna.

Then Svona put the tray of food to the side and told me it was time to make me beautiful. I've had a lot of lessons in that already and so I could do most of it, but Svona helped me put my hair into braids so I had two big balls on the back of my head and then the rest of my hair going down my back. I put some kohl around my eyes and picked out a necklace with a red stone that matched the ribbons on my dress. When I was all ready, Svona turned down the big light and lit candles. He told me it was time for me to lie down and wait. Soon, very soon, they would send up my partner.

I didn't know who it would be. The only thing the administrators had told me was that it would be one of the new instructors they had brought here. I hadn't met any of these new hara, because of course I've been in my room for a few weeks now, ever since they were hired. So before he came, I tried to imagine what he would be like. I knew he wouldn't be like me, since I'm going to be a hostling, but that was about all I could guess.

I was very, very happy with who it was. He came into the room and as soon as I saw him, I knew that I would probably be having a very good night. He introduced himself and said his name was Vlaric. He had pure white skin, as white as mine is tanned, and black hair that was cut short and stuck together in spikes. He had wide shoulders but a thin waist and overall was very slender, although from his arms and chest, I could tell he was strong. It's amazing how quickly I noticed all these details, but I guess I knew it was important.

Vlaric did everything right. I'm not going to write every single thing but there are some things I will write because I want to remember them more. I remember that first of all, he came and sat at the end of my bed, where I was lying on top of the covers. He reached out and put his hand on my knee and talked to me in a soft voice. He told me he was going to be teaching me a lot in the next few weeks, but that this first time, it was only about pleasure, not about making pearls. Aruna was magic and we would be making magic.

He asked me if I was ready, and I said yes, because I really was. I could even feel my body actually aching for him, wanting him to touch me. He was so beautiful, and then he did it, he touched me, and not just on my knee. He ran his hands up my thighs and then he slid up next to me, putting his arms around me, his hands under my dress, and then as he unbuttoned the dress and took it off, he was stroking my back and my chest.

Then his hands were on my face, so gentle, and we shared breath. It was magical, like nothing I'd ever known, and the more we did it, the more I wanted to make it so it would never, ever stop. He laughed a little bit, in a good way, and said I was "insatiable" before sharing breath some more.

We got under the wonderful silk sheets and shared breath and touched each other for quite a while, but even though I loved it, after a while I was feeling desperate, like I wanted even more. I knew there *was* more, after all. Vlaric was perfect, and right at the moment when I was ready to ask, he all of a sudden got up off the bed, pulled off his pants and was naked. His ouana-lim was much bigger than any I'd seen before, although of course that had only really been the other harlings that time or those pictures from lessons. I was actually a little wary of it, because it really was big.

Vlaric could read my mind, I think, because immediately he told me not to worry and then he came back to bed and let me feel it. It was so soft and looked like a violet flower. I could see in his eyes how good I was making him feel, and soon I could feel it in how he was no longer soft but had almost started to blossom. By then he was panting and grabbing my arms, telling me to stop because he was ready — ready for me to be soume! I was ready too and had been for a while, since after being touched so much all over, everything had slipped up inside of me, and so when Vlaric moved on top of me, I knew he would find me willing.

Right at first, it really hurt! The teachers and doctors had told us it would hurt a little bit, but it hurt worse than I thought. I could tell that Vlaric was trying to be gentle though, and he shared breath with me while he pushed inside, making me feel better until after a couple of minutes, the pain had faded and I felt that pleasure I had always hoped for. Inside of me, I felt that special feeling that the teachers said felt as good as a flower looks.

And that was just the physical part. I haven't even written about how I was feeling! The sharing of breath wasn't like touching somehar, but like mixing with them, and actually the whole aruna was like that. We weren't just touching, we were mixing ourselves together. I could taste Vlaric and he could taste me. We were like two souls wrapped together. Of course I'm sure I only got a very beginning taste of this, since I'm just starting, but even in the first few minutes I was learning that special magic of aruna, and at the end it was like we had taken a flight up to the stars.

Vlaric really was good to me. Actually after that first time we shared about five more times, all night long! It was a mutual thing. I wanted more and he wanted to give me some lessons, a little bit of practice. We tried different ways of lying together and he showed me different things the ouana might want or might do to me. He began to tell me some special techniques for moving my inner muscles. We didn't talk about the seal or pearls at all, just the more basic things, which was good because I needed it, and because it really was wonderful, just that part. I can't imagine how good it must feel to conceive a pearl if just regular aruna already feels so absolutely wonderful.

Chapter Six

Pansea led Swift through the sprawling wings of the building to a room far removed from the noisy classrooms, where various groups of harlings were singing or playing word games. Pansea knocked politely on a pair of wide paneled doors that were decorated with large crosses of fading gilded paint.

"Enter," barked Paran.

As his visitors entered the room, he stood. "Ah, tiahaar Swift, I wasn't sure when you were coming so I started passing on the latest instructions from General Aldebaran. Let me just finish writing out these orders and then we can discuss them — if that's okay with you of course."

Swift made a motion with his hand for Paran to continue with his work and glanced curiously around the office. The room was impressively large, slightly bigger than the dining hall at *Forever*, in Swift's estimation. The ceiling was vaulted with a criss-crossing of dusty wooden beams. One end of the room was filled with rows and rows of old metal file cabinets in various dull colors. At the other end stood two large tables and well over a dozen rolling chairs. Presumably this had been a meeting area for the breeding facility's administrators and staff. Raised on a large dais at the far end of the room, the desk where Paran worked was a very large and grand old structure of dark mahogany. There was only one small window, fitted with panes of colored glass that threw cheerful splashes of red and blue and yellow across the walls of what was otherwise a rather somber and dim room

Pansea turned to Swift and said his goodbyes. Just as the young har dipped into another of his elaborate bows, Paran glanced up from his desk and said, "Pansea, don't go anywhere. I'd like you to distribute these for me."

Pansea approached the desk. "Certainly, Captain Nemish. I'd be happy to take these for you. How many are there?" Swift noted a hint of fake politeness in Pansea's voice, but watched as the harling leaned eagerly to see the documents, inadvertently getting between Paran and the portable lighting units needed in the dim room.

"I'm not done yet," Paran said, "and I can't concentrate with you in my way. Go wait over there." He pointed to the opposite side of the room.

Pansea blushed and began staring at his feet dejectedly. "Sit here with me until Captain Paran has time for us," Swift said to him, partially because he generally felt sorry for the harling. But as they settled at the second large table, Swift was also pleased to see that the edge in his voice had encouraged Paran to scribble his orders a bit faster.

After remaining silent for nearly a minute, Pansea said softly, "Thank you for being honest with me about what's going to happen." The harling paused as if debating whether to say more, then added, "I love Lis very much but he won't tell us anything!" He frowned, his hands clenched together on the table. "He thinks that he's keeping us from being scared by not telling us things, but *not* knowing actually makes everything *scarier.*"

"Lisia doesn't know what will happen either," Swift said. "He simply wouldn't want to tell you something that might not be true."

"I suppose," Pansea muttered. His expression clearly showed that he was not completely placated, but he remained silent.

"All right," Paran said. He rose from the desk, grouping together a short stack of sealed envelopes. "Pansea, find these hara and give them these right away. Remember, they are not for anyhar to read, other than the hara whose names are on the envelopes. And do it quickly."

"Excuse me, captain, but didn't you say we would be *discussing* these orders?" Swift interjected, as he watched the envelopes handed over.

Paran shrugged. "Oh, these orders in particular are nothing to worry over, tiahaar, just some general instructions. I meant we would discuss Gelaming orders in general. We're eager to move on, away from this place."

"I see," Swift said, irritated at Paran's vagueness.

Pansea's departure staved off any further discussion of the orders. "Goodbye again, tiahaar Swift," the harling said on his way to the door. "Will you be leaving soon too?"

"I'm not certain how long I'll be staying."

"Well, maybe you could come back and visit again later," Pansea suggested. He studied the floor and shifted his weight in a shy manner that was wholly contrived in comparison to the earnestness Swift had seen in the stairwell.

Swift smiled then. Pansea was certainly going to grow up to be a charmer. "I can't say yet," Swift replied. "But I'd be delighted to take supper with you this evening, so we can talk further. Perhaps you have more questions I can answer?"

Pansea's resulting smile was wide and genuine. "That would be wonderful, tiahaar! There are bells that ring for dinner times. I eat at the third bell."

"Then we'll meet in the dining hall at the third bell," Swift said. "Oh, and why not invite some of your friends to join us? I'm sure they also have questions and things to say."

Pansea's mood deflated visibly at hearing this, and Swift couldn't help but smile again and add, "It was a great pleasure to meet you, tiahaar."

"Thank you, tiahaar Swift," Pansea responded. "It was a great honor and privilege to speak with you." He swept into another of his elaborate bows, but Swift caught him by the arms and straightened him up.

"There's really no need for quite all that," Swift chided. The harling blushed in embarrassment, so Swift winked at him and whispered, "It's not as if I'm some stuffy Gelaming."

Pansea smirked then and at just that moment the "stuffy Gelaming" present cleared his throat to indicate that he was ready to talk with the Megalithican ruler. Pansea smiled and waved from the doorway and then literally ran from the room with his deliveries.

Paran sighed theatrically and declared, "Honestly, tiahaar, I'm surprised that you encourage him."

Swift turned and frowned at the captain. "What do you mean?"

"That awful *flirting*," Paran said, pronouncing the word as if it were profane. "It's perverse."

Swift just laughed, but stopped abruptly when he realized that Paran was serious. "Why does it bother you? It's perfectly harmless. He's not really flirting — not in the way you imply. He just wants a little attention, a little reassurance."

"By batting his eyelashes and slinking around suggestively like a kanene?" Paran returned sarcastically. "With all due respect, tiahaar, I think not! But perhaps you are familiar with such things..."

Swift raised an eyebrow inquisitively and stared at Paran, silently daring him to elaborate on his insinuation. When the captain said nothing, Swift said, "Pansea's simply mimicking the sort of behavior he's always seen around here. He thinks he's being grown up. And besides, Lisia explained to me how the older harlings used to entertain the soldiers and keep them company — it was part of their training. They *just* want approval and frankly they aren't getting it from you or your hara," he added, eyeing Paran sternly. "You make them feel abnormal."

"They *are* abnormal."

"No, they are perfectly normal," Swift said, his voice firm. "They just need to be educated and exposed to a healthy Wraeththu lifestyle. I guarantee they'll adapt in no time."

"I think you're right about that," Paran agreed. "But that's why we need to break these old habits. The quicker they adapt the better. You know that flirting, or approval-seeking, simply won't be acceptable in the outside world."

Swift rolled his eyes. "Really, captain, I'm telling you it's fine." Adding silently, *Thank goodness all the Gelaming aren't as uptight as you.* Aloud he continued, "Didn't you — well, just trust me; this is an area where I have more experience. Older harlings flirt — it's normal and healthy."

A sharp knock at the door interrupted their conversation.

"Come in," they both said.

A Gelaming soldier entered the room looking slightly put out. "Captain Nemish, there is a har here who has just arrived from Galhea. He's waiting in the downstairs hall. He says that he needs to see Lord Swift."

"Did you ask his name?" Paran asked expectantly.

"Yes, captain," the har answered stiffly. "But he just brushed right past me without giving it! I would have used force, but I got the impression that he was somehar rather important since so few hara would even know that we're here and he traveled by *sedu.*"

Paran and Swift both frowned. "Well, send him here," Swift replied. "He must have been sent from *Forever* so it's probably important." For a brief moment Swift experienced a slight twinge, an anxious feeling of puzzlement at who it might be; a suspicion darted briefly into his mind but he quickly chased it away. He'd find out soon enough and he felt sure that if something were wrong at *Forever* he'd somehow sense it.

The har left to retrieve the visitor. Swift turned back to Paran and approached his desk. "And before we have any more distractions, I want to tell you that I disapprove of the way you've been telling the harlings that they're going to be taken permanently into Gelaming custody — or anywhere else, for that matter. Despite your implications, nothing has been decided and at this point I'm not so sure that I want further Gelaming involvement at all!"

Paran's face registered surprise. "As far as the Hegemony is concerned, it *has* been decided," he countered, handing Swift a small sheaf of papers — the newly arrived instructions from Immanion.

Swift snatched the papers from Paran's hand and glanced through them quickly. A multitude of comments came to mind as he scanned the text; none of them were polite. After several moments of silence he spoke tightly, "If the Hegemony wishes to withdraw their resources from aiding this facility, then Parasiel will simply use our own means. However, they would do well to remember that all these harlings are Parsic citizens and furthermore, wards of the state. The Hegemony has absolutely no authority to take them anywhere."

"Be reasonable, tiahaar! The Parasiel don't have the expertise to—"

"To what?" Swift interrupted. "Care for our own harlings? I find that assumption intensely insulting, Captain. The hara here come under my jurisdiction and I will provide for them. You might be unable to forget the past, and what Parasiel came to replace, but remember who put me in this position. Thiede trusted me to be governor. Or do you suppose you know better than he does?"

"I think I know quite a lot, having been assigned to Megalithica for over a year," Paran replied, crossing his arms. "Whether you keep the harlings here — which I must say is a revolting idea — or let them out among the common hara, without protection and education, they're going to end up being used and objectified. For all we know, this cycle of exploitation will continue. Of course that's assuming that any of *your* hara here would be able to incorporate the breeding data."

"And that's all you're really concerned about, isn't it? That the breeding data falls into the *right* hands. Well, in this case the 'data' includes Parsic harlings and I'm not going to let them fall into just *anyhar's* hands," Swift insisted loudly. "They're not going anywhere without my approval and assurance that the relocation is in *their* best interests." Swift paused, his face flushed slightly in anger. "Besides, I'm not sure yet whether they're going anywhere. I think it's perfectly plausible to leave them here — for a time anyway."

Paran looked aghast. "You keep bringing that up, tiahaar, but you must realize that's hardly a practical prospect. This situation calls for the involvement of advanced experts and you surely can't expect that sort of har to crowd into some musty old human building in the middle of nowhere."

"All these harlings need are competent caregivers and proper resources. There's no security threat at this facility. Perhaps if it were the military training complex, I could accept the Hegemony's concern, but—"

"But you have an obligation to see to it that these procreation breakthroughs are studied by the most advanced minds," Paran interrupted smugly. "It's not just about your tribe, it's about what's best for all Wraeththu and we both know that means Gelaming involvement. Just think what a har like Lord Thiede could do with this knowledge." Paran paused as if pleased with himself for his reasoning. "Besides," he added, "these harlings are at such high risk considering their upbringing; they need to be protected from a society that will consider them inferior."

Swift's eyes narrowed. "Why? Because they're so soume?" Swift shook his head dismissively. "They don't need deprogramming, not what you're talking about. That's as barbaric as any Varr practice. It's my precise intention that *all* Parsic harlings *will* be nurtured and protected, whatever their behavior. And I'm not the har insinuating inferiority here!"

Paran opened his mouth to argue further and then paused, staring in the direction of the door. Swift turned. His mouth dropped open in surprise. "Cobweb, what are you doing here?"

Cobweb breezed into the office, his elegant travel cloak hanging behind him. "Parasiel is a free tribe, is it not? I decided to do a little sightseeing," he said airily. He eyed Paran and then Swift, who was still flummoxed by his hostling's unexpected arrival. "Come now, I only wanted to see what all this business was about. Besides, I believe I might be of use here."

"Indeed," said Paran. "Welcome, tiahaar Cobweb. Given your own former occupation, you no doubt *could* be of some use."

"And you are?" Cobweb demanded icily.

"I am Captain Paran Nemish, currently in charge of this operation. I think your son needs a calming influence right now, somehar to help give him a little perspective before things become unnecessarily difficult."

Cobweb studied his son, who had crossed his arms and was now glaring at Paran, seething at the captain's rudeness. "Becoming 'difficult,' Swift?" he asked, arching an eyebrow. "Whatever reason could you find to argue with the esteemed Gelaming? We all know they're *always* right."

Swift sighed. He and the captain both ignored his hostling's sarcastic comment and the last thing Swift wanted was for his hostling to turn a political scuffle into something personal. "Cobweb, must you get in the middle of all this? Paran and I were just having a discussion—"

"An *argument*, Swift," Cobweb cut in. "I could hear you out in the hall. Something about the harlings?"

"There is simply a difference of opinion regarding who will decide the fate of the harlings," Swift said, dismissively. He was now eager to leave the office and sort out Cobweb's sudden arrival.

He approached the desk and leaned over it, planting his hands squarely on the front edge. He stared into Paran's eyes with as much power and authority as he could muster. In times like this he felt he drew on his father's strength. "I want a copy of these latest Hegemony orders for my records. In the meantime, you may contact the Hegemony and tell them that regardless of what aid they do or do not give, *I'll* be making the final decisions here. Leave if you must; the harlings will be staying here until I say they are leaving. They will be rehabilitated, but on Parasiel terms, not Gelaming. As General Aldebaran said himself, this is a domestic concern."

"If you say so, tiahaar," Paran replied, unflustered. "You'll have a copy before we leave."

The response was not truly a concession, but Swift knew that Paran wasn't really the har who would make final decisions anyway and he didn't want to waste any more time discussing the matter with him. "Thank you, Captain. Now," Swift turned to his hostling, "I believe Cobweb and I could do with a little catch-up session. Paran, I'll collect additional reports from you later."

"Yes, fine," Paran said, taking up papers with feigned interest.

As soon as they left the office, Cobweb enfolded Swift in a quick embrace. "I'm glad you put that pompous Gelaming back in his place."

Swift stepped back, feeling a little uncomfortable with the parental hug given that there were soldiers in the area. "Me too. Now tell me how you got here. How did you even know where this place is?"

"I have my ways," Cobweb said slyly. "After you and Seel went to bed, I made a decision to follow you. I saw the perfect opportunity to flee the stifling safety of *We Dwell in Forever*. It wasn't difficult to coax assistance from that messenger. I just had to—"

"Stop right there, Cobweb, say no more," Swift interrupted. He wasn't sure he wanted to know his hostling's particular methods of gathering intelligence. He did, however, want to know how Cobweb had managed to escape his responsibilities at *Forever* and arrive not far behind him. He shook his head in mock disapproval. "You're going to get some poor Gelaming decommissioned one of these days. So, what, you woke up this morning and got everything ready for a trip? Without any of us knowing?"

Cobweb nodded and began to head down the hall. "Yes, of course. Can we go this way, find somewhere to talk?"

Swift followed him. "Yes, I haven't had a chance to see the rooms in this wing yet. We can talk while I explore."

As they made their way down a flight of stairs and then down a hall, Cobweb filled Swift in on the details of his departure. Cobweb confessed he was glad he had been trained to ride the *sedim* so he could travel the otherlanes like the Gelaming; otherwise the journey would have been impractical. "Packing and preparing and consulting with the staff was the easy part. I got it all done while you were busy readjusting your work schedule and Seel was doing whatever it is that he does with those reports. Of course, after you'd left I had to borrow Seel's *sedu,* which was the only minor difficulty in my plans."

"And just what did Seel have to say, after you announced you were leaving?" Swift asked. They'd come to a long hall with doors identical to the classrooms he'd seen before. All these rooms were quiet, however.

"He was quite displeased at first, but then I reminded him that he had chosen to stay home anyway, and Bryony and the rest of the staff can take care of the domestic chores without supervision for a few days; and they will likely look after the harlings most of the time as well. After that, it was just a matter of his weighing the likelihood of his needing his *sedu* in the next few days against the benefits of not having me around. My success was guaranteed," he added dryly.

Swift shook his head, trying to imagine the conversation in his mind. "Now tell me, why *did* you come after me? And, did it ever occur to you to simply tell me that you wanted to come along?"

Cobweb looked circumspect. "Well, after you two left I couldn't help thinking about this... abomination. I told you, your father had mentioned it, but I never knew it had actually been organized and been so—" his mouth dropped open for a moment as Swift cautiously opened one of the doors, "productive!"

"I hadn't really gotten a good picture in my head," Swift said softly as they walked into the room. It was a dormitory room, the sort Lisia had grown up in until his feybraiha. Although the room was half the size of the office they'd just left, it was packed with about ten narrow beds. The head of each bed was placed against the longer walls, creating a sort of alley down the middle of the room. In between each bed was a small chest of drawers.

"I know I could have just asked to come with you," Cobweb continued, "but I didn't want to argue about it. You know, I was aware of some of the more mercenary acts Terzian and the other Varrs committed, but I was always able to shield us somewhat from that darkness in the safe fortress of our home. After thinking about it a little, I decided I should come out and see some of the darkness for myself, as you've been doing. Seeing it makes it real for me, and making it real means that it can be confronted. And, of anything you've discovered," Cobweb gestured over the rows of old wooden furniture, "this has really been the first thing I've *wanted* to see."

Swift was eager to see more as well. Slowly, almost reverently, he and Cobweb explored the rest of the rooms. In one room they actually discovered a couple of the older harlings taking well-deserved naps. Swift and Cobweb quietly backed out of that room and made an effort to keep their voices down as they moved on.

All the dormitories were the same size, though the number of furnishings varied. Cobweb pointed out how neatly all the beds were made. They were covered with what appeared to be standard military blankets that had been dyed a garish pink; in some rooms dolls were carefully placed atop the pillows. The numerous windows had similar heavy woolen blankets nailed up as curtains, but these were tied back and most of the windows were open to the summer breeze. Swift also noticed that a few portable lighting units had been supplied by the Gelaming in order to make the harlings more comfortable when they used the rooms at night.

"In some ways this all seems so familiar, and yet it's so foreign," Swift said as he fingered one of the many trifling childhood treasures displayed on a dresser top — a small seashell fossil that was imprinted in an otherwise unremarkable pale rock. The dresser tops in each room were packed with such items — dried flowers tied with ribbons, an old plate full of assorted beads, colorfully painted pinecones, various little trinkets and cheap jewelry.

"Yes," Cobweb responded with a wistful smile, "I remember you had a big jar full of all sorts of rocks and shiny pebbles and bits of old broken china."

Swift sat on the edge of one of the beds, the stone still in his hand, and gazed out of the nearest window.

After several moments of silence, Cobweb prompted, "What are you thinking about?"

Swift shrugged and did not speak for several moments more. "You know I still have that jar tucked away in the attic. I meant to throw it out when I was moving my things into Terzian's room, but I had this strong impulse to keep it." He looked up at Cobweb, whose expression remained blank. "I was just thinking about how closely I can relate to these harlings in some ways. I was talking to one right before you arrived and I felt such a deep understanding of what he was going through. I didn't think anything of it until just now, when I realized that I was that young only four years ago."

Cobweb sat on the bed next to Swift. "But you've come very far from the harling you once were, Swift, even if it has been in a very short time."

"Yes, that's true, but not so far that I can't remember and understand. The more I think about it, the more I realize that I understand these harlings in a way that the Hegemony never could." His fist tightened around the stone and his jaw clenched. "But that's the very reason why they won't take me seriously, isn't it?"

"I suppose your age may be one of the reasons," Cobweb said neutrally. "I think also that the Gelaming find it inconvenient when hara have opinions that differ from their own."

"In other words, I was given my position because nohar ever expected me to defy the Gelaming's wishes." He looked again to Cobweb, who had become uncomfortably silent. "I'm not completely

117

oblivious, Cobweb," Swift said ruefully. "This is just the first time it's mattered."

"So, what do you intend to do?"

Swift moved to replace the fossil he'd been holding. "I feel strongly that the wishes of Lisia and the harlings should be a priority in any final decision. Experts should be consulted certainly, but from what I can tell the Gelaming want to take all the harlings away to conduct some grand genetic study. I don't think it's in the harlings' best interest to be subjected to that. Plus, the Gelaming will want to turn them all into dispassionate, philosophical little Aghamists. Look around." He gestured to the beds. "These harlings have grown up with this as their entire world and they thought it was normal. They've been through so much trauma since being abandoned. Could it possibly be healthy to send them — especially the older harlings — off to live in a culture where they'll be regarded as freaks or as obscene harling kanenes?"

Cobweb nodded. "It does seem reasonable that they will adjust better to the changes if they're allowed to cope with them together and in familiar surroundings." He frowned. "However, you must acknowledge this place is tainted, Swift. I'm not sure that what was done here can ever truly be erased."

"Perhaps not," Swift conceded. "Regardless, I want to consult more with Lisia. I've read his diary and earlier I met with him. He's remarkable and he already has many plausible ideas for converting this place into a wholesome and nurturing environment."

"What's he like?" asked Cobweb.

"Who, Lisia?" Swift paused to reflect a few moments. "Well, he's very self-assured, hard-working, and dedicated — absolutely *dedicated* to these harlings. It's like he's hostling to *all* of them."

Cobweb pondered this. "I can't imagine. How else would you describe him? I mean, how does he act? Judging from that first report, I gather the Gelaming don't think much of him."

"Well, they're being overly judgmental. Paran and Ashmael both seem to make such a big issue of what they term Lisia's 'appallingly hyper-feminized' manner. Lisia told me this himself, although he doesn't even know what 'feminized' means, poor thing. Anyway, they're not completely wrong — Lisia certainly has been shaped by his upbringing — but at the same time, I feel Paran specifically overlooks his good qualities. It took a lot of courage for him to take charge of this facility. He, too, will need some help in making the adjustment to normal Wraeththu life, but I still think that he should remain involved the decision-making process and in the harlings' lives. And, I fear that taking them all away from him now would kill him — he told me so himself."

"I'd like very much to meet him," Cobweb concluded.

"We should have some time to find him between now and dinner. In the meantime I'd like to go around, do a little more observation. I'm sure Lisia will be busy until later anyway, as he has a lot of charges to fuss over. 182, can you imagine?"

Cobweb, following along, shook his head. "No, as I said, I really can't."

For the next hour hostling and son continued their exploration of the building and its grounds. Swift showed Cobweb the nursery and they also observed a number of classes through the windows inset in the classroom doors. For the most part the harlings appeared happy and well-adjusted.

With the afternoon wearing on, Swift led them back in the direction of the hostlings' wing where he'd last seen Lisia. Before they entered the stairwell, Cobweb froze in place, staring at a darkened hallway that they'd so far ignored. Cobweb reached out and grasped Swift's shoulder. Swift turned and saw his hostling's grim expression. "What's down there?" Cobweb asked.

Swift frowned. "You know, I actually haven't been *there* yet. It's so quiet it just seemed like it wasn't being used." He started forward and after some hesitation Cobweb followed.

As they went further into the hall, they noticed a large sign nailed to the wall. It read, "Except for Emergency, Do Not Enter Without Authorization." Swift realized that they had likely stumbled on the area where the pearls had been delivered and incubated. "What's that smell?" he wondered aloud as his fingers ghosted over a doorknob, worn brownish with age.

"Antiseptic," Cobweb answered absently, "—and pain."

Swift glanced at his hostling before slowly opening the door. They stood in the doorway, eyes adjusting feebly to the darkness. The windows here had been boarded over and while a faint gleam of sunlight squeezed out from around the edges, it was still too dark to make out the interior. Cobweb dug into the deep pockets of his cloak and pulled out a small Gelaming glow stone. While the stone only illuminated a few feet around them, it brought a narrow raised cot into clearer view just ahead of them. Silently they moved forward into the room. It was large and appeared to be refurbished from a communal bathing facility like the one they'd seen on the dormitory floor.

The flickering light revealed the same tiled walls and floors that the other room had, although it was impossible to tell whether these were the same sickly shade of green. The floor dipped inward in spots, where shower and overspill drains had been inset. The grout was deeply discolored in patches and paths leading to the drain, but the room did not smell of mildew. Underneath the lingering noxious cleansing fumes was a faint odor that reminded Swift of death. "How ironic for a place whose purpose was to bring forth life," he thought.

The shower stalls lined the wall directly ahead of them; the showerheads still glinted dully on the walls. Clearly, every other stall wall had been removed to create three larger stalls where six had once been. The remnants from the removed walls had been shoddily mortared to extend the existing stalls, creating room-like pockets, each containing a narrow medical cot. Swift squinted at the strangely patterned sheets that covered the mattress before him. Just as he realized that he was looking at faded bloodstains and not an artistic rendering, there was a loud crash behind him.

Swift jumped and quickly turned to Cobweb, who was bending to hold the light up to something on the floor. "My cloak caught it," Cobweb explained. Beside a low bench with peeling paint, a metal tray was overturned on the floor and light glinted off an assortment of perverse-looking metal tools that had scattered across the tiles. Swift recoiled slightly and thought, "I certainly wouldn't want any of those touching me if I were trying to deliver a pearl."

Glancing up, he gestured to the wall behind his hostling and asked, "What's that?" Cobweb held up his light to a series of large, elaborately scripted signs. One contained terse birthing instructions, advising hostlings to push with contractions, bend their legs, and so on. A more enthusiastic series contained messages such as: *Remember to breathe! Visualize your flower opening to release the pearl. It gets easier with every pearl!*

"What are you doing in here?" boomed a loud voice.

For the second time in only a few minutes, Swift spun round to investigate. A tall har stood in the open doorway. Swift took Cobweb's light and approached him. He was dark, his skin almost black in the dimness, and he wore a healing emblem on his Gelaming-style clothing. "I'm Lord Swift, governor of the Parasiel tribe. My hostling, Cobweb, and I are inspecting the facilities here before carrying out a permanent solution for the victims." He held out his free hand. "You must be the medic."

The medic smiled warmly and bowed to Swift while taking his offered hand appreciatively. "My apologies, Lord Swift," he said, smiling. "I thought some of the harlings were in here and I didn't want them getting into mischief. My name is Colden. I've set up in an office down the hall. There's really more to see in there than here — literally, as I've actually got a light."

"Thank you, Colden, we've seen enough here," Cobweb said, quickly brushing past Swift and nearly shoving Colden from the doorway.

"What else is down here?" Swift asked. He felt he should look around some more, but it seemed pointless without a proper torch since all the windows were blocked out.

Colden paused and pointed to each door in succession. "Birthing room number two, incubation, recovery, supplies, and healers' offices and private examination rooms." He led the way to the very end of the hall where faint light could be seen around the edges of the door.

"Who was it?" a cheerful young voice asked as they filed into the room. A harling, between five and six years old was half-reclining on a bed like the ones Swift had just observed in the birthing room. Thankfully this one appeared clean.

"Visitors," Colden responded. He went to the child and gently pushed him so that he lay back down. "Very important visitors. This is Lord Swift, the new ruler of your tribe, and his hostling, tiahaar Cobweb."

"Really?" the harling asked in amazement. He struggled to sit back up.

"In a moment, we're almost done." Colden turned to Swift and Cobweb. "Please have a seat, tiahaara. I apologize, but I'd like to finish up with Blackberry here."

"Certainly," Swift said and immediately walked toward a stack of binders filled with papers.

"Is everything well with Blackberry?" Cobweb asked.

"Mostly well," Colden answered cheerfully.

Swift noted that the Gelaming had a charming bedside manner for a field medic.

"Blackberry had a nasty burn on his hand and arm here and I was just giving it a little extra healing energy."

Swift looked over to where the hara were gathered and saw Blackberry holding out his damaged limb for Cobweb's inspection. The harling, a winsome thing with straight, shiny black hair and a moderately brown complexion, was obviously what Lisia referred to as a Lily of the Valley, a harling designated to become a hostling. "I burned it really bad on the stove last month," he was saying. "Tiahaar Colden says that maybe he can fix it so that it won't look so ugly anymore!"

"Ah, but with such a lovely face, I'd have never noticed it," Cobweb told Blackberry.

Swift smiled at his hostling's thoughtfulness and returned his attention to the binders. He opened one. The first pages contained long lists of what appeared to be codes.

"Oh, you won't find much of interest in there, tiahaar," Colden said. "Half of it is just coding protocol and the rest is pretty dry medical reading."

"That's all right, Colden, I've grown highly accustomed to dry reading over the past few months," Swift replied, undeterred. Each sequence was paired with a name, generally flowery. As he flipped through, he found entries for each name that contained a daily journal describing feybraiha progress. Swift was surprised at the thorough nature of the notes, some of which even included suggestions for a few remedies and often-quoted things the harlings in question had said about their feelings and symptoms.

"Well, I think we're all done for today, Blackberry," Colden said. Blackberry thanked the medic and, bowing to Swift and Cobweb, backed from the room.

"These records are amazing," Swift said after Colden's patient had gone. "I didn't even realize that anyhar kept records on feybraiha like this."

Colden nodded and sat gracefully behind the desk. "Indeed. One thing I have to credit these particular Varrs for is their medical recording and the overall attention to detail."

"And all the records seem to be intact?" Swift asked. "I thought they were all in code."

"I can't say for sure whether everything is here. I have no way of knowing. And it's only the files upstairs that are encoded. But these don't divulge anything of state interest — they're purely medical."

"But it is of interest," Swift said. "It's horrible what was done here, but don't you think this information would be valuable to Wraeththu nonetheless? So many hara still suffer and struggle with feybraiha and pearl delivery." He turned to his hostling who remained apart and silent. "Cobweb, you should see some of this."

"I'm not sure that I should be letting you view these, tiahaar," Colden said. He came forward to his desk and closed an open blue binder, returning it to a metal bookcase just behind him.

Swift gritted his teeth for a moment before he could speak in a civil tone. "Tiahaar Colden, you are obviously forgetting my position here. This facility, the harlings and all its contents are Parsic. Regardless of the Gelaming's interest in these records, they technically belong to my administration, not yours. I'll read whatever I like."

"Certainly, tiahaar," Colden replied in a clipped tone. "I meant no offense. I'm simply doing my job."

Swift half smiled. "I assure that you won't be blamed, Colden."

Cobweb had walked behind them and removed the blue binder that Colden had put away. After flipping through a few pages he spoke in an almost reverent voice, "These are reports written by the hostlings themselves."

Colden was silent for a few moments, seemingly wrestling with his duty. "They include all sorts of innovative ideas for dealing with pearl delivery," he offered, shrugging slightly. "Granted, it's not my area of expertise by any means, but I feel certain that there is data in these binders that even our most advanced healers don't have. After all, nohar has ever done so much work with conception and delivery."

Swift swapped binders with Cobweb, who took the feybraiha data silently. Eagerly Swift opened the blue binder to leaf through it himself. "I'd like to make sure that this information is available to our *Parsic* healers," he said. Soon he was lost in reading the hostlings' writings. The three hara remained in the office until they heard the faint ringing of the first dinner bell.

Paran strode from the stables back to the main building. He was not a happy har. He'd wanted to find Tarkan and have him deliver a message to Immanion before ferrying additional temporary supplies from the nearest large Gelaming camp. But the har had already left and for once Paran cursed his efficiency.

As he walked through the main hallway, Paran saw Edrei exiting one of the classrooms. He did not look cheerful either. "What's wrong?" Edrei asked, falling into step beside Paran.

Paran shook his head, irritated, and replied in a low voice, "It's Swift Parasiel. He arrived this morning and has managed to turn everything upside-down. He's refusing to condone the transfer of the harlings to Imbrilim and is questioning our right to conduct studies of them at all. He says that he's considering a variety of options, but I can tell that he's got his heart set on keeping them all here."

"Here, as in right here?" Edrei asked.

"Right here," Paran whispered fiercely. "Isn't that ridiculous?" Edrei's face registered the proper dismay so Paran continued, "It's all the doing of that hostling, Lisia. He's convinced Swift that the harlings are all perfectly normal and happy and that we should just subsidize this place with staff and supplies. I suppose I should be grateful that Swift doesn't have the foresight that we do about medical studies and their potential, or he'd simply be insisting that the Parsics have more right to the breeding technology. The last thing we need is for them to figure out how to get this program going again – especially before we have that knowledge ourselves." As Edrei took this in, Paran led him towards the wing where their rooms were located. He didn't feel comfortable discussing this matter with the other hara.

Edrei had a thoughtful expression on his face as they entered their room. "Well, keeping them here *would* probably work as well."

Paran cast him a scornful glance.

123

"With the right teachers and guides, I mean."

"Edrei," Paran said in a tone that came across slightly patronizing, "there are 182 harlings here and as far as we have been able to determine, almost all of them have been brainwashed or neglected. The Parsics have no idea how to handle them and they certainly don't have the experts to study them, which I suppose is a blessing."

"Actually, I'm not quite sure the harlings are as brainwashed as they appear," Edrei said. "It's very difficult to get a clear reading on all of them, but to my mind they seem to have normal instincts. I think they just need somehar working with them more closely. As for the experts, we could probably compromise and have our hara study them here. As far as I can see, it would save an awful lot of trouble in moving them."

"And trust the Parsics to facilitate things properly?" Paran countered. "They've never exactly built up an educational system out here — at least not a morally decent one! And what about the older harlings? They're the ones who've been most thoroughly conditioned, having gone through the beginning stages of this facility's *training*. They've grown to exhibit the most shocking mannerisms, flirting like kanenes, not to mention simpering and fawning over jewelry, prettying up their hair, and wearing skirts. It's like they're not even Wraeththu, they're... *little girls*. The Parsics haven't graduated enough from their Varrish ways to provide the sort of monitored environment that those harlings need. Their influence would probably skew the studies."

Edrei smiled slightly and spoke soothingly. "I've noticed the harlings' behavior, but I think perhaps you're overreacting a little, Captain." He used the formality playfully and placed a calming hand on Paran's shoulder. "From what I've seen, the harlings are probably normal within reason, given what they've been through. And in any case, they're young and flexible enough to change, if they're so inclined, as most of the Parsics have been doing most admirably. Certainly they need further education and especially interaction with the outside world, but that could be done from here *or* in Imbrilim. The way I see it, what we are dealing with here is a kind of family; moving it or breaking it up would be yet another trauma for them."

Paran could hardly fathom what he was hearing or how they'd ended up even having this conversation. The last person he'd expected to support this travesty was Edrei, who was always so sensitive to the injustices they'd encountered in Megalithica. He'd never expected him to argue with the basic assumption they'd all made from the beginning — the facility was supposed to be broken up and the harlings were to be removed to undergo deprogramming and be studied, along with the medical records. He pulled away from Edrei's touch and walked across the room with his arms crossed defensively. "Of course it will be traumatic, Edrei, but that's hardly *our* fault! It's the fault of those Varrish monsters who put them in this situation to begin with. I think you've got it all wrong. Have you been meeting with Lisia or Swift secretly behind my back, letting them work their arguments? You *must* see it's not in the best interests of anyhar for these harlings to remain here! It goes against our entire purpose for being here."

"But what if they're happier being the way they are? They may in fact choose to stay predominantly soume, but if that's their choice and nohar is forcing them into a role or forcing them to stay here, it seems to me we should respect that."

Paran responded with an incredulous snort. "And let them all grow up to be like that Lisia? I think not. How are hara like that ever going to bring Megalithica out of its backward human tendencies?"

"That's harsh, Paran," Edrei chided gently. "Lisia is an incredible har. Despite his outward appearances, he's quite strong-willed and highly intelligent as well. Aren't you amazed with what he's accomplished here? And he's nothing like the Varrs. He's deeply compassionate. In my opinion, that's exactly what Megalithica needs."

"Don't be ridiculous, Edrei, that creature was raised practically from the pearl to think of himself as nothing more than a tool in the war effort, a supplier of goods. His caste training is practically non-existent, comprising nothing beyond aruna and the conception of pearls. I don't expect he really has any idea of the full context of this situation. How can he when he's never even been beyond these grounds? How can he possibly help anyhar?"

"He saved the lives of all these harlings."

Paran could think of nothing to counter that.

"Besides," Edrei continued, a slight edge creeping into his voice, "I think you're being incredibly hypocritical about this whole situation."

"What do you mean?"

"You know very well that some hara are simply more inclined toward one element or another. After all, you're more than a little ouana, yourself!" Edrei held up his hands placatingly as Paran opened his mouth. "There's nothing wrong with that. Anyhar should be able to emphasize one part of his nature if that's what he wants."

Paran shook his head again. "None of this debating may matter at all. The general has indicated that the Hegemony is eager to involve itself in this situation."

Edrei frowned slightly. "But you said Swift was refusing to have them sent to Immanion. What can the Hegemony do? Regardless of anyhar's feelings on the subject, the Gelaming simply do not have the authority to make decisions regarding Parsic harlings. Do they?"

"I think we're about to find out," Paran replied dryly.

Chapter Seven

I'm all curled up in bed and cozy under the blankets as I write this. I don't even know if I'll be able to stay awake long enough to finish writing everything I want. I've just been exhausted. I never would have guessed that hours of meditation could be so tiring! Of course there is the aruna too. Whatever the reason, I just feel like lying here and going to sleep.

I've been in training for a full week now. Even though it makes me tired, I wish I could have lessons every day, because I want to learn everything so badly, but right now I have to be patient. There are only three instructors, and since they have to work with six of us hostlings, I only get lessons every other day. I was hoping at first that I would just work with Vlaric, since I already knew him and felt comfortable with him, but of course they switch the instructors around every time. I know this is for the best, since I need to get used to being with as many different hara as possible. Besides, I know it's selfish of me to have a personal preference.

Anyway, I was kind of surprised to find out that even if they're a bit more complicated, the lessons are basically very similar to what I expected. I know that seems odd an odd thing to say, but usually when you think you know how something will be — like with my feybraiha — it turns out to be very different. So this time I'm kind of surprised that I was right.

At this point I've learned that the purpose of lessons is to learn the three levels of aruna needed to make pearls. Level 1 is the easiest, since it's nothing more complicated than learning all the best aruna techniques. There are all sorts of lessons in Level 1, some of them broad concepts but others ones just small techniques — like learning to become soume whenever we want. That's pretty easy to do. All I have to do is think about aruna really hard and it happens naturally. I mentioned that and one of the instructors, Tinnesh, said that this was because I had the proper mindset for a hostling. Apparently becoming soume isn't so easy for all hara. That makes sense, I suppose, but obviously if it wasn't easy for me, then I wouldn't have been picked to be a hostling to begin with. Anyway, Tinnesh told me that the hara who come to plant the pearls in us will want us to be soume before we even undress. That's a little bit harder, but still not so very difficult.

I must admit that one thing I like very much about these exercises is that the more I practice being soume, the less I have the embarrassing tendency to feel sensations in my ouana-lim. It's like I'm growing up, and as I get older my body gets smarter and knows exactly how it needs to be. During my feybraiha tiahaar Laran told me this would happen, but now I really, really believe him. Anyway, I think the instructors must know all about this and that's the real reason why they have us practice it so much. That's fine with me. I think the instructors are very smart when it comes to aruna matters.

Another part of Level 1 is learning about the seven energy centers of the soume-lam. This is something they never taught us in the classroom because you really have to feel it to understand. Right now they're teaching me how I have seven special spots inside me that are used during aruna. Five of them are easy to reach and I should be able to experience them one by one during aruna, at least if I'm practicing good techniques. The other two centers are a lot harder to reach, though, since they're hidden deep inside me where my seal is, and I want to open my flower to make pearls. In order to feel those energy centers, I have to master Level 3.

Level 3 is hard! It's a lot harder than I'd hoped, but all the instructors say that I am doing very, very well. In fact, Vlaric told me that it would take a har who wasn't special like I am years to master this technique. That makes me feel better, but it's still discouraging. I'm pretty sure that I've only actually managed opening the flower up once so far — I'm not even sure since obviously I can't see it open.

I think that's what makes it so hard — not being able to really see it. I do see it in a pretend way, though. That's a big part of the lesson — visualization. I have to meditate, which means I get very quiet and still, and pay close attention to all the things that are going on inside of my body, like my heart beating and my breathing and even the food going through my stomach. Then I become soume and go through the five energy centers. I try to follow the sensations of arousal to the inner seal and picture it inside me. Then I'm supposed to see it open in my imagination, like a flower, and that's supposed to make it open for real.

I thought it would be as easy as becoming soume, but it's not. Vlaric assures me though, that it's much easier to do during aruna, when the proper energies are flowing between hara. It seemed funny that we don't practice finding the seal during aruna, so I asked Genvert, another instructor, about it. He laughed at me, of course, and said that since I wasn't fully trained we might make a pearl by accident that way. I felt very stupid then, but he said that actually it was probably possible to open the seal without making a pearl, but it's very difficult and because I'm not ready, it probably would make me uncomfortable or be scary for me, at least right now. I wonder if we'll be trying that later.

This week I've been learning a lot more about the art of aruna. It's so strange. I never really thought that aruna itself would be so complicated but it really, really is. After doing a lot of Level 1 work and starting on Level 3, I already know a lot of different techniques and my aruna instructors agreed that I had mastered them so now I needed to study Level 2. This one is all about concentration and going through with aruna no matter what is happening around you or how you might feel. Genvert explained that before it's been easy for me to have good aruna because all three of them are well-experienced and know how to work with me. But, he said that some of the hara who I will be partnered with will not be as good. So, I need to know how to still have good aruna even if I don't like what the other har is doing.

At first, I had a hard time imagining that aruna could be bad, but then we started practicing and I understood. We would start having aruna like usual and then one of the instructors would do something on purpose that he knew I wouldn't like or that would be distracting. It could be all sorts of things, like they might say something rude or stupid, or start going too fast or too hard, or touch me someplace strange. At first I'd get so startled that I'd stop what I was doing or say something. They all pointed out that this was very rude. It's impolite to ask, "What are you doing?" and I'm not supposed to laugh either. It's really hard to just keep quiet and not say anything, but I can see why it would be mean to complain. It's not like the soldiers get special training for aruna like we do, so it wouldn't be their fault if they make mistakes. I just hope they're not all that bad. I asked Tinnesh about that, but he told me that because souls and minds tend to mix together during aruna, most of the hara will know what I want without me having to tell them because I can just send the image to them.

Anyway, after a while it almost got to be fun to try to fix the aruna when it started to go wrong. If they can't find out what to do from sharing breath or being connected, the proper way to do it is to very softly say which things you really *do* like the har to do. Also when they do something stupid, just try and guide them back into doing the right thing by moving your body the way you want to or guiding them with your hands.

One thing we are allowed to say is if they do something that hurts. It's not rude to speak up then and the instructors were very, very clear that our ouana partners are not supposed to do anything to us that hurts. If they do, they will get in big, big trouble, which obviously they should. But anyway, if the problem isn't that they're hurting us, but just that they're not very good, there's a secret for that too. I even managed to figure it out all on my own without the instructors telling me. I just make believe in my head that I'm enjoying myself and think about times I had aruna that was very, very good. That usually works pretty well and I manage to really enjoy myself at least some of the time.

I am so proud of myself. Today, I made a lot of progress in finding my seal and opening it for sure. Tinnesh was my instructor and he decided it was time to do a new sort of exercise. We had aruna like normal, but he warned me ahead of time that we were going to work together and open my seal. He said he would be helping me. I didn't understand how he could help but he said he would do it through the special connection of aruna — and that I would have to trust him and just follow along. He told me that as soon as the seal was open, I was to be very, very still and just concentrate on what I was feeling so that I'd know how it was supposed to feel. I was still a little nervous about it and I asked him if we were going to be making a pearl. He said no, we wouldn't because he would be very, very careful and not plant any seed in me.

So we had the aruna and it really was very wonderful, then Nesh told me to relax and so I did. Right after that, I felt this wonderful, incredible feeling of love and hope and then along with it, a movement deep inside of me. It felt so strange and incredible. Before he could even say anything I cried out and I said, "It's open!" And he smiled and said "yes," and then next thing I knew he was out of me. As soon as he moved away, the seal closed up again and I felt funny, like I was missing something and it suddenly kind of hurt, like a bad cramp. I almost started to cry, but I stopped myself because I knew it was such a good thing I'd finally had the seal open. So instead of crying, I told Nesh it hurt and he rubbed my stomach for a while until I felt more normal. Then he told me just to relax for a while so I would be rested and ready to try again.

So we just laid down on the bed, I guess about a half an hour, and talked a little bit about different things like what was for dinner and what I'd been doing with my friends on the days I didn't have aruna lessons. I told him how on those days the ones of us that were free would either help with the smaller harlings or work in the gardens. After a while we stopped talking and started to share breath again. I was very glad because I was feeling better and really wanting to have aruna again instead of talk.

This time was a little different. As soon as we started to have aruna together, Nesh started talking to me in my mind. This had happened before a few times, since the instructors tend to prefer to say things through the aruna connection, but this time he was with me in my mind and I was in his mind as well. He told me to concentrate on my body while we were having the aruna, just like I would concentrate if I was meditating. This wasn't too hard. So I did that and this time when the seal opened, I felt him actually doing the visualization to make me open up.

For just a moment, I was filled with such a feeling of magic, but then he pulled out again and we laid back, very tired. I was sore again, feeling like I'd slightly twisted something inside, but it really wasn't as bad as the time before. When Nesh sat up and said he was hungry, I got up with him. We both decided to take a break and got dressed and went to the kitchen for a snack. After we ate, we sat in the hostlings' lounge for a little while talking again, but I was distracted because I knew that we were going to go back to my room and open my seal again. I was so ready that I even started becoming soume just sitting there. Genvert was right. Opening the seal is a little bit scary, because it makes me feel so strange, but that magic feeling was so very good. I just want to do it again and again!

Finally he took me back to my room and this time when we took aruna, everything was the same except that he told me to open the seal by myself, to "make it happen." It took a lot of concentration, but I did it! I was so proud that I hardly even minded that we had to stop again and I hardly noticed any pain. I just lay there and smiled and smiled. Nesh said that I had done very well and that we would be stopping the lesson for that day. He said that once I was able to open the seal by myself during aruna, twice in a row, even with distractions, that I'd be through Level 3 and ready to host.

Today I learned something that really surprised me. It wasn't something the instructors taught me but something I figured out myself. I had training with Vlaric today and I found it pretty easy to open my seal, even though he was trying to make aruna "bad" (though it's hard with him, he's so good normally). Anyway, this time when I opened it, it was open for a little longer than usual and because of that, I had more of a chance to concentrate on how it feels. It's interesting, because I finally realized it doesn't really feel like a flower opening, no matter what the instructors have been telling us. I mean, it's sort of similar and the good feelings are like flowers, but actually the feeling of the seal opening is more like a door opening. I know it can't be a real door, but it feels like the seal is like a door and when it opens, there's something behind it like a room. Of course, I had to let the seal close again or else Vlaric might have gotten his seed into the room and I'd be hosting!

I'm starting to get a little frustrated with all this training. I really feel like I'm ready to conceive a pearl all on my own. I'm getting much better at opening the seal during aruna. I can do it almost every time I try now and I've been given lots of lovely gifts as rewards. But still, the lessons are slowing down and that's making it harder. The problem is that some more of the harlings have passed through feybraiha and need to start training. That means that the instructors are available less and I have fewer lessons.

On the bright side, I have more time to spend with my friends. When we're not busy helping with the younger harlings, we spend a lot of time in the gardens. But a lot of the time we just go outside and instead of pulling weeds, we talk a lot. We've all been doing well with our aruna lessons and we've all had lots of funny stories about the "bad aruna" parts. Mostly, we just talk about the same things we always did. We wonder a lot about what the ouana hara will be like and whether we will like them. I wonder what the harlings that comes from my pearls will look like and what they will grow up to be. I wonder what it will feel like to have a pearl growing inside of me.

Finally, after waiting for so many months, I am finally a real hostling!

Really everything seemed to happen so fast this week. The lessons had slowed down a lot and it's not really spring yet, so we were getting bored since there's much less work to do outside. Then one day, tiahaar Botbek called all of us hostlings together at dinner. He said that we would be given our final tests and that the soldiers were coming in just eight days! Those of us who passed the test would be able to take aruna with them and host our very first pearls. We were all so excited.

I must admit that even though I had been doing really well, being able to open every time, I was nervous for the test. After all, three of the administrators actually came into the room and watched to witness that I passed. I was a little embarrassed because it seemed so strange to have aruna with others watching, but Genvert reminded me that I needed to be able to perform well even with distractions. So, I concentrated very hard and opened the seal both times! I was so pleased.

I was also very happy for all my friends — everyhar passed the test. Tonight, after dinner, all the staff and instructors and administrators came to announce that we were officially hostlings. We got to share a lovely cake and everyhar stood up and cheered for us. Rosea was so happy that he cried. I just couldn't stop smiling. By the time I came up to my room, my face was hurting.

I have had many happy, important days in my life, but I think this has been the best day ever so far. I'm so full of joy. I feel like I am finally fulfilling my purpose as a hostling. After all this learning and training, I have finally created a pearl — there is a new harling living inside of me and soon I will deliver him and he will grow up to be a another Varr helping our tribe to stay strong.

As incredibly wonderful as it is to be hosting, just meeting the soldiers for the first time was exciting too. We were all waiting together in the lounge when the soldiers came. I was so nervous, but I couldn't stop smiling. Then the hara came up the stairs and I felt like my heart was going to jump right out of my chest, I was so excited. The head administrator, tiahaar Upsari, led the group of hara and gave us a little talk. He went over the rules quickly, which were all very obvious anyway. Then he said that because making a pearl is very, very difficult, we might not all succeed on the first try. This made me very nervous, because it was something that I had worried about, but he said that we all had until dinner to get it right. Then, he said that we should get to know one another and that as soon as they were ready, the hara would get to pick which hostling they wanted. That made me nervous too. I was so afraid that I would get picked last. But, thankfully, I got picked right in the middle.

I liked my har very much. His name was Aeroka, but he said that all his friends called him Rok. He was very tall and had short brown hair and brown eyes and dark skin with freckles. He asked to go to my room as soon as he picked me. I must admit that I was so nervous, my hands were shaking a little, but I smiled the whole time and I don't think Rok ever guessed how scared I was about making a mistake. On the outside, everything looked perfect. I had on my special dress with the red ribbons and lots of beautiful jewelry that sparkled and the beautiful silk sheets were on my bed. And to make everything even better, Rok was so polite. He opened my door for me and told me over and over again how lovely I was and how he'd never forget what I looked like. He really made me feel special. It was obvious that he knew how important I was because I can make pearls.

But then the most awful thing happened. Everything was going great. I was soume right away and I could tell Rok was very aroused when he took off my clothes and we shared breath. We began to take aruna together and it was very nice. I was all the way through the first five energy centers when I started concentrating on my seal, which always feels so very, very wonderful to me. I was thinking of how the door would open and rather than having to close it quickly, I would finally be able to keep it open and make a pearl. I was sharing that thought with him to encourage him, but then as soon as I started to do that we reached the pinnacle too fast and it was over before I had a chance to open up.

I was so embarrassed. I couldn't believe it. Once we had gotten started, I was so sure that it was all going to be all right. I felt so ashamed that I started to cry. But Rok was so kind to me. He put his arms around me and said that I shouldn't feel bad. He even said that it was his fault. He said he was just too over-excited and anyway he was nervous about doing it since he'd never fathered a pearl. I know that should have made me feel better, but I couldn't stop crying, which made Rok laugh a little. Then I realized that I was being childish and I made myself calm down. But all that crying had made me tired and Rok was tired too, so we got under the covers and went to sleep for a little while.

I woke up after that because Rok was rubbing himself against my thigh. As soon as I opened my eyes I realized that I was ready to try again. This time, I decided not to open up my mind to Rok when I opened the seal. It worked! And it was so wonderful. It was the most fantastic aruna I had ever had — and, of course, I had a lot of aruna during lessons. Usually, I'm not very loud, but I couldn't help but shout out a bit when I felt him move past my seal and plant the seed there. It was beautiful. When the seal opened, it was like the door to another world and the feeling I had made me feel like I was a beautiful flower opening up — like being music and all the colors of the rainbow and wrapped up in soft warm blankets all at once.

I was a little embarrassed at having been so loud, but Rok just laughed and said he liked that. We lay down together for a long time after that, but then my muscles were aching to get out of the bed. Rok seemed to be getting bored too, so I suggested that we get dressed and I would show him around the facility. He said that sounded nice and so that's what we did. He didn't really have much of anything to say, but he let me tell him all about the harlings and the things that we did when we weren't having lessons. Then he saw another soldier walking around and went to go visit with him. I didn't see him again until we all had dinner together that night, but it really didn't bother me. I was too excited thinking about my first pearl!

Today, a week since my aruna with Rok, tiahaar Botbek performed an examination and confirmed what I already knew: I'm hosting! I've waited a long time for this and now that it's happening, it's like I'm dreaming.

I went over for my examination right after breakfast. One of tiahaar Botbek's assistants had come over to me with a note while I was eating. I was so excited I couldn't really eat any more. My friends told me none of them had got an exam yet and it made me happy because I'm never first to do anything. After I saw tiahaar Botbek finish his breakfast and leave, I waited around five minutes, then I told everyhar I had to go. Coral said he hoped I got good news. I told him I was sure I would, but as I was walking down the hall, I actually was a little nervous. After all, how did I really know I was hosting? I felt it in my heart but I couldn't really feel it in my body.

Anyway, I walked down the hall towards the wing where all the doctors' offices and exam rooms and everything are. I had only been there for that one appointment at my feybraiha and that time I was too excited, and I guess too young, to have really noticed everything. This time was different because I realized that soon it would all be very important to me, since I would be there a lot more often. I looked at the signs on the doors. Some said they were delivery rooms and some others were recovery rooms. Then I saw another door that said it was for incubation and I wondered what would be in there, but by that time I was worried I was going to be late for my appointment, so I hurried up and went to see the doctor.

I found tiahaar Botbek in his office, standing behind his desk filing some paperwork. I said hello and he nodded at me and told me to go into the exam room next door. He said he would be coming in a few minutes, so while I was in there I should take off my clothes and just lie down. Five minutes later, I was lying on the special exam table and tiahaar Botbek came in with a clipboard with a notepad on it. It was a lot like the feybraiha exam I'd had with tiahaar Laran, so I wasn't very worried, even though I still nervous about what the doctor would say.

So finally he started the exam, telling me to put my legs up and relax with slow, deep breaths. "You know you're the first Lily of the Valley to be examined for a pearl," he told me. Again I felt very special and proud. He then asked me questions about my aruna with Rok. He wrote everything down, then when I was done telling him he told me he was sure he'd have good news for me.

All the same, he said he needed to verify it by doing an internal exam to locate the pearl. After he spread my legs, he told me again to relax and then he asked me to use my training and become soume. He said he needed me to do that so that it might be easier. I wasn't really in the mood since this was a doctor's exam, but I managed and so then he put lotion on his hand and went up inside my soume-lam. Even with the lotion and him being gentle, it felt strange and uncomfortable. Finally I started to feel a little cramp and that's when he said his hand was by the womb, which holds the pearl. He then told me to let out my breath so he could press down and feel for the pearl. I was scared that it would hurt but he said it wouldn't hurt much, so I let out my breath while with his other hand, the doctor began to press down on my stomach. I felt a bigger cramp, but it only lasted a couple of seconds before the doctor stopped pressing and took out his hand from inside me. He said he definitely felt the pearl and that in seven weeks I'll deliver it.

I was so happy I wanted to jump up and do a dance, but I really couldn't with him standing there so I just thanked him for telling me. He gave me some advice then about taking care of myself during hosting, but I didn't hear a word he said, honestly. All I kept thinking was how it was the most amazing, wonderful thing and I just wanted to go tell everyhar in the whole world. As soon as he said I could get dressed, I grabbed my clothes and I think I must have been dressed before he even reached his office. I called out goodbye and just ran down the hall. I was almost to the stairwell when I stopped running, realizing I shouldn't be running since I'm hosting.

I went up the stairs very slowly, just feeling like I was living on a cloud. I stopped half-way up, on the landing, and looked out the window, just so I could have time to savor the moment and how I was feeling. Out the window I could see a big group of harlings playing and I thought to myself, "Someday there will be a group of harlings like that and they will be harlings I have made." I really can barely describe how it feels now, knowing I will be making harlings. I've always known that, I'm a Lily of the Valley, but until now it was not quite so real.

Finally, I decided it was time to go up and tell all my friends. When I got to the lounge they were actually all there, waiting for me. Calla was the first to ask me: "So, are you hosting?"

I smiled my biggest smile and said yes and they all came up and hugged me and kissed me.

"Stand back, let me see!" Coral said.

I stepped back and they all looked at my stomach, though of course they didn't see anything since the pearl is still very, very small. "You should go for your exam," I told Coral and he smiled and said I was right; he had a note of his own saying to visit tiahaar Botbek right after I was done. I wished him good luck and he went downstairs.

Now it's after dinner and I still keep having the same thoughts over and over again, how amazing it all is. Inside of me is something that will grow and grow and become a little harling and then later a har. I'm trying to imagine how small the pearl must be now. I'm thinking about all the diagrams from my lessons and so I bet it's not even as long as the first joint in my thumb. Still, it's alive and growing and in seven weeks it will have grown to be a big pearl, as big as a ball or, so Vlaric told me, a har's head. I wonder if I'll feel different then.

It's been a while since I last wrote. I'm almost halfway through my hosting and finally, I can really tell. Ever since I first found out for sure, I've been checking myself every day and finally around five days ago, I was lying in bed and pressing down on my stomach with my hands, trying to feel it, when I suddenly got a cramp and felt the pearl, a hard lump. The next day when I was getting dressed, I looked at myself in my big mirror and for the first time, I thought I could see a change; my stomach was a little bit rounded.

I've been keeping this to myself, wanting to wait until I got a little bigger to really share with the others, but today I just couldn't help it. All us real hostlings were out in the garden gathering flowers for some decorations. I wanted to pick some of the pansies so I bent over which, of course (how silly of me), made me right away have a cramp in my middle. I sort of yelped and stood up. Everyhar stopped what they were doing and looked over at me. They looked scared, thinking something was wrong, but then I just patted my stomach and smiled. "It's just the pearl," I said. "I guess it's getting in the way." Then everyhar laughed and came up to me. We all started talking about how our stomachs were growing and how we could feel our pearls. Seagrass surprised us all when he said he had felt his harling moving inside the pearl. None of us had felt that yet or even really knew we would be able to.

Tonight I'm going to try very hard to feel the harling moving. I think when I do, it will make everything feel even more real. Every day I get closer and closer to my dream and only a few weeks from now, I'll see my very first harling.

I love my pearl. And I think it loves me back. This afternoon I went for a nap in my room and while I was just starting to fall asleep, I felt the harling. It was like a sort of ripple inside me, like when water splashes on you in the bathtub, only it was inside me and it made me feel so warm. I put my hands on my stomach and rubbed it. It moved a little more then and I felt another kind of ripple then, like an actual feeling. My pearl was happy! I could just tell.

So I kept on rubbing my belly and then I started talking to the pearl, very nice and quietly. "How are you doing?" I asked it. "I hope you're all comfortable there, all warm and snuggled up inside your pearl." Even though I was talking and the harling can't possibly hear me from inside my body, I was so sure that the harling would understand me, just feel what I was saying through my body. I think he did too because I just felt even more happy and peaceful.

I sang to the harling. At first it was just some simple songs we'd all sung as harlings, but then I started on some songs of my own. I can't remember all the words to what I sang, because I was making them up as I went along, but the main one I sang had a chorus like this: "It's dark in here, but I've no fear, for soon it will be light. I'll come into the pretty world and then I'll learn to fight. Of course before I learn to fight I must be born and hatch. But for now my hostling and I are a perfect match."

Things are not going to happen the way I thought. Today tiahaar Botbek, tiahaar Laran and a couple of administrators told us we won't be able to see our pearls or our harlings. I really didn't understand it at first. They had invited us all to a meeting in one of the classrooms. We're all six weeks now and walking over, some of us thought we were going to get some more lessons and instructions. We still haven't been told very much about delivering the pearls. Anyway, once we were all in there, tiahaar Botbek explained it to us. He said that as soon as the pearls are born, they will be taken away and cared for by other hara. There's a special room where they will all be kept warm and safe. Once the harlings hatch from their pearls, they will be kept in a nursery and then other staff will be taking care of them. Tiahaar Botbek said they wanted us to know now so we wouldn't be surprised.

I was really shocked by this! We all were. All along, I had thought that I would be taking care of the pearls and the harlings. We've all been trained to take care of harlings, after all, and we make the pearls, so of course we would take care of them. But, we found out, that is not the plan. We were all angry, I think, and Calla interrupted the doctor before he was even finished and asked him why things had to be that way. Tiahaar Botbek was very calm when he explained it. He said that taking care of our pearls and harlings was not our job. As soon as we delivered our pearls, we would be getting ready for another conception and then we would be hosting. Hosting is our job. Calla spoke up again and argued, saying we had worked with the harlings all the past six weeks, but tiahaar Botbek said that was different.

Calla asked why it's different (he was really being brave to ask!) and that's when we finally understood. It was actually one of the administrators, tiahaar Phaden, who answered. He told us the reason we can't take care of the pearls or harlings is because they are ours. That seemed the exact opposite of what we hostlings had all been thinking, but what he said was that they were going to separate us from the harlings for their own good. Almost all these harlings are going to be soldiers and workers for the Varrs, not Lilies of the Valley like us. In three years they will be sent away to go into training. They're not going to stay here. Because of this, the harlings should not be allowed to get too "attached." If they always had hara like us taking care of them and knew where they came from, then they might not want to go. Plus, how would we hostlings feel when we had to say goodbye to our harlings? It was better if they were treated nicely — but not by us.

It was obvious all of us were still upset so that's when Phaden made us a promise. He said that although we wouldn't be able to care for the pearls or the small harlings, once the harlings were older, we would of course still see them around, even if we weren't specifically taking care of them and wouldn't know which harlings were ours. Also we will always keep training the younger Lilies and helping with their lessons. They weren't going to prevent us from taking care of harlings altogether.

Afterward we all left the room and didn't really say anything. That was until we got upstairs. Coral asked, "Why didn't they tell us before?"

Then Calla laughed and said, "Because now it's too late!"

I don't know what to think.

It's been a week since we got the news about our pearls. Surprisingly, I feel a lot less upset about it than I did originally. I guess I just had to think about it. When I first heard the announcement, it was just a jumble of words, but the more I think it over, it does make sense. We can't be selfish and want the harlings for ourselves. The harlings are for our tribe and we have to remember that. It's just like with aruna — we can't always be with one particular har, even though we might really like him. We have to share and accept. It's part of our duty as hostlings, our job.

I haven't just changed my mind from thinking, though. Today I was in a classroom with some harlings who are close to feybraiha, and tiahaar Nemish was having me tell them what it's like to host a pearl. Talking in front of them, I realized that even though those harlings aren't my own harlings and I never saw them as pearls, I still love them. I think I'll be able to do my job just fine after all.

Coral had his pearl last night! It was early and a big surprise to everyhar. Yesterday afternoon after lunch, we hostlings were all outside. Even though we're all obviously round in the middle and feeling a lot more tired than before, it was a nice spring day out and we weren't too tired to enjoy it. We were spread out around the yard doing various things when there was a big commotion. I was sitting on a bench telling a story to a small group of harlings — the story with the ugly duckling growing into a swan — when I heard somehar shout. I looked up and saw hara crowding together by the spring lily patch. I heard somehar shout to get a doctor.

I wanted to go over and see what was happening but because I had the harlings, I couldn't just run over. I waited a few minutes and tried to see what was wrong. All the harlings kept asking "What's happening? What's happening?" I told them to be quiet and just wait. Finally I saw tiahaara Botbek and Laran rush out of the building and over to the hara. Then I saw them supporting a har by the arms. I saw the har's curly blond hair and knew right away it was Coral. I also knew what was happening.

As soon as the doctors went inside with Coral, I told the harlings the story would have to wait. I told them to come with me so I could find out for sure what was going on. When I got there, everyhar was in shock. Calla actually had tears in his eyes.

"What's wrong?" I asked.

Calla said that Coral was going to have his pearl.

"But that's wonderful!" I said. That's when they told me that Coral had fallen on the ground. He was in a lot of pain and had been crying. To me, that wasn't that surprising since the doctors said delivering the pearl would hurt, and that's what I said.

Then Rosea shook his head and said, "I think he was in more pain than we imagined."

After that, we talked some more but we really couldn't concentrate on anything we were doing. I took my group of harlings back to their room. We hostlings all wanted to go to the delivery room to see Coral, but there were staff standing outside it who told us we weren't allowed. We went upstairs and waited and waited in the lounge. It was hours and hours we waited. Finally it was time for bed. None of us wanted to sleep though. We all just wanted to know about the pearl. We were all talking about it. During all those hours, I had an idea about why Coral had seemed to be in so much pain. I think it's probably because the pearl came early and his body just wasn't ready yet. I wonder if maybe Coral did something wrong, like run or lift something heavy, to make it come early. I hope the doctors will explain it to us later, since I don't want that happening to me.

Anyway, it was very late when we heard somehar coming up the stairs. I almost thought it would be Coral, but instead it was tiahaar Botbek. He looked very tired and also was very messy, like he'd gotten dressed in a big hurry. His hair was sticking out in all directions and he was sweating. "Well," he said, "Coral's had his first pearl." It was so wonderful and we all hugged one another — Calla even hugged tiahaar Botbek. We asked if everything was OK and the doctor said both Coral and the pearl were fine.

Calla asked if we could see Coral now (I really wanted to myself, just to ask him what it was like!) but tiahaar Botbek said Coral had to sleep. In fact, today we were told we won't be able to see Coral for quite a few days. He has to stay in a special room by himself for a while. I asked why and tiahaar Botbek said they just want to be sure Coral is healthy and well adjusted before he comes back to live regularly and conceives another pearl. I know just a few weeks from now a group of hara is scheduled to come and a whole new round of pearls will be conceived. In a month I'll probably be hosting a brand new pearl. Time goes so quickly!

Finally the pearl is almost here. Yes, it's been a whole two months. It seems I've been waiting forever and ever for this pearl to be born, but at the same time, things have gone pretty quickly. Besides, I'm just glad that I'm not delivering it early like Coral did.

Up until last week, I wasn't even feeling different, except for feeling the harling move sometimes and being a bit tired. This last week I'm a lot more tired, which makes sense, since hosting takes energy, especially now when the pearl is so big. I'm also hungrier than I ever used to be. Instead of having regular meals, which kind of make me sick if I eat too much, I'm given smaller meals, like snacks, throughout the day and it's all very good food to make sure I'm healthy and the pearl can grow.

I think it's wonderful that things are going so well. The pearl really must be big because bending over has gotten a lot more awkward and it's certainly harder for me to get comfortable when I sleep. Still, none of it worries me because very, very soon, I'll deliver the pearl and I'll be so happy.

I've never been so miserable before in all my life. I feel like everything I thought I knew about my life is a lie. I was so happy just a few days ago. Everything was perfect. Now I don't think I can ever be happy again.

It's been three days since I bore my first pearl. It doesn't really hurt any more but I feel sick. I feel like there's a great big hole inside of me where the pearl used to be. It's like I wish the pearl was back inside, so that I could feel it and hold it inside myself and love it. They wouldn't even let me see it. They told me it was healthy, but I don't even really know. They wouldn't lie about that, would they?

But then they didn't tell me how awful, awful, awful the delivery would be either. I knew it would hurt — but not like that. They said that about my first aruna too, and it only hurt for a little while and then it was wonderful. They said that knowing I'd delivered a healthy, beautiful pearl would make the pain worthwhile. But I don't feel worthwhile. I just feel empty and lonely and afraid. They said that deliveries were all perfectly natural and that my body would know just what to do to make the pearl come into the world. But I didn't know what to do and I don't think that it was natural at all. This was just horrible. I thought I was going to die. I really did.

It started right before dinner. I got this pain that was a lot like I had during feybraiha. I knew it was time for the pearl to come and I wasn't that scared at first. I was kind of excited. I thought it would be all right and one of the serving hara saw that I was hurting and called for some administrators to come. I didn't even get to eat. I wanted to tell my friends that it was happening, since I was going to be the second delivery after Coral, but tiahaar Botbek came rushing over and took me to the delivery wing away from everyhar else.

They put me on this special table and by then the pain started getting worse and I started worrying because I knew that it might take hours for the pearl to come and I didn't know why the pain was getting worse. I thought something was wrong. But then tiahaar Laran came and examined me and he said everything was fine. But it just kept getting worse and worse. I started to cry and they told me that I was being immature because I'd known it was going to hurt. I kept telling them that something must be wrong because it couldn't possibly be proper to hurt so much. I remembered about Coral, but I still thought I would be different, because I was really ready; I just couldn't believe it. They said I should be calm and still and then it wouldn't hurt as badly.

I tried, I really tried hard, but whenever I'd relax a great pain would pull down on my middle and it felt like the pearl was going to pull loose everything inside of me and it made me scream. Tiahaar Botbek said that I mustn't scream because I would scare the other hostlings. And I said that they *should* be scared because this was the most horrible thing in the whole world. Tiahaar Botbek didn't care at all. He said that the pain was only going to get worse and that I'd wear myself out by carrying on like a spoiled harling.

I got so angry then. I started screaming at him and said this was all their fault and they hadn't told us the truth and that the others should know, and I said I didn't want to have pearls anymore and that I would die if this didn't stop. And he put his hand over my mouth and said if I didn't stop he'd tie my mouth shut. I tried to be quiet, but then the pain came again and it felt like I was bleeding. I got scared and screamed again. And he did cover my mouth. They tore a sheet and put it in my mouth, and tied it tight in back, so I couldn't talk or scream so loud. In a way, that was better because I bit on the cloth and it helped a little.

It was the worst feeling in the world. The muscles in my body just kept squeezing and squeezing and I had no control. There were times when the pain would stop, but it was never long enough. When the pains came, I would shut my eyes and think really hard how much I wanted it to stop. I didn't like the time in between pains, because then I'd open my eyes and would notice all the blood on the doctors' hands. After a while, I stopped opening my eyes.

It was hours and hours and hours and the pain went on and on. I was so tired. I thought surely I'd faint at last from all the pain and being so tired, but I never did, even though I kept hoping I would. I just wanted it to be over, over, over. The pain continued all night long and finally, after the sun had been up for a long time, tiahaar Laran held my hand and told me to take a deep breath and push down with my muscles to make the pearl come out. "Just one big push," he said. I didn't even open my eyes, just pushed until I thought I was going to die. And finally, finally it came out.

Suddenly I opened my eyes. I was so relieved, I started crying all over again, which I had stopped doing from being so tired. Through the tears, I tried to see the pearl but tiahaar Botbek was in the way. His arms were covered with blood. I forced myself to sit up and tried to reach for the pearl. I knew I couldn't keep it, but I wanted so badly to see. I wanted to touch it and know that it was all right. But tiahaar Laran and the assistant pushed me back down and then tiahaar Botbek took it away.

Tiahaar Laran left then and it was just me and the assistant. He took out a cloth and began to wash me off. I was all covered with blood and realized I was in a lot of pain. "You're a bit torn up," the har told me (I don't even know his name). I swear I didn't even care, all I wanted was to see the pearl. A few minutes later, tiahaar Laran came back and said the pearl was healthy and that I'd done very well. While he put medicines on me and did some stitching (which for some reason I didn't really feel), I told him that I didn't think I had done well at all. I told him that it all went wrong but he said that it hadn't.

And then he was done and said I would be "as good as new." I looked at him. I felt cold all over because I knew that I'd have to go through this again and again forever and ever. I'm a hostling har and this is my duty. My whole purpose is to make pearls and bring them into the world, and I've always wanted to do that so much, but now I know it's such a horrible thing and I don't want to do it again.

I told that to tiahaar Laran and he said that I was just tired and scared and that I would feel better soon, all healed. After I'd had a few pearls it wouldn't be so hard as this first time. I told him that it wasn't fair for pearl bearing to hurt so much. He said that it was the price I paid to be a hostling and live in a nice room with pretty things and have no work to do but aruna. He said I should feel thankful that I'm protected and will never have to fight and toil. And then he said that I should think about what he said, and that I would have to stay by myself until they were sure that I wouldn't go to the other hostlings and frighten them with scary stories and exaggerations.

After being in the recovery room a half a day, I was brought up to my own room. Since then, I've been here all alone, except for when the doctors visit and hara bring me food. I feel like nohar cares about me and I'm all hollow and cold inside. I wish I could see the pearl or go down to the harling rooms and play with the little ones. I think that would make me feel better, but I'm not allowed. I know I must be good and do what

I'm told, if I want to stay here and be treated like a hostling. I don't want to go and fight or work in the fields all day, but I don't want to deliver any more pearls either. He said it wouldn't be so bad after a while, but how do I know that's true? I think they're just telling me that so I'll be quiet. It's cowardly and mean and I hate them for not telling us the truth.

But I'm trapped. I'm supposed to take aruna with a new har in a couple of weeks and then I'll be hosting. There will be another pearl in two months and then this all over again. And it will always be this way. I'm so scared that it will never hurt any less and I'll never stop feeling empty inside. I just wish I could make it all stop. I wish the delivery had gone wrong. I wish I were dead.

Chapter Eight

Swift leaned back in his chair and studied Cobweb's expression. For the past ten minutes, his hostling had been gazing out of the window, his eyes alternately focused and unfocused. Swift sensed he was gazing into the present as well as the past.

After reviewing the medical records, they had given Colden their thanks and returned to their rooms for some rest before dinner. The second bell had already rung but, assuming the second shift was as long as the first, they still had twenty minutes.

"So are you glad you came?" Swift ventured.

It was a few moments before Cobweb replied. He did not turn from the window. "I'm not sure 'glad' would be an appropriate description. This place is and was... *foul.*"

"I know," Swift said. He went over to the window and stood to Cobweb's right. Outside, the youngest harlings, who had eaten at first bell, were enjoying an after-dinner recess. "I read Lisia's journal and spoke with him at length. I know what went on."

Cobweb glanced at his son. "I didn't have to gather any facts, read anything, have any interviews. I *know*. I can *feel* it. I can *smell* it. It's repulsive, revolting... like carnage." His hands gripped the sides of the window frame, flexing with tension. "If this place can be so bad... I can't imagine what Fulminir was like."

Swift put a hand on Cobweb's shoulder. "Well, fortunately you didn't have to see that. I did." Outside, the harlings were now being rounded up to return inside the building. "It's strange, actually, thinking of the atrocities there and then the crimes perpetrated here. Fulminir was horrific, violence not even concealed, depravity right on the surface, while here life was peaceful, ordered, and wreathed in flowers — but the motivation behind this place was just the same."

Hostling and son remained at the window a few minutes longer, then went to their individual rooms to freshen up for dinner.

Later, Swift found his hostling standing in the lounge, his hair woven in a loose plait down his back. "The third bell should be ringing shortly," Swift said. "Let's head down."

The dining hall, which they had both visited earlier that day, was at the back of the building, but by the time they reached it, they were still early, so most of the tables were empty. Pansea and his friends, however, had already found seats. The harling face lit up when he spied Swift coming in through the doors.

"Those are our dinner companions," Swift announced, waving across the room. "I met with the redhead earlier today. Nice harling. I promised to have dinner with him."

They arrived at the table, which was round, with seating for seven. Pansea beamed and stood up to gesture to the remaining seats. The other seats were taken up by four additional harlings about the same age. Like all the older harlings Swift had seen, they were wearing embroidered blouses with skirts or silky, flowing pants, fingers full of cheap rings and their hair, which apparently they'd done up especially for dinner, pinned up with pretty barrettes and combs.

"Good evening, Pansea," Swift said, as he and Cobweb sat down. "May I introduce a special guest who's come to visit? This is my hostling, Cobweb."

All the harlings' eyes went to Cobweb. "Lord Swift's hostling?" A couple of the harlings' faces registered pure awe. "I'm truly honored to meet you, tiahaar Cobweb," Pansea said earnestly before introducing his friends. "There used to be a lot of hostlings here but now they're all gone. We miss them."

"I'm sure you do," Cobweb replied. "My son has been taking me around the building and grounds. He's told me a little about the harlings here and how you all live together. He told me he spoke with you this afternoon."

Pansea nodded, eyes downcast demurely. "Yes, tiahaar Cobweb. He was very kind to me."

Swift was amused to see the harling once again playing at flirting. "All I did was listen," Swift assured Cobweb. "Now, Pansea, stop looking down like that. It's okay to look hara in the eyes; generally it's considered polite."

Pansea raised his eyes. "I'm sorry, Lord... sorry, *tiahaar* Swift, I'm just not used to being with older hara any more."

"Don't worry about it," Swift assured him. "Now do any of you have any questions?" He addressed the entire table, a group of eager almost-hara obviously burning with curiosity. A black-haired harling at the far side of the table raised his hand. "Yes?" Swift prompted

Like Pansea, Cissus was shy, glancing down as he spoke. "Well, I was going to ask something else, but now I have a question for tiahaar Cobweb. How many pearls have you had?"

Swift flinched inwardly at the question, knowing Cobweb would be taken aback, but was relieved when his hostling managed to conceal any reaction. "Um, just one — Swift."

Cissus frowned. "Oh."

"I do also have another harling, whom I've adopted," Cobweb added.

"Adopted?" Pansea asked. "Adopted from here?"

The harlings seemed to have a way of posing awkward questions. "No, it was a harling from somewhere else. His parents—" Cobweb began, then stopped himself. "His hostling wasn't able to take care of him, so I did it."

"Oh," said Pansea. "I see. That's good, because harlings need somehar to take care of them. Before everything changed here, we took for granted that there would always be hara to take care of us all. We didn't think about the things that we can't do without adults. We're lucky that Lisia stayed to take care of us. It's like he's adopted us."

Cissus suddenly looked very upset and spoke in a fierce whisper to Pansea. "It wasn't just Lisia. Don't forget Peony and the others!"

Pansea reached over to put a hand on his friend's shoulder. "I'm sorry, Cissus, I didn't mean to." All the harlings looked uncomfortable. Swift and Cobweb were confused until Pansea noticed their expressions and explained. "Some of the other hostlings like Cissus' mentor Peony stayed too, but after a while they had to leave and try to get help."

Swift had intended to question Lisia about this earlier, but the subject had not come up. He wasn't sure whether he could offer any comfort to the abandoned harlings.

"Obviously, Lisia, Peony and the others cared about you all very much," Cobweb said softly. "They are brave, strong hara."

The harlings nodded and Swift offered his hostling a smile of gratitude. By this time, more hara and harlings were filing in for dinner. At that moment, there was a stir as Lisia entered the room, surrounded by half a dozen older harlings. The dinner bell broke the somber silence.

"That's him," Swift said softly. "At the entrance, wearing the orange silk."

Cobweb studied the figure, who was moving toward what was obviously considered the head table. *My, but he's skinny,* Cobweb said in mindtouch. *Though, he has rather wide hips.*

Swift chuckled aloud at his hostling, ever unpredictable, but replied silently. *He hasn't been eating much these last few months, and as for his hips — well, he* has *hosted 24 pearls, you know. They must have gotten wide on their own.*

A twinge of Cobweb's pity and outrage filled the mental connection, which they then allowed to disintegrate, so they could concentrate on their meal, which a few of the harlings had helpfully brought over from the serving line.

Fifteen minutes later, they were still half-way through their meal, listening to the harlings' questions, when Lisia rose up from the main table and approached them.

"Good evening, Lord Swift," he said, tilting his head in acknowledgement of the harlings and arching an inquiring eyebrow Cobweb. "How is dinner?"

"Very good," Swift declared, although in truth it was fairly standard Gelaming army fare. "Tiahaar Lisia, I would like to introduce you to my hostling, Cobweb, who has decided to pay a surprise visit. Cobweb, this is of course tiahaar Lisia, of whom I've spoken."

"It is a pleasure to meet you," Cobweb offered graciously, laying down his fork and gracefully extending his hand.

"Oh, the pleasure is all mine, tiahaar Cobweb," Lisia responded, accepting the handshake, then taking a seat. "I've heard so much about you."

Cobweb smiled uncertainly. "About me?" he asked, looking at his son. "What did you tell him?"

Swift shrugged, equally curious. "Nothing. Lisia, who told you about Cobweb? Was it General Aldebaran or Captain Paran?"

"No, it was long before any of this," Lisia replied . "We'd hear about the legendary Cobweb now and then when we discussed consorts, Varr rulers, that sort of thing."

"I see," said Cobweb, sounding slightly icy. "And what exactly was said? If I may ask?"

"Oh, different things. Sometimes they'd talk about you as an example of a beautiful hostling, the kind that was good enough to live outside the facility and produce heirs for our rulers." Lisia shifted in his seat and glanced at Swift. "I told your son earlier how they made us aware, to a limited extent, of the larger world. Anyway, you're quite famous and different Varrs would mention it to us, as well as our teachers. Other times, we'd just hear about you when hara talked about Terzian." Cobweb and Swift both stiffened but did not interrupt. "We heard over and over how you had produced a beautiful son who lived with you in Galhea. I didn't know his name then, that he was Swift, but it *was* mentioned. We always assumed you had more sons that they just didn't tell us about."

Cobweb's hands gripped the edge of the table. "No. The opportunity never arose again," he said slowly.

Swift was sure Cobweb had been tempted to growl.

Lisia nodded uncertainly and thought on this. "Hmmm, strange. I mean, Terzian always took the opportunity to make pearls here."

Swift stared. *Terzian visited this facility?* That thought had tickled his mind intermittently over the course of the day, but until that moment, Swift had never managed to face it. Now that he had, he was fairly sure he didn't want to hear any details.

Cobweb pushed back from the table and the metal feet of the chair scraped unpleasantly against the tile floor. "Do you mind if we take this outside?"

Lisia was somewhat startled by Cobweb's stern reaction. "Certainly, tiahaar Cobweb," he answered, "we can speak wherever you'd like." Rising from his borrowed chair with quiet grace, he motioned for Cobweb and Swift to follow as he headed for the nearest exit.

Holding the door open, Lisia glanced back and saw Cobweb and Swift were still over by the table. At first, he assumed they were saying goodbye to the harlings, but then noticed that Cobweb was holding Swift's wrist and glaring, clearly wishing his son to stay put. Swift shook his head and said something Lisia couldn't hear, the words lost in the chatter of the crowd. Lisia was about to head back over and see what the delay was, when Cobweb suddenly turned away from his son. He pulled his thick braid over his shoulder and stalked towards the door.

Cobweb passed Lisia wordlessly, like a black cloud. Swift followed closely behind him. Lisia felt vaguely troubled by the hostling's behavior, but then he reasoned that the former consort must still be grieving the recent loss of Terzian. This could result in a gruff manner and short temper. Lisia was aware that he himself had been exhibiting similar mannerisms ever since their facility had been so graciously "liberated."

In the hallway outside of the dining hall, Lisia smiled at Cobweb in a way that he hoped was reassuring and sympathetic. "What is it you would like to discuss?"

"Terzian fathered pearls here, at this facility?" Cobweb asked in a harsh whisper. "You know this for a fact?"

Swift held up his hand to cut Lisia off before he could respond. "I really don't think that the hallway is any better a place for this discussion than the dinner table." He gave Cobweb a warning glance, then turned back to Lisia. "May we take this up to the lounge where you and I talked before?"

Lisia nodded and again beckoned for them to follow. Once his back was turned, Lisia allowed his cordial smile to falter. Why would such a simple matter be the cause of such secrecy and distress? The answer came to him suddenly. For whatever reason, Cobweb had only produced *one* pearl. The fact was perplexing, given his great beauty. Lisia had assumed immediately that Cobweb's lack of pearl production had simply been normal in relation to life outside the facility. Things in the outside world were very different. However, now that Lisia could see that Cobweb was rankled over the matter, he wondered if perhaps there was more to it than he knew.

Lisia was determined to make amends for his presumably thoughtless comments. As soon as they reached the lounge, he opened his mouth to offer Cobweb his condolences and apologies.

But before he could utter a word, Cobweb beat him to it, fixing him in his gaze and demanding, "Tell me everything you know about Terzian's activities here at this facility."

Lisia paused for several moments, trying to choose the best answer. He wanted to offer his sympathies to Cobweb, before discussing the possibly disturbing information about Terzian. However, he decided to respect the manner that Cobweb had adopted and answered the question directly and without elaboration. "To my recollection, Terzian visited here four times to contribute to the project. As far as I know, a pearl was produced on each occasion. There may have been more visits that I don't know about, perhaps when I was preoccupied with deliveries, but I don't think so. Any visits by high-ranking officers were always major events."

Cobweb was silent for a moment, his attention fixed upon fluffing a sofa cushion, effectively preventing his companions from gauging his reaction. Eventually, Cobweb looked up at Lisia. Calmly, he asked, "You never serviced Terzian personally? You never bore his pearl?"

"Oh no," Lisia answered matter-of-factly, "he always pre—" The hostling stopped himself in mid-sentence, realizing that he was about to say that Terzian had preferred blondes, which would most likely be insulting to Cobweb. "...Preferred more beautiful hara than I. It's obvious where he developed his high standards," He offered a conspiratorial smile.

Cobweb appeared unimpressed with the flattery. "And, as far as you know, Terzian never had any difficulty in conceiving these pearls?" It was more a toneless statement than a question.

Lisia couldn't help but smile at that. He thought Cobweb must have been making some sort of a joke. When he saw Cobweb eyeing him expectantly, he was rather confused. "Well, as far as I know, there were no problems." Lisia recalled that Terzian had chosen Calla as his hostling twice. If there had been anything out of the ordinary about the great leader's performance, Calla would have been sure to tell everyhar else about it. "You know, the ouanas have little to do with conception, so his performance wouldn't have mattered. It's the hostlings who make it all work."

Cobweb grimaced and turned his head away, so that Lisia could no longer see his face. Lisia wondered what he could possibly say next, without once again causing offense.

"Lisia," Swift said, "I'm afraid this is another lie that you've been led to believe. Outside of this facility, most pearl conception is actually the product of a more mutual union, where both partners are important, not just one. The soume har may help, but rarely in the way that you and your fellow hostlings seemed to be doing here. Yours was a totally unique situation."

For a few moments Lisia could only stare. He was shaken by this revelation. Aside from the few times his instructors had used visualization to guide his seal into opening during his initial training, it was his experience that the opening of the seal was controlled solely by the soume har.

"But we always did it for them," Lisia explained, feeling slightly annoyed. After all, surely he had more experience with conception than either of these two hara. "Most of the ouana soldiers didn't know anything about making pearls or opening seals. A lot of them weren't even much good at aruna. Our job was to make it easy for them, no matter what. We were all trained to open our seals whenever we wanted to. Isn't that how all hostlings do it?"

Swift shook his head. "No, Lisia, no other hostlings do that. As I know you've already been told, any har with proper caste training can conceive a pearl. However, the soume har does not usually control conception and certainly it's not common for hara to conceive with such frequency. It was only for the sake of this project that you were taught such a skill."

Lisia felt dizzy, disoriented, as this knowledge settled coldly in the pit of his stomach. Ever since being told that all hara could conceive pearls, he'd felt smaller and less secure. His entire self-image centered around the fact that he had possessed this important, rare ability. Now he realized that the skills he possessed were abnormal as well. And yet, it was so hard to believe. He turned to Cobweb. "But you're like me, aren't you?" He was unable to keep a pleading tone from his voice. "You conceived Swift. You were a consort. You're not like these Gelaming — you're like us."

Even as he said these things, a dark suspicion began to cloud Lisia's mind. He knew Cobweb wasn't really like him. He wasn't a simple hostling whose various virtues won him the elevated status of consort.

151

Why else would he have asked about Terzian's performance? Cobweb had only hosted one pearl.

Cobweb's jaw was clenched tightly. "No, I am *not* like you," he answered, his voice nearly a growl. "Yes, I was a progenitor, but I wasn't some sort of breeding machine!"

"Breeding machine?" Lisia erupted, indignant. The words stung. "I wasn't a machine, I was a hostling! It was my job, what I was raised for. Before the Gelaming and you two arrived, I was valued and respected, at least for the most part. I'm sorry you're so jealous." Lisia scowled. He was frustrated, and tired of trying to placate this combative har, however high Cobweb's status might be. "You only had one harling because Terzian didn't want any more heirs. But you could have had more if he'd wanted. You must have received the training somewhere! Didn't you learn any of the techniques that I have? You were obviously raised to be a hostling."

Cobweb laughed aloud at that notion, confusing Lisia utterly. Swift rose from his chair and stood behind his hostling. When Swift placed his hand on his hostling's shoulder, Cobweb brushed the hand away. "Don't you get it yet? This place is nothing like the rest of the world. You were the only ones trained in this manner." Cobweb laughed again but his voice quickly became hard. "I wanted more harlings but I couldn't make more. I don't know how! Of course I was never trained the way you were. I'm not pure-born. I was raised to be a *boy!*"

Lisia sat mute and looked to Swift for reassurance. "I see," Lisia said, trying to show a confidence he did not feel. "So... Terzian chose you to be his consort even though you had been trained to be a 'boy' instead of a hostling. I suppose it's because you're so beautiful."

Noting no change in Cobweb's expression, Lisia attempted to turn their discussion towards more conversational tones. "Was it a difficult adjustment? Exactly what kind of a job is being a 'boy' anyway? I think I remember hearing the term once or twice, but I never thought to ask. Is that some sort of farming or merchant trade?"

Lisia watched as the Parasiel leader's face registered a look of astonishment. "By Ag, haven't any of the Gelaming explained to you about humans and inception yet?" Swift asked.

Lisia squirmed in embarrassment. In truth he'd heard the terms once or twice — boy, human, inception — mostly since the Gelaming had arrived, but a few times earlier, in occasional comments from teachers and administrators. "Well, I gather that humans were an old tribe and inception was some sort of ritual of theirs."

Suddenly Cobweb reached out to Lisia and took hold of his hands. "Oh, you poor, misguided innocent," he said softly. "There's so much we need to explain to you."

Lisia saw pity in Cobweb's eyes. He braced himself, guessing he was about to learn yet more painful truths. He guessed correctly.

Although he hadn't planned it, Swift found himself suddenly thrust into the role of teacher. In the space of an hour, Swift and Cobweb laid before Lisia as much Wraeththu history and background as they judged he could absorb.

They went back to the beginning, telling him the story of the Aghama, whose name Lisia had heard in oath but whose significance, so he explained, had never been revealed. Cobweb told the isolated pureborn his own story, explaining how he had been incepted, changed from a human boy, with only something like an ouana-lim, into a har who had produced a pearl. They spoke of humans and their differences and deficiencies. Cobweb explained the way humans and hara had fought and how that led to the rise of the Varrs in this part of the world and other Wraeththu tribes elsewhere.

Swift offered a basic summary of how he'd gone to the Gelaming with the intention of helping his father, but then had ultimately decided to help the invading hara overthrow Ponclast in order to bring peace. He spoke briefly of the powerful aruna magic, Grissecon, that the Gelaming had taught to him, and how he and his consort had used it to vanquish Fulminir. He told of the horrors that had been hidden there. Lastly, Swift explained how the Gelaming and Parasiel were now proceeding with reforms.

As these explanations were offered, Swift watched the hostling's face flicker through a variety of expressions — shock, surprise, wonder, curiosity — but when they were finally done, Lisia was hardly readable. Apparently he was too stunned to speak.

"So, Lisia, what do you think?" Swift asked gently.

For a few moments Lisia didn't turn his head, but continued to stare at the floor, as he had on and off throughout the conversation. Finally, he looked up. "I don't know, Swift." His voice was soft, almost a whisper, and he shook his head. "I don't know what to think except..." He put his hand over his mouth.

"What is it?" Cobweb asked. "Any questions you have, we'll answer. Anything you have to say, we'll listen."

With a sharp intake of breath, Lisia closed his eyes. "They lied."

There wasn't much either Swift or Cobweb could say to this and so they waited for Lisia to go on.

"They lied to me all along." In Lisia's voice, there was a hint of anger, mixed with shock and disbelief. He opened his eyes. "Sometimes, when I was younger, I felt it. I would always ask so many questions and wonder about things, but the answers I got always sounded so believable.

And now you tell me — You've got to be kidding!" Lisia looked to the hostling and son for consolation, but there was none. He let his shoulders droop. "Or maybe not. Maybe I'm just an idiot."

Swift reached out and patted Lisia's right hand . "No, Lis, you're not an idiot. You're a very good har, very smart, and very strong. There's no way you could have known any of this. I didn't even know everything until I met the Gelaming. You said it yourself — they lied to you."

Cobweb cleared his throat, a vaguely uncomfortable expression on his face. "Remember how I said I wasn't trained to be a hostling? Well, Lisia, let me tell you just how under-qualified I was." His tone became grim. "I didn't even realize I was hosting until the time came for me to deliver Swift's pearl."

"You didn't know?" Lisia asked, shocked. He paused for a few moments, more questions evident on his face. Finally he sputtered, "And then you went through delivery, with no preparation?"

Swift frowned. He was glad Cobweb was sharing this story since it would surely make Lisia feel better. But although it had been related to him before, nohar enjoys hearing what a horrible ordeal his delivery had been. Not that he felt guilty; Swift still couldn't fathom how Cobweb had been so unaware.

Cobweb nodded. "Unfortunately yes, that's how it was. Terrible. I barely knew what was happening, I was so shocked and in so much pain, and when they put me on the table, they found out I couldn't do it, there was some problem — I think I was too small — and they had to cut me." He averted his eyes from Lisia's gaze. "They ripped Swift's pearl right out of me. When they gave him to me later, at first I didn't know he was mine. I'd never even seen a harling before!"

Lisia was amazed. "I've never heard of such a thing! How horrible that must have been. I never had anything like that."

Cobweb nodded. "You were led to believe that, as a consort, my hosting skills surpassed yours, but in truth you have far more knowledge than any har I know. We were both forced to play roles that suited the Varrs. It was largely circumstance that placed you here and me with Terzian. And who's to say which of us is more stupid? I played my role, even though I knew something of the real world, while you, shown only what they wanted you to see, played yours."

Lisia sucked in his breath. "It's something I often suspected. There were a lot of things that made me wonder... but eventually I accepted most of it and I was happy. I thought I understood everything and knew why things were the way they were. Not that I liked everything, since there were bad things — I haven't told you, but there *were* bad things — but no matter what, I was used to it and it all made sense. Now..." His words trailed off.

Swift squeezed Lisia's hand. "A lot of things will be different now. Don't be frightened and don't call yourself stupid."

Lisia squeezed Swift's hand in return. "I'll try not to." Swift heard in his voice the echo of the Lisia he had encountered in the journal, the obedient hostling who had tried so hard to obey his doctors' orders, to be quiet and good even during the agony of his first delivery.

There was a long silence before Cobweb broke it. "Lisia, there's something I must ask. I bring it up because it has to do with emotions. Emotions can have great power, like poisons."

"What is it, Cobweb?" Lisia asked warily.

"Now that you have a bigger picture, how do you feel about the hara who ran this facility?"

The words were calculated and Swift shot his hostling a warning look. He sensed Cobweb was trying to incite something in the pure-born, who was obviously shocked but still had not exhibited a truly strong reaction.

Lisia put his hand to his chest. "How do I feel about them? I— I— Well, I don't know. How should I feel?" The hostling grimaced and tugged on his yellow forelock. "They're not here anymore. They left us here. They were supposed to destroy this whole facility, but instead they left us here *still* not knowing *anything!*" At these last words Lisia had raised his voice. "Sorry, but I'm so, so—"

"Angry," Cobweb supplied. "As well you should be."

Lisia's eyes were flashing, his face red. "They lied to me so much, put me through so much... and I did everything they asked. I always tried so hard and now I find out—" He clamped a hand over his mouth.

For the first time, he was showing how upset he was. Swift sent out a wave of calming energy, but Lisia only drew away from it. "I know what you're doing to make me feel better, but no thank you. I need to think this through, feel it. Cobweb is right. I'm angry. I can hardly stand it. My mind is just screaming — it's been like that ever since the Gelaming found me here. You know what I keep thinking?" He clasped his hands together. "I keep thinking... they did all that, put together my whole education, gave me this life, and I thought they were being so *good* to me and that I was *special* yet *all along they only wanted my pearls!* They didn't care what they did to me! They just used my body, stole my harlings from me! I mean, we all knew that was the truth of it really, but at the time, it didn't seem sinister — it just seemed normal. We thought we were doing something good, giving something good to the world. We thought we were helping the Varrs..."

Swift felt nothing but sympathy and regret.

Lisia glanced at him. "But it's all come to nothing, hasn't it? Half my... half my harlings, so many, have already been sent off to become soldiers, workers. Where are they now? Gone." He pressed his hands into his eyes, which were welling with tears. "Gone. I used to feel so empty, every time they took the pearls away, because..." Lisia began to weep, his words coming with difficulty, "because I wanted to *keep* them, even though I knew I couldn't... From the very first I wanted to be able to see them, to hold them, to keep them. But I went along with it, stopped fighting it, because I thought it was because that was my lot in life, that was the way it was."

Lisia released a series of wrenching sobs, his body contorting in what looked like physical agony. His shoulders heaved. His arms were crossed tightly across his stomach. "My little harlings," he kept moaning, "my pearls."

Cobweb wrapped Lisia's body in a comforting embrace. Swift didn't speak, but sensed it was time to take action. Once again, he concentrated on offering up some calming energy. It was important that Lisia had expressed himself and brought his true feelings out into the open, but letting such painful thoughts continue seemed cruel.

Swift locked eyes with Cobweb as the Lisia's sobs finally began to die down. Cobweb was stroking Lisia's back, which was hard and lean from malnutrition. "I know it hurts, Lisia," Cobweb said. "I've been very hurt myself at times. But the important thing is, you're here now and have more knowledge than you did. You've had to be strong before, and now you're going to be so again." He kept stroking for a few more moments, then gently pushed Lisia away. Lisia's face was swollen from crying. Cobweb reached out and touched his cheek. "I wish I had a handkerchief to clean you up. You need it."

Lisia's hands went to his face, catching Cobweb's hand. "Do I? That bad?"

Cobweb nodded and smiled. "Yes, but you needed it. How about you go and wash your face and get changed? I could use it too. We're both soaked with tears!"

Lisia ventured a slight smile. "Thanks, I'd like that. My room is just down the hall here. Come with me."

Once Cobweb and Lisia had left, a feeling of exhaustion crept over Swift and he sprawled across the sofa, sighing. Closing his eyes, he pressed his cool fingers to his forehead, which was pounding. He'd managed to focus his energies on Cobweb and Lisia, but now that they were gone, one thought repeated over and over in his mind: He had four other half-brothers. The thought unsettled him greatly. What had become of those harlings and where were they now? The knowledge that Terzian had created and abandoned four harlings to an unknown fate gave him a new perspective on his own childhood. Swift thought back, trying to remember whether any of the harlings he'd seen here had borne any resemblance to Terzian. Perhaps there were just too many of them for him to have noticed. He considered briefly the older harlings like Pansea. Had one of them looked familiar? But quickly he dismissed that thought. It seemed impossible to believe that any harlings fathered by Terzian would have been destined to become hostlings. Besides, what would he do if he did find Terzian's other sons? Would Cobweb be interested in adopting them as he had Tyson? These wouldn't be newly-hatched harlings, but older children who'd been subjected to the same lies and mental conditioning as Lisia.

Swift didn't feel prepared to deal with this new revelation. He wished fervently that Seel could be there with him. His chesnari would doubtless make him feel better with his words of wisdom and calm strength. But, of course, Seel was back at *Forever* and Swift knew that this was something that he was going to have to deal with on his own. "And later at that," he thought. At the moment he had other responsibilities to consider.

As if responding to his thoughts, Cobweb and Lisia re-entered the room with clean faces and fresh clothes. Swift sat up and smiled at them.

"I apologize for getting so emotional," Lisia said immediately. "I should have dealt with my feelings days ago, when the Gelaming first arrived, but I think I was just too shocked to have a proper reaction."

"There's no need for apologies," Swift said. "You have every right to be upset and you shouldn't expect to put these things behind you immediately. You've lived your entire life based on false pretenses, and it will take time to reconcile with your new reality. We certainly don't expect you to make all the adjustments overnight."

"You are not alone, Lisia," Cobweb added. "I know the Gelaming and their sanctimonious attitudes can be hard to take, but please accept the aid that the Parasiel have to offer. We are your tribe, after all."

Lisia smiled hesitantly. "I trust you both. You're the first hara who have revealed the whole truth to me and I know you have the best interests of the harlings and me at heart." He clasped his hands together . "Now, it's getting late. You've given me so much time and comfort that you've missed dinner — or at least were pulled out of the dining room before you'd finished eating. Why don't I go down to the kitchen and bring us something to eat?"

Swift hadn't realized how hungry he was until Lisia mentioned it. "That sounds like a wonderful idea, Lisia. Thank you."

"I'll be back in a few minutes," the hostling replied and headed for the stairs.

Once Lisia was gone, Cobweb sat next to Swift on the sofa. Swift searched his hostling's dark eyes for any hint of emotion, but was surprised to find Cobweb's face unreadable. "Thank you for what you told Lisia," Swift said. "You got through to him more than I could have."

Cobweb merely shrugged. "I only told the truth," he said. "This place needs it."

Swift had to ask. "Cobweb... are you disturbed by what we've learned tonight about Terzian?"

Cobweb made another dismissive gesture and uttered a short, mirthless laugh. "Why should I be?"

Swift looked at him incredulously. "You certainly seemed to be disturbed earlier. I thought you were going to throttle Lisia!"

Cobweb shook his head. "Give me more credit than that. I knew it wasn't Lisia's fault."

Swift did not alter his expression.

Cobweb made a frustrated sound. "All right, yes, I *was* angry, but not at *him*. I was angry at Terzian." He paused for a few moments and became thoughtful. "No, that's not true either. I'm angry with myself. I knew exactly what Terzian was capable of. Why should this surprise me after what I watched him do with Cal right under my own nose? What upsets me is that I always chose to look the other way. I chose to accept the blackness and injustice in exchange for... for what? For safety? For comfort? For convenience?"

"For me," Swift answered.

Silence. Hostling and son stared levelly into one another's eyes.

"Well then, that would make it worthwhile," Cobweb replied.

Swift swallowed with difficulty. "I'm sorry... I'm sorry that you were never able to have more harlings."

Cobweb shrugged again. "It's not your fault."

"In a way it is."

Cobweb frowned. "What do you mean?"

Swift looked down at his hands. "You must have realized this before. It's not that Terzian didn't want any more harlings. He just didn't want any more harlings with *you*. I think that's because he was so disappointed with the way I turned out." Swift glanced at his hostling, but only for a moment. "If I had been the sort of son he could have been proud of, then things might have been different. I suppose he thought that a har like Cal had a better chance of producing a harling who would be a suitable Varr leader."

"I can't believe I'm hearing this!" Cobweb exclaimed. "And I never want to hear it again! How can you sit there blaming yourself for the way I raised you? Nothing that happened between Terzian and me is your fault. I don't want you torturing yourself like this. Ag's blood, Swift, I..."

Swift stayed Cobweb's hand, which had reached out to touch his shoulder. "I haven't been torturing myself, Cobweb. These things have only just occurred to me. I certainly don't have regrets about who I am, or the path I've chosen. I'm just sorry that I had to cause you pain along the way."

"You've brought me far more joy than pain," Cobweb said. "And keep in mind that I made choices too. There's no need for blame." He smiled slyly. "And besides, you're wrong."

Swift raised his eyebrows inquisitively.

"Terzian didn't get Cal with pearl because he thought he'd bear him a mighty Varr heir," Cobweb said. "Terzian was madly in love with Cal. Of course, we all know that Cal was no meek progenitor, but Terzian created Tyson in a feeble attempt to pass him off as one, make the relationship seem more acceptable. Cal merely went along with it in order to secure his position, no matter what he felt about having harlings."

Swift nodded. The events they were discussing had occurred only four years earlier, but they seemed another lifetime away. "I never really thought about it," he admitted, "but I suppose that's true."

"There's something else that needs to be said," Cobweb said. "You're a smart har, so I won't lie to you and say that Terzian was proud of the way you turned out. But you were important to him, certainly more important that what he created here. He cared about you and—"

"Don't say it, Cobweb," Swift interrupted. "I know. I've always known, but it's easier to pretend that he hated me. I did betray him after all. I don't regret it and I'd do it again, because I have no doubt it was the right thing to do, but it still hurts."

"It seems the most precious things in life are always paid for in either blood or tears," Cobweb mused.

Swift didn't reply. Words no longer seemed important.

Chapter Nine

It's been a full seven days since I delivered the pearl. I feel like I'm losing my mind. I can't sleep. I know I should eat, but food just makes me feel sick. For a little while this afternoon I was very thirsty, but now I can't even bear to drink water.

I just keep thinking about the fact that my harling is probably going to hatch from his pearl today — about seven days is what they've always told us. It could have happened already by now. In fact, it probably *has* happened already. I wonder what he looks like. I wonder who was there when he opened his eyes for the first time and took his first breath. I keep straining my ears to hear a harling mewling. I've been dreaming about it all week. I'll dream that I can hear my harling crying for me and I want to get up and go to him, but I can't wake up. I can only lie here asleep.

And then I wake up feeling terrible inside. This empty feeling won't go away. It's even worse than anything else sometimes. I'll wake up in the middle of the night and start crying because it feels so terrifying to be empty like this. It may be silly, because I always loved having this special room all to myself, but all of a sudden it feels lonely, because I'd gotten used to talking to my pearl when I was here all alone. I wonder if this feeling is permanent, something that happens to all hostlings after their pearls are gone. I wonder if this will start to feel normal, like being a full-grown har felt normal after my feybraiha.

I'm tired now, probably because I haven't eaten like I ought to. But at the same time, I'm restless. I keep pacing around, going through my things here in my room. Nothing makes me feel better. In my dresser drawer I saw my fancy special dress with the ribbons and, instead of making me feel proud like it usually does, I felt like just ripping it into pieces. There's also a big vase of beautiful flowers that the administrators gave me, to show how pleased they are with me. I just look at them and wish that the flowers would die and shrivel up so that they'd look the way I feel. In fact, just about everything in the room makes me feel angry or frightened. I wonder if I'm becoming crazy. I don't know how that happens, but I remember tiahaar Neydish talking about insanity in lessons once.

I know I don't feel like Lisia any more. I don't think like him. Lisia was never angry or disobedient. I know that I've become wicked somehow. I keep wanting to do bad things, like scream and carry on, and I get so angry sometimes that I want to throw things around the room and break the window. I don't dare to do it though. I know I'd be thrown out for sure if I did. I've decided to pretend to be good, so they'll let me be with the other hostlings again. I need to talk to them. Maybe they can make me feel better or understand what's happening to us. I think I could maybe learn to be a good hostling if I had them to help me — if we could do it together like before.

Every day, the doctors and administrators come to me and talk and ask if I'm ready to stop sulking and be with the rest of the hostlings. I always say that I want to be with the others, but then they ask me questions and know that I'm not really ready, because I'm still angry and sad. I've decided that today I am going to lie when they ask me questions. I will pretend to be like I was before the pearl came. I know this is wrong — I'm not a proper hostling and I shouldn't pretend to be. But I need to be with the others. I need to talk to them about what happened and how I feel. I feel like once I talk to them again, I'll be able to decide what I want to do next. Then I'll tell the truth about what I want to do from now on.

Finally we're all together again. After more than a week of being forced to stay in our rooms almost the whole time, with meals brought to us, today at lunch the administrators let us downstairs so we could all sit together in the dining hall. We didn't really get to talk like I wanted because the administrators were all right there watching us. I could tell that everyhar was nervous or unhappy, but we all tried to pretend like we weren't. I'd seen a few of the others a few times over the past few days, in the hall or in the bathroom. But the doctors have said that we all need plenty of rest and there's constantly somehar around to make sure we're not wearing ourselves out by standing around and talking. We're supposed to be in our rooms resting, except for when we meet with the doctors or the instructors.

Anyway we've talked to each other when we can. Every one of us seems to have had a terrible delivery. I guess that should be scarier, since it means that all deliveries must hurt like that, but in a way I feel better that I wasn't the only one. I was afraid that maybe mine hurt so bad because I wasn't meant to be a hostling. Everyhar says that they were told that it would be easier next time. Coral said that he wished he could just skip the next year and get to the point when it won't hurt any more. Rosea said that he doesn't think they'll make us host again so soon at all. I don't know what gave Rosea an idea like that! I started to tell him that he was being stupid, but I didn't because it seemed mean.

I had a nice long talk with Genvert today and he said something that I am really thinking about. I don't know whether it makes me feel any better, but it makes a lot of sense.

He had come in and asked me how I was feeling after the delivery. He wanted to make sure that I could still control being soume and opening my seal. I haven't even thought about it, of course, because I haven't tried since the pearl came. He made me try for him, just to do it on my own while lying on the bed, and asked me if anything hurt when I did it. It's odd, but even though I don't want to host any more, it scared me to think that I might not be able to. I got scared that all my bad feelings would prevent me from being able to open my seal, but I tried it and it still works.

Nothing hurt when I tried, but I decided to tell Genvert about the empty feeling I have inside of me. I've told the doctors before, but they've always acted like it isn't important. In fact, tiahaar Botbek told me that the empty feeling is all in my head. At first, Genvert looked angry when I told him about the empty feeling and I started to apologize, because I thought I'd done something wrong. But then he told me that it was natural for me to feel empty when I wasn't hosting, because I *am* a hostling and my body craves to have a pearl inside it. He said that the only way to make the empty feeling go away would be to make another pearl.

So it seems that I must go through another delivery in order to make this emptiness go away. It's not fair at all. I can either feel like this for the rest of my life or host again and just have the horrible pain of delivery and a couple weeks of emptiness every two months. I really don't know which is worse. I'm hoping that maybe the emptiness will go away on its own after a while.

Well, this is it. Today is very probably the last time I will ever write in this journal. I've thought all night long about what Genvert told me about being empty forever unless I host another pearl. And I really do want to do the hosting part again. I loved conceiving and having the pearl inside me.

But I'm still afraid of delivering. And I'm still angry that the teachers and doctors never told us that the deliveries would be so painful and that they didn't seem to care that it hurt. But deep down I know that I'm wrong to be so angry and afraid. I know that the hara just didn't tell us the truth because they didn't want us to be afraid — that's what Laran told me. I know that, as a good hostling, I'm not supposed to feel angry and think all the hateful thoughts that I've been having. But I just can't seem to stop feeling this way. I know these thoughts would be bad for a pearl if I was to try hosting again. I know I'm a bad hostling.

That's why I've decided to see Upsari today. I'm going to tell him what's wrong with me and that I can't be a hostling after all. I'm terrified of what will happen to me, but it just wouldn't be right to stay here and pretend to be something I'm not. Besides, it might make the pearls come out wrong and that isn't something that I could ever live with.

I really don't know what to think now. I saw Upsari in his office. I wasn't sure whether he'd have time to talk to me but he did and he was very nice to me or at least didn't punish me. I tried to be very calm and grown up when I told him about my decision, but I couldn't help but start crying before I could even come close to getting to the point.

I thought he'd get mad at me, but he just told me to go ahead and cry and then he went back to work and waited until I had calmed down enough to try again. So after a while I was able to calm down and I told him everything about how I had been having all these terrible thoughts and I didn't think that I could be a hostling anymore. When I was done he just sat there looking at me as if he expected me to say something more, so I suddenly had an idea and volunteered to stay on and do staff work like Hyacinth instead, since I already know a lot about taking care of harlings.

He laughed then, but in a way that made it clear that he didn't think anything was funny, he was just trying to pretend that it was. He asked me if I was having any trouble opening my seal and I told him no. Then he smiled and brought me a handkerchief to dry my eyes. He said that I wasn't a bad hostling at all, and the very fact that I was so worried about being good and doing what's best for the pearls proved that.

I wasn't so sure and I told him that I didn't want to take a chance. He just patted my shoulder and told me that I was the most dedicated hostling at the facility. He said it would be extremely selfish of me to quit just because I was scared, because then all the other hostlings would probably want to quit too, and then there wouldn't be any more pearls for a long time and all just because I was over-reacting.

I still wasn't sure, but I didn't know what to say. Finally he just sighed and said that he had important things to do. He said that my request was denied. I couldn't quit.

The other day in tiahaar Upsari's office I mentioned that if I didn't host anymore I could do staff work like Hyacinth. It's funny I said that because today I actually talked to Hyacinth. Ever since he was taken out of the Lily program, none of us has really spoken to him. We were really afraid we'd just make him sad, especially when we were hosting. I know every time I saw him I'd sort of try to make myself invisible or not make it so obvious how happy I was (which before the delivery, I was).

Anyway, today after lunch I went outside to just rest a bit and think, on my own, nohar else around. I'm still trying to believe everything tiahaar Upsari said. So I walked out over to where there's a nice bench and who do I see there but Hyacinth, raking the grass! Since he saw me at the same time I saw him, I couldn't really just turn around, so I decided to go over to the bench anyway and just wait until he went away.

As it turns out, he didn't go away. It's true he did keep on raking, but around a minute after I'd sat down, he turned around really slowly and looked at me. I certainly couldn't be invisible! "So, Lisia, how've you been doing?" he said.

To cover up my surprise, I smiled and said, "Oh, just fine." And then, to be polite, "And how've you been doing?"

Hyacinth didn't smiled back at me. Instead he came over to sit on the bench next to me. "I think you know how I've been. Don't act like you're a stranger, Lis! You *all* act like that and I hate it."

I felt too ashamed to look at his face, so I looked down at his hands, which were still holding the rake. I noticed they were all rough from working. "I'm sorry," I said. "I just don't know what to say. Though now maybe there's something I can tell you." Finally I looked at his face. "I know you were very upset when they said you couldn't host. I would have been too... *at the time*. But I think maybe it was a good thing after all."

As soon as the words were out of my mouth I realized just how mean I had sounded, so I jumped up from the bench just to get away — I thought he'd get really angry!

"How can you say that?" he demanded. He was all red in the face and I could actually feel how shocked he was I'd said that.

So I explained. I told him how even though he'd wanted to host, just like me, that actually, truth be told, hosting isn't all wonderful. The deliveries are the most terrible, terrible thing in the world.

He didn't believe me at first. He'd noticed the other hostlings had disappeared after the pearls came and he knew we didn't seem too happy, but since none of us were talking to him, he hadn't actually heard any details. And so I told him all about mine, from beginning to end, how the pain had just got worse and worse and the doctors didn't care and even tied my mouth shut. At the end of it poor Hyacinth had his hands over his mouth, he was so shocked. Finally he said. "You're not lying to make me feel better, are you?"

I said I definitely wouldn't lie about that.

He hugged me then and kissed me on the cheek. "Thanks for talking to me," he said. Then he said he would see if there was any way he could help us. I didn't understand what he meant and definitely didn't want him talking to the administrators about what I'd said, but instead, he told me he wants to see if maybe he can help out in the infirmary. "Maybe someday I could help you in the deliveries. Even if I can't host, maybe I can still help somehow, make it better."

I thought that was just about the sweetest thing. I got up and hugged him again, then walked back to the building while Hyacinth finished raking the leaves.

Despite all my thoughts against it, I'm hosting again. I can hardly believe it. We hardly had any advanced warning this time about the soldiers coming. It's probably a good thing, too, because we were all so nervous about going through this process again. It was easy to see that, just looking around the lounge while we were waiting for the soldiers to come upstairs. Everyhar looked nervous and sad, but Calla laughed suddenly in a funny sort of way and told us all that since the delivery was going to be such agony, we deserved to enjoy the aruna at least. He said to try and just forget about what would come later.

It was good advice but very hard to actually do. In fact except for the pinnacle, I hardly enjoyed my aruna at all. I was just too nervous. In my head I kept changing my mind about whether or not I would go through with opening my seal. And then before I knew it, the soldiers were there. It turns out that these soldiers were actually very important officers from Fulminir, which is the biggest city in Megalithica. They were nice enough but at the same time, they had a way of making me feel very small inside — it's hard to describe, but they didn't seem to think of us in the same important way that the first soldiers had.

I very much wanted to excuse myself from the group, but the way the soldiers looked at me, I was just too ashamed to speak up. And then I found myself in my room with the one who picked me. I know I wasn't doing a very good job of pleasing him and making him aroused and all of a sudden he said, "I hope you don't plan on shirking your duty, hostling." I don't know how he knew it, but I had been thinking of just pretending that something was wrong with my seal and I couldn't open it anymore. But the way he looked at me when he said that scared me too much to even think of doing something deceitful like that. It was like this har could read my mind! I don't know how I managed it, but I opened the seal right away. Even feeling scared like that, the feeling of conception was just incredible. I felt like I had shot up to the stars. Afterwards the har just smiled at me and left. I don't even know what his name was.

Today I am starting to feel like a hostling again. One would think that I'd have felt like a hostling as soon as I conceived the pearl, but somehow it felt less real this time than the last. I have to admit that the reason for this is that I have been trying not to think about the life growing inside me. Last time I was so happy. I thought about the pearl all the time and I was filled with such a sense of love. I think that love makes you feel the pearl stronger.

This time I've been afraid to feel that way. It's not that I don't love the pearl — how could I not? But I tried not to think about it. Genvert was right that I wasn't as empty once I had another pearl inside me, but the feeling didn't go away completely and knowing that the emptiness was coming again was still bad. I figured that if I didn't love this pearl as much as the last one, maybe I wouldn't be so sad and upset when they take it away.

So I tried not to think about the pearl this time and spent more time with the other hostlings instead. And because I'd been thinking about these sad feelings, I started to feel sorry for Aster. I realized that this must be even harder for him than any of the others because he's younger and he's the only one from his Lily group who's hosted yet and the administrators won't let him spend time with his friends until they are hostlings. But Aster isn't really one of our Lily group either so he's alone a lot of the time.

I decided I ought to make sure that he's not too lonely, so I made a point of talking to him. He and I had a very good long talk. He told me that it was very, very hard being without his friends but that his pearl made it easier because he was never truly alone. I told him that was a very sweet thing for him to say but that he probably shouldn't get too attached to his pearl since that would make it harder once it's gone.

Aster looked at me very sternly then, and said that we had to love our pearls because that's why we're hostlings. He reminded me that we spent all that time taking care of harlings when we were younger so that we'd know how to have love for the pearls and that his pearl needed to be loved in order to grow into a proper harling.

I'm not sure who taught that to Aster, since in all my lessons it was never explained to me in quite the same way, but deep down I knew it was true. I was a little ashamed that a younger har had to be the one to tell me how to be a proper hostling, but I'm glad he did. Tonight I let myself think about Pearl 2 and I even talked to him. As soon as I did I couldn't help but start feeling that love inside me again and that made the emptiness go away a lot more than before.

My pearl is going to be born sometime next week and knowing what's ahead is making me sad and scared again. I keep talking to the pearl so much because I know soon it will be gone. Tonight I also wrote a short poem, which I keep repeating to myself. I am going to copy it in here for my memories.

> *Speaking to you in the dark of the night*
> *Without words you call my name*
> *But when you are born in the dark of the night*
> *It will never be the same*

Well, I've lived through another awful delivery. I hardly even want to write about it, but I've got nothing better to do and somehow I feel like I should make some mention of it. Bearing a pearl is such an important thing, I feel like I owe it to the harling to write it down.

It started in the early hours before the sun rose. At first I didn't want to get out of bed or summon help, but I knew that I must. I knocked on Calla's door because I didn't think I could make it all the way to the delivery floor by myself. Calla was very kind, though groggy at first from being woken up. We went to the infirmary and Calla rang the bell for a doctor, then helped me to a delivery room. When Laran arrived he could see how much Calla wanted to help me feel better so he let him stay. I think that helped a lot.

The birth was just as painful and bloody as last time, but at least it was faster. The pearl came just before lunchtime. I didn't rant at everyhar like I did before — I knew there wasn't a point. I did scream, but surprisingly they let me this time. Calla stayed the whole time and held my hand and stroked my hair to help me feel better. He even stayed with me after the doctors left and then he whispered in my ear that he'd caught a glimpse of the pearl and it was very beautiful, even with all the blood. That made me cry for some reason, but not for very long.

Another good thing is that the doctors aren't making us stay in our rooms after the deliveries like last time. I know the only reason they kept us apart before was that they wanted to keep the pain a secret. I also asked tiahaar Laran if I could stay with Calla while he bore his pearl since Calla had been so good to me. He said that I could if I promised to be good and helpful.

As if I wasn't already still tired from having my second pearl two days ago, last night I stayed up all night long with Calla for his delivery. I was just about to go to bed, coming back from the bathroom, when I heard this awful moan coming out of his room. I went inside right away and found him huddled on the floor by the bed. He was having trouble talking but he said the pains were very, very bad even though they had just started. He had tried to get out of the room but it hurt him too much.

I knew he had to get to a delivery room right away and so I told him I would take him there. I had to work very hard to pull him up off the floor and even then, he was bent in half. He was only in his nightgown so I took a blanket and put it around him as I led him into the hall. He was holding onto my arm so tight, and he could only walk a little bit each time before he had to stop and wait for the pain to die down. When we were almost to the stairs, Seagrass happened to come out of his room and saw us. It was lucky he was there because it was hard to get Calla down the stairs. I was very worried about him. He had started to cry and it made me want to cry myself but I couldn't because I knew it was an emergency.

Finally, after about fifteen minutes, we got to the infirmary. Seagrass went and rang the bell and I took Calla to a delivery room. He was so relieved to lie down, even though the pains were just as bad as before. Finally tiahaar Botbek came in. At first he didn't want Seagrass and I to stay there, but I told him tiahaar Laran had said I could and that it would make Calla feel better. I don't think Botbek really understands how much it hurts. Anyway, Seagrass and I stayed all night long. We thought up different ways to calm Calla down and even sang a few songs. Botbek actually left the room a few times because he said he knew it would take a long time and that we were doing a good job helping.

Just at dawn, Calla started to really scream and Botbek said it was time for the pearl to come. He sent Seagrass to get the other attendants, like the incubator, while I stayed with Calla. I let him squeeze my hand and I told him it was almost over. Finally the attendants arrived and just then I saw the pearl come out. And I really did see it, looking right down between Calla's legs. It wasn't that bloody this time and to me the pearl was like a big, glistening black ball. It made me ache inside to look at it because I had never really seen a pearl before. Calla was so tired he just fell back onto the delivery table. I don't think he even really got to see it before the attendants took it. I saw it though, and Seagrass saw it too. We both told Calla it was all over and we hugged him. He was crying for a little while, but finally he was so tired he fell asleep.

Seagrass and I stayed in the room anyway for a couple of hours. Finally we went back up upstairs. We told the other hostlings what had happened and that we were going to bed so we could sleep all day. It's almost time for dinner now but I only woke up about an hour ago. I guess I should get ready.

I've just come to realize something that I find very shocking and disturbing. Several of us were out in the new northern gardens tending the flowers. Coral, Seagrass and I are all three weeks hosting our fourth pearls, but the others aren't because more soldiers won't be free to visit for another week. I kind of like it better now that we're not always hosting together at the very same time, because this way there are more of us able to help with each delivery. Helping with a delivery when you are two months hosting or have just birthed a pearl is really too hard.

Anyway, we were all in the garden and Rosea had asked if anyhar had heard where the next couple soldiers were being sent from. I hadn't, but Coral made the joke that Rosea ought to hope they came from the same place as his last one had. A bunch of them started snickering and Calla told Coral to tell us all about it. So then Coral started bragging about how tall and strong his last har had been and how he had the most lovely blue eyes and that he had been so skilled with his hands.

In fact, Coral was being so specific in what he was saying that it made me a little uncomfortable. I started getting even hotter — though it was warm in the sun to begin with. But even more disturbing was that thinking about what Coral was talking about made me almost start to become soume! I had to hurry up and start pulling a bunch of weeds to take my mind off of it. Tiahaar Botbek has warned us that thinking thoughts like that while we are hosting is bad for the pearl. Aruna is something just for making pearls, so if we are already hosting, it's not something we ought to think about.

But Coral was still talking and then he said something that made me pay attention again. He said, "I guess Enevier was just so handsome that it was disrupting my concentration and that's why it took me three long tries before I could finally manage to get that silly seal opened up." I couldn't help but look up at Coral and I was so surprised by the way he just said that. I mean, if I took three whole tries, I would have been so embarrassed and I certainly wouldn't be telling everyhar! But Coral was smiling in a way that showed he was actually very proud of what happened and everyhar else was smiling and giggling and Calla said, "Good for you, Coral."

And then Seagrass shocked me even more and said, "You know sometimes, I'm not even completely sure that the seal really got opened, so we have to do it again just to be sure."

Again everyhar laughed and I just couldn't stop myself that time. I said, "Seagrass, how can you possibly not tell when your seal has opened? I mean it's just so obvious. How can you not know?"

Everyhar started laughing at me so hard. Calla and Rosea both rolled over on the ground they were laughing so much. So I asked what was so funny because I really didn't have any idea and Rosea just tossed his hair and got all haughty and said, "Really, Lisia you act like such a harling sometimes!"

Suddenly everything just became so clear and I felt my face getting very, very hot. I couldn't believe what I was hearing! They were having extra aruna on purpose! And even after conceiving, which I know is very, very bad. I just said, "You know you're not supposed to do that!"

They all kept laughing then, all except Calla, who got very serious and told me that I better not tell on them. I felt kind of guilty then because I felt like I ought to tell, but I certainly didn't want to get my friends in trouble either. Then Seagrass grabbed my hand and begged me to promise not to say anything, so I nodded and said I promised. Then Coral just laughed again — but it was a nervous kind of laugh — and he said, "I bet the administrators know anyway. They don't care as long as we get with pearl and keep the soldiers happy. I bet they're glad we do it."

And really, I can't help but wonder about that. I guess maybe it doesn't matter if we do have aruna a little extra before we make the pearl. I mean, we did all that practicing when we were learning and that didn't hurt anything. Still, I don't know if I'd have the nerve to try it. What if the soldier said something? And what if the har just thought I didn't know how to open my seal very well and then the administrators decided I wasn't a good hostling after all? I think it's better to just do what the administrators tell us to do.

I've hardly had any time to write in here lately since I've been so busy writing other things. Laran suggested since we'd been doing such a good job helping one another with deliveries that we should keep on using our skills to make one another feel better. I've been asked to write poems about how noble and important pearl-bearing is. These are going to be recited to help hostlings stay positive during deliveries despite being in pain. I've also written a lot of poems that don't have anything to do with pearls or harlings, but are just pretty, because I know sometimes a har doesn't want to told he should be positive when he's in so much pain. Last time I said something like that to Coral during his delivery he threatened to shove my notepaper down my throat!

Of course he didn't really mean it. Often hostlings say all sorts of angry things during deliveries because of the pain. I remember how I used to behave. I think that's why the doctors are content to let us help one another — they want to stay away as much as possible! Botbek said that he didn't know what was worse — the screaming or our singing. I shouldn't say so, but he's just not a very nice har, though he is a very good doctor.

Tonight I just helped Lark through his very first delivery. I feel a little shaky now that it's all over. It really made me think again about how hurt and upset I was after my own first delivery. I don't think about that as much now, because the hostings and deliveries just seem kind of normal now. But, I'm glad I wrote down all the bad thoughts that I had at the time. I don't want to forget those things. Sometimes I do forget though, because I'm just so busy with everyday little things.

But tonight reminded me. I really hated to see poor Lark so scared and hurting. Aster, Coral and I were the ones who stayed with him and Botbek. This month is the first time that the rest of Aster's Lily group is delivering pearls. I know that he's thrilled to be with them again. But, that means we've been very, very busy because we have our own births, plus theirs to help with. Last week Calla and Seagrass actually delivered at the same time! Hopefully in a few months the new hostlings will be helping in deliveries too.

There's really not that much to do in a delivery, but it's still hard work all the same. It makes you tired to have to stand there for hours and be calm when somehar you like is screaming with pain. It was especially hard with Lark. I must say that he was very brave about it, but it was an extra long delivery. For some reason he carried the pearl a few days longer than we'd expected and it was a little bigger than normal (at least that's what Botbek said since I wouldn't know exactly). But there wasn't much for us to do except hold his hands and rub his arms and body a bit to make him relax. We tried to calm him down with songs and poetry and looking at the pretty paintings that have been brought in. I'm glad Aster was there; he told him encouraging things and explained what was happening as the delivery went on. We also took turns wiping him with a damp cloth and giving him advice on how to sit and how to breathe.

Then when it was all over, just as usual all we hugged each other and cried for a little bit. I'm not exactly sure why we always cry, because by then the worst part is over with. Of course, there's always the empty feeling, but I think those of us who've been hosting for a while are so used to it that we hardly notice. It'll be hard for Lark and the others his age for the first few pearls, but we keep telling him that he'll get better too. It just takes time to get used to it.

I'm starting to think that the other hostlings don't like me! I don't know how I should feel right now. Why must everyhar be so difficult and mean? It all happened today in the garden. A bunch of us hostlings were working together in the garden – nothing heavy since all of us were hosting. And then Dande just sort of tossed aside his basket and said how he couldn't wait for his pearl to come and the next soldiers get here because he was "just dying for a good roon."

I felt my face get all red when he said that and I told him, that a proper hostling shouldn't ever say anything so common. "The correct term is *take aruna*," I said "and you certainly shouldn't be wanting it right now. You should be thinking only about your pearl." But everyhar just laughed at me! I was so angry. I don't know what's wrong with them sometimes – they hardly act like hostlings at all and I told them so.

Then Coral just rolled his eyes and told Dande, "Don't mind Lis, he's just morally superior to the rest of us." And then Coral said to me (well he didn't look at me when he said it, but I know he meant it for me), "I've noticed the soldiers like it *very* much when we tell them we're 'dying for a good roon.' And I'm sure even the administrators would agree that if it makes the soldiers happy then there's nothing bad about it."

I couldn't really think of anything to say to him in response – at least not anything that they wouldn't just laugh at anyway. I know they've always been a little jealous of me because our teachers always rewarded me so much, but today was the first time that they hurt my feelings just because I try to behave properly. I'm not all that surprised by Coral, though. I love him and Calla very much, but they've always tended to be mischievous. I thought they'd grow out of it once they started hosting, but I guess not. What does surprise me is how even the younger hostlings are behaving. It's like everyhar else started to act less like a hostling once he actually became one! Ah well, there's no point in getting angry about it. I bet Dande will remember what he said during his next delivery pains and then he'll regret having been so glib.

Life has been so busy. The past year has just flown by and I've hardly even thought about writing in my diary. Most of the time we spend at least half of our day with the oldest Lilies, teaching them proper etiquette and working with them on dancing and beauty and arts and crafts. And of course there are the deliveries. Lately, the hosting has been divided up so that only a third of us conceive at a time. That way we don't get overwhelmed with too many deliveries at once, and there are always hostlings able to help with the deliveries and to handle the regular duties. We've also set up a schedule for which hostlings are "on call" for delivery help on each day. It was the only fair way to do it, because some hostlings were being asked to help all the time and others weren't getting to learn.

The administrators seem very pleased with all the pearl production. It really is amazing. Sometimes we see the little harlings that we made here,

173

but not often since they don't go outside that much and don't have lessons.

With all the Lilies still waiting to become hostlings, I can see that in a few years we'll be producing hundreds of harlings! The administrators are already preparing for it. We've been getting more supplies for all the little ones, and some hara have come in to construct pavilions out on the edge of the grounds to make room for larger groups of soldiers since there are more and more hostlings available now. It's really not anything fancy — the soldiers are used to staying in tents. When they started work on the pavilion, Upsari called a meeting and told us that eventually we'd be so productive that we'd have whole separate buildings for hostlings and staff and Lilies and little ones. I'm not sure how I feel about that. I don't want to have to move into a new building — I like the way things are and I'd miss my little room. But, if it would give more space to the harlings, then it's for the best.

I have to admit that I feel pretty proud of what we've accomplished. Despite what ouana hara may think, being a hostling is very hard — physically and emotionally, but all of us hostlings have been doing our duty well. I think we deserve all the nice things that we've been given.

I can hardly bear to write this down.

Sometimes when I write in this journal I get scared. There are so many bad things in here, so many things that would get me in trouble, if anyhar knew. Bad thoughts, thoughts I should banish from my mind. I try to stay happy, to dwell on the positive, to have the right attitude, do my duty. I really do try. I should be writing poetry or stories, at least according to my training. Still, no matter what, there are things I feel I must say, if only to myself. If anyhar finds out, there will be trouble, but it's too late now, much too late. I've said so much, I might as well say this.

I don't know where to start except to say I had a dream. It was two nights ago. I wanted to write about it before, but I was afraid. I was so afraid. I picked up the pen to write, but I couldn't. I thought if I wrote it down it would be too much for me. I don't want to think about this, I really don't. As I said, I'm trying to be good and these thoughts, that dream, it's too much for me. But finally I have the pen and I'm going to write it.

I remember bits and pieces, some of it very clearly, other parts blurry. It started out and I was in my bedroom, lying on the bed, dressed in my latest special outfit and there with me was the har coming to me to make a pearl. It was the same as always, I suppose. Something else important is that when the dream started, I was seeing out through my eyes. I can't remember what the ouana har looked like really except that his hair was brown and he probably looked quite handsome since I would guess I'd dream about a handsome har.

So then I was talking to him, the usual protocol, bringing him out, trying to seduce him, and everything went quickly. Soon I had his clothes off and he was pressing me back into the bed and my clothes were falling away. I am so skilled at this I don't need to think about it and it was just like that in the dream.

Everything was normal up to this point. I was on the bed, looking up, and soon we began to share aruna, soon he was inside me and I was doing my work, pleasuring him, coaxing him, guiding him to the ultimate goal. It was going well, very well, the pleasure taking hold and he smiled at me, leaning down to share my breath.

That's when everything changed. I was locked to his mouth when something happened in the dream, like part of the dream just jumped forward and suddenly I wasn't where I was before. Well, actually I was — I was there on the bed, but I wasn't seeing out of my own eyes anymore, I was seeing myself from outside! I was still having aruna with the soldier, panting and sweating, and I knew this because I swear, I was seeing it as if I was the soldier.

It was so strange. I was looking down at myself as if I was another person and I was sharing aruna with myself! I don't know where this dream came from. I really don't know. Do I want to know? I don't think so. I shouldn't have dreamed that, but that's what I dreamed. I was sharing aruna but I was the soldier. When I think about it now, I realize that, strangely, I didn't feel any different at first. In the dream I felt the aruna just as always, as if I were soume and not ouana. Then I was looking at myself and started to panic because I knew that I still needed to conceive the pearl and so the soldier had to release his seed. I was in the soldier's body and so it was my job. I had his body!

Suddenly I remembered how it should be. I couldn't be the soldier and feel soume! How could two soumes create a pearl? It was impossible. I had to change what I was doing. I had to become ouana. I had to remember what I was doing. Things were already started and so I didn't have to worry about the beginning. I was already inside and it seemed I was doing fine. The soume was doing things to me and I don't know if that's really what it feels like and I can't remember now how I thought it felt. It was a dream and it's not the same. I was imagining it all, how it would feel. In my mind though, in the dream, I knew it felt good, very good to be ouana like that. Mostly I just kept thinking about how I had a goal to reach and how I needed to let the soume bring me to that goal, that special level, then when the seal opened, I could do what the ouana is supposed to do.

Finally I could tell it was time. I knew that in my real body, my soume body, the seal was opening up and it was time. The other body, the soldier body, got very excited, throbbing and pulsing, and then suddenly there was a whiplash of sensation all over me and just as I've felt so many ouana do, I delivered forth my seed. I remember I was shouting, so happy that I had done it and that there would be a pearl. I was happy, just feeling very successful.

After that, there was another one of those strange gaps. It's in the middle of the dream and I had fallen asleep and woken up. I was still in the bed, still on top, but now I was spent, lying there, having slept a little. I was worn out. I knew in the dream that I was still the soldier, that I was lying on top of myself. Suddenly I remembered that I should really withdraw, get off from on top, because I'd been sleeping on the soume or, really, myself.

Without even really looking up, I pushed myself off and that's when I felt it. My leftover seed ran out, all around my ouana-lim. I was wet with it. I've never been wet with seed before. Never. Not my own. I haven't even ever seen my own! I don't know why I had to dream that. It was horrible. I saw it and I knew it was wrong. I shouldn't have been seeing that. I was seeing what I'd seen before obviously, but this was perverted. I was imagining it was mine. Well, really, it was the soldier's but it was mine since I was the soldier. It's so confusing but I knew it was bad and I got scared suddenly, even in the dream, that somehar would find out what I'd done.

That wasn't the worst thing, though. No, right after that was the worst thing. I had pulled out and was lying there next to myself feeling upset, when I looked up and saw who I was with. It wasn't me, Lisia. It was Calla. Calla! I was so shocked. I have known Calla since I was little. We grew up together, learned to be hostlings together. He's helped me with my deliveries and I've helped him with his. We work together. We're friends. And look what I had done!

I don't know how it happened or why it happened, but in the dream Calla was there smiling at me, happy. He was thanking me, telling me how good I was, how I'd been such a good ouana and had made him happy. I had planted a pearl in one of my best friends! I couldn't believe it. When I did it, I thought I was the soldier and I was making a pearl with myself, but then I knew that actually I'd been tricked. I'd been ouana all along and Calla had been with me. I had wanted Calla and he had wanted me and...

Words fail me almost. I am so ashamed. I don't know what to do. That's all of the dream there was. After that I woke up, tangled in the sheets, sweating and most horrible of all, my ouana-lim was throbbing, absolutely throbbing. It was such a terrible moment because as soon as I felt it, I remembered Pearl 10. I'm at four weeks now. Four weeks! The pearl is still very sensitive. It's important for me to be thinking the proper thoughts and if there is a worse thought than that dream I had, I don't know what it is. I couldn't sleep. I tried to think about my pearl, tried to think about proper aruna, to go over all the lessons. I tried to school myself into the right thoughts, to create a good environment again. Eventually I fell asleep but when I woke up, I felt the guilt. I also worried. What if anyhar found out what I'd been thinking? I felt so different, like I was a harling who'd broken something and was waiting for somehar to find out.

It's been the same since then, I guess, although sometimes now I'm a little less shaken. The worst is when I see Calla. Actually that hasn't been very often since my friends don't seek me out to talk and do things together like they used to because I'm "too good." This used to bother me, but now I'm glad and I'm avoiding Calla on purpose. But on the day after the dream, he sat across from me at lunch and it was like the dream came back to me. My ouana-lim came alive right there at the table and it was like the dream, me looking at this hostling thinking he was beautiful. It was like I was going crazy, somehar else's mind taking control of my own. I made some excuse and left the table. I only came back later when he was gone. I need to eat for the pearl — can't starve myself.

They avoid me because they think I'm too good to be fun. How ironic. If only they knew the awful truth! But they'll never know – not if I can help it.

Anyway, that's what I was so frightened to write down. I didn't want to think about it, but actually I'm glad I got it down, even though it's dangerous and if anyhar finds it — no more hosting for me, no more life. Out to the fields, out to the war. I am useless otherwise, outside of hosting. That dream of mine — a nightmare. I am a hostling and that is all.

It seems winter has come yet again. It's strange how I barely noticed the weather turning colder until suddenly it started to snow this morning. I guess it's because I've hardly had a chance to go outside lately. Ever since tiahaar Upsari decreed that the project needed to become more self-sufficient, we've been stuck learning "practical" skills like knitting and sewing. First off, I don't know where they found the har who came to give us the first lessons in making clothes and blankets. He barely seemed to know what he was doing himself. In fact, if he's the best instructor the tribe had to offer, it's easy to see why most Varrs dress in simple leather instead of fine fabrics.

Well, that's not really fair of me to write. I know that most hara need durable clothing, unlike us hostlings, who have a less strenuous lifestyle.

Even so, leather is not practical for harlings or for bedding. I never really thought much about it before, but I've also figured out something about our clothes. I knew that our nice things come from far away, but I didn't realize until recently that when we were small, our clothes were all very old. Everything always had yellow or brown coloring to it and the fabric would tear very easily if we weren't careful. I guess that's why we had to be so reserved in our playing. Or else, maybe the old clothes made us behave more like proper little hostlings since we had to be so careful not to ruin what we had.

Anyway, there aren't enough of the old but pretty clothes around for all the new harlings so we're having to make them ourselves. It's a good thing because from what can tell, the very small ones that we've birthed are pretty much allowed to play very rough and be quite messy. I guess that's fine since they're going to grow up to be soldiers and workers. I guess they may as well be used to being messy and rough, but if they're going to be that way, our old dresses certainly won't do for them to wear.

Fortunately, being hostlings, we are smart and have learned to improvise on the meager lessons we got. Otherwise, the poor little ones would probably end up going naked! I have to admit that my first few creations were pretty ugly, but I'm getting better. At first I found both sewing and knitting to be so boring that I wanted to scream, but now that I'm figuring out more and able to create some nice things, I actually enjoy it.

To be honest, I'm thankful for the distraction. Instead of just idly visiting with my friends, I keep myself busy with work. It seems like a good way to keep the bad thoughts from creeping in.

It's been well over two years since I conceived my first pearl. It's hard to believe. I don't know if I would have even realized it except that Laran said something to that effect while I was delivering Pearl 12. He said that because Zinnia was commenting on how much easier deliveries seemed to be for me than for him.

I'm glad that they're now allowing some of the younger hostlings to attend our deliveries. They're not all that helpful yet, but it's good for them to see that deliveries really do get easier with time. I remember that when I was Zinnia's age I didn't believe it would ever get any easier. Of course everything seemed different when I was Zinnia's age. It's hard to believe that was only a couple years ago. It seems like a lifetime.

I remember back when I used to get so excited about a group of soldiers arriving for a conception session. I used to put the soldiers on such a pedestal. I was so worried about what they thought of me. Now I tend to take comfort in the fact that they don't seem to think much at all. I don't know which ones I feel more frustrated with — the ones who are thoughtless and crude or the ones who are so sweet and try to impress me.

I suppose I shouldn't be so hard on the nice ones. They mean well, and I know this is an important privilege for them. I try to keep the proper mindset, that each one of them is very special, and treat them that way, but it's hard. Each pearl is important to me during those precious two months when it's a part of my body and I can hold it inside me. But what's so important about the soldiers? They're just a necessity. Most of the time they're not even any good at aruna. Thank goodness I know how do it properly! Honestly, I kind of feel sorry for the soldiers. Their lives must be very dull and rough.

I just flipped back and read my entry about my first conception. I had to laugh. I wonder whether Aeroka remembers me like he said? I should hope he does. After all, how hard is to remember the har with striped hair who made your pearl! I must admit I can still remember him, though the details are vague.

It's kind of a shame. I wish I could get excited about aruna like I used to. Now it's just part of the routine.

It took the longest time for my hands to stop shaking so that I could write this down. Part of me knows how stupid I am to actually put this on paper where it could be found, but I simply must write it out. I'll just need to be extra careful about hiding this journal.

I feel dizzy when I think about it. I can hardly believe what I've done. There's no going back now. I'll never be able to tell myself that I'm a good, pure hostling again.

It all happened so unexpectedly. It was a beautiful day today, the nicest one since winter ended. I just couldn't stand to be stuck indoors. I needed the fresh air and the sunshine so badly. So I put aside my sewing and decided that despite the priorities, I was working in the garden.

It was still a little cool but all the snow had melted, and the sun was shining beautifully. I didn't even look my best at all. I wore my gardening clothes and threw on one of the first sweaters that I'd made, since I really didn't mind getting it dirty, ugly as it is.

Truthfully, we hostlings are only supposed to work in the flower gardens, but there wasn't much to do with them at this time of year. No weeds to pull and it was still a little too early to plant the bulbs outside since it could easily snow again. So instead of that, I decided to go out to the potting shed and plant some seeds in pots that could be started indoors and then moved outside. I was in a very good mood, because the pots would give me an excuse to visit with the lessons-age Lilies. They'd be happy to take care of the seedlings, and the instructors like that sort of thing, so everyhar will be happy.

Anyway, I was sitting on the ground in a sunny patch just outside the doorway to the potting shed, with a dozen pots spread all around me and a wheelbarrow full of potting dirt. I was taking my time because I didn't want to go back inside. I sat there singing to myself as I worked.

I don't know how he managed to get there without my noticing. I guess I must have gotten very intent on the seeds. Anyway, I noticed somehar was blocking my sunlight all of a sudden. I was startled for a moment, but I looked up and it was Vlaric. I couldn't help but smile at that. I've always been very fond of Vlaric. How could I not be, since he was the one who took me through my very first aruna?

So suddenly Vlaric was standing there, looking just as handsome as he could be. He really is a vision. Of all the hara I have taken aruna with so far, he is the one who has left me with the fondest memories. Actually, the aruna with soldiers is more profound, because I open the seal with them and that brings a pleasure far more intense that just practice aruna, but there's something about Vlaric that is slightly different. Whenever he's around, I feel my attention turning to him. I feel sort of like a flower that turns itself to follow the sun as it moves across the sky. My eyes always want to follow Vlaric when he is near me. I've noticed other hostlings doing it too. I think it's because he moves somehow almost like a hostling. It's hard to explain, but when he walks into a room or smiles at you, you get the feeling that he's thinking about taking aruna with you. I guess that's just normal since that's his job. And we all can't help but remember how very good he is at his job.

He was just standing there smiling in that way that makes me all flushed, and I was hoping that he wouldn't notice the reaction he was giving me because we both would know that's extremely improper. I am hosting after all, my fourteenth, and I'm not supposed to be having such feelings and especially not about Vlaric. So, I tried to be calm and I smiled and said something like, "What a surprise to see you out here, Vlaric. You haven't started giving aruna lessons in the potting shed, have you?"

As soon as the words were out of my mouth, I wanted to just sink under the ground. I couldn't believe I'd said something like that. How could I be so stupid? He was bound to guess what sort of terrible thoughts I was having. And he did know, because he laughed then, not in a truly funny way but in a dark, private sort of way. And then he said, "I hadn't thought about it before, but now that you mention it, I think the potting shed would be an inspirational place," and then he paused and looked right in my eyes before saying, "for lessons."

My first reaction was to say, "But I don't need any lessons," but I realized that would be obvious. I'm not stupid. I knew that Vlaric was flirting with me. I know what that's all about. I do it all the time; it's part of my job. In fact, Vlaric taught me a great deal about the art of it. But I didn't for the life of me know why Vlaric would be flirting with *me*. So, I just said, "Now you're being ridiculous, Vlaric. The potting shed is no place for lessons except maybe gardening lessons. Besides there aren't even any flowers in here yet. It's mostly a bunch of dirt."

And then Vlaric walked past me, almost brushing against me with his hips as he moved around where I was blocking the door. He walked into the potting shed and leaned against one of the worktables with that loose, flowing way he has. Then he looked at me and said, "Come in here and this little potting shed will be graced by more beauty than any mere flower could provide."

I started laughing then. "Oh, yes, I'm a real beauty with my hair all tangled, and this crooked sweater, and work clothes, and dirt all over my hands! Really, Vlaric you shouldn't tease me like that, it's not nice." But for some reason I stood up and took off the garden gloves and went into the shed with him. I think part of me knew what was happening, but I pretended that I didn't. I pretended that this was just a friendly conversation, like we might have in the dining hall. I couldn't help myself. I wanted so badly to hear the things that Vlaric was telling me. I hear this sort of talk from the soldiers all the time and not for a long time has it meant a single thing to me. But when Vlaric said it, it made me feel warm and tingling.

And so I walked in there and stood right in front of him as if daring him. And he took the dare! He said, "I think you're beautiful. You're the most beautiful hostling here." I frowned at that, because it was so blatantly untrue. He must have guessed what I was thinking then because he reached out and took my hands and said, "You're the most beautiful where it counts, on the inside. You're the smartest hostling I've ever met, and you're so kind-hearted and dedicated to your position."

I smiled at that. It was the most perfect thing he could have said to me. And before I could think of something to say back, his mouth was on mine and we were sharing breath. I couldn't help myself, I just shared back and then we were holding each other and it felt different from any other sharing that I've ever had. It was so deep and intense and I felt like he was desiring me so much and I felt powerful, feeling I wanted him too and my whole body tingling and surging from wanting to take aruna. In fact, as we stood there sharing breath, I even started to become soume, and that's when I all of a sudden got alarmed. I remembered my pearl and I struggled to pull away from him.

I was terrified. I said, "My pearl. Vlaric, we'll ruin it!"

And Vlaric just laughed and said that it wouldn't harm the pearl in the least.

I frowned at him and he accused me of not trusting him. I told him that I did, of course, and he cut me off before I could say, "but." He said that he knew what we had been told but that he knew better. He pointed out that I knew very well that the administrators were often stupid and there were many things they didn't know about.

Right after that he moved to share breath with me again, but I wasn't comfortable. I whispered fiercely at him that this was not allowed and that even thinking about aruna when I was hosting was wrong. I could be thrown out or punished in some other way if the administrators ever found out. And Vlaric laughed and said that nohar would care as long as we were discreet. I looked at him and frowned, because I knew what he meant, but I still wasn't sure I wanted to admit anything. Then he said then that he knew the other hostlings took extra aruna with the soldiers and that we shouldn't have to be lonely just because we're hosting.

I said, "This is different. You're not a soldier."

And then he said in that low voice of his, "No, I'm better than a soldier and you know it. You deserve this, Lisia. You've been so good for so long. Why don't you just enjoy yourself for a change?"

I looked up at him and couldn't decide. I was so afraid. I was afraid that I would change somehow if I did this. That everyhar would know that I wasn't as good as I used to be. But I wanted it so badly by then.

He looked deeply into my eyes then and said, "Please, Lisia, I need you, please."

That undid me completely. Nohar has ever, ever said those words to me. I told him to close the door to the shed. He did and he blocked it with some heavy pots. I wasn't sure then how far this was going to go, but I knew that I really didn't care. I couldn't think at all. We started to share breath again, deeply, and we were touching each other frantically. He had on a long coat. He took it off and laid it on the ground. Without a word, I laid myself down on it reached out to him.

It was like nothing else. I felt like a wild creature of some sort. I'd never felt so free before and yet, Vlaric was in control completely. In the very back of my mind, beyond all the pleasure, I was a tiny bit worried about the pearl being harmed, but Vlaric would tell me with his mind that there was no risk at all. Even so, he laid with me in a way so that there was no pressure on my stomach, so eventually I forgot about it altogether and was soaring with him up to one of the best pinnacles of my life, besides the ones for conception. Afterward I felt utterly weak, more than usual, and it frightened me at first, but Vlaric held me in his arms and said that I would be fine. It had just been such a long time since I enjoyed myself so very thoroughly, plus the hosting makes me tired anyway. We lay there together for a short while, but we quickly began to feel the cold and decided to get dressed again.

Once we were dressed, he pulled me close and looked into my eyes. He told me very firmly that I mustn't tell anyhar about what had just happened — not even my friends. I nodded without even thinking. Of course I wouldn't tell anyhar! Then he said, "This is something beautiful. Something sacred, just between you and me alone. I love you, Lisia, but we must protect one another by keeping this secret."

I agreed quickly and told Vlaric that I loved him too and would never, ever say anything. And then we tried to tidy ourselves up. He left first and I stayed behind and finished the work I had started. I was shaky for the rest of the day and after I brought in the flowerpots, I avoided everyhar else. I was so nervous that somehar would notice something, see the dirt on me and guess what I'd done.

But once I was in my room, I couldn't stop smiling. I feel so excited even though I'm also scared. I know that a very important thing has happened to me today. I should be quiet and reflective about it and savor it. But mostly, I just keep wondering about when we'll be able to do it again.

I feel almost as if I'm no longer really living my life anymore. It's like I'm somehow watching myself go through the everyday routines of knitting and sewing and dance lessons with the older harlings. But my mind is never really on what I'm doing. My thoughts are always on Vlaric and the time we spend together. I avoid the other hostlings, when I can. I know I'd be tempted to tell them, or even just hint to them, about Vlaric — especially since they've always teased me about being so good and so proper. Even though it's a terribly wicked thing for me to do, I think they'd actually be proud of me for it. But I cannot tell, so I try to keep away even though I know this hurts their feelings. I can't help it though. Besides, they aren't a part of this wonderful new part of my life and somehow it makes me feel hollow to be around them.

The only time I really feel alive is when I'm with Vlaric, but I can't be with him nearly as much as I'd like to be. We can only manage to meet a few times a week. The potting shed is still a haven for us because the administrators haven't hired a garden staff for the spring yet and nohar usually goes out there. When he's visiting the new hostlings for their aruna lessons, he slips notes under my door telling me when to meet him.

Aruna with him is amazing. He is so skilled and so attentive. It has been so long since I was able to truly enjoy aruna. Oh, and I've decided that I really like his nipples. Just writing that now has made me think about the look he gets when I start playing with them. He likes that very much.

I've come to realize there's a price to pay for having such wonderful aruna with Vlaric and that is that I'm missing it now. I'm in the last two weeks of my hosting, and Vlaric said we shouldn't indulge just in case it should cause a problem. And what's worse is that then we'll have to wait even longer until I'm hosting again. Vlaric seemed to think that it would be safe to take aruna after I heal from this delivery, but I have to admit that during my pinnacles, I've felt the impulse to open my seal to Vlaric. Of course that can't happen since I'm already with pearl, but I worry about what would happen if I wasn't. I don't want to take the chance even though it will be misery to wait so long to be with Vlaric that way again. I've never craved aruna this way since I completed my training. But at least we have still spent some time together, just talking.

Vlaric is more fascinating than any other har I've ever spoken to. He's not a Varr. His tribe are the Serpent Hara, which is a different tribe from far away. He won't tell me much about his tribe, even though I've asked him several times. I think it makes him sad to talk about them. He said that he could never go back to them again. His tribe used to travel around instead of living in buildings like ours. I asked if they were soldiers, since I know that soldiers travel a lot and live in tents, but Vlaric said they weren't. He did describe for me what some of the lands that he's been to look like. He told me about huge rivers that went on and on, and places where there was nothing but tall swaying grass as far as the eye could see. It sounds like there are many strange places out in the world. I wish I could go out and see them, but I know that I never will.

This is my home and I know that if I were to leave, I probably wouldn't ever be able to come back again. I used to dream sometimes that I would be discovered here by some very important har, who would be so pleased with me that he'd take me away to be his consort and I'd live in a great big house with one har and make heirs for him. But ever since Vlaric and I have started our special relationship, I've decided that I'm happy with the way my life has turned out.

I've been thinking a lot about some of the things that Vlaric has said. Back when he told me about his tribe, I asked him why he had come to live with the Varrs instead of staying with the Serpent Hara, since he seemed to miss them. He got a very dark look on his face and said that unlike his brethren, he didn't want to die. When I asked him what he meant by that, he smiled in a sad sort of way and said that I wasn't meant to think about those things. He told me to think about my flowers and laughing harlings and pretty things and then he shared breath with me.

I didn't ask him about it again, but I couldn't help but think about it. I finally figured out that hara in Vlaric's tribe must have been killed by the bad Wraeththu like I read about in that letter when I was a harling. I know that there are bad hara out there in the world and that they do terrible things. The teachers explained that to us when we were older. That's why we need soldiers to keep us safe. I'm glad he told me what little he

did. Now I feel better about the important work that I'm doing here —
my harlings are going to grow up to protect hara like me and Vlaric and
all the hostlings and Lilies. That makes the sacrifice worthwhile, even
though giving them up is a very hard thing to do. I think that's why Vlaric
and I are so drawn together. I sense that we are alike in some way — he
misses his Serpent Hara the way I miss my pearls.

When I was thinking all this, it occurred to me that Vlaric would have
made a good hostling. He helped teach us all the aruna techniques and
how to open our seals, after all. So, I asked him today if he resented that
he couldn't be a hostling like us because he wasn't raised as a Varr. And
he laughed at me, which I thought was pretty rude! He said that he
wouldn't want to be a hostling. At first I assumed that this was because he
is simply a ouana har and doesn't have the proper instincts. But then it
dawned on me how lucky Vlaric is. He gets to live here on these pretty
grounds just like us, and he doesn't have to fight or work. He is protected
and his job is having aruna all day. Only, the instructors do all this and
don't have to bear pearls!

It just doesn't seem fair at all. I can't help but wonder what my life
would be like if I were an aruna instructor — or maybe even a lessons
teacher or an administrator. That really wouldn't be so bad. And I think I
know enough to teach others — but then I'd have to be ouana, which I
just can't imagine. I guess there's no point in thinking about it. I was born
to be a hostling and nothing will change that. Besides, if I weren't a
hostling then Vlaric wouldn't love me like he does.

The most astounding thing has happened. I'm so shocked that I can
hardly believe it. Today after dinner tiahaar Botbek called an assembly of
the hostlings. He explained that the reason we'd had fewer soldiers
coming for conceptions was because the Varrs are preparing for a great
war with the Gelaming. That alone was terrifying but he had much more
important things to say after that. He told us that from now on we could
expect fewer groups of soldiers and that the same soldier would probably
be planting seed in several different hostlings on each visit. That in itself
isn't bad except that it makes all the deliveries come at the same time.

But the most important thing he told us was that in order to stay
productive when the soldiers couldn't come, some of us hostlings would
be making pearls among ourselves! I really didn't understand what he was
talking about at first, but then he went on to explain that a few of us
would learn how to be ouana. He said that they weren't really sure
whether it was going to work or not, but that they'd try with just one
hostling to begin with. Then Botbek said that the hostling they'd selected
was Odill and that he'd take a few lessons from Vlaric to learn how to be
ouana!

Then he started talking about how we were all going to have to take on more responsibilities because we wouldn't have as much staff anymore, since some of our staff hara were being sent to work for the army. But I wasn't really paying attention to any of that. I was too busy thinking about the idea of a ouana hostling! All I know for sure is that I want to ask Vlaric about this right away. I don't think I'll even be able to sleep tonight.

Today I was finally able to meet with Vlaric. He said that he was sorry but he had been extra busy and couldn't get away any sooner. Before I could stop myself, I asked if he'd been extra busy with Odill. After I said it I was embarrassed and I thought he'd think I was jealous, because Odill is such a pretty hostling. But he just laughed and said that actually he only needed to give Odill one lesson. I wanted so badly to ask him how he'd taught Odill to be ouana, but I didn't want him to think that I was too interested in that subject.

But I could tell he wasn't going to talk about it unless I asked, and we couldn't just sit there not talking and not taking aruna (which we still can't do until I'm hosting again). So I finally asked if Odill being ouana was going to ruin him from being a regular hostling again. Vlaric said no and that as long as Odill didn't become ouana often, he could still be a good hostling.

Then I sighed because he wasn't making things any clearer and I said, "I still don't understand. Odill isn't a ouana har — he doesn't have that scar on his arm!"

Vlaric just stared at me then, like I had said something very strange, so instead of waiting for him to explain, I kept on talking and said, "I thought that hostlings couldn't be ouana at all — maybe by accident when they're young, but not for aruna!"

Vlaric still kept quiet, but I could tell he was thinking about how to explain it to me, so I tried to be patient. Then he said, "It's not that you *can't* be ouana, it's just that for hara like you, being ouana would make you unhappy. It would make it harder for you to open your seal so easily. That's why you never learn how to do it. But it will be okay for Odill, since he'll only do it a few times."

I looked at him, frowning, because it was all so hard to believe. "And you say you taught him in only one lesson!"

Vlaric nodded. "Yes, I didn't need to teach very much. The lesson was mainly for him to practice."

And I got confused again and asked if another hostling had been there for that and Vlaric just laughed again and shared breath with me. Then he smiled and said, "I love you Lis, you're just so cute." He said it in that way that I knew I'd said something silly, and then my mouth dropped open because I realized what had happened.

Vlaric had been soume! I couldn't believe it. Well, actually I could, because right away I started imagining it and immediately I became very, very flushed and I started getting sensations in my ouana-lim for the first time in months. It was so embarrassing. I made up an excuse that I just remembered I had to meet some of the Lilies and I got up and left as quickly as possible so that Vlaric wouldn't notice.

Now I kind of regret running away so fast. I've thought about it (and thought and thought and thought about it) and it makes sense that Vlaric would know how to be soume since he taught us all about it. I just thought he knew from being ouana with lots of hostlings, but I guess that being an instructor makes him special, that he can be both. I guess that's why he seems so different.

But the more important thing is that he said that being ouana just a few times wouldn't hurt a hostling. Oh, I know it's very, very wicked of me, but I can't help but wonder if he would let me do that with him. I'm not really sure if I really want to or not. The idea makes me so scared. What if he thought I were a horrible hostling to ask him for such a thing without a good reason? The last thing in the world I want is for him to think I'm bad. Still, I just can't stop thinking about it and it's making me miserable. I actually ache from thinking about it so much. I don't know how I'll be able to be with Vlaric again without him knowing about these terrible things I've been imagining. I know I should stop, but I just can't help it.

They did it. The hostling they chose is Phlox, one of the young ones who's only in his first year of bearing pearls. I suppose they chose him because, like Odill, he's especially pretty. He's also had an uncommonly easy time with births for somehar so inexperienced.

I wouldn't have even known that they had done it except that Phlox told his friend Violet and he is quite the gossip, and soon we all knew. So earlier tonight I was woken up because I heard noise and giggling out in the hall. This is not so unusual. We're all supposed to stay in our rooms and go to sleep after the lights are turned off, but once we feel sure all the other hara have gone to sleep, we often get up and visit one another to talk and gossip.

I hadn't joined in a secret visit in a long time. It's always made me uncomfortable to break the rules like that, so I don't usually go visiting unless there is something very important to talk about. Since I haven't been spending as much time with my friends lately anyway, in recent weeks nohar has bothered to come tapping on my door or has even told me something that might make me want to go talking with them.

But tonight when I heard all the commotion in the hall, I knew what they were going to be talking about and I got very excited. I wanted to know too, so I threw off my covers and ran out the door to catch them before they disappeared. I asked where they were going and they said Odill's room, so I asked them to wait for me while I went to get slippers.

It seems like just about every hostling was in Odill's room. I went to stand next to Coral and Seagrass, who were surprised to see me, but made room for me, even though I could tell that they were hurt I'd been keeping away. I asked Coral what I'd missed and he said not much. I looked over at Odill and the poor har looked like he wished he could crawl under his covers. I'm sure he had been told not to talk to us about his experience because he seemed very nervous.

Just about everyhar was begging him to tell us what it was like. He was offered just about every bribe there is — cleaning his room, jewelry, makeup, barrettes, clothing, doing his chores. Finally he just sighed and said he'd tell us, but we had to promise we wouldn't ask again because he'd get in big, big trouble for talking about it. I knew we shouldn't be putting him in such a bad position of making him tell, but I couldn't help it. I just smiled and nodded with everyhar else. So he told us how the trick had been to start touching his ouana-lim before he even got thinking about aruna enough to turn soume. Then he just had to do what the soldiers do and let Phlox do all the work. I noticed that Phlox wasn't with us, but I thought maybe that's because he was sleepy — hosting can do that even early on.

And then Coral asked, "But what did it feel like?"

Odill blushed and said it felt good. He said it was hard to describe, that it still felt good like regular aruna, but it was different to be going into somehar instead of somehar going into you. He said he didn't want to talk about it any more than that, because he was supposed to be forgetting about it.

And then Calla flopped down on his bed and said, "You could always give us a demonstration instead!"

And everyhar just groaned and laughed. Calla always says things like that.

Odill rolled his eyes and he said if we wanted to know anything else we'd have to ask Phlox.

And one of the hostlings, I think it was Violet, made an impatient noise and said, "What could he tell us that we don't already know?"

And Odill just smiled and said, "Well, nothing really, but he did say that he enjoyed it very much!"

And then we all laughed again, and Jonquil asked if Vlaric had enjoyed it very much too. That startled me a bit. I guess I should have felt jealous about it, but then I noticed how everyhar started smiling and murmuring and I realized how much everyhar likes Vlaric and I realized how lucky I am. If only they knew the truth!

I know this is terribly wicked of me, but I just haven't been able to get the thoughts about Vlaric and hostlings and soume and ouana out of my mind. And you know we're already being wicked by sneaking around and taking aruna together. I know that should not be an excuse for thinking about something even more terrible, but what Vlaric and I have together doesn't feel bad. I think it's something wonderful that the administrators just don't understand since aruna isn't their job. So maybe being ouana just one time wouldn't be bad either. But, I don't really think I'd ever have the nerve to try — I'm not even sure that I would like it.

I can't believe what I found out today. My head is just spinning from it. I doubt I'll be able to sleep at all. It happened because I took a chance. Vlaric and I were meeting together — this time we had to sneak out to the stables, since the staff is working on the gardens all the time and the shed isn't safe. We had just taken aruna together and were lying together all comfortable and so it seemed like a good time to bring it up. So, I asked Vlaric if he had enjoyed being soume for Odill. I tried to make it sound really casual when I asked him, but I think we both held our breath until he finally answered me. He said that it wasn't as good as when he and I are together.

Of course I knew that! So, I asked him if it felt weird for him to take a role that wasn't natural for him, and then, so he wouldn't feel bad talking about it, I told him that I had wondered what it would feel like to be ouana. He just shook his head and said that he wasn't like me. And then I got a little impatient and I told him that I knew that — that's the whole point. But then he said that it wasn't difficult for him to be ouana *or* soume! I must have made a really funny face because he laughed. Then I got mad and told him that he'd said before that anyhar could switch once or twice. And then he smiled at me in this way that I knew meant he thought I was being silly, and he asked me who I thought the administrators took aruna with.

At first I thought that was a stupid question. I told him administrators don't take aruna at all — they don't make pearls. And then he really laughed and he said, "Are you and I making pearls together?"

Then I felt really stupid and I didn't ask anything else. Vlaric was having aruna not only for lessons but also with the administrators! That didn't make sense to me, so after a little while, I asked why the administrators would make so many rules about aruna if it was something they did too. Then Vlaric got kind of serious and he said there was power in taking aruna, and they wanted hostlings to put all that power into making pearls and not keep any for themselves.

I've thought about all this a lot and I think it sort of makes sense. I know that I do feel more powerful when I take aruna with Vlaric. And the administrators must be powerful hara or they wouldn't be in charge of something so important. It still seems bizarre to me that Vlaric can be ouana or soume all the time. I know it's not fair of me to think it, but it seems sort of perverse. Not that I love him any less for it. I guess that it was just something he was born into, like I was meant to be a hostling. That must be why he's an aruna instructor and why he's been given such an important job even though he isn't Varr.

And I don't like the idea of administrators or teachers taking aruna at all — that just seems weird. All in all, I'm sorry I ever even started thinking about being ouana. Just knowing these things is giving me a headache!

I am so angry that I can't stop crying. I must be the biggest fool in the world. And to think how he told me that I was so smart! I'm such an idiot and Vlaric is just so, so wicked. I should have known better than to think that I was special, that anyhar could love me in that special way when I'm just an ordinary hostling and not some sort of consort.

It's a miracle I didn't lose my mind and attack that stupid little hostling Jonquil. And Salvia too! I hate to imagine for how long I would have gone on being a fool if I hadn't happened to overhear those two in the gardens. I should have known. I've been so stupid. I wonder if Vlaric laughs at me for being so easily fooled.

I overheard it all out in the gardens today. I was pulling up some grass underneath the tall bushes and they didn't see me on the other side. I guess they should have been more careful considering what they were talking about. The were swapping stories about Vlaric! It sounded like Salvia used to think he was the only one too until Jonquil confided in him. But now they think it's great fun to both be taking aruna with him, and it sounded as if they knew of others too. I almost made myself known just so I could ask, but I was too shocked and embarrassed. I feel so stupid. I've spent enough time with ouana hara that I should have known the truth. Vlaric seemed to think he could play with us all forever. "Tell nohar" indeed!

But I must calm down. This sort of upset surely isn't good for my pearl. Still, I can't calm down! I just want to scream! I'm very tempted to go straight to tiahaar Upsari and tell them what Vlaric's been up to. But that would be stupid. I would only bring terrible trouble onto myself with that sort of confession, and it wouldn't be fair to those young hostlings who were also seduced by Vlaric's sweet words.

I don't know what I'm going to do. I'm so terribly angry and when I don't think about being angry, there's a deep hurting inside me that feels much, much worse. I don't want to lose what I had with Vlaric. I really love him. But he couldn't possibly have ever loved me. It hurts, but I know in my brain that I'm not losing anything at all except for a wicked, selfish fantasy that a good hostling shouldn't have had to begin with. Maybe this is all for the best. But it still hurts so badly.

I saw Vlaric at dinner tonight and I told him that I needed to speak with him urgently. I could tell that he knew something was terribly wrong. He actually looked a little afraid, which somehow made me feel better. I told him to meet me in the first level classroom after dinner because I knew it would be empty. When he met me, I didn't waste any time telling him what I'd heard in the garden between Jonquil and Salvia and that I didn't want to take aruna with him anymore.

I didn't know how he would react. I honestly didn't think he would care. I thought he would laugh in my face and tell me that he was surprised that it took me so long to figure out. But he looked sad and scared and miserable. He asked me if I was going to report him and I had to laugh at him for that. I said, "Is that all you care about? Well, I'm not going to report you, but only because I'm not going to get the young hostlings into trouble."

As I write this now, it suddenly occurs to me that what I said isn't true. I could go to Upsari and tell him that Vlaric had been taking aruna with me and me alone. The younger hostlings wouldn't be exposed, and when the truth came out, they would realize that they'd been doing a very dangerous thing. I know it would be the right thing to do, but I can't. I'm afraid of what would happen to me for telling such a thing. I think they'd be very angry at me, and they might even lock me up so that I wouldn't do it again. And I don't know whether Vlaric would even get into trouble since he's such a good instructor, but he seems to be scared about it and as angry as I am, I don't want anything really bad to happen to him.

After he asked whether I was going to tell on him, Vlaric seemed really sorry that my feelings were so hurt. He said that he didn't mean to hurt me but that we could still be together if I just wouldn't be jealous. I laughed again at that. I told him that I wasn't jealous that he took aruna with other hostlings or even some of the administrators. He's an instructor after all and has to do his job, what other hara tell him to do. But what hurts me is that he lied and he tricked me. And on top of that he lied specifically only to me. I absolutely hate being lied to and looking like a fool and that is exactly what he did. There is nothing I hate more than that.

And he tricked me with those lies too because he knew I would never betray my position as a hostling without a good reason. He made me think that I had a good reason, that I was something special. And now the truth hurts even more than before because I know I'm not special at all. I'm just stupid.

Tiahaar Botbek made a comment while I was delivering my sixteenth pearl that the first group of harlings would be taken away for soldier training at the end of this summer. I'm proud to know that we've been so successful and soon will reach such an important step, but I can't help but feel sorry for all those little harlings, destined for such a hard life. Whenever I used to ask about that, or worry about it in the past, our teachers would just say that the harlings will be happy with their lives as soldiers because that's what they are meant to be and it will suit them. I used to believe that, but now I don't know whether that's really true. After all, I'm not always happy with my life as a hostling even though it's what I'm meant to be and it's actually a very, very good life. So, if I can be unhappy with such a wonderful life, how can the little soldier harlings be happy with such a hard life?

You'd think that after all these weeks have passed I wouldn't miss Vlaric anymore, but I do sometimes. I miss the aruna. Sometimes I wake up after dreaming of his hands on my body and I want it so badly that I'm tempted to reach down and touch my soume-lam. Every once in a while I actually hurt from the desire. That can't be good for my pearls.

A few times I've been weak and stimulated the energy centers. But I know that's not proper since I'm far past my lessons and have nothing to practice for. It's not the same anyway.

I am trying so hard to be good and keep away from all the confusing thoughts from being with Vlaric. I know now that nothing good comes from breaking the rules — it just brings heartache. I'd give anything to leave this torment behind and go back to being a good, pure hostling like I dreamed about being when I was still a Lily.

The most unimaginable, terrible thing has happened! I can't believe it, but I know it must be true. Calla has conceived a pearl with somehar other than a soldier. I'm not sure when it happened. I didn't know anything about it at all until I started noticing that Calla was nowhere around. Two days went by and I didn't see him in the dining hall or in the gardens or in the lounge. I thought maybe he wasn't well, so I checked his room a few times, but it was empty. So then I saw Coral and I asked him if he knew where Calla was and Coral got really nervous and told me to come to his room tonight and he'd tell me.

So I was just there and Coral told me the shocking news. Apparently, the administrators have taken him away somewhere to keep it all a secret. Poor Calla! I feel so sorry for him; this must be so humiliating. At the same time, though, I'm angry with him too for doing something so foolish. We all had lessons and lessons on how conception works. How could Calla possibly have let something like this happen? He should know better.

I said that to Coral and he just shrugged. He said that was the way Calla is. Then he told me something even more shocking. He said that the father of Calla's pearl is one of the administrators. He said Calla told him so and that he hadn't been worried so much about the pearl, because he could not possibly be punished for taking aruna with an administrator since they make the rules to begin with. Calla wouldn't say which one it was though and now Coral was worried that they had done something bad to Calla.

I find that hard to believe. Maybe the administrator has decided to make Calla his consort and that's why he's not here anymore. I know that's a silly thing to think since things that nice never really happen, but I can't help but hope for it, and I think that if it were to happen to anyhar it would be Calla. I bet they are just keeping him locked up in one of the far-away rooms until Calla promises not to tell anyhar else that it was an administrator who broke the rules and took aruna with him. That's what's making Coral so nervous. We mustn't let anyhar else know that we know the truth or they might lock us up too.

I am so angry and horrified that I'm sick. Really, I went to the toilet and threw up all my lunch right after they dismissed us. Tiahaar Upsari called a meeting of all the hostlings and even all the Lilies. He said that Calla was guilty of conceiving a "bastard" pearl and had been sent away. He can never be a hostling again. I was so shocked I couldn't think of anything. I felt like somehar had thrust a big icicle into my stomach.

And then Rosea shocked me too, because he spoke up and asked if Calla had been able to keep the pearl. Upsari was very angry about that question and he said certainly not. He said that Calla had birthed the pearl here before being sent away and the pearl will be treated no differently than any other and that they were showing a great mercy since it ought to have been destroyed.

I should have realized Calla had birthed the pearl and gone, since he'd been missing for so long. How awful it must have been for him. They must have kept him locked up and made him deliver that pearl all alone, knowing that he would never see any of us again and that he was going to some awful fate far away.

And it's so unfair! Coral and I know very well that whoever fathered the pearl is just as much to blame as Calla. In fact, Calla shouldn't be punished at all for doing something that an administrator said it was okay to do. It's just rotten. I'm shaking, I'm so angry. And all the administrators were there, so I know nothing bad has happened to any of them. I can't believe that they would treat one of us this way. Calla has been a faithful and productive hostling for years and now he's thrown out for a simple mistake. What harm was really done if they're keeping the pearl anyway? It just doesn't make sense. It's like they did this just to be cruel.

It makes me so scared when I think of all the times I took aruna with Vlaric when I wasn't supposed to. That wasn't any different from what Calla did, except that he was foolish enough to conceive. Part of me wants to go out tonight and tell everyhar that it was an administrator's fault that Calla was sent away, but I'm afraid of what they might do to me if they found out. It frightens me. I'm so thankful that I broke off my relationship with Vlaric when I did. I would just die if I were made to go away from here.

I can't believe it. I never had a chance to tell Calla goodbye. None of us did. And I just remembered that awful dream I had about him so long ago. It makes me feel even worse. Almost like I'm even guiltier than poor Calla. I've known him all my life and he was my friend, and now I think of all the times I avoided him because of that stupid dream that wasn't even his fault. And now I'll never ever see him again and he'll be miserable forever for something that wasn't even his fault.

Chapter Ten

Swift was about to get out of bed when an instinct told him to stay where he was. A few moments later, the door opened and in came Cobweb, wrapped up in a robe.

"You *could* knock first," Swift said in mock anger.

Cobweb merely made a dismissive gesture and closed the door. "It's not like you could possibly have anything to hide."

"Actually, I do," Swift said. He turned onto his side and reached under the mattress, sliding out the black book that contained Lisia's journal. He held it out briefly, making sure Cobweb saw it, but then tucked it under his blankets. For all he knew, Lisia could be next to walk into the room and he wasn't prepared to explain why he had the item in his possession. "If I had any sense, I'd have slipped this back into Lisia's room last night while he was getting our snack." His face took on a thoughtful expression. "But maybe it's for the best that I didn't. Would you like to read it first, Cobweb?"

Swift was surprised when his hostling's mouth settled into a stern expression. He crossed his arms and stared down at his son. "Swift, I can't believe you'd offer such a thing. Who are you to offer up Lisia's private journal as if it was some sort of schoolbook from a library? I thought you held Lisia in more regard than that."

Swift ducked his head. Cobweb was one of the few hara whose disapproval could sting him, and in this case he realized that the harsh words were well deserved. "You're right. I wasn't thinking at all." He looked up, only to see Cobweb still glowering with disapproval. "I do think very highly of Lisia, and much of that is based on what I've read — so much so that I don't think of it as an invasion of privacy, but something that's helped me. I know that you've begun to develop some sympathy and understanding for him, and just now it occurred to me that reading the journal would help you to understand him even better."

Cobweb's face softened, but his posture made it clear he was not relenting. "Yes, I suppose it might," he agreed, "but I will content myself to understanding Lisia through that which he chooses to reveal to me himself. His rights have been trampled on enough. I'm not going to subject him to more dishonesty and manipulation." Cobweb ran his fingers through his sleep-tousled hair, "Besides, didn't Paran read the journal, too? I don't think it's helped *him* to understand Lisia any better."

Swift gestured for his hostling to sit on the end of the bed. "True, but I don't think he looked at it too closely. Perhaps he would respect Lisia more if he had really *read* this, instead of just skimming." He patted the blanket, under which the journal lay hidden. "At any rate, I'm sorry for suggesting it. I just wasn't thinking"

"Don't apologize to me," Cobweb replied, giving Swift the look that always signified a word of advice was on the way. "You should apologize to Lisia."

"Lisia doesn't know that there's anything to apologize about," Swift answered curtly, "and I'd like to keep it that way." He glanced over to the door, thinking of Lisia and the conversations of the day before. "I can't afford to lose his trust by letting him know that his diary was pilfered and sent to me in Galhea!"

"Ah, but the trust between you and Lisia will be shadowed unless there is honesty between you as well." As he spoke, Cobweb leaned forward and quickly snatched the journal from Swift's blankets.

He was already out the door as Swift fumbled for his robe, whispering angrily, "Cobweb, what are you doing?"

Cobweb had already been admitted into Lisia's room by the time Swift left his own room and stared down the empty hallway. He knew he could not stop his stubborn hostling from revealing his deception to Lisia. Muttering curses, Swift retreated into his bedroom and closed his door. If he was going to face Lisia's indignation, he'd at least be properly dressed before he did it.

A few minutes later, Swift knocked softly on Lisia's door. Cobweb admitted him, his expression grim. Lisia was sitting on the bed, the journal clutched tightly to his chest. He glanced up at Swift; his expression was a disheartening mix of hurt and anger. Their gaze only connected for a few moments before Lisia turned away.

"Go away!" he said sharply. From the choked quality of his voice and the shining redness of his eyes, it was clear that he'd already been weeping, if only briefly.

Swift was dismayed to see all the trust he had built destroyed in a matter of moments. He stepped closer to the bed, looking straight at Lisia, even if the hostling would only stare at the wall.

"Lisia, I am sincerely sorry," Swift began. "I didn't mean to deceive you—"

Immediately Lisia snapped his gaze in Swift's direction. "You *didn't?*" His face was flushed with rage. This was not going to be easy.

"Well," Swift admitted, "I suppose I *did* mean to deceive you but—" and here he held out his hand, asking for patience, "only because I didn't want you to be even more upset than you already were." Once again, he stepped in closer, keeping his eyes focused on Lisia, hoping that somehow he could say the right thing. "Please understand that I read the journal before I came to know you and respect you. I know I should have been honest once you put your trust in me, but you were already upset about so many things that I just didn't see the wisdom in adding to it."

"Then you shouldn't have read it at all!" Lisia snapped. "You're almost as bad as the administrators, just doing whatever you want for your own reasons, treating me like a harling." Lisia scowled and tightened his grip on the journal before going on. "No, maybe you're *worse!* At least they allowed me my private thoughts."

"Now, Lisia," Cobweb soothed, "keep in mind that *Swift* did not sneak into your room and steal the diary from you. *That* was Paran. Swift was sent the journal as an important source of information."

Lisia's face twisted into a mask of anger. "I should have known *he* would do something like this. I hate that har. I want nothing more to do with him."

Swift swallowed and proceeded hesitantly. "Truly, Lisia, your anger with Paran, while certainly understandable, is somewhat misplaced. I admit that I don't like the manner in which he has interacted with you, but don't fault him for taking the journal. It's my opinion that at the time, it was the right thing to do."

Both Lisia and Cobweb looked up at him incredulously. Swift raised his hands in a placating gesture. "Please understand, Lisia, that when the Gelaming first came here, they didn't fully understand what had been happening at this facility. Their first duty was to the mission — to ensure that this place presented no danger to the security of Megalithica. Their second duty was to understand what had been going on here so that they could understand how to make things right."

Swift took a deep breath before continuing and tried to deliver his words as non-confrontationally as possible. "They tried to get answers from you, Lisia, but you were understandably distraught and then emotionally exhausted. You seemed unwilling and unable to provide the information needed. Paran had to find some other way to discover the details of what you and the harlings had been through, in order for both the Gelaming and me to know how to help you. He didn't intend to steal your journal, but when he found it, he couldn't pass up the opportunity it provided."

Lisia's face lost some of the anger, but he still sulked. "There was nothing of any importance in that journal about the facility. Those were my private thoughts."

"Well, that's not completely true," Swift said. "The journal is about you, but it makes us — or me, really — aware of things that we wouldn't have thought to ask about otherwise. And more importantly, it helped me to understand you and to know that you don't think in the same way that the administrators of this place thought. Unlike them, you have the best interests of these harlings in your heart and—"

"Of course I have their best interests at heart — I'm their hostling!" Lisia interrupted angrily. "You should understand that just from talking to me."

"I do understand that now," Swift replied smoothly, "but Paran could not have known that you would open up to me any more than you did to him. I don't think he read very much of the journal himself, but he knew I'd be one of the hara making the decisions about the welfare of the harlings, so he made the right decision in sending the journal to me."

Swift paused to glance at Cobweb then, who had moved to sit on the bed next to Lisia and lay a hand on his arm. "As it turns out," Swift continued, "I didn't really need to read it, but I'd be lying again if I said that I regret it, because it touched me." Swift would never forget some of the passages he had read in the journal. He'd lost a lot of innocence in the space of a year, but this was the first time he'd truly caught an unfiltered glimpse of what life had been like for a har coping with the old Varrish regime.

"I only regret that I was not honest with you about this sooner. I chose to test you to see if your answers would match what I had read." Swift shrugged as if in defeat, then rested his hand on Lisia's dresser. "Then, when I realized that you'd come to trust me, I was afraid to lose that tenuous relationship." He looked into Lisia's pale green eyes unwaveringly. "I admit that I became very thoughtless. I *was* treating you like a harling almost, and that is similar to what the administrators did, and you have every right to be angry. But do believe me when I promise you it won't happen again, and even if we cannot always agree, I sincerely have the best interests of you and your harlings in my heart."

Lisia was silent for several moments and then, looking down at his lap, mumbled, "I have no good reason to trust you."

Cobweb squeezed the hostling's hand gently. "Do you trust *me?*" he asked. Lisia looked up and nodded slightly. "Then believe me when I tell you Swift is sincere. Has anyhar else ever admitted to you when they are wrong? Swift is a powerful har. He doesn't need your trust or your friendship, but he sincerely wants them." Cobweb smiled at Lisia reassuringly. "He just made a mistake. None of us are perfect. Besides, he's still young."

"Hey!" Swift cried indignantly, but Lisia smiled at Cobweb's comment and soon Swift did too.

Lisia sighed dramatically and said, "I suppose I can forgive you this one time."

"Thank you," Swift replied, meaning it.

"Well, now that we're all committed to honesty and forgiveness, why don't Lis and I get dressed?" Cobweb suggested. "I'd like some breakfast."

Once they arrived at the dining hall, Lisia made the rounds of the tables, checking in with the various groups of harlings, and being affectionate with the younger ones. Eventually, Lisia seemed content to leave matters in the hands of the Parsic volunteers on duty and found a table in the corner where he and his companions would be allowed to eat in relative peace.

"It's amazing to see so many harlings eating together like this," Swift remarked. "They're remarkably well-behaved."

Lisia surveyed the scene and shrugged. "I suppose. I mean, we're *all* very well-behaved, aren't we? We were trained to be that way. Meals in the dining hall were just a part of our routine." He paused, taking a bite out of a slice of bread and chewing on it thoughtfully. "The only time it was difficult was, of course, the last four months when we had no staff to manage things. At first the situation was very chaotic, but then we all had to take charge, more or less."

The hostling's journal from that time period had indicated as much, and not wanting to dwell on such painful memories, Swift let the remark pass as they moved on to other topics. They were almost through with their meal when Edrei approached them.

After greeting them as a group, he turned to Lisia and told him that Paran had important information for him and he should report to his office as soon as he was done eating.

"Oh?" Lisia asked, sounding worried. "Something urgent?"

"Well, it's information I'm sure you'll want right away. I agree, you really should go right over," Edrei urged.

Lisia's expression suddenly changed; he was now eyeing the har impatiently. "If it's so important, why don't you just tell me now, if you know?"

Edrei considered a moment before sitting down. "I suppose I could. Maybe I could do a better job of telling you anyway. I'm aware that you and Paran don't exactly get along."

Swift raised an eyebrow. "We've been trying to work on that."

Edrei nodded. "Good. I'm sure some mutual empathy will make the work here much easier."

"Indeed," Lisia said. "Now what is this *important* message?"

"Well," Edrei began, hesitating slightly, "actually it's more like a relay of some information. Lisia, you know we've been examining all the records and files we can find, trying to find out what we can, possibly track down the hara responsible for this facility."

"Yes, of course I'm aware of that," Lisia replied curtly. "And?"

"And we had discovered a huge number of files, only they were written in code. It took quite a while, but now we're able to confirm that a large proportion of the records are medical in nature." Edrei glanced at each of them in turn. The suspense in the air around the table was thick. "Late yesterday our specialists began working with these particular files and started deciphering them." Edrei leaned forward confidentially. "Lisia, we now know these are records of all the pearls produced in this facility — when they were produced, who the parents were, what the harlings looked like when they were born. Once we decode them all, we could link up every harling to his parents. Paran wanted you to come over to find out about your harlings."

Lisia froze. "*Mine?*"

"Yes, Lisia. There must be some harlings here who are—"

"No, Edrei, there are *not*," the hostling cut in sharply, having pulled himself out of his immediate shock. "They are not *my* harlings." He paused, perhaps recognizing the confusion on the faces of those around him. "Well, I do *call* them that, 'my harlings,'" he explained, "but only in the sense that I feel responsible for all of them, as if I'm their one and only hostling. But understand, I don't mean that in the possessive sense. They are not *mine*. They *never* were. And they never *will* be."

Edrei could not hide his surprise. "But we can decipher the records and link the harlings up using their breeding codes. It would be—"

"Hideous," Lisia spat. "I won't do it. Tell Paran. I won't see those records. As far as I'm concerned, he can burn them all."

For the first time since Edrei had arrived, Swift spoke up, looking at the hostling questioningly. "But why?"

Lisia, who had pushed his food aside, clasped his hands together tightly, staring at all three hara. His calm and even tone belied the look of deep pain in his eyes. "Simple. Because I do not wish to know. I was never intended to be their parent and I never have been. Their fathers are... also lost." His voice had become tight and he shifted his clasped hands on the tabletop. "I don't want to know which are mine. I really don't want that."

Edrei turned to Swift and Cobweb for help or comment. Both of them shook their heads. What could they possibly say?

"What about the harlings?" Edrei asked gently. "Don't you think *they'll* want to know?"

Lisia straightened in his seat. "I wouldn't know, Edrei," he replied darkly. "I was taken from my own parents and never knew them. I've not spent much time wondering either." His eyes shifted uneasily. For the first time, Swift wondered where exactly Lisia had come from.

"I think the harlings could get along without knowing," Lisia continued. "After all, what would they do if they *did* know? I'm the only hostling left you can track down — the rest of them either left with the administrators or disappeared after they went for help." He paused, kneading his hands together once again. "So what are you suggesting, Edrei? That the dozen of them left here that are indeed 'mine' become... *special?* That I claim them as my own and forsake the others?" He shook his head. "Well, I'd rather none of us knew." He paused again. "Maybe later... when they're older, and if they want to know, but certainly not now! Surely you can understand this."

"I respect your decision," Edrei said. "I will let Paran know your feelings on the matter."

"No, I'll tell him myself," Lisia declared. "I can manage it. Not right this moment, since I have many other—"

"Excuse me, Lis?" broke in a voice. They had all been so deep into the discussion that they had missed a young har's approach.

"Yes, Tilithia?" Lisia asked. "I'm surprised to see you here. You must have something out of the ordinary to tell me."

Swift observed the speaker. From the way he was dressed and his apparent age, Swift judged that this was another of the trained harlings, but older. This was the first time he'd seen this particular Lily. He wondered if he had passed feybraiha, as he seemed fully developed.

"Forgive me," Tilithia said, bowing his head. "It's only that I was just talking with the others and..." His words trailed off.

When he did not continue, Lisia sighed wearily. His expression was apprehensive.

Tilithia looked up, and obviously still nervous, he blurted quickly, "They sent me here to say we really need to talk to you."

"I see," said Lisia slowly. "Would it be all right for me to come by in an hour or so? You'll be in your room?"

"Yes, Lisia," Tilithia replied with obvious gratitude. "That would be very nice. Thank you, I'll tell them." With that the young har bowed his head once more and departed hurriedly.

Swift ate the last of his breakfast quickly. He was eager to meet with Captain Totral to discuss progress and then had plans to interview various hara who had been assigned to caregiving. He wanted to hear their observations on the harlings. Before saying his goodbyes he turned his attention back to Lisia. "What was that about? Are the older harlings having problems?"

"It's hard to say," Lisia replied slowly. "I'm not sure what they'll want to talk with me about specifically."

"Don't you?" Edrei asked accusingly. He leaned back in his chair. "It's obvious. He's *ready*, Lisia."

Lisia did not reply.

"Feybraiha," Edrei prompted. "I decided to read him because I was surprised I'd never seen him before. He's definitely ready — through with it for a couple of weeks actually." Edrei paused and frowned deeply. "As you well know."

Swift peered at Lisia, who appeared decidedly guilt-ridden. The Parsic leader tried to work out a motivation for the hostling to neglect Tilithia as Edrei had implied. "Lisia?" he prompted.

"I... know," Lisia admitted bitterly. He dropped his head into his hands. "Yes, I know. He's ready. Several others are almost ready as well."

"So, why did you hide him from us?" Edrei demanded. "You know that we asked to interview all of the oldest harlings here and yet you specifically hid Tilithia away from us, didn't you? And others as well? With all your training surely you're aware that once a harling passes the point of sexual maturity he begins craving aruna. Hiding him away like that! It's... cruel."

"I would never do anything intentionally cruel to these harlings," Lisia countered, clearly discomforted.

"But what were you planning to do about this?" Swift asked. "Why hide him away?" To let harlings pass through their feybraiha without any acknowledgement or arunic initiation was unthinkable.

Lisia shrugged. "You must understand that I'm aware of a young har's needs, but how was I to know whether the Gelaming were to be trusted? They're the enemy — or at least I thought they were. I was afraid they might take advantage of Tilithia's needs."

"But surely you trust us now," Edrei said, his voice more gentle than before, "at least some of us."

"Yes," Lisia replied, nodding wearily. "I — I should have said something yesterday. There's just been so much going on at once." He glanced away as he continued. "But really, I'm very grateful that there are hara here to take care of him and the others."

Lisia tugged on his blouse nervously, seeming to gather up courage to speak. "When I first realized Tilithia was changing, I hoped some of the others would change along with him and they would have each other. And thankfully some of the others started to mature as well. I know it's not the proper way, but I let them all share a room together and sort of hoped nature would eventually just take its course." He sighed. "But Tilithia was far ahead of the others, and even when they caught up, they were all too well-behaved to try anything, so my plan didn't work. Finally I was just about to, um... take care of that, but then you and the general and the army showed up... and so I decided to wait."

Cobweb, who'd been merely listening all along, finally spoke. "So were you going to do it yourself, Lisia? Take that harling through his feybraiha?"

Lisia sighed again and wrung his hands together. "Yes, Cobweb. I was *going* to. I finally had talked myself into it. It was very difficult."

"Why difficult, Lisia?" Edrei asked. "You make the consummation of feybraiha sound terrible. The harling's welfare aside, I would think you would have looked forward to it, since you were apparently all alone for weeks without aruna."

There was a silence as Lisia stared at Edrei, then blinked. "That in itself is not unusual," he stated flatly. "Normally I've only ever taken aruna about every two to three months. To conceive pearls."

"Oh," Edrei said. "I hadn't thought about it that way."

There was another silence. Swift looked from face to face and concluded that Cobweb and Edrei were just as confused by Lisia's reactions as he was. Based on the hostling's journal, he found it hard to believe that Lisia neglected the completion of the harling's feybraiha just because he wasn't in the mood.

Seeming to sense Swift's thoughts, Lisia blurted, "Well, it's not as easy as you think. You're overlooking something rather obvious — I'm a hostling!"

Cobweb nodded. "Yes, I see, Lisia. You didn't think you could do it because you hadn't had any experience in that area."

Finally Lisia looked relieved. "Yes! I'm glad *somehar* understands! Goodness, could it not be more plain? What happens at feybraiha? Assuming I'd gone about things the usual way, the traditional way, I'd have to have gone to him and—"

"Become ouana," Cobweb finished for him. "I—I can understand, Lisia. You're not used to doing that and it might be difficult for you."

Lisia surprised them all by flashing a nervous smile. "Well, yes. I've... *never* done that. I'm guessing from what I've heard so far that apparently that's a very strange thing, but that's how I've been raised. It's not something I'm comfortable with."

There was a moment's silence as Cobweb and Edrei, neither of whom had read the hostling's journal, absorbed this information. Swift guessed they had not realized just to what extreme extent Lisia had been raised to be soume.

"I suppose it's just another reason to be glad we arrived when we did," Edrei said, half to himself. "But eventually you would have done it?"

"Yes," Lisia sighed. "I would have had no choice." He looked across the hall. Most of the harlings were being led out, as breakfast time had ended. "Although that wasn't the only reason I waited. There was another... no, two actually."

"What was that?" Swift asked.

"Well," Lisia said, turning his head slightly, "First, it just seemed like it would be too strange — aruna simply isn't part of my relationship with these harlings. Second, I thought to myself that aruna really isn't something you should learn from the *only* available har... and a *hostling* at that. We always had aruna instructors who did it and were excellent. So you see, I wanted the experience to be very good and with me, I really couldn't be sure it would be. Well, not if I were ouana at any rate."

"I understand now why you waited, Lisia," Edrei said, "though I wish you'd alerted us to the situation sooner. But I'll take care of it."

"How so exactly?" Lisia asked.

"Tilithia will be initiated into the ways of aruna," he said. "By me."

"By *you*?" Lisia asked, incredulous.

Edrei nodded. "Yes. I volunteer — with your permission, of course," he added, inclining his head slightly to Swift and Lisia.

"Oh," Lisia replied. "That is quite... generous of you, tiahaar." The hostling paused uncomfortably, glancing from har to har. "So, you don't think it necessary to summon a special instructor? I mean no offense," he added quickly, "it's just that I want the best for my harlings."

Far from insulted, the Listener fought to suppress laughter, though he couldn't quite hide the smirk on his face. "Trust me, Lisia, I want the best for the harling as well. But it really won't require a specialist." He crossed his arms confidently. "I'm positive that I will be sufficient."

"For all of them?" Cobweb interrupted.

Edrei did chuckle then. "Well, no, I don't have *that* much time. I mean at least the one, Tilithia. His need is immediate."

Lisia's surprise was fading, and now the hostling's expression was serious. "Very well, but what exactly will you do?"

"*Do*?" Edrei queried. "I think it's obvious what I'll do. You're pure-born and went through feybraiha yourself. That was—"

"Totally different," Lisia interrupted. "I think. I mean... Things aren't the same now, are they? Lita isn't going to be raised the way I was raised. He's not going to be what I am... was. That's why I want to know what you will do. I don't know, but I'm guessing that your idea of feybraiha is probably different from mine, what with all your ideas about the soume and the ouana. I mean, for me feybraiha was wonderful but you know... we had our own way."

Cobweb nodded knowingly. "You were soume— only." Based on what Lisia had said earlier, it only made sense.

"Yes," Lisia agreed. "It was the only lesson we needed to learn."

Edrei got to his feet. "Well," he announced, "from me, Tilithia will learn his full abilities – soume *and* ouana."

Lisia stood as well. "I—I don't know what to say except... thank you." He hesitated a moment and then asked, "Can we go to them now and explain?"

Edrei considered. "I suppose I have time."

As Lisia led him to the oldest harlings' room, Edrei reached out with his inner senses. He turned to Lisia abruptly, fighting to keep his tone from sounding scolding. "Lisia, haven't you spoken to Tilithia and the others about — well, anything?"

Lisia halted. Edrei could see plainly the tension returning to the hostling's posture. "Edrei, I assure you that the harlings understand feybraiha. Despite what you may think of Varrish ways, we were very well-educated about the workings of our bodies." Lisia turned and fixed Edrei with a level gaze. "And, I certainly haven't ignored *all* their needs. I remember how uncomfortable feybraiha was for me. Despite having all these young ones to tend, I *have* made time to check in on my oldest. I offered as much comfort and reassurance as I could *and* answered their questions."

"But not lately," Edrei countered softly. "You haven't spoken to them about what's been happening since we arrived, have you?"

Lisia turned away and continued down the hall. "They're going through enough — dealing with the tumultuous changes inside their bodies. I didn't think it would be appropriate to burden them with the changes to their lives as well. Especially when I still don't know for certain what will become of us."

Tentatively the Listener reached forward and put a hand on the hostling's shoulder. "I understand, Lisia. I shouldn't have judged you so harshly."

Lisia did not respond. They'd reached their destination.

Once inside the room, the harlings greeted Lisia and Edrei with nervous, polite voices, though some smiled at Edrei with undisguised interest and even longing. Looking closely at the group, Edrei realized with dismay that it wasn't only Tilithia who had gone through feybraiha, but four others as well. Another four more were right in the middle of it: weary, hot, moody and scratching.

Tilithia began stammering, trying to broach the awkward subject, but Lisia made it easy for him and said that he knew what was on their minds. He decided to get directly to the point and made the pronouncement the young hara had all been waiting for: Yes, those that were ready would receive the long awaited rite of passage.

Edrei decided to speak up then. "I think it's clear who among you have completed your progress into adulthood. However, I think it would be appropriate for our medic, Colden, to perform an examination first — just to be sure." He paused and observed that none of the harlings present seemed at all intimidated by that prospect. He continued, "I had already volunteered to partner with Tilithia for his first aruna because I sensed his need when I saw him just now at breakfast." The Listener paused to smile and send a psychic wave of appreciation and reassurance to Tilithia, who was blushing but also smiling eagerly. "However, I don't think that I can be there for all of you. With Lisia's permission, I'll see if I can find some of the Parsic hara to be there for the rest of you. If you like I can come back with those hara later today so that you can get to know us and pick which har you'd like to be with."

This comment did elicit a startled response. "Is that proper, Lis?" asked a thin young har with sleek chestnut hair. "Can we really do that?"

Lisia was clearly slightly flustered himself, glancing to Edrei then back to the harlings. "Well, Starling, I know it's not the way feybraiha was handled in the past, but these are new times." He paused a moment tugging nervously at his sleeves. "I regret that I haven't had more answers to share with you before now. I know some of you must have already ascertained that our circumstances have changed once again. I promise that I will stay up here with you and answer your questions as best I can. As for your first aruna, if you are comfortable with choosing a har to be your partner, then nohar is going to object. If making the choice is uncomfortable for you, then I'll see to that decision."

Another harling, the pale one that Edrei recognized from the nursery, spoke up then. "Lis, from what I've gathered, the ones like tiahaar Edrei are Gelaming, which we know are very different from us and have all these new ways of doing things." He paused and took a deep breath before continuing. "But the hara who came after them, the Parasiel? I was told that they used to be Varrs like us before we lost the war. So, what I was wondering is, will aruna will be different depending on whether we pick from the Gelaming or the Parasiel?"

Edrei cut in with a response. "That is an excellent question, — er, what is your name?"

"Juni," the harling supplied.

"Juni. Yes, what Juni asked makes sense. Every har is a little different in how he likes to perform the act of aruna. That's part of what makes sharing ourselves so wonderful and exciting. But the Parasiel hara will not be adhering to the rules of aruna that you were taught. They will initiate you into the same things I will, which is to be soume and also ouana."

As expected, this announcement again caused a tumultuous stir. All the young hara were talking at once and some looked quite distressed.

Lisia didn't need Edrei's prompting. Choosing his words carefully, he said, "I know this comes as a shock to you. I promise that despite what you've always been taught, including what I've taught you, it will not be a bad thing for you to be ouana." The hostling turned to Edrei. "Perhaps we can get Colden to come and help me explain it all before he examines them?"

Edrei nodded. Clearly these young hara were accustomed to obeying authority figures, but they had also been taught to believe certain falsehoods about their own biology. A doctor was the ideal person to convince them of their natural sexual duality.

Lisia went on to assure them that despite their initial mistrust of the Gelaming, the hara who would attend to them were honorable and experienced. He then prompted them to take turns asking their questions.

"Um, tiahaar Edrei," Tilithia asked, "I don't mind so much if you want me to be ouana, but you will still teach me how to make pearls, right?"

Edrei fought the urge to groan in frustration. Instead he smiled warmly and said, "That's an excellent question, Tilithia. Lisia, why don't you explain that while I go and fetch Colden."

Content that Edrei and Colden were now handling the young hara's questions, and relieved that he'd finally enlightened his oldest hara to the truth of the Wraeththu world, Lisia next went to see Paran — alone. The matter of the birth records was something he felt singularly qualified to discuss and besides, the matter was personal. *Very* personal.

"What in the world are you thinking of, wanting to open up the records and linking everyhar up?" Lisia demanded.

Paran's expression of annoyance morphed into one of genuine confusion. "Don't you want to know which harlings are yours? Don't you think the harlings want to know?"

Lisia forced himself to calm down, telling himself that the Gelaming captain had no way to understand fully his feelings on the matter, as obvious as they were. "The present situation does not favor linking pearls to their natural parents, Captain," Lisia said patiently. "After all, except for me, those parents are now absent, moved elsewhere into Megalithica and no doubt scattered or possibly even dead. Of course, the soldiers shouldn't even be a factor in the matter. They never had any personal interest in the harlings."

"But what about you, Lisia?" Paran asked. "I know you have a more than personal interest."

"Even harlings I produced myself would be better off keeping with their status as products of the facility, not of any specific hostling. I do not see any benefit in permitting certain harlings to be called mine and not others. I love all the harlings and I don't want to give special treatment to those who happen to belong to me biologically. I want to continue being hostling to all of them. It's only fair."

Lisia crossed his arms defiantly as Paran remained silent for long moments after the hostling's impassioned explanation. The captain leaned forward, propping his elbows on the desk and resting his chin in his folded hands. "So what you're saying is that to avoid preferential treatment or jealousy, you don't think that your biological harlings should be singled out." Paran nodded his approval. "I can see why you'd want to avoid such attachments at this point. I have the utmost respect for your decision, Lisia. You're developing a very healthy Wraeththu outlook."

Lisia's mouth dropped open for a moment. The last thing he'd expected was approval — especially from Paran. "So you will not share this decoded information with the harlings then?" he asked cautiously.

"No," Paran replied. "We'd originally wanted to extend the courtesy simply because we assumed you'd insist on knowing. But I see no reason to inform the harlings if you don't want them to know." He reached over for a stack of papers to his right, which Lisia presumed to be the records in question. "Besides," he said off-handedly, "now I'll be able to get these off to Immanion immediately rather than wasting more time."

"Why do you want to keep the records?" Lisia asked. To him it seemed like a waste of time to bother with them at all.

"Well, to you these may just be about simply parenthood, but to the scientific mind there is a wealth of information in these records about genetics. As we continue to study the harlings, among other things we'll learn a great deal about what traits tended to dominate."

Lisia's face twisted into a distasteful frown. "How surprising," he spat, "I thought the noble Gelaming would have no interest in our barbaric traditions like breeding." Before Paran could reply, Lisia turned sharply and left with his head held high.

Later that afternoon, Lisia knocked with difficulty on the door of the oldest harlings' room, because his arms were heaped with clothing and other supplies. A nervously giddy Tilithia admitted him to the room and immediately hugged the hostling's neck despite his precarious armload.

Lisia felt tears pricking the corners of his eyes. "Oh Lita, I'm so happy for you," he said. "I was afraid you'd hate me for making you wait so long and then shattering all your dreams on top of that."

Tilithia gently took the bundle from Lisia's arms. "Oh Lis, don't cry!" Lisia found himself embraced on all sides.

"Don't be upset," said a young har named Mossy. "We wish you'd told us sooner, but we understand."

"And anyway tonight is supposed to be about celebrating," Glade added.

Lisia wiped away his tears. "Yes, yes. Tonight *is* for celebration." He gestured to the clothing and accessories that Tilithia had heaped on a bed. "I want tonight to be as special for all of you as it was for me and my friends." He walked to the bed and gestured for the others to follow. "It's been ages since any finery was sent here to us, so I decided you should have some of our things." He pulled a milky white dress from the stack and brushed away at wrinkles. "Lita, you've been so patient and brave throughout all of this. I want you to have my feybraiha dress."

"Oh, Lisia, I couldn't possibly take your dress," Tilithia replied breathlessly, though he fingered the silky fabric reverently. "It's your special dress; it should belong to you for always."

Lisia smiled. He couldn't help but admit that part of him was relieved. "Well, perhaps not," Lisia said. "But I'd be honored if you would borrow it for tonight. I've always thought white is so fresh and charming against dark skin like yours. And here," he pulled a silver ring from his finger and put it on Tilithia's outstretched hand, "I insist that you keep this at least."

After the young har gratefully accepted, Lisia turned to the others. "Glade, Cirrus, I know that you were both very close to Rosea " He paused and swallowed thickly. "I know he'd want you to have these. Glade, this is the dress that Rosea wore for his feybraiha. Cirrus, I know this dress is plainer, but it was Rosea's favorite; he loved this shade of blue."

The emotional impact of this time was almost overwhelming for Lisia and the young hara. Lisia had never felt the loss of his fellow hostlings, his friends from his earliest memories, as deeply as he did now. But the one remaining hostling refused to allow the special time to be overly marred by sadness. Mossy chose a special gown that had belonged to Chrys, and Hasta selected a favorite of Honey's. As Lisia and the other older harlings helped them dress and prepare, the hara filled the afternoon with both laughter and tears, anticipation and remembrance. When Cobweb came to the door announcing that the time had come,

Lisia was surprised that the celebration, which would usher in a new beginning for his harlings, filled him with a strange sense of closure as well.

That evening the dining hall played host to a special ceremony that Lisia and the Lilies had never witnessed: a feybraiha celebration. Though Lisia was at first uneasy, as the transition had been a very private affair among hara raised at the facility, Swift assured him it was commonplace and nothing that should be hidden.

Lisia had noted that despite the unfamiliarity of the coming ceremony, the young hara had been very excited and eager to get on with the evening's events. He was thankful that Edrei and Colden had apparently answered all their questions and put any of their worries at rest.

All five harlings were given their own table, which had been heaped with flowers gathered from the fields. Cobweb had accepted the honor of officiating the actual ceremony. The young hara were clearly ecstatic that the fabled consort stood before all eloquently announcing their ascent to Neoma, though it was doubtful that they fully understood just what the words meant.

Lisia's heart swelled with pride as he watched the bright-eyed, smiling young hara as they beamed at Edrei and the other chosen hara. He had to admit that if any hara deserved an honored celebration, it was these who had worked so hard for their fellow harlings, even while suffering the pain and frustration of feybraiha.

At the end of the meal Cobweb brought each young har to the center of the room to join hands with his chosen. Singing and dancing followed, and then one by one the young hara were escorted away to rooms that had been specially prepared in the old administrators' quarters. They probably would be not seen again until noon the next day, Lisia thought to himself.

After they'd gone, Lisia sat with Swift and discussed a variety of topics, including the new concept of feybraiha celebrations. Lisia felt it was a perfect example of how much he and the others still needed to learn about the outside world. He spoke of his determination both to receive his own education and plan that of his charges.

As other hara came to join their conversation, Swift and Cobweb and various Parsic hara offered Lisia what amounted to a short course in the nature of the Wraeththu world. There was so much Lisia wanted and needed to know — the background of all the different tribes, common rites and ceremonies, Wraeththu history, geography, and all the other information regarding the outside world that the hostling had heretofore either been denied or misled about.

Lisia was eager to know enough to answer the harlings' questions and possibly fears, at least until they began their own educations, which they would do shortly, if he had anything to do with it. The hostling reiterated his opinion that after keeping the harlings safe and fed, education was his greatest priority and he was adamant that wherever the harlings ended up, they would receive the sort of education they deserved.

"Something else they deserve is proper caste training," Paran interjected, unexpectedly pulling up a chair to join the small group. Swift had already introduced the topic to Lisia before, but he listened with interest as Paran described the concept more deeply. Although Lisia still resented the captain, he was eager to hear more about Wraeththu's natural abilities.

He spoke up after Paran extolled the virtues of speaking mind to mind, which Lisia had always presumed was strictly a part of aruna. "Do you think I could have talked to my pearls that way?" he asked. "Through the mind? Would they have understood me?"

Paran said it was likely that the pearls would have at least understood projected emotions. Lisia smiled in wonder, then shook his head, laughing softly. "Good, because I always did talk to them, thought things to them." He reflected back on those bygone days, before he had known the truth. "I thought I was crazy, but I guess I wasn't. I just knew it was my only real chance to care for them as my own, and so I used to try to tell them things, like to be good or to have hope or to be happy. I also used to worry when I would get angry or upset because I felt it would affect the pearls. I suppose my instincts were correct."

"It's obvious that with *your* instincts, you'll go far with proper caste training, Lisia," Paran said. He ignored the surprised expressions his words conjured in his companions. "The same is true for all of the harlings here. It's the opinion of the Gelaming that you and the hostlings were specifically chosen for your potential. That's one of the reasons we feel you should all receive the best training and education available, which with all due respect to the Parasiel, is with the Gelaming."

"Then I suggest your best Gelaming instructors volunteer their services and come here to teach them," Swift replied, his tone clipped.

Paran raised his hands defensively. "I know we haven't been seeing eye to eye on this matter, but the Gelaming are not above compromise. I think we could construct a wonderful school for the harlings in Imbrilim. That way they wouldn't have to leave Megalithica."

"Imbrilim is a distinctly Gelaming town; it may as well be across the ocean," Swift argued. "Furthermore, this isn't a question of geography, Captain Nemish. It's a question of autonomy and choice."

"Which is why General Aldebaran has made arrangements for you and tiahaar Lisia to present your case before the Hegemony," Paran replied smoothly.

"He expects me to come to him in Immanion?" Swift asked, clearly unimpressed. Lisia looked shocked.

Paran shrugged. "It's really more that he wants Lisia to come to Immanion. After all, you speak of choice, and you want to make decisions based on the hostling's recommendations. But how can Lisia make an informed choice without really debating his options with the Gelaming?"

Lisia felt that even if it meant he could present his argument, the prospect of leaving the facility was still very daunting to him. "But I can't go to Immanion," he said. "I have to stay here with the harlings. Surely we can't all go. And I don't even know how to ride one of those special Gelaming horses that you say can fly. I've never even ridden a *regular* horse!"

"I'm sure Swift would be willing to take you there, Lisia, you don't have to ride alone," Paran explained. "And you wouldn't be gone very long. I'm sure somehar else can handle things here. After all, it's not like this facility hasn't run perfectly well in the past without your express guidance."

Lisia frowned. If on one hand he felt eager and excited about this opportunity, why, then, on the other hand, did he feel that leaving, even to argue for his harlings, would somehow amount to a betrayal?

"Besides," Paran added, "Colden wants to bring that little harling with the crooked hip to have him cured by the best healers. You said that you wanted us to do that, but do you really want him to go through it alone?"

Lisia turned to Swift, his expression pleading for guidance. "I don't know. Swift, do you think it would help if we went before the General's Hegemony?"

Swift's face betrayed little emotion, but he crossed his arms in a guarded posture. "Very well, Paran, Lisia and I will go to Immanion. But I'm putting Cobweb in charge of this facility and all the harlings in my absence."

That evening, as he prepared for an early bedtime, Swift drew out a piece of paper and a pen. Before leaving for Immanion, there was an important message he wanted to send back to Galhea.

Dearest Seel,

I'm sending you this message to let you know that I'm traveling to Immanion for a few days. The Gelaming have been trying to step over my authority ever since they stumbled across this place and I just can't have that.

They've thrown out the opportunity to present my case to the Hegemony like it's some sort of concession. I'm no fool! The only reason for the invitation is that they intend to dazzle Lisia and convince him that giving the harlings over to the Gelaming will be in their best interest.

I'd prefer to dig in my heels and make the Gelaming come to me for this little debate, but I just can't spare the time that would take. And I suppose I do owe it to Lisia to let him see what the Gelaming have to offer. I feel pretty confident that I'll be able to convince the Hegemony of Parasiel's right to determine the fate of our own hara. Of course I could always take the matter directly to Pell, but I'd rather win this without the Tigron's support.

I do wish I had your support, though. I miss you very much. This has been much more difficult than I'd first anticipated — not only dealing with the Gelaming, but confronting other things in this place.

I discovered something disturbing. Terzian visited this facility. He fathered four harlings. Lisia was the first to tell me but then I checked the records when they were decoded. All of them were sent to that military compound that we can't even find, so there's no trace of them. Two of them are around six years old, one five and one four. They don't even have names— just code numbers.

I've already assigned hara to work with the Gelaming's intelligence tracking down the other facilities. It's a top priority and perhaps the harlings will be found. So what do I do then? My heart says that if my half-brothers are found that I should take responsibility for them. It's what I want to do. I don't know what Cobweb would say about that. He knows about the harlings and he took it pretty well since it's not personal like with Tyson. But I don't know how he'd react to having more of Terzian's offspring in the house.

And that's not the only reason I'm not free to make that decision. I hate to admit it, but I realize how dangerous this information could be for Parasiel politically. We both know there are plenty of hara who'd much prefer following a traditionally military-trained son of Terzian. And I shudder to think of what sort of training my brothers did receive. I haven't missed the irony that, assuming they weren't slaughtered, the sons that my father abandoned to an anonymous fate no doubt exhibited blind loyalty to the Varr regime, while the son he nurtured and protected betrayed it.

I know the smart thing to do would be to deny my brothers' existence even if they are found. But wouldn't that make me just as ruthless as the hara who instigated this vile breeding program in the first place? I suppose I am worrying over nothing — they're probably all dead and the Gelaming certainly won't let the secret out.

Still, I have to admit that this is all eating away at the back of my mind. It would be such a relief to have you here. Please give my love to Azriel. Let him know that I'll be home as soon as I can. I love you.

Swift

Chapter Eleven

Everyhar has been gloomy and resentful and quiet since they sent Calla away. We've had plenty to do to keep us busy since we don't have half the staff here that we used to. I remember what it used to be like. Back when we were treated with respect. When we hostlings didn't have to work unless we felt like picking some fresh flowers. Back when we filled the long days of hosting with genteel activities like singing, dancing, arranging flowers, sketching or painting. I can't remember the last time I bothered to arrange blossoms in a vase or strolled the halls to admire all the paintings and drawings that the more talented among us created.

Now all I do is knit, sew and occasionally tend vegetables. Well, honestly, I shouldn't complain. The work I do is pretty easy since the older harlings and the younger hostlings are usually assigned the harder tasks. But, I enjoy being outside, doing the vegetables, so I do it as often as possible.

None of it really takes my mind off of Calla though, not like I wish it would. I'm still so angry and miserable over what happened to him and what it means for the rest of us too. I guess it's selfish of me to think that way. I should just be sorry for Calla, but I'm sorry for all of us too. I thought that we were important to the Varrs, special, even sacred — like in the old words. But, now it seems like we're not very special at all. Obviously, we're not very important if they can just throw Calla away for something that wasn't completely his fault anyway.

I wonder sometimes if it's just this way at our facility, though. Maybe things are better in other places and the administrators here are just bad. They just did this horrible, cowardly thing to cover up their own mistake of letting Calla host for one of them. But why is it such a crime? It's just one pearl out of so many. I'm on my 19th right now. Why can't I be allowed to have just one of my own if I wanted it?

Well, I know the answer to that. Because I'm just a hostling and my pearls aren't heirs. And that's the proof, I guess, that we're not really important after all. If we were, none of these things would be happening. Calla would still be here, I wouldn't have blisters on my hands from pulling weeds, and I could have a real relationship with a har other than a soldier. And even if I can't keep any, I would at least be able to visit with the little harlings.

But I shouldn't be feeling sorry for myself. At least I'm better off than poor Calla. I wonder where they sent him. I really can't imagine at all. I hope that maybe he's in one of the interesting places that Vlaric told me about. We've asked but nohar will tell us anything. I hope they haven't decided to make him into a soldier to fight in this awful war. I can't imagine Calla as a soldier having to fight those horrible Gelaming. I hate them. If it wasn't for hara like them, we probably wouldn't have to have any soldiers at all and we wouldn't have to send all the little harlings away to learn to fight and Calla and the rest of us would be safe.

Today, Violet, Seagrass and I were down in Tolea' classroom to spend time with the harlings in that group who hadn't started feybraiha yet. Before we finished, Neydish came and asked if I could come to his classroom when we were done. That was unusual, but not all that strange. Sometimes the instructors just like to say hello to some of us.

A little later, I went to the classroom and he was at his desk. All of the harlings were gone, except one who was sitting in the back and looked nervous. I'd seen him before, but I didn't really know him. Neydish said that he (his name's Pansea) had caused a great deal of trouble two days before, when his group of Lilies had been helping with some of the small harlings. Because of that he isn't allowed to help with small ones any more.

I must have just stared in shock when Neydish said that. I couldn't imagine having done anything so bad when I was that age. Neydish just sort of smiled nervously and said that there had been enough disappointment and scandal here recently and they didn't want to lose another potential hostling. That's where I came in. He wanted me to start mentoring Pansea.

I hardly heard the rest of what Neydish was saying. I was too busy fighting this sudden anger. I took a hard look at Pansea and I knew without a doubt that he was being given special treatment. He's very pretty and will no doubt make a beautiful hostling, the kind that all the important hara will want to request. And obviously the administrators didn't care that he doesn't have the natural bond with small harlings that would mark him as a good hostling. They just care that he's pretty. If he weren't, he'd have been taken out of the facility without a doubt. I'd seen it done with others his age, and with Lilies who were good but not as pretty as they could be, like poor Hyacinth. I looked at this Lily with his perfect hair and perfect face and I was just disgusted. I found myself hoping that when the time came, it would turn out that he was too stupid to learn how to open his seal at all.

It must have shown on my face, what I was thinking, because Pansea started looking like he wanted to hide under his desk. I took satisfaction in this at first, but then I couldn't help but feel a little sorry for him. Neydish was saying that I was to start mentoring him during the hours when he would have been helping with the harlings. I was to be excused from all other mentoring to give special attention just to Pansea, who is actually still younger than any of the others I've ever worked with.

And then I realized suddenly that Pansea probably wasn't any worse than Calla. And even if he was lucky right now, he could still end up like Calla, if nohar warned him against it. But how can I really show him how to be a good hostling when, deep down, I was guilty of things that should get me thrown out as well? I wanted to tell Neydish to find somehar else to mentor Pansea. But then I thought about Calla and I just couldn't. I certainly couldn't risk telling Neydish why I'm not a good mentor, and I couldn't deny the harling a second chance. I just hope I won't end up leading Pansea more astray than he already is. I suspect that neither of us really ought to be here at the facility. I guess in a sad way we're a perfect match.

Well now I feel pretty stupid and guilty about the way I've treated Pansea. I haven't really been mentoring him like I'm supposed to. I've just been dragging him along with me on my normal routines, not talking to him very much, except to show him how to knit and sew. It's not just that I resent him for his special treatment, but I really have no idea how I can possibly advise him.

This afternoon, we were all sitting in our lounge knitting, when Pansea turned to me and said, "Don't you ever do anything other than this damn knitting?"

It was really embarrassing, because all the other hostlings and training Lilies turned and stared, so I took us both outside for a walk. He was still being a brat, so I let my temper get the better of me and said, "Well what do you think we do all day, Pansea? These days, being a hostling isn't all flowers and glamour. Besides, you ought to be thankful that you're being taught any of the soume crafts at all. I've never seen a Lily more unsuited to being a hostling in all my life!"

Then he said that he wasn't going to change, because he knew he wouldn't get kicked out, and besides he didn't want to be a hostling at all — he was going to be a *consort!* At first, when he said that, I laughed at his presumptuousness. Then he said that he'd overheard some teachers talking and they'd said that there were plans for some of us hostlings to become consorts eventually.

My mind was working quickly then, while Pansea stood there and fumed. I immediately started hoping that I could be one of the ones chosen, and then I got angry again because I knew the prettiest ones like Pansea had the best chances, and I really hated that. But still, I started to think of what I could do to increase my chances of being chosen, and wondered what it would be like to be a consort.

With all the haughtiness I could muster, I told Pansea that he was a vain, self-centered idiot and that if it were up to me he'd be thrown out altogether or better yet, put to work in the kitchens. And then I blurted out that it was disgusting that a Lily like him was being given special treatment just because he's pretty. And Pansea just looked at me all smug and said that I was just jealous.

That took me aback for a moment, because I know deep down that it's at least partially true. But it didn't change the way I felt and I told him that I would tell Neydish that he was a hopeless case who couldn't be trained. Then I reminded him that times had changed, and if an excellent and incredibly beautiful hostling like Calla could be dismissed, then so could he!

Pansea snapped back that he knew that times had changed. He said, "I may still be a Lily but I'm not blind and I'm not stupid." He said he didn't want anything to do with the way things had become and that he *would* become a consort and that when he was, he would be in charge of his own harlings, and he would make sure that they were happy and cared for and that nohar would ever hurt *his* harlings.

Something about the way he said that gave me a bad feeling deep in my stomach, so I asked him if he'd seen anyhar hurting harlings.

It was then that he told me the whole story of what really happened to get him banned from the small harling rooms. It's not that he was bad with the harlings at all. It's just the opposite. He saw some stupid staff worker hitting a poor harling for no good reason. Pansea said it wasn't the first time it had happened, but that for some reason this time he just got too angry and he shouted at the staff worker to stop. When he didn't, Pansea went over and took the harling away from him. But of course that didn't go at all well and the whole thing turned into an awful squabble.

I'm just furious and sad about the whole thing. I know that the harlings we created don't get special treatment like we did, but it really upsets me to think that they're being hurt and neglected. I even cried a little. Pansea assured me that it's not that bad all the time, but he said that it's hard, because there are just so very many little ones and there are fewer workers now, and they lose their patience more and more. He also said that nohar bothers to try teaching the little ones how to behave, and so it just makes it all the worse.

I hate this. I know that most of the harlings aren't meant to be special like us and that they can't all be treated the way we were, but I agree with Pansea. It's not fair.

I was so wrong about him and now I'm sorry that I judged him so badly. I took back everything I'd said and told him that no matter what happens he will be an excellent hostling and I'm very proud of him for trying to help the little ones. I know that he wants to leave here and be a consort. If anyhar has a chance, it may be him. I've promised myself that from now on I'll teach him whatever I can to help him.

Pearl 22 came today, this morning after breakfast. I was working in the gardens, on the far side, with Pansea. He was helping me to do the low work, since I was much too far along hosting to be comfortable bending down. When the pain came, I fell right onto the ground; it was so strong. I knew right away that there was no way I could make it back to the building for the delivery – I could feel the pearl dropping down! Pansea was staring at me, not knowing what to do, so I managed to tell him to get a doctor for me. He looked so scared and said he didn't want to leave me by myself, but I told him I would be fine, that I really didn't need any help.

It was getting hard for me to talk, but finally I convinced him to go. As he was running for help, I felt the pearl moving down and I knew it would only be a matter of one or two minutes. I was so relieved Pansea had gone because I really didn't want him to see me deliver the pearl. I'm not sure he's ready to see a birth yet, not at his age. It could really frighten him, even if my births are very easy. I still always end up screaming at the end, which is what I started to do in the garden, right in the middle of the potatoes. I didn't care who might hear because it really made me feel better.

I was pushing out the pearl and yelling, when far away I heard Laran calling for me. I didn't look up or stop, just kept on pushing until finally it came out. I had pulled off my skirt and put it between my legs to keep the pearl from coming out onto the ground, and when Laran saw it, he smiled at me and congratulated me. After so many deliveries, he told me, my body doesn't have to strain at all, and really I don't much need a doctor any more, except of course to examine the pearl and make sure I'm OK afterward.

He asked me how I was and I said I felt fine. Then he let me watch while he examined the pearl. This was the first time I've ever been allowed to really see a pearl of my own. I wanted to curl around it, hug it next to me and to keep it warm. Meanwhile Laran said the pearl was undersized. From seeing other pearls, I saw he was right. Probably this can be blamed on my diet, but it still made me feel disappointed in myself.

It makes me so angry that our supplies have been so low recently! I was far more tired during this hosting than usual, and I know it was for lack of the proper nutrients. I must be more careful about getting enough to eat or the pearls might not be healthy. Or maybe the burden should be shifted — could we institute a priority system to give the hostlings first choice of the food? Harlings and staff need food as well, of course, but if we hostlings aren't given what we need, we will fail in our purpose.

Laran sent Pansea inside to get me fresh clothes and said that he would stay with me until I felt strong enough to stand. It was about ten minutes before Pansea showed up with one of my skirts, so I could get redressed. Then Laran wrapped the pearl up in my old skirt and took it away. But before he did, I got to watch it change color and texture as the shell sat in the open air. I even think it got bigger and there were little movements. I've never seen a pearl for so long and it actually started to upset me to look at it, knowing there was a harling inside that I would never see, at least not until later maybe and then I wouldn't even know it. Once it was gone I was almost glad.

Then Pansea helped me get up and go back inside for a bath and then to lie down in my room. It's so strange how easy it is now. All those years ago, when I first started, it was so hard but now it's just almost another normal day.

Against all odds Pansea and I are really becoming close. Once he realized that he and I have the same feelings towards harlings, he became much less of a brat. Sometimes, I almost wish he was still in his sullen phase, because now that he trusts me, at times he never seems to stop talking. He's still restless with many of the more tedious chores that we have to do, but he hasn't been complaining.

I really feel sorry for him. He definitely misses being able to help take care of the small harlings and I can relate to that. Even worse, the Lilies his own age are reluctant to be too friendly with him since he got into trouble. So, I've been letting him spend a lot of his free time with me so he won't feel so lonely.

It's nice to be around somehar who's still so young and full of hopes and dreams. Spending time with him reminds me of when I was young and used to stay up late at night with Calla and Coral, and sometimes the others, whispering about the future.

I've hardly had time to write lately. We've been so busy since almost all of the staff have been sent away. Tiahaar Upsari and a couple other administrators went on a trip yesterday. They took a lot of the things we'd knitted and a lot of our silver and even some of the paintings off the walls. They loaded up the horses and the cart and went somewhere to trade those things for supplies. I hope they bring back a lot of food.

I'm not sure if it's true yet but I heard that Aster lost his pearl last week and has been very ill since then. I've never heard of such a thing happening before, but it wouldn't surprise me. I feel so terrible for poor Aster.

At least they've gone back to staggering our hostings, so that we won't all be delivering at the same time. It's a good thing too, because I don't know how anything would have gotten done during those last few weeks otherwise.

I can't sleep! I've been trying all night but I just keep thinking about my pearl and what happened today. I'm so frightened and also so angry I could scream. I almost lost my pearl today. I'm only at five weeks but I almost had a delivery. That should never have happened!

If it had actually happened, I wouldn't have blamed myself; I would have blamed the administrators. They should have known when they had us conceive that it's not right for us to be hosting anymore, not when there have been so many problems, when there's so much work to do. Why couldn't they have waited until things are better again? They also shouldn't make us work like they have been, but they always say it's for the greater good and so we help. Well, today I almost had my pearl, and I know if it had been born that early, it would have died. I just can't stop thinking about it!

I was working out in the vegetable garden. Everyhar was out there with me, adults and harlings, since it's a very big job to sow the soil and plant everything. The only ones who weren't there were the few hostlings in their last week, since at least the administrators let them stay inside. I was there with Coral helping to dig a planting ditch. We both had shovels and had been going at it for a long time. The ground seems harder this year and I was getting really sore. My back and shoulders were hurting and I had gotten a blister next to my thumb, which was making me have to hold the shovel funny. We still had about a quarter of the ditch left and I was thinking I would be aching all over by then, when suddenly I had something a lot worse to worry about: birth pains.

Birth pains! I had just stuck the shovel in the ground and given a push with my foot when I felt a birth pain. It wasn't that strong but it was obvious enough. I stopped what I was doing and stood there, hoping I'd been wrong, but then I felt another one. I turned to Coral, who was in

221

the middle of a dig and didn't notice me there, holding my stomach. "Coral, my pearl is coming!" I said to him, not really loud, but really urgently. I felt another pain.

Coral spun around and stared at me. "What?! You're not..."

I went over to him and grabbed him around the shoulders. The pains were coming more quickly. "No, Coral, it's coming."

We weren't very far from the potting shed so I asked him to take me there, so I could go behind it. I didn't want to have it happen in a dirty ditch. Walking over to the shed seemed to take forever. The pains weren't very strong but they weren't stopping. I was in such a panic I started to cry. Then suddenly Pansea ran over, seeing me, and I couldn't manage to explain. Coral told him to go get a doctor as soon as he could and to send him to the shed.

Finally I got to the back and lay down in the shade. "Coral, I don't want it to come," I said. "It can't come, it can't, it's not ready!" Coral told me he knew how I felt, since his first pearl had also come early (although only by a week), and he also said he had thought of a way I might be able to stop it. During aruna, we can have a lot of control over our muscles, and since the womb, where the pearl is, is just another kind of muscle, probably we could control it as well. He told me to use as much power as I could, do the strongest visualization ever, and make my muscles relax and stop contracting and pushing on the pearl. I was in such a panic and still wanting to cry, but what he said made sense. Just like at a birth, he sat there and held my hands, guided me through it. It was really the opposite of what you do in a delivery, since the point of it was trying to hold the pearl in and not push. I never imagined fighting a delivery like that.

His idea worked and after about ten minutes, the pains finally stopped. Laran came at the very end. We told him what had happened and he was very sympathetic. He has told me to stay in bed until it's closer to the right time for my pearl to come, and do no more work except for some knitting I can do in bed. I'm happy enough with those suggestions, because I don't want my pearl to come early, but it makes me so angry he didn't say anything about any of the *other* hostlings. How can they possibly keep making us work so hard when we are hosting?

Pearl 24 finally came. I really hope and pray this is my last pearl for a long time. This hosting was the worst I've ever had and the birth was the worst since my first year. After what happened in the garden, I have been mostly stuck in bed, but I still had pains two more times. Plus I was so tired. It was like I was sick and it's never been like that before. I just worried so much about everything and then, when the birth finally came, it was just the worst.

When it started, I was eating dinner that had been brought up to my room. I was scared to try to get to the birthing rooms, because I thought the delivery would be so quick, like the last few. Unfortunately, it wasn't. Once I was taken downstairs, it took almost fourteen hours! It was as bad as my first pearls. I know so much now, but it didn't help. It was like I had lost everything I had gained from going through all of those births. I had a lot of trouble concentrating and instead I kept worrying. I know what's important during a birth but instead of thinking of those things, I was thinking about how my hosting had been so bad and my pains were so much worse than they had been. Then I worried about the pearl and what would happen to it.

And what's going to happen to me? There haven't been any soldiers here for weeks now. What's going to happen to us hostlings? All during the birth I thought about it. The pearl was a few days late, but still it came out small and the delivery was so difficult. Coral was there with me and he said his last birth had been hard as well. Anyway, I don't want to do this again. Not for a long time.

I'm almost glad that I can't sleep because I want to write this down now while I have the chance. I suspect that soon I'll be too busy to write much in this journal at all, but this needs to be written down.

I look back at so many times in my life when things have happened that were bad and I thought that I could just curl up and die in grief and anger. Now I realize that those events were nothing compared to what I'm facing now — what we're all facing, though the harlings don't know yet. And it's funny but even though this is much, much worse than anything that has ever happened before, I've hardly cried about it all. It's like I can't. I think it's because I'm still too shocked. I just have this painful empty feeling inside — just like the emptiness after I've delivered a pearl.

Some of the other hostlings said that they had suspected something like this would happen. I don't believe that. I think they're just saying that to make themselves feel better — so they won't feel so helpless. But I'll be honest and say that I never, ever dreamed anything like this could happen.

When Upsari called another meeting for all the hostlings in the dining hall, I assumed that he would tell us that the soldiers were going to stop coming for a while (which was obvious, since they'd already stopped) and that we'd need to sell more things to get supplies.

But I soon as I saw the expressions on the faces of the administrators and the teachers, I got a prickly cold feeling all over my body. I thought they would say that the Gelaming were coming, but what Upsari said was just the opposite. Nohar is coming, they are leaving.

I don't understand all the reasons, but he said that messengers had come from Fulminir and had told him that the Varrs had decided they could no longer support this facility. The war with the Gelaming has taken all of their resources and Gelaming forces are already moving at will through Megalithica, having already taken Galhea. The Varrs can't afford to support us and they don't want the Gelaming to take us either.

But instead of just moving us someplace safe, they have ordered the administrators to leave. It doesn't make any sense. I guess it shouldn't surprise me, since soldiers are rarely very smart, but I would expect better from our leaders. Upsari said that they'd been ordered to destroy all evidence of the military breeding project. At first, I didn't even know what they could mean by that. What good would it do to destroy the facility when all the harlings are the evidence and they can't be destroyed?

But then, as I looked at the faces of the hara — the administrators and doctors and teachers who I've known for as long as I can remember — I knew. Some of them had been crying — even Botbek, who I'd have sworn was biologically incapable of tears or sympathy. And the rest of them looked so very sad, and scared and guilty. Upsari kept talking and finally he said it: The military meant to destroy the harlings, as if they were some sort of enemy or common animals that had no souls. A few of the hostlings started crying then and some became hysterical.

Upsari tried to calm everyhar and said that they had discussed the orders and decided to defy them. They said that they could not harm any of the harlings, or us either. But then he said that we were all in serious danger. What he said next really proved how serious this was. He said that they had killed the messengers who had been sent to deliver the orders and see them carried out. He said the messengers will be missed eventually, and then the military would come down with greater numbers.

I started crying a little then. It was like being trapped in some sort of nightmare. I still can't believe that this is actually happening. I can't believe that the soldiers who had come here and shared aruna with us, who had helped create those precious little harlings, would come here and coldly kill us all. It just seems impossible and I don't understand any of this.

Then Upsari was saying that we were going to leave this place and go far away where we couldn't be found by the military. But they couldn't save us all. He said that the journey would be difficult and the harlings would slow us down too much. And he said that so many young ones would attract too much attention that might cause the soldiers to find us.

I could hardly believe what I was hearing. He was saying that all of us adult hara would flee, but we'd leave the harlings and the Lilies behind. Again there was so much shouting and crying that it was difficult to for anyhar to be heard. I shouted too and asked what would happen to the harlings. We couldn't just leave them all alone! A lot of the hostlings were saying the same things.

Then it seemed like everyhar was talking at once. I actually started feeling dizzy. One har was saying that we needed to keep our voices down or we'd send the harlings into a panic. I remember thinking that was an extremely cowardly thing for him to say.

And right at that moment, I knew that I would not leave without all the harlings. Once I knew that, it was almost exciting. I don't understand why I felt that way, but I did. I stopped crying all at once. I stood up and waited for Upsari to look at me and when he did, I looked him right in the eyes and I said, "I'm not leaving."

He was flustered for just a moment and then he said, "Very well, that is your choice." He stared at me then like he expected me to change my mind and when I didn't, he called for everyhar to get quiet. Then he said that I would be staying behind to take care of the harlings. At first, there was just silence, but then there was murmuring and I couldn't follow all of it. Laran was arguing with Upsari, many of the other hostlings were telling me not to do it — that I needed to escape with them. I looked up and saw Vlaric sitting with the teachers and he looked so sad. He motioned for me to go up to him, but I turned away.

And then I heard another voice say loudly, "I'm staying too." It was Peony. Then Hyacinth said that he would stay too, which is truly beautiful considering that they wouldn't even let him be a hostling to begin with. And then a lot of hostlings were murmuring about whether they should stay, and Upsari all of a sudden said that everyhar who came could take one harling with him and so they'd be saving some of them. He pointed out that staying behind was almost certain death and that each hostling who left with them would at least be saving the life of one harling, which would be better than throwing their lives away by being stubborn and staying here. I still don't completely believe that. I think he just said it to scare the hostlings into going with them, but I didn't say anything, because I didn't want to be responsible for anyhar else staying behind if it turns out he's right and the soldiers are coming to kill us all.

There was still a lot of murmuring going on and then Upsari was telling everyhar to collect a small number of things and get ready to leave. I wasn't sure what to do then. The whole dining hall was in chaos; nohar was filing out in the normal orderly way. Everyhar was pushing and shoving. I went over to help Rosea, who was still very ill from his last pearl delivery, which had gone badly. I was trying to help him so that he wouldn't get knocked down.

Then I saw Vlaric coming towards us, and I was trapped because I didn't want to talk to him and I couldn't just abandon Rosea either. I tried to be very casual with him as always, but he grabbed my arm and said he needed to talk to me. Rosea nodded and told me to go with him. Vlaric told me not to stay, that I deserved better than this facility and always had and that it would be tragic for me to just throw my life away when I finally had a chance to be free.

I didn't know what to make of what he was saying. I mean, how much would things really change if I left? We'd still be with the administrators, after all. But, maybe not. I hadn't thought of that. I asked Vlaric what he was going to do and he said that he was leaving with the rest, but that as soon as he could, he'd go away on his own. He didn't say it, but I knew that he'd help me get away too if I asked — not just me, but that didn't matter.

I was tempted. I felt like my heart was breaking all over again, but I wouldn't let myself think about the possibility of running away with Vlaric. I shook my head and said that I could not abandon the harlings. Vlaric got frustrated then and he took me by the arms and shook me a little. He said I didn't understand; that I didn't know what the Varrs were really like. He said that I was crazy if I thought somehar was going to come and help us and feel sorry for us. He said that nohar but the military even knows that we're out here and that if they came, it wouldn't be to help. I glanced up at him and I could tell by the look in his eyes that he really, really meant what he was saying. He was scared for me and I have to admit that it made me scared too. But I just couldn't abandon the harlings. I'd never be able to live with myself. I was shaking by then but I looked in his eyes and just said, "I'm a hostling."

He got very exasperated then and said something angry that I didn't really catch as he walked away from me. Then I turned and saw Rosea was standing right near me. He said that he was going to stay too. I was surprised, but I didn't argue. I just hugged him.

The next hours were a blur. I said goodbye to so many — hara I'd known all my life and friends I'd grown up with. Everyhar was crying. A few times the harlings woke up and came to see what was going on, but they were just sent back to bed. They must have known something was happening though, because so many of them were being snatched from their beds and told to get dressed. I don't even know for sure, who was taken — different harlings of all ages. And then we were all standing outside, and the administrators were giving orders. They gave one last chance for us all to decide who would stay and who would leave. Before they left, Upsari said that I was in charge of the facility.

Five other hara stayed behind with me: Rosea, Hyacinth, Peony, Chrysanth, and Honey. We all stood by the gates and watched them leave until they disappeared into the woods beyond, where the road fades away. Rosea was so upset that he got sick. I suggested we try to get some sleep and that we go and wake up the oldest harlings right before dawn to tell them first what had happened.

But I never did go to sleep. I'm very tired, but I just can't relax. The thought of going to sleep seems ridiculous. I just lit a candle and wrote all this down. Now, it's starting to get light outside. I could write more, but I need to stop. I need to go and get the others so that we can tell the harlings who are old enough to help and then figure out what to do now.

The harlings did not take the news well. I don't know what I was expecting really. I was so busy being scared and shocked and worried, that I was not prepared to deal with their fears and grief. Thank goodness I'd had enough sense to tell the others to keep quiet about the orders to destroy us all. I just told them that the administrators had been sent away because of the war and they took most of the hostlings with them because they were needed at another facility. I didn't like lying to them, but I didn't want them to be terrified — it was scary enough just being left with no supplies and all these harlings to take care of.

We got together the oldest ones first — the seven- and eight-year-old Lilies who haven't gone through feybraiha. I told them how much we are going to depend on them since they know more about taking care of little ones and doing the chores that we need to keep things running. Once we started talking seriously about making teams and groups to get the work done and sharing ideas, they seemed to calm down a little and they really were very helpful and brave. It's strange — they look so grown up and know so much that I almost forget that they are still just harlings. I have to remind myself what a shock this is for them — they have never before felt like the entire world is changing around them.

Today I took care of small harlings for the first time since I went through feybraiha. It should have been a joy. If I had thought about it, I would have cherished the moment that I walked into that nursery and picked up a tiny harling for the first time in years. It might have occurred to me then that one of those harlings had to be one of my own, from my very last pearl. But, I was so busy trying to remember what needed to be done that I didn't even think about it until later. Actually, it was Pansea who pointed it out, because he was saying how happy he was to be able to be around them again, too.

I know it's selfish, but I must admit that I'm glad nohar chose Pansea as their harling to take away with them. I know Pansea would have liked the opportunity to see the world and maybe get his chance to be a consort without a breeding program. But, I'm still glad. I need him here with me. He's such a great help. Really, all the older harlings are. They're younger than us but they've taught so much to me and the other hostlings — things we'd forgotten and some things we never knew. I'm so grateful for each one of them.

Now on top of everything else, I'm sick. It's been this way ever since the others left. I'm tired all the time, but I can't sleep because I'm sore from work and I have too much to think about. I know I should eat, but the thought of food makes me feel ill, which is for the best since we have to save our food supplies. Anyway, when I do eat my body doesn't usually handle the food very gracefully. But, I feel weak from not eating — I get dizzy all the time. Sometimes I feel very hot and sometimes I feel very cold and I get aches — it's worse than hosting. I guess I shouldn't complain. At least I'm doing better than poor Rosea, who was already doing poorly before.

We are coping as well as can be expected. Most of the harlings seem to be more upset about their missing "lings" than the missing hara. I suppose that reaction makes sense considering none of them have been told the full truth and have no idea of the extent of the danger we're in. They've a vague idea that new hara will eventually show up to take over when times get better.

Of course, they're not completely convinced of this. Harlings are not stupid. The oldest Lilies are especially suspicious and I can sense that they are resentful of the hostlings who left. I can't blame them. I feel a little resentful myself, though I try not to be. Still, it hurts much more to be abandoned by dear friends than by hara from whom I didn't expect much better. But I can't allow myself to dwell on that. If I do then I'd constantly be in a bad frame of mind.

And oh how we must work to keep up a good frame of mind. I swear the building never used to be as noisy as it is these days. I constantly have a headache. There's so much tension in my body, Chrys said he could feel it coming off me in waves.

Thank goodness we're able to rely a good bit on the older harlings. Every Lily has been given assignments to help keep things running. We've formed a committee, together with the oldest and some of the most reliable, and meet regularly to come up with ideas and evaluate the various situations. It's been a real battle, though, to prod some Lilies into taking charge and thinking for themselves. I'm amused to note, however, that many of the Lilies who shunned Pansea for being outspoken before now tend to look to him as something of a leader.

Every time I think that things have gotten as bad as they can possibly get, something all the more terrible happens. Rosea has died. I didn't really see how weak he was. I was too busy looking after the harlings to really notice how he was sickly and struggling.

Well, that's not completely true. I knew that he'd been hurt by his last pearl delivery and I saw that he was struggling. We did our best to assign him tasks where he could sit as much as possible, because we could tell he was in pain, though he tried to hide it. But the last pearl deliveries had been hard on all of us, and since I recovered quickly and everyhar else seemed to also, I just assumed that Rosea would be all right. If only we'd known. I keep wondering that if he'd gone with the others, maybe he would have gotten help and been okay.

I found him this morning. I went looking for him when he didn't show up to help with breakfast. I knocked on his door, and when he didn't answer I got worried and went in. I'll never forget the way he looked lying there. He could have just been sleeping, half curled up on his side. He'd even taken the time to tie up locks of his hair in coils to set them in dark ringlets. But, his face was so pale. Not pale in a beautiful way, but sickly, like his skin had spoiled somehow.

And there was blood. I could smell it and saw it had seeped through his blanket. At first I thought that maybe he'd secretly been with pearl and had lost it, but I could find no evidence of that. I went to him right away and shouted his name and tried to shake him awake. He felt cold. I'd never heard anything about what a dead har looks or feels like, but somehow I knew. It was obvious and it was terrible.

I don't know how I made it through the day without collapsing into tears. I'd decided to keep Rosea's death a secret from the harlings. They've been through too much and I think this would push them beyond the limit. I told everyhar that he was very sick and asleep in his room and nohar was to disturb him for anything.

Later, I spoke to the other hostlings and told them the terrible truth. We met in his room after all the harlings were asleep. It had already begun to smell horrible. I had intended that we would sneak Rosea's body out of the building during the night and bury him just beyond the grounds, and then we'd just tell the harlings that Rosea had left to join the other hostlings because he was too sick to keep working here.

But, the others didn't want to go along with that. Hyacinth was very angry with me for suggesting it. He said that he would never tell a lie like that and let the harlings think that Rosea had abandoned them when he actually worked himself to death caring for them. I knew that Hyacinth was right. We'll have to tell them the truth. I just hope one of the others will be the one to explain it; I just can't.

It's strange how I was able to hold myself together until Honey broke the news to the Lilies in our meeting today. They refused to believe it at first.

I can't blame them; it seems so unreal. I'd never heard of anyhar ever dying except in battle.

I honestly don't think that Rosea himself had any idea that he would die. When we were wrapping him up to take him out and bury him, we found a pile of bloody clothes in his wastebasket. He must have been bleeding for a long time, maybe ever since his last delivery. But surely if he knew how sick he really was, he would have said something and not have hidden it? None of us ever imagined we would or could die like that.

Anyhow, the Lilies couldn't believe it either. Cirrus started shouting at us and screaming that it wasn't true and we were all liars. And then Glade just crumpled up and started sobbing in the most heartbreaking way. And that's when I started crying. I cried like I've never cried before in my life and I swear I didn't think I'd ever be able to stop.

Some of them took me into my room and I must have fallen asleep eventually. Pansea came and woke me up much later to bring me some soup and I felt terrible that I'd broken down that way. I felt like such a harling and there was Pansea trying to be comforting, saying that I'd been Rosea's friend since my first year and nohar blamed me for taking his death so hard. He said they'd all agreed I should take the day off and try to rest.

I feel a little guilty for it, but I've done just that – crying most of the time about Rosea and everything else too. Earlier tonight Hyacinth came up and offered to stay here in my room with me if it would make me feel better. We stayed up late, talking about old times, very long ago, when we were all young and together. Eventually it was Hyacinth who was crying and me rubbing his back.

He's asleep now. I suppose I should try to sleep too. I know I can't waste another day tomorrow.

Something truly horrible has happened. It all just makes me want to scream. One of the very small ones was terribly hurt a few days ago. (We call him Two because the youngest little harlings hadn't even been given proper tattoo codes before the administrators left, so we named them One through Ten.) I've been with Two almost constantly since then.

Even with being so overwhelmed, we've tried our very best pay special attention to smallest harlings, but somehow he managed to sneak out of the nursery and get into an empty classroom. There was the most horrible crash and then the most pitiable wail. Peony and I ran in there and saw a bookcase had fallen on Two. Probably he pulled it over by accident. Peony lifted that entire bookshelf off Two like it weighed nothing.

It was horrible the way Two's leg was all twisted. The bone had actually broken through the skin. I thought I would be sick for a moment. Thankfully, Two was pretty dazed and couldn't see how badly he was hurt. Peony picked him up and ran with him to the doctor's office, which made Two shriek over and over. I went too and Peony told me to find some medicine. I know there was a bottle of something that they used to give us to make us sleep when somehar needed stitches after a delivery. I went into the storage closet and just tore the place up looking for it. There's hardly any medicine left and most of what little there is here is a total mystery to all of us. I was able to find one bottle with a little of the sleeping medicine left in it.

In the meantime, some of the Lilies had come and one of them remembered that when a small harling had broken his wrist once, the doctors had wrapped bandages with straight wood around it, to keep it still while it healed. So we broke up a wooden chair and put the pieces around Two's leg, after we made him sleep with the medicine. We straightened out his leg as well as we could, but it just looked so terrible and his skin was so mangled and it felt very hot.

Two didn't wake up for a long time after that and we thought he might actually die. But later he woke up and he has hardly stopped moaning and sobbing since. I wish we had more medicine to give him. What's worse is that we might have what we need, but I don't know which bottle to use because we hostlings were never allowed to work with the medicines.

At one point, Hyacinth came in and told me that we ought to just put a pillow over his head and smother him so he wouldn't suffer. It was the most horrible thing I'd ever heard of. I started thinking that maybe it *was* the right decision to prevent Hyacinth from being a hostling. But I guess maybe having to be a worker all those years has made him think more harshly than the rest of us.

Besides, I hate to admit it, but there were moments when I actually was hoping that Two would die because the dear little thing was in so much pain and there was nothing that we could do for him. Thank goodness, he seems to be getting a little better now. I think he'll be all right after all.

I'm so exhausted. We're having so much trouble keeping up with all the little ones and managing everything else as well. At least we finally seem to have settled into something of a routine. There's so much I'd like to write about how wonderful the little ones are and how proud I am of the Lilies and how close I feel I've become to the other hara who have stayed here with me. But, I'm barely able to write; I'm so sleepy.

We hara had a meeting today and talked about how concerned we were that the supplies are running out and that we have no way to help anyhar who gets hurt or sick. Honey made the very good point that if soldiers were really going to come, then they probably would have done so already. He also said that us being a secret out here was going to be the end of us all.

Then Hyacinth spoke up and said that he knew there was a village that wasn't too far away. He said that the other kitchen hara he used to work with had passed through there when they first came here. He said that some of us should try leaving, in the same direction that the administrators had gone, and that probably we'd run right into the village and find some hara who would be willing to help us.

I didn't really like that idea. I was afraid that the hara in the village would simply alert the soldiers to our presence and have us killed. But Hyacinth said that most hara wouldn't be like that and that many would probably be willing to help us for the sake of the harlings, and those who didn't do it from the goodness of their hearts would help if we worked off our debt to them after. I must admit that he made a good argument. Then Honey pointed out that it should be done now, when the weather is good, rather than wait until we start getting more desperate and too weak to make the trip.

I don't really like this, but all of the other hara seemed to agree. I think it's what happened to Rosea, and then to Two, that has made the difference. Anyway, they seem determined and they feel very confident that they can find a town and convince somehar to help us. I can't stand the idea of losing more friends, but they have convinced me that it's for the greater good.

They feel pretty sure that they can be back soon, since the administrators hadn't packed lots of food or supplies when they left. So, they've decided that all the other hara will go, but I'll stay here with the older harlings to help me keep things running while they're gone.

It's been over a month. They should have come back by now. I can't believe that they would abandon us here. Something terrible must have happened to them.

Until now, I've refused to write my thoughts on paper, because somehow I thought that would make it real. But I can no longer deny that they are not coming back – not to myself and not to the harlings.

Some of the oldest Lilies have volunteered to go into the woods and look for them, but I have refused. I will not lose anyhar else. I cannot.

I never thought I would have to kill anything in my entire life, but then again, I never thought any of this would happen. Every day is something worse, like a nightmare, only it's real and I can't wake up. I never thought it could ever get this bad. I thought somehar would have come for us by now. But nohar has come and maybe nohar ever will come.

Two days ago, I had to kill our mule. I didn't think we could really use it for travel and we were having to give it food, which we really couldn't afford. Most importantly, we haven't had any meat in a long time. So I went out to the stables, knowing what I had to do. Whatever I felt about anything, I had to forget it.

I ordered all the older harlings to make sure everyhar stayed inside until I came back. I didn't want anyhar to hear it or see any blood. I even took a change of clothes, so when I came inside they wouldn't see. I wore my oldest, worst clothes. Having thought about it for a few days, I knew what other things I had to take with me. I had taken the wheelbarrow from the potting shed and filled it with heavy stones. I had also collected heavy pieces of wood from the edge of the forest. And from the kitchen, just before I went out, I took all the big knives I could find.

Everything in my whole mind and body was telling me I didn't want to kill that mule, but I made myself go in there. A while ago we named the mule Clover. Well, Clover looked at me and I almost think he knew what I was going to do and was scared. I couldn't even bear to say anything or look at Clover too much, just put down all my things and got to work. I went to the stall and I took the ropes there and tied him down, so there would be less of struggle. Then I took out a big rock, so big I had to use two hands and balance it on my hip, and I went over to Clover and I threw it down on his head as hard as I could.

It was worst moment. There was a thud and a crack and Clover bucked up, pulling on all the ropes, and made a horrible sound. Still, it obviously wasn't enough, so I had to try another rock. And another one. Each time there were horrible noises and eventually there was a lot of blood. The ropes almost came undone (and I was so scared Clover would get loose!) but by that point I was almost finished. Finally Clover fell over, but the body kept shaking, legs kicking, and so I had to keep taking the bloody rocks and smashing them onto the poor thing's head. I also used the big log and just batted it over and over. After a long time it finally seemed done.

Still, I knew I had to do more. I waited a while, to be sure there wasn't any more movement, and then I got to work with the knives. I thought if I sawed off the head then I would be sure Clover was dead. I threw up more than once while I was doing it. The body was still warm and there was blood everywhere. I cut and cut and cut. It was incredibly hard to cut through all those muscles and then all those other things I don't know anything about.   The stink was terrible.   I had to snap through tendons and bones and everything else, and there was a pool of blood, blood spattered all over. Some squirted all over my face and I screamed; I couldn't help it.

When I was done, I just wanted to run out of there, but as I was leaving I remembered the blood all over me, and I threw off my clothes and put on new ones. Then I did run out of there. I didn't want to do any more. I didn't want to do anything except kill myself for what I had done, even though I knew I'd had to do it. I ran back to the building. As soon as I went in, Pansea was there, where he'd been waiting and watching, and he stared at me. There was still blood on my face and hands and even in my hair. He was so frightened but I told him it was all right; we had meat to eat.

Later that day I took several of the older harlings in there and we cut the animal into pieces, then set about making it into dinner. Then we thought of ways to preserve what was left for later, like drying it or salting it. There were a few books in the kitchen that talked about it. I don't know if we did it all right, but at least that night we had a good soup. That is the only good thing about it.

Chapter Twelve

I'm so glad I've got this journal back — and just in time, too! Tomorrow morning I'm going with Swift to Immanion!

When Paran first talked about this at dinner tonight, my stomach just about leapt into my throat. I know the Gelaming have been very determined to have their way, but forcing me to leave here and go to their city? I never dreamt it. They said it was an invitation, from that Hegemony of theirs, but I know an order when I hear one. Besides, it's not like I have a choice, because of course, I must do everything I can for the harlings. And I guess if that means I have to ride with Swift on a magical horse, and go thousands of miles away to visit the home of the tribe that used to be my enemy... well, then I will.

A couple of hours ago, Swift visited me here in my room. I'm still not exactly sure what to make of him, since I'm still getting used to this new sort of hara, but I really believe he's going to try his best for me and the harlings. He seems determined, just like me, to keep us all here, where we belong, and then to just help us get back on our feet — not to move us away or study or change us like the Gelaming are saying.

Swift also described Immanion to me. Honestly, half the things he said about it sound like harling stories to me, they were so unbelievable. I can't imagine any place really being so big and then everything being so beautiful! A huge palace on a hill? Everything all white and full of light? The city's even on the water, with a harbor. I wonder if I will get to see all those water things we learned about as harlings, like coral and seagrass. I suppose it's funny that Coral and Seagrass and the others all left here while I stayed, but I bet I'll end up traveling further than any of them have.

I have trouble imagining all the hara there. Swift says the Gelaming soldiers here aren't entirely representative of the hara in the city. He talked to me about most Gelaming being even more "balanced." He also said that I shouldn't be too shocked if they are quite flirtatious or bold, but on the other hand many of them will probably be very condescending, and perhaps treat me almost like a harling. They may be more "balanced," but it sounds to me like most of the Gelaming are just very mixed up!

Anyway, we're leaving tomorrow morning. I think I'll make an announcement to the harlings during their breakfast breaks, so that they won't be upset when I'm suddenly not around. And then while we're eating, I'll have to talk with Cobweb about running things while I'm away. I'm glad that Swift thought of putting Cobweb in charge; I trust him more than any other har here.

Swift says the trip to Immanion will only take a short time, using the *sedim*. (I can't imagine what that will be like either and I'm afraid to think of it in case it keeps me up all night!) Once we get there, we'll probably only stay a few days — just go to have the meetings about the harlings and me. I'm kind of happy about that because I don't want to be away from here very long, no matter how the city turns out to be. Swift said he'll try to arrange for us to have a little tour maybe, but that's it. I suppose that's for the best, too. Hopefully, I'll be able to use what I learn to start teaching my harlings about the real world right away.

Even though it will probably be a short trip, I've spent the past hour working at packing my things. Actually, I had to borrow a travel bag from Cobweb since I've never gone anywhere in my life. The one he loaned me is beautiful, made of very fine black leather with all kinds of symbols and patterns worked into it. I still might change my mind tomorrow, but for now I've packed the orange silk outfit, two other blouses, two other skirts and a dress. I tried to pack only summer clothes, since Swift tells me it's warmer there, in Almagabra. Although, Cobweb also insisted on loaning me his lovely cloak. They said that traveling by *sedim* gets very cold no matter what the weather is like — I guess from flying around so fast! Oh, and yes, I packed a bit of jewelry and makeup, too. I may as well try and look nice since they're all going to be judging me. I won't look very Gelaming, I guess, but I couldn't look that way if I tried.

It's the middle of the night and I can't sleep. I did sleep a little at first but then I started dreaming about Immanion and when I woke up, I started thinking about riding a *sedu*. That sounds completely bizarre to me. Traveling around by magic? I hope I'm smart enough to do it. Swift says I don't have to worry since he'll be in charge, but I just can't imagine how it works or what it will feel like. In a way, I almost feel like it's the night before my feybraiha, I'm so nervous, wondering what will happen.

On another note, since I couldn't sleep, I just was lying in bed looking through this diary. Reading through it now, I feel like saying what Cobweb says — "By Ag!" Some of my ideas about the world, especially from when I was a harling, are just so silly. When I look at the older Lilies now, I can see they are already a lot smarter than I was about things. They seem to know more about how the world really is. I hope they keep on learning.

But now, I've got to go to bed. Even if it's not a long trip, I want to be at my best.

This has to have been the longest, strangest, most busy day of my entire life! I'm in Immanion, and it so much like what Swift said. I'm not so sure what to think about the hara, but the city is just amazing.

Even though I'm very tired now, I really want to tell it all from the beginning, right from this morning. Just like we planned, Swift and I got up early and met with Cobweb. I gave him instructions on how I wanted things done, as well as what I did not want done. I was a little nervous that Cobweb would be annoyed with all my rules, but he seemed to approve of my being thorough and even asked about a few details I'd overlooked. I also told him the Gelaming aren't to do any "studies" on the harlings or start teaching them anything especially "Gelaming." Swift was adamant about this too. Cobweb said he'd go around and observe everything to make sure our wishes are obeyed.

Next, I waited around in the dining hall to talk to the harlings. Breakfast is the one meal where the oldest harlings eat first, so they can get started on tasks early and the younger harlings can get more sleep. Today things got pretty disorganized, because many of the harlings stayed through more than one meal shift because so many were asking me questions — once they started asking about when I was coming back, it seems like they felt the need to ask me all sorts of questions that had been preying on their minds. I tried to answer as best I could, but without frightening the younger harlings.

Unfortunately, I didn't get a chance to talk to our new young hara, because they did not come down for breakfast at all. I suppose it's for the best since they should still be enjoying their first arunas and not worrying about Hegemony meetings.

Finally, Swift, who was coming back from meeting with his own hara, said that we had no more time for me to answer questions. At that point, I sat down with Two while he was finishing his breakfast and explained to him about the trip and how he'd have to be gone a few days. At first, he was upset about having to leave his lings, and frightened, too, but Swift told him he was sure the Gelaming would be able to fix his leg and then he couldn't help but want to go. He also was pleased when we told him the har he'd be riding with would be Branad, the Gelaming who'd been working in the nursery a little. Two seems to get along surprisingly well with that soldier.

Once outside, we were met by Branad, who had gotten the special horses ready. With him was a group of Lilies wishing us goodbye and good luck. Looking back, I almost wonder if I should have taken some of them with us, so they could see all this, but at the time I hadn't thought of it. We all just hugged and went to the stables.

Swift's horse, Afnina, is such a magnificent creature and I was somewhat excited about the chance to ride her, but with my skirt and not having any experience, I was terribly clumsy. With help from Branad and Swift, I finally managed to get on her back. After that, Swift rode around the yard very slowly, so I could get used to it. It was the first of many things I had to get used to. Two seemed to bond with Branad's horse, or I guess I should call it a *sedu*, instantly and was chattering to it like crazy, naturally!

Then came a surprise. The night before, Swift and I had only talked of he and I, Branad and Two going on the trip, but when we made it out from the fruit grove, we were met by Paran. I tapped Swift on the shoulder and said, "Is he coming too?" Paran had a travel bag so the answer was obvious but Swift still said yes. I looked over at Paran and smiled, even though, really, I was not happy at all he was coming. That other important Gelaming, Edrei, seems much nicer and wouldn't fight us so much, but I guess he was too busy with Lita to go.

"Well, shall we be off, then?" Paran asked us. "I hope it's not too uncomfortable a trip for you, Lisia," he added, coming up close to me, "but we do think it's important for you to make this visit."

After giving some basic instructions to Two and me, Swift had all three horses line up at the end of the field. Branad called me over to help him with Two, who needed to be put on the horse a special way, because of his hip and being so small. He couldn't sit on the horse properly at all. Fortunately, Branad had thought up a clever sort of sack to wear across his front. I helped put Two inside and told him not to worry, which is funny because *I* was getting so nervous. Once I was done, Swift told me to hold on to him tightly, around the waist. And then we were off!

Well! Then came the incredible part. I don't really know if I have the words to describe what the trip was like. At first, we were just riding, but then I got this strange feeling that things looked funny and then... I couldn't see properly at all and it was like I'd gone into a dreamworld. Actually I shouldn't say it was a dream, but just like going someplace very, very strange. In a way, it was like aruna or even conceiving a pearl. All reality was different, my body didn't exist; I didn't know where I was. There were colors and shapes all around me, fields of flowers, sounds like voices that I couldn't understand. I couldn't even think during it, I was so overwhelmed. All I could do was feel it and wonder — and hold on tight!

Then, after what was quite a short time, as Swift had promised, suddenly it all began to fade and I was in the real world again... although it was hard to know for sure. Immanion is hardly the "real world" I'm used to.

We landed in a special field they have dedicated to comings and goings of the *sedim*. It's a meadow, sort of like the ones at home, but the things around it are nothing like anything I've ever seen! We were right near the palace Phaonica, and it hurt my neck to actually look at it all, with its tall spires and turrets. I had to squint my eyes against the light and the bright white stone shining in the sunlight. All around us, the buildings were white and perfect. Down the hill, the buildings just went on and on. I would have stared at it for probably a whole minute, but then Swift asked, "So what do you think?"

I turned to him and said, "It's incredible, beautiful; just like you said."

He laughed and said, "True, but I meant 'What did you think about the otherlanes — the traveling?'"

He had the widest grin when he asked that, and I couldn't help but smile in return and exclaim, "That was the most amazing thing I've ever done!" Then I realized that he looked funny. "Are you cold, Swift? There's ice all over your cloak!"

He just shook his head and said, "Yours too."

I looked down and he was right. I'd been so enthralled by everything that I hadn't even felt cold! But then I remembered little Two. Just then I heard him demand, "Let me down! This bag is cold and all crunchy... and I want to see the flowers!"

I turned my head and saw Branad getting down from his horse with Two squirming in his sack. Swift said, "Shall we?" and got down before me, then offered me his hand. Once again I was awkward and my skirt got tangled in the stirrup, but I didn't fall.

Once I was standing, I said, "I can't believe it. This is really Immanion?"

Swift nodded. "No place else like it."

That was when Paran appeared. "So, Lisia, impressed?"

Honestly I was, but I didn't want to be too nice to him so I just said, "Well, yes, so far, but I'm not just judging the buildings, am I?"

By then, Two had gone over to the side of the meadow to look at some flowers – so different from the ones we grow at home. Swift, Paran and I walked over to where Branad was standing, watching. I'd never seen flowers like them before, and even said so. Paran reminded me of just how far away from Megalithica we are, how the plants and flowers in various parts of the world are different, just like the hara are different in some ways. I guess that's a good way to think of it, but it would be nice if hara like Paran remembered that nobody tries to change how flowers are.

My, but this journal entry is going to take forever to write if I go into such detail about every little thing! Maybe I can speed up a little? Let's see, first we brought the *sedim* to a stable to be cared for, then we took our packs and went into the streets of Immanion. I think that overwhelmed me just as much as seeing the Phaonica and all the buildings. I kept bumping into carts and hara and things, because I was looking all around, trying to take everything in and even just figure out what was what. I've seen books with pictures of streets, read a few stories set in towns or cities, but I hadn't really any idea what it all looked like. Now that I've seen it, I don't think the city life is for me at all, but I can see how some hara might find it very exciting.

Paran led us to a tavern, where he said we could have drinks and something to eat before going up to the palace. At that point I took charge of Two, whose eyes had got so big I was sure he was even more overwhelmed than I was. The inside of the tavern was strange to me, just like the outside had been. There were all kinds of furniture and decorations I'd never seen the like of before. Even the smell of the cooking was different. We waited for a moment and then a har came up and guided us to a table by a window.

I could hardly decide what to look at — the fruit market across the street, with all the fruits I'd never heard of, or the har standing by the table. The har was very, very Gelaming. His hair was blond and went long down his back, like a hostling's, but his clothes didn't match being a hostling at all. I wouldn't say they were soldier clothes, but they were different and not like those that the administrators and staff used to wear. He wore a lot of leather, similar to what soldiers wear, but he didn't act like a soldier at all. And his leather was different from any kind I'd ever seen. It was very, very tight — it couldn't possibly have been comfortable — and almost shiny. And yet his shirt didn't seem to match — it was puffy and silky. It didn't seem practical at all! Paran ordered us all drinks, and when the har walked to the counter the way he walked reminded me of Vlaric — almost like a hostling but not.

I had so many questions, but I didn't want to appear foolish — especially not in front of Paran. So, I tried to act as if I ate in a tavern in a big city every day. Fortunately, Two had no such reservations and began asking question after question about everything he'd seen. I expected the other hara to be annoyed with this, but they seemed to find him quite amusing and soon they were telling us both all about life in the city. I actually found myself relaxing and having a very good time. After a few minutes, during which we were all chitchatting, the har came back with drinks. Thankfully mine wasn't alcohol, because I'm sure being drunk was more than I needed, given how the city was making me feel.

At that point, I had a bit of an awkward moment. I had Two sitting in my lap and while the server har was pouring my juice, he said to Two, "You've got such pretty, dark curls! You must take after your other parent, then."

I froze then, feeling hideous, and didn't know what to say. Fortunately Swift spoke up and said "Yes, perhaps" and made the har go away by asking for something extra for his drink.

The next few hours were a blur. Once we were done eating (sandwiches filled with all sorts of exotic ingredients I'd never tasted), Paran led us up and up towards Phaonica. The closer we got, the bigger it got, until we were going through the gates and I felt like a little ant compared to what was around me. This place is absolutely like nothing I have ever dreamed of. As we went in, the colors were black and gold, and all around, everything was made of different kinds of stone and carved in beautiful patterns, shining and polished. There were huge towers and hallways, and steps going up and down. It was hard to believe any hara could actually live there.

When we got to the entrance some very serious-looking hara were standing there. When Paran said who we were, they said that we were expected and became very courteous. We were shown into a very grand hallway, where we waited for just a minute before another har came to show us to the rooms where we would be staying. I was a little flustered — I knew we'd be coming here, but I didn't know that we would be staying *in* the palace! I guess that's the benefit of traveling with an important har like Swift.

Oh, I should mention a little bit about what the inside of the palace looks like. Actually, I could probably write for pages and pages about it, but I'm getting tired of all this writing so I'll make it short. Everything was bright and shiny — there was polished marble all over — walls and floors. All of the metal seemed to be gold and all the furniture was shaped very strangely — lots of exotic woods that looked like they just grew into the right shapes. I couldn't see how anyhar had actually put them together. But it was all very comfortable.

Even though Paran and Swift both did their best, pointing out our surroundings and explaining things, I was quite dazed until we reached the guest quarters. That's when Paran said he would go to General Aldebaran to announce our arrival and get some details on the meeting and the procedure for Two's healing.

As soon as he was gone, I went to the bed and stretched out. Such a wonderful bed it was! Two came over and snuggled right next to me.

Swift and Branad sat on the other bed. "So, what do you think?" Swift asked.

I told him it was all very interesting, especially the buildings, but again, I'm wasn't going to just judge the buildings.

"Good idea," Swift agreed. Then he and Branad said they were going to their own separate rooms, which were across the hall.

Two had a nap for almost an hour but I tried to and couldn't. Finally the har who had shown us to our rooms came back to take us on a very nice tour of most of Phaonica. It's funny that I could hardly sleep at all then — I kept waking up thinking about everything and full of energy, but I can hardly stay awake right now. I guess I really should stop this entry and go to sleep. Hopefully, I can catch up writing tomorrow, maybe in the morning. I definitely must continue on, though, so much happened after that!

Well, lucky me, I've woken up in the middle of the night, sleepless, but I can still write, thanks to these wonderful Gelaming lamps. Swift pointed out how to use them when we first got here. They're round like moons and all you do is press them and they come on and make a nice soft glow. It's perfect for writing but at the same time, it's not so bright that it'll wake up Two.

Anyway, now's the time to write about the rest of yesterday. Let me start around mid-afternoon. That's when Paran came by and told us the "agenda" for the day. First, Two would be taken to the infirmary. In the meantime, I was invited to tour the gardens, which he was sure I'd enjoy. Finally, we'd all get together for dinner and then a reception with members of the Hegemony. Swift rolled his eyes at some of this, since apparently the Gelaming are masters of trying to impress hara with their way of life, but I was polite and once I had taken a moment to fix my hair, I said I was ready to go.

Branad knew where the infirmary was and, as Two is fine with him, I was happy to let them go off together, while Paran led me on a tour of the "unparalleled" gardens. I must admit, he hadn't exaggerated. Even if you compare them with how our gardens *used* to be, before the bad times, the ones at Phaonica are quite wonderful. Most of them have a different style to the ones back home, being more formal in layout, but flowers are still flowers and the Gelaming's are so healthy.

We must have been visiting different gardens for an hour when suddenly something happened to change our plans. The garden we were in was actually a bit wilder than the other ones we'd seen, with bushes all growing together and tall vines growing up trees. I was looking at flowers like Lilies of the Valley when somehar (I never got his name but his hair was dyed the most amazing shade of blue) came up to us and said, "Excuse me, are you tiahaar Lisia? I was just looking for you!"

I couldn't imagine how anyhar in Immanion would know me, but then he started explaining that the healer from the infirmary had sent him. Immediately I was worried, thinking something was suddenly wrong with Two, but he said no, it wasn't that, but there was a doctor who needed to talk to me. The har, who said he was a healer too, brought us all to the infirmary, which was quiet and had walls in a lovely soft almost-white color. We went down a hallway into a room with more of those glowing lamps like in my room. Two was lying on a very comfortable-looking bed and Branad was sitting on the end of it.

The doctor got my attention right away. He had very dark skin and, with the white robe he was wearing, was one of the most striking hara I'd ever seen. "Ah, you must be tiahaar Lisia. Come, have a seat."

I sat down and the har introduced himself as tiahaar Sheeva, chief surgeon at the infirmary. He had just completed an examination of Two and had formed an opinion on how best to heal him, but before just going ahead, he wanted to talk to me and get permission.

This was another surprise. It never occurred to me that the doctors would talk to me about how to fix Two's leg. After all, they are the experts and not me! It kind of made me nervous — like I was somehow going to be responsible if Two didn't get better.

I got even more nervous when Sheeva started explaining things to me. He told me that after looking at the hip, he decided he'd have to reset the joint and then heal it back. I asked him what he meant by "reset" and he said it meant they'd have to break it, then make it go back how it should be. My first reaction was that of course they couldn't do that, it was too horrible and painful, but then Swift and Paran and Branad all nodded at the surgeon. Two wouldn't feel much pain, Sheeva said — he'd have hara taking all the pain away and making him feel like he was someplace far away and happy. Plus there were medicines they could use.

"Really, Lisia, I've had surgery myself," Paran said. "and trust me, it can be done with only the smallest amount of pain."

Swift was smarter than to say that — much smarter. He said, "Lis, I know what you're thinking, about the doctors you grew up with, but I swear, this one isn't lying to you."

I had to think about it for some time, but Swift was confident in Sheeva and so I believed him. I said okay to it, but I insisted that I be in the room with Two when they did it. I told them that I'd put a stop to it if they were hurting him too much! They scheduled the surgery for the day after tomorrow... well, the day after today. We should be done with our meetings by then.

We were all just starting to leave when Sheeva came up to me and asked if I'd stay behind in the room for just a moment so he could speak to me. It was for something private. Swift said they'd wait for me by the front. Once they'd gone, Sheeva asked me to have a seat again and then he brought up something I did not expect at all, although now that I think about it, I was incredibly stupid not to have. He asked me about making pearls. Specifically, he asked me if I would talk to him about it and let him examine me. "Anyhar who can open the cauldron of creation at will is somehar I certainly want a look at!"

I'm sure he didn't think there was anything wrong with asking this, but I got very angry with him. "You want to study me?" I said to him. "Well, the reason I came here is because I don't want to be studied. Not me, and not my harlings."

Sheeva argued with me, gently actually, and said I have knowledge beyond that of almost all hara. "So much is unknown to us," he said.

I said it wasn't "unknown" to me, but that at the moment, I didn't feel like teaching anyhar — especially not the Gelaming. I just want to be myself.

Sheeva didn't argue anymore, but simply said I should think about it. He's been trying to learn about Wraeththu reproduction for a long time and he would keep trying in the future, he said. "Perhaps sometime later, you and I can talk again."

Well, after that, I wasn't too eager to stay in that office, so I left quickly and met up with the others. I didn't say anything about what I'd been asked and they didn't pry, though from the way Swift looked at me, I suspect he could tell I was flustered. Paran told us that it was late and we ought to go back to our guest quarters to get ready for the evening. He'd come to get us when it was time to leave.

Branad took Two out to the gardens for a while, so that I could have the room to myself to bathe and pin up my hair without distractions. I'm really glad I had that time alone, because it gave me a chance to really think about what Sheeva had asked of me. All day, I'd been feeling so ignorant and helpless, even though I tried to hide it. And even though Sheeva made me angry, I realized that despite what everyhar has told me about how anyhar can make a pearl — I'm starting to get the idea that maybe I really *am* special, or at least all of us "project" hostlings are. I know something that the mighty Gelaming don't — I know how to control the "cauldron of creation" better than they can! I bet I know more about a lot of other things too — like hosting and deliveries and even taking care of harlings. It turns out that I was happy for what Sheeva had asked. For the first time in a very long time, I really began to feel the power that I have as a hostling.

Of course, that feeling didn't last very long once I got to that big fancy Gelaming dinner. Now let me just skip straight away to that, because that was the most amazing part. Paran showed up and escorted us. He told us were going to one of the "smaller dining halls" used for entertaining representatives from visiting tribes. Well, if that was a "small" dining hall, I think their big ones must have to be in separate buildings! Also, even though Paran said it was going to an "intimate gathering," there were about fifty hara there, all Gelaming. Only some of them were Hegemony, and at first I didn't know which. To me everyhar there was like an exotic bird or a jewel. I was truly dazzled by the crowd.

I worked hard to give a good impression, but I didn't talk to anyhar because seeing all of them made me painfully aware of how ignorant I am of what "normal" hara are like. And besides that, I know that I look simply dreadful after all these months of hard work. I didn't want to call attention to myself, so I just stayed at the sidelines of the gathering with Swift.

In the meantime, Swift had asked Branad to look after Two again, saying he didn't want me to be distracted during this special night. Not be distracted? I was relieved when hara started to take their places at the tables, because then they all stopped moving around. But then I realized something awful — Swift was a special guest and so we all had to sit at this big table way out in front of everyhar! I felt so conspicuous — like everyhar there was judging me and thinking of me as simple and plain. When the food was served, it turned out to be distracting too, which is good because I was able to stare down at my plate and not look at all the hara staring at me. The Gelaming food was, as I should have expected, something quite different than what I'm used to. Paran told me I've been raised on "rustic food" and that what we had was "cuisine." I agree there was a difference, though I didn't like everything put before me.

As soon as we were through with dinner, a little band came in and began to play some music, though not the kind of music for dancing, which would have been fine since I can dance very well. But this was a kind of soft gentle music that seemed to encourage all the hara to get up and walk around talking again. I think I would have been happy just to watch the musicians — they had such strange, elaborate instruments — nothing like the simple things we'd grown up with. At the same time, lots of wine and other kinds of liquor were brought out on trays and along the side of the room they set up long table all covered in sweets. "Go try some," Swift said, and sent Two along with me.

To my surprise, when I got to the table, hara made room for us. "You first, tiahaar Lisia," said one of them, a har with beautiful tawny hair. For a moment I was dazzled (these Gelaming have a magic power to dazzle) but then Two was up at the table reaching for desserts, so I went after him.

Once Two and I had our plates heaped with food, I turned back to where our table had been, only to find the tawny-haired har touching me on the shoulder. "Excuse me, wait a moment, tiahaar, I'd like to talk."

This was what the reception was for, talking, so I smiled and followed him to a table. The har introduced himself as tiahaar Chrysm, a member of the Hegemony. Immediately I became as poised as I could, since he's one of those I'm talking to tomorrow at the meeting. So, after some small talk about the desserts and telling Two how pretty he is, Chrysm said to me, "I've been hearing a lot about you." He'd read reports from Paran and Ashmael of course.

I was actually thankful for all that training I'd received for talking to the soldiers who came for aruna. I didn't get nervous at all. I just let him lead the conversation so he'd feel smart. I expected him to ask me about making pearls or moving the harlings. I was prepared in my mind with what I would say in turn, but he just asked me about what I thought of Immanion and all these new hara. He must have guessed what I was thinking, because after a while he said he wasn't going to ask me about any details, just wanted to know me "as a har." I saw Swift watching from a distance and he was smiling encouragingly, so I let myself relax.

After that, Chrysm and I talked for a long time. Mainly we talked about Immanion. I told him all I'd done, everything I've just been writing, except about what Sheeva said. Chrysm was easy to talk to, so easy I almost forgot a couple of times he's Gelaming. Anyway, finally he offered to take me around the room and introduce me. I asked about Swift, and Chrysm said Swift would be busy doing some "politicking." Sure enough, I did see him with a group of hara talking together quite intently. I took Two back to Branad and Chrysm led me round the various groups of hara. I met everyhar there, I think, or at least they met me. By the end of it, I'd become less dazzled, as I'd got used to all the elegant clothes and silver jewelry they seem to like so much.

But just as I was getting used to things, in came the most incredible looking har I'd ever seen! He wasn't very tall, but it was obvious he was of very high rank. General Aldebaran was standing beside him, and although he's very impressive himself, beside this new har, he looked almost understated. This har had more jewelry than any hostling ever did at home! His earrings were enormous black and silver teardrops and around his neck, across his chest really, he wore a matching necklace of teardrops all hung together. His shirt and pants were of silver and his arms were hung with bracelets. Oh, and his hair, light blond, was all perfectly coifed, with another great big teardrop pendant hanging down onto his forehead.

Before I could ask "Who's that?" I got my answer.

That's the Tigrina, Caeru Meveny, Chrysm said, speaking directly into my mind. I stepped away from him, surprised he'd done that, and then he said (into my mind again), *Excellent, you have natural ability.*

I didn't have time to think about this special mindtouch, however, because soon the whole reception turned into something more. The groups shifted around, some moving towards the Tigrina, some away. Chrysm took me to talk with groups closer and closer, until finally we were just one group away. And then Caeru stopped what he was saying and came over to us!

Considering how all my life I've idolized high-ranking hostlings, this was a big moment for me, so big it almost didn't seem real. It didn't even matter to me that this was a Gelaming hostling and not a Varr, I just thought, "This is what I always wanted to be." How wonderful the Tigrina looked. I wondered how long he'd spent on his makeup; it was so perfect. In the meantime he began speaking to me, friendly talk that I could tell was meant to impress those around him. Some of it was jokes I didn't understand, but other parts I did, and I was most polite in everything I said. In fact, I was just thinking to myself how well the meeting was going when suddenly the Tigrina asked me something that shocked me. "So, tiahaar," he said, moving closer to me and holding a large wine glass, "do you see anyhar here you'd like to host pearls for?"

I didn't answer him at all, just pretended I was either confused or just really didn't "see anyhar." What kind of question was that? Honestly I was angry. That seems like a very undiplomatic thing to say to somehar. As if I'm here in Immanion looking to make pearls! And I thought the Gelaming were supposed to be aghast at the very idea anyway!

Thankfully, Chrysm was sensitive enough to talk our way away from the Tigrina with the minimum of politeness. And then, even better, he managed to move me across the room, to a door that led out to a terrace. "Go have a look at the view," he said. "Have some fresh air. You could use a rest from all that, I think."

I thanked him and turned away. The view was predictably impressive, overlooking a great swathe of the city and the harbor besides. But my mind wasn't really on the view, it was on Caeru and what he'd said to me. I suppose that, without realizing it, I must have thought he might be the one Gelaming with whom I could relate, like I did with Cobweb, but it was not to be. Why must everyhar only ever think about that one thing? First, all the Varrs who raised me, then Ashmael and Paran, then Sheeva, and then the Tigrina.

"A bit lacking in judgment at times, aren't they?" a new voice said.

I whirled to the right and there was a har even more incredible (is there some other "bigger" word?) than the Tigrina. He was standing at the side of the terrace, where vines were growing up from below and white flowers were blooming. He was very tall, with red hair like flames, even flying up on top like fire does. I just stood there stupidly a moment and then I nodded. "Yes, some were rude to me."

He stepped toward me and it was an effort for me not to back away. He was certainly the tallest har I'd ever seen. And he was certainly Gelaming. "I'm sorry about that, Lisia," he said. "I hate to see you suffer after all you've been though."

That made me suspicious. "I've never met you before," I said, feeling bolder than I'd felt most of the night. "I'm sure I would remember it. You weren't inside just now. Who are you? And how do you know who I am?"

He laughed then. He had lot of white teeth. "Who am I? Oh, just a visitor. I don't want anyhar to know I'm here." He stepped towards me again and put a hand on his chin, seeming to study me. "And how do I know who you are? Well, that's simple. I've heard your name over and over, and I wanted to meet you.

Then the conversation got strange. "You care for your harlings?" he asked.

I asked him if he meant all the harlings left at home or just the ones whose pearls I created, because I didn't know which were mine, I cared for all of them.

"I understand, he said. "I have many, many children myself, though not all of them are mine. I can't control what they do. And often they are without mercy and do terrible things."

I couldn't work out what he was saying, except maybe he had been a hostling himself, but before I could ask him any questions, there was a sound behind me, and I turned to look. I thought it would be Chrysm or somehar else, but there was nohar there. When I turned back to ask the redheaded har to explain what he meant, he was gone!

In some ways, I think maybe I just had too much wine or was overtired, but then again, I think I only had two glasses, which shouldn't affect anyhar like that. In any case, I just sort of looked around for a minute, even down from the balcony, looking for where the har could have gone. I didn't see him anywhere, though, and there wasn't even a plant moving or anything to show he'd even been there. Finally I just shook myself and went back to the party. Things had actually died down a bit, some hara were leaving, and I told Swift I'd like to go back to our rooms, and besides Two really needed to go to sleep. Swift asked Branad to take us back. I guess he still had more "politicking" to do.

And here I am. I wonder what time it is. It's still dark out, I can see out the window, so hopefully I'll have some hours more to sleep. I will need to be strong today, for as that strange har said, sometimes hara can be without mercy.

Chapter Thirteen

Swift came to my room early this morning to tell me what to expect in the Hegemony meeting and to discuss our presentation a little more. He also said that he had heard about what the Tigrina had said to me last night and that I shouldn't take his words too seriously.

I just said to him, "Well, if that's the Gelaming's idea of a hostling, then it's no wonder that Paran and the others treated me the way they did! And to think how we were taught to aspire to that sort of thing!"

Swift just sort of shook his head and said, "Well, now you know a little more of the truth, Lis. In fact, I don't know that many, but aside from Seel, I've never met a consort who was happy with his relationship or his role. That aspiration was just another myth."

I'm glad he told me that, because it just makes me even more determined that my harlings will be free to learn and make their own way in life. I'm actually eager to go into this meeting.

I don't think I've ever been more nervous in my entire life and that's really saying something, given all that I've done and been put through. We've finally made our presentation before the Hegemony. Now we're waiting in this very ornate room (I swear I don't know why these Gelaming must make all the ceilings so high — you'd think they were giants — but, then maybe that's the point).

At any rate, I feel that we really did a good job of presenting our opinions and I can't see how the Gelaming could go against what we said. It wasn't at all easy, though. I really had to fight for it and definitely so did Swift. I suspect that this could be just as big a victory for him as it is for me and the harlings — or a defeat. But, I shouldn't think about defeat right now. I want to describe everything that was said while I still remember it clearly.

And very much was said. I hate that it's taking so long for them to make a decision, but we have given the Hegemony a lot to think about. Besides, Swift told me that even if they decide right away, they'll make us wait for a few hours and pretend like it was a tough decision!

We started work early in the morning, just after breakfast. Swift sat down with me and we had a talk about what it was the Gelaming were planning and what we wanted instead. It's funny, I think Swift was surprised by some of the ideas I'd developed just since yesterday. He simply seemed to be against moving, but he didn't have any idea what to do if we stayed. But I did. And, he really liked my ideas, too.

So, unlike what I expected, I was able to go into the meeting feeling pretty confident. There we were, in a fancy conference room, with a giant table and a ceiling lamp made out of glass, and I thought, "Okay, I'm with the governor of Megalithica, and he and I will do our best."

Once Swift and I were seated, I was introduced to all seven members of the Hegemony. They all had very impressive names, but the only ones I can remember are Ashmael (of course), Chrysm, Cedony and a name starting with an E. I think I only remember Cedony because of his eyes and hair, which were an orange color like I'd never seen. Anyway, Paran was there too, representing more of the army perspective and prepared to offer his opinions about what he'd observed back at the facility.

Naturally, unlike the dinner and reception last night, this gathering was formal and businesslike. Ashmael was in charge and gave a summary of what we would be discussing first. "Do we allow this Varr atrocity simply to remain in place and heal itself, or do we make the best of it by taking it apart, learning from it, and helping those left behind?"

I wanted to answer him right away and say "What's wrong with the first option?" But instead I sat and listened as Ashmael continued.

First he offered up a summary of his own discoveries on his visit, which I'm sure everyhar there had already heard. After that, he let Paran speak, updating everyhar with what had already been fixed and what they'd discovered. Most of what he said was what I had expected and not that inaccurate, like about how the water supply had been mended and how they'd discovered the secret to the records, but then he got to talking about the hara.

Well, that's when I had to speak up. Paran actually had the nerve to call my harlings "brainwashed" and "neglected," right in front of me! I didn't want to talk out of turn but when I looked at Swift, he gave me a look that said, "Go ahead."

So I said, "Excuse me, but what do you mean by that?"

Paran didn't seem too upset I had interrupted, and in fact I think he expected it. So he answered, "The older harlings have all been taught according to the same Varr teachings you were."

And I said, "Well, yes and no, they're being taught differently now already." I explained to the Hegemony about the feybraiha ceremony we'd just had, and how even the aruna had been different.

Paran didn't take that as a good argument, however. "But I don't just mean aruna, Lisia, I mean their outlook altogether, how they dress and how they act."

This is exactly what Swift told me he thought might happen — Paran was all concerned about hara being too soume! I was not about to apologize, however. I actually stood up because Paran was standing already and I wanted to be as tall as him. "You say you have a problem with their outlook altogether and how they dress and act. Well, that seems flawed to me on a number of levels. First, it's stupid to assume that my harlings are 'brainwashed' just because of the way they're dressed. Tiahaar Swift, and even Paran himself, have told me that there are many different tribes of Wraeththu, with just as many different ways of acting and dressing. I've been told that this 'diversity' is supposed to be something we should admire. So, if my own tribe, the Parasiel, don't have a problem with our being a little different, why should you?

"Secondly, you can't very well expect all the harlings to magically obtain new clothes and a completely new way of acting overnight, simply because the Gelaming army happened to show up! Maybe you have the ability to produce finery and fancy clothes out of thin air with magic, but it's unfair to expect everyhar else to. You're judging us when we're not even at our best! Once we have the materials we need and have had time to teach the harlings about the outside world, I'd certainly allow them to adopt whatever clothes and 'balanced' mannerisms they like. That is *if* they want to change when the options are presented to them. Some hara just feel more comfortable accentuating the soume half of their natures and it's very likely that this will simply be more comfortable and familiar for many of my harlings."

I paused then and continued, "There isn't anything wrong with that, tiahaar, is there?" I looked around the table then and saw all the Gelaming looking uncomfortable. "Is there?" I asked again.

Chrysm was the one who answered me finally, I think because we talked last night. "Ideally, hara should be living to their fullest potential, that potential being both soume and ouana." He then repeated a whole bunch of things I remember both Paran and Swift explaining to me about Wraeththu.

"That's very nice," I said, "but really I don't see how it matters."

Paran stiffened in his chair. "Of course it matters!"

I asked him if the Gelaming had gone and moved all the Varrs in Megalithica into special schools. Ashmael spoke up then, saying of course they hadn't, because that was different.

"How?" I asked.

Ashmael then told me that they couldn't hope to recreate a whole culture at once. It would take years for the Parasiel to adjust.

This was when Swift chose to stand and add his voice to the debate. "Years, you say? That's interesting," he said. "And they don't have to be closely supervised by the Gelaming throughout the process? Why is it, then, that you desire to do this for the harlings at the breeding facility?"

Ashmael looked most annoyed then and he said, "As you well know, harlings don't have years in which to adapt to new ideas. They simply grow up too fast, and if they retain this brainwashing into adulthood, it will be all the more difficult for them to adjust to the real world. We simply cannot take the risk that they will be further contaminated by Varrish indoctrination. Can you imagine how difficult your rule would become once an entire generation of these engineered harlings come of age?"

Swift had the most interesting expression then. He seemed to become taller somehow, and older. He said, "Ah yes, this all comes back to the 'Varr problem,' doesn't it? And yet you've actually made my argument for me, tiahaar. Continued Varrish indoctrination would complicate *my* rule — not yours. I most certainly concede that the harlings need to be protected, and supported, and properly educated. This term 'brainwashing' has been bandied about quite a lot lately and I really think it's misplaced. The harlings have been taught according to the standards of their tribe at the time. Their tribe is now Parasiel, and I will see to it that they are taught according to our standards, which you must agree are mostly in tune with those of the Gelaming. And, even if you don't agree, is it really any of your business?"

Ashmael seemed very put out. By that point Paran and I were both sitting down again. It was almost fun to watch Swift talk. A few of the Hegemony members looked rather taken aback by Swift's words, but most of them showed no reaction. These were definitely formidable hara and it would take more than Swift's impassioned arguments to change their minds. After pausing to consider Swift's words for a moment, Ashmael said, "I think you underestimate your tribe, Swift. If the Gelaming didn't consider Megalithica to be our business, then we wouldn't be there rooting out defunct breeding facilities to begin with."

Swift paused to drink some water and then told Ashmael, "I like to think of the Gelaming presence in Megalithica as mutually beneficial. I am grateful for much of the assistance you have given me and my hara. However, if our alliance is to continue, our relationship must be one of mutual respect."

Then the har with the E name got all haughty and said, "I was unaware that showing an interest in the well-being of harlings showed a lack of respect."

I couldn't help but speak up again at that. I said, "Maybe not, but when you imply that we don't want what's best for them, or that we aren't capable of taking care of them — well nothing else could be more hurtful or degrading!"

Swift turned to me and nodded slightly to acknowledge what I'd said, then turned back to the Hegemony and said, "If I've learned one thing about my hara, the Parasiel, these past months, it's that they are passionate. They are also quite stubborn and naturally independent. As sensible hara, they are open to good ideas when they're presented to them and they are quite capable of embracing change when it suits them. But if those changes are forced on them by outside authority figures, they will fight against them. It doesn't matter if it's military aid, or political authority, or a school for liberated harlings; I cannot and will not support any Gelaming influence or interference that circumvents Parsic autonomy. Parasiel is your ally, not your colony."

One of the other Hegemony hara, whose name I never did catch, spoke up then and said, "I don't understand why you're turning such a simple matter into some overblown assault on your sovereignty. If you'd put aside your stubborn, independent pride, you'd see that the bigger picture. What General Aldebaran discovered out in that wilderness is nothing short of a breakthrough for all of Wraeththu. It could be the key to ensuring the permanent success of our very race, and that should be the 'business' of everyhar."

Then Swift went into the real issue that the Gelaming cared about. I think he had been planning it all along. He said that in doing his personal investigation, looking at records, and speaking with both soldiers and harlings, he'd concluded that the Gelaming didn't have only the good of the harlings in mind when they meant to move us. "There is something that just about everyhar should have an interest in — Wraeththu procreation. But it seems to me that you want to be the hara who obtain this knowledge, to be used or distributed as you see fit. I was told, quite openly, that you want to make a study of these harlings. You're interested in genetics and special traits they might have."

I knew that of course, since Paran had said as much to me too, but then Swift went on and said that the Gelaming weren't just after the harlings, but rather the "breeding technology" that had created them. This was something that I'd suspected as well, after meeting with Sheeva. The Gelaming's hypocrisy really makes me furious. I couldn't help but cross my arms and frown.

255

"Tiahaar Lisia," Ashmael said, "you seem uncomfortable with that prospect. Do you really not think you should share what you know?"

It was like back when the administrators, Upsari chief among them, had tried to intimidate me. But this time, I didn't get scared. I said, "I have no problem explaining it, but I don't like the idea of being used! You act as if there's something wrong with me and my harlings. You attack my training and accuse the Varrs of 'breeding hara like animals,' and then you want to *copy* it?" I turned to the rest of the Hegemony. "I think we have a better plan. And, one day, it might even include sharing what I know. Do you want to hear about it?"

Suddenly, it was as if I was on stage. Everyhar was quite for a moment and then Ashmael said, "That's why we're having this meeting. Any objections to allowing tiahaar Lisia to present his case?"

Nohar had any, and after Ashmael said to Swift that he should help me explain if it was needed, I went ahead and presented my case. Let me try to remember what I said — or at least as much as I can. Even if I don't get it exactly, I'll try to get it close.

First I said that we wanted to stay in our same building. "Not only do we already have the proper accommodations in place, but it's what we're all used to. There will be great changes in the function of the facility, but many of our routines will remain the same. The classrooms, dining hall and gardens will all continue to serve us. We may need to rearrange some areas, but overall we should have enough room to accommodate new staff and the harlings as they grow."

When nohar interrupted, I continued on and said that in addition to that advantage, this would prevent any further disruption in our lives. "We can stay together and start over, and we'll be someplace safe, away from the rest of the world."

Ashmael questioned this. "Do you think it's wise to keep yourselves so isolated?"

"Oh, no, I don't mean to cut us off from the world," I explained, "only to keep us from some of its shocks." I told them how we would definitely be letting the world in. I want the harlings to learn everything they can. "Swift and I have talked," I said, "and as part of his staff recruitment, he will set up guidelines to look for instructors from various tribes. As I said before, now that I am aware of this concept of diversity I am in favor of it. After all, many of us hostlings were probably taken from other tribes, as were our instructors." It was a bit painful to recall, but I mentioned how Vlaric had come from the Serpent Hara.

"Bring in hara from other tribes?" Cedony asked. "That's an interesting concept. As you've noticed, we Gelaming have done a lot of that ourselves."

"And some of our staff may even be Gelaming," Swift added wryly.

I couldn't help but smile at that, but I got back to business. "I did notice that, tiahaar," I said, "and in part we think we'd like to emulate that. There would still mainly be Parasiel on the staff, like the local hara, but we still want to create a place that's diverse. I think that would be for the best. It will give us the maximum number of options."

"This will work well, don't you think?" Swift asked, looking around the table. "I've thought about the recruitment and think we should be able to find plenty of hara willing to go up there, especially since the situation will be explained and they'll know what they'll face. What a rewarding challenge! Also it is quite a picturesque location, so perhaps some city hara might see it as a way of getting away from the hustle and bustle."

"That's not all, however," I said, not wanting to slow down in presenting my plans. "We have to be careful about the recruitment. All the instructors will have to be qualified in specific areas and pass some basic guidelines. One of the biggest requirements I have personally is that no staff will have been former Varr soldiers."

Here I got to present a lot of the ideas I'd already told to Swift on what sort of educational program we could put together. For the older harlings, young hara, myself included, there would be some "remedial instruction," since I know perfectly well there are many areas where we had, as the Gelaming claimed, been "neglected." As for the rest of the harlings, they'll be taught the full range of what Swift said were the standard subjects — reading, writing, history, mathematics, sciences, and the like. Possibly, there will also be a way that many of them can be prepared for eventual work in useful trades, so that when they come to adulthood they could make their way in the world. I also insisted that all harlings past feybraiha would be introduced to caste training, passing up through at least the basic levels.

"And what level do you want to reach, tiahaar?" Paran asked.

"Ulani at least," I said.

To my surprise, Paran actually grinned.

And then I introduced our secret surprise. "I think some of my training would be very useful," I said. I explained my idea for the long-term future of the facility. Once all the harlings come of age, they will most likely leave and begin new lives as adults elsewhere in the world, in Megalithica or wherever they desire. In the meantime the facility could shift its purpose from being a school for harlings to being a school for adult hara.

"What do you mean, a 'school for adult hara'?" Paran asked. "What on earth would be taught?"

"I thought all you Gelaming were convinced I had so much 'special knowledge,'" I said, enjoying his confusion. "And now you think I can't teach it? Only if your Gelaming are the ones controlling it, I suppose."

Before he could interrupt me, I went on. "There are certain lessons I could teach that would be useful to other hara. Not only conception, which Swift tells me isn't necessarily easy for all hara, but hosting and of course birthing."

Those Gelaming looked pretty unhappy with me then. Swift was smiling, however. I kept on talking. "Swift and Cobweb have both told me that there hasn't been enough time for Wraeththu to amass much literature or knowledge of hosting or pearl delivery, but I think I can make up for that. I'd like to pass on what I know and if we turned the place into a school for adults, such as hara who want to be parents or train to be doctors, I could do just that. We could even teach harlingcare, and explain how harlings develop and grow."

We had quite a discussion of my ideas after that. Surprisingly, I found not all the Gelaming seemed to be against it. I think really it was just a matter of them deciding not to be selfish.

But Ashmael was not so easily convinced. "All this philosophizing and planning makes for pretty speeches, but you're forgetting one very important thing, tiahaar Swift. Your tribe simply does not possess the funds, or the means, or the organization, to support this school you've proposed, in any form. How do you plan to pay these teachers or stock supplies? Your idea is completely dependent upon further support and subsidizing from Immanion, and you've gone quite mad if you think you're going to have all this your way and give absolutely nothing in return. Keep your secluded location if you must, but I must insist that you allow us to conduct the medical and genetic research that could very well prove to be of benefit to all hara."

"Actually, I think that you are the har who has forgotten something, General,' Swift said. "When Fulminir fell, we confiscated a very large stockpile of valuable goods and wealth — ill gotten, I'm sure. Even though my first instinct was to bury it all with the rest of the rubble, Lord Thiede had a more practical suggestion. You may recall that he purchased the goods with a decent treasury account, on the condition that I administer those funds strictly to alleviate suffering imposed by the old regime. I'm sure we can all agree that caring for these abandoned harlings qualifies."

Then it was Cedony who spoke. He said, "I'm sure that will be enough to get you through the first year or two, but it'll take much more than that to implement the kind of plans you've discussed here."

"You're correct tiahaar," Swift said. "That's why I discussed the matter with the Tigrina last night. He's already quite interested in the prospect of sponsoring a series of charity events. Even if the Hegemony is unwilling to support us, I'm sure Almagabra has no shortage of comfortable hara who will feel quite good about themselves if they heap money into the coffers of the poor harlings who were mistreated by the Varrs."

I hate to admit it, but I lost track of exactly what was said after that. I was too busy wondering about the Tigrina telling Swift that he would help us! But there wasn't much more to say on either side, and before I knew it the Hegemony dismissed us, so that they could discuss the matter in private.

And so now here we are, stuck in this room and waiting. I must have sat around for a whole hour before I even started writing this. Well, maybe not that long, but it certainly seems like it. At least I had the chance to ask Swift about what he'd said regarding the Tigrina. I can't imagine why that har would help us, except that maybe it will make him seem nice to his hara. But I really wasn't sure I wanted his help and I told Swift so. I told him how I didn't like the idea of all these Gelaming having parties, where they stand around and talk about how sad and "neglected" my harlings are and discussing our business. Swift kind of laughed a bit at that and said that I don't have to worry. He said that most of the hara who participate would hardly remember what they were donating the money for in the first place. That seems hard to believe to me, but then anything is possible with these crazy Gelaming!

Swift just saw me taking out this journal and said, "Don't leave anything out, Lis, it's too important."

Well, as if I would! After all, writing down today is going to be practice to tell all the harlings back home — which is going to stay our home!

Now that all the discussion is over, it feels almost anti-climactic to write it down, but none of it happened by accident. I want to write it all out just to savor it. If victory had a taste, today would be very sweet.

It all happened so fast! A har came to bring us back to the meeting room and then Ashmael, who was still standing, looked around the table and asked if anyhar had any objection to the plan Swift and I had presented. The official vote was all in favor!

It was like we'd worked magic on them, honestly. The big, powerful Gelaming had somehow let a "neglected," "brainwashed" formerly-Varrish hostling and a "stubborn," "proud," "independent" young har interfere with their plans!

Then we had a whole discussion of budget issues. In the future, I certainly will have to pay attention to this, but I hardly want to go word for word on what was said. Mainly, Swift and Ashmael discussed what could be done with the funds from Fulminir. Ashmael cautioned Swift against over-committing resources.

One thing that's clear is that we'll never have any of the sort of luxuries back home that I've seen here in Immanion. We'll always have to conserve supplies, and share work, and probably eat "rustic" food and wear castoffs, but we'll be together — and we'll be free in a way that we didn't even know that we were missing.

And now that I stop and think about it there are other things we can do to support ourselves as well. We've always done a lot of knitting and sewing. What if we made goods to trade? The administrators did that and I think we could too. I can make wonderful blankets and sweaters. A lot of the older harlings are already trained as well. It's not hard work, but even doing it part time, there are enough of us that we could come up with a decent stream of goods for trade. Plus, it will be an excellent opportunity for the harlings to visit towns and learn first-hand about the outside world. I'll definitely have to talk to Swift about this later. I'm glad I've written it down so I won't forget.

On the subject of things I don't want to forget, one more thing happened before the Hegemony dismissed us again. Chrysm said something that I need to remember.

"Lisia, I know that you have misgivings about outside hara coming in and changing the way that the harlings behave," he said. "But, I really think that, in addition to teachers, you should have some counselors on hand."

I frowned at this, but he continued in his gentle tone. "As they learn more about the outside world and come to understand what happened there, the harlings and young hara are surely going to be confused and possibly resentful. It wouldn't be fair to expect academic teachers to handle the reactions alone. Counselors could go a long way towards helping them cope and have healthy futures."

I knew that he meant well, but I still wasn't happy with his suggestion. "Well, as the hostling, I think that calming their reactions is my job," I said.

But then Swift put his hand on my arm and said, "I think Chrysm makes a good point." He told me that while I'll be the most important person that the harlings come to with their questions and anxieties, I will probably need help. "You can't be there for each of them all the time."

I thought about it and suddenly it sounded all right. I told them all that counselors sounded like a reasonable thing and thanked Chrysm for the suggestion.

Tonight, as a celebration of our victory today, Swift took me to a very nice place to have dinner away from the palace. It wasn't like the tavern at all. This place was beautiful but in a way that wasn't as grand as Phaonica. And it was right over the harbor, so we could watch the water in the moonlight. I could even smell the salt and hear the waves! To eat we had many different types of seafood, which hara brought out on big platters. It seemed almost obscene to have so much more food than we could possibly eat, but I was glad because I'd never had this type of food before and I was able to try different things and find out what I liked.

It wasn't all fun, though. Swift wanted to discuss some important things about our school that he didn't want to say in front of the Hegemony. "It's important for us to deal with the residue of the past," he said, "and to make sure your school presents only a minimal burden on the Parasiel government." He paused to take a sip of water from a glass that had been poured by a serving har. "I know that we both agree that the days of mass pearl production are over. But I have to go a step further and ask that no pearls be produced for at least the next seven years."

By that time all the harlings will have matured. He also said that if any pearls are produced, the resulting harlings will be the sole responsibility of hostling and father, to be raised as part of a family, not as simply another resident harling. The Parasiel government will not support those harlings, because he doesn't want to "create a permanent cycle of dependency."

I sat through this speech without saying a thing. Once Swift was done, I said quietly, "This has been one of the most difficult issues for me personally. I understand why such rules are necessary but it's still hard to imagine life without constant rounds of new harlings or, more to the point, constant hostings and births. I won't be passing my aruna training on to any of the harlings unless they ask. After all, nohar really wants to be a 'breeding machine,' as your hostling called it."

"True, although you wanted that, Lis," Swift said.

I nodded. "Yes, but I wasn't given any other option. My harlings will have a whole world of choices."

By the time we had our wonderful dessert (chocolate!), we were back to talking about things that were happier. I told him about my idea for the harlings and I to sell our knitting and sewing. On top of that, I suddenly had an idea about having livestock, not only to eat (chickens and cows) but for the knitting — we could raise sheep for their wool! He thought that it was an excellent idea and told me lots of hara around Galhea would be able to help us get started. "You'd probably be good at breeding the animals," he said, "ironic as it sounds." I'm not sure how similar delivering baby cows or sheep would be to delivering pearls but I guess I will have to investigate. Selling livestock could make us a good bit of money over time, Swift said.

I thought of something suddenly. I think the first thing that we'll do with the money we raise for ourselves is to erect a memorial to the hostlings who gave their lives by staying behind to care for the harlings. I just know the older harlings will think it's a beautiful gesture.

It's been a whole day since the big decision was made. The Gelaming totally back the new plan and all day they've been organizing things to help us once we return back home. I'm quite tired out from it actually, but we're leaving tomorrow morning, so by then it will be all arranged. I know I have a lot of years of work ahead of me, but really it's almost like there isn't anything to worry about. As long as I'm not being used or told what to do, it's all fine with me.

The big news today wasn't any plans we made for the school, however, but what Sheeva did for Two. I am truly amazed with what Gelaming healers are able to do. Two didn't even cry when they "reset" his hip! He was given a cup of some sleeping medicine and then when he was nearly asleep, a group of healers knelt around him and formed what they called a "circle of calm." Even in his sleep, Two wouldn't feel any pain. Sheeva and another har did the actual work on the hip and while I hated to know what was happening, they finished very quickly and immediately concentrated on healing him. I could almost feel what they were doing; their power was so strong. Finally, after what must have been a couple of hours, Sheeva looked up and said, "It is done."

Two was asleep for the rest of the afternoon. I sat in the room with him. He looked completely peaceful. When he started to stir, I worried about how things would be, but everything was perfect. He simply woke up and after a moment said, "Am I better?"

Sheeva was there in the room and explained that while he might be sore, the hip was in the right place. "See for yourself," he said.

Two sat up on the bed and smiled, then slid off and walked over to my chair. "Lis, he fixed it!" Then he went up to Sheeva and hugged him around the legs.

Chapter Fourteen

I'm back home and happy beyond my wildest dreams. What a homecoming we had. We arrived in the back meadow at mid-morning and as we rode the *sedim* over to the stables, harlings ran over to us calling out, "What happened? What happened?"

I didn't answer them, but waited until we'd all come down from the horses — and unstrapped our travel packs, which were heavy with gifts and special supplies from Immanion. By that time there was quite a crowd, mainly Lilies. I made my announcement. "I'm pleased to tell you that we're going to be starting a new life — right here in our old home! We get to stay!"

Everyhar cheered and then, all at once, the whole crowd of harlings rushed up to me like a swarm of bees, only instead of attacking, they kissed and hugged me. "We love you, Lis!" and "Thank you, Lis!" and "Thank you, Lord Swift!" was what they were all saying. My eyes filled up with tears, I could hardly handle all that. Overwhelming!

After a couple of minutes of this, Pansea was at my side talking about how I had to go over to the dining hall to see something. I said I just wanted to put my things back in my room but he was insistent I go right away. "There's something we've been wanting to do and while you were gone, we decided to do it."

"Do what?" I asked.

"Just come!" Tilithia urged. He took my hand and starting pulling me towards the building. "You have to see it!"

So I shrugged and went along with it, letting the crowd escort me inside. Once I got to the hallway, I saw immediately that every harling in the facility was packed inside. Even the smallest harlings were there, and Two actually ran up to his lings to hug them.

I was still out in the hallway. "What's going on?" I asked.

Those harlings are devious though, and wouldn't tell me. "You'll see," Tilithia said, and gestured to Pansea, who had stepped behind me. "Or rather, you *won't* see," Tilithia added.

Then Pansea clamped his hands over my eyes!

I started to get nervous. "Pansea, what are you doing?" I sputtered. I knew it couldn't be bad, but I'm not sure how I feel about surprises.

Well, this was the best surprise the harlings could have thought of. It was a mural. The day after I left, all the harlings had been drawing pictures to give me, Pansea explained, and then he and the older harlings decided that they could all make a picture together as a kind of present. But it was Cobweb who'd had the idea to paint a mural in the dining hall and all the harlings were happy to join in the task. Gathering up all the paint they had remaining, and with some assistance from a few of the village hara, they'd gone ahead and made me a gift that would last a long time.

I saw some truly breathtaking art in Immanion, but this mural is the sweetest thing I've ever seen. It's a scene of happiness. There are crowds of smiling harlings and behind them smiling hara, hostlings with long hair and skirts, some of them (even me, I saw a har with striped hair) holding knitted sweaters. One of the hara is dancing. Everyhar in the mural is standing in a field of pink and yellow flowers by a big brick building — our home. Above everything, floating in the big blue sky, are words in white, written as clouds: "Harling Gardens: A Happy Family."

"That's our new name for this place!" Pansea explained. "Harling Gardens! Tiahaar Cobweb thought of it — isn't it just perfect?"

I couldn't help but burst into tears again, tears of joy. I told them all it's a beautiful name (we never had a name for home before!) and thanked them all over and over. But they wouldn't have me thanking them, and once again rushed up to me with the kisses and hugs.

Off to the side, I saw Swift and Cobweb looking on and smiling, evidently as happy with the turn of events as I am. And I also saw that way back behind everyhar else Paran and Edrei were reuniting; they were sharing breath quite enthusiastically. It hadn't even really dawned on me that they liked each other!

I'm in my room and, unlike how it's been for months and months, I've got the luxury of being able to write without worrying. Of course, at the moment I wouldn't have this opportunity if it weren't for the harlings, since it was Pansea who told me I should take some time off and have a nap. I looked tired, he said. I almost laughed because I certainly am tired, but I didn't want to have to explain why exactly. In fact, I don't even want to explain it here, not right now, because who knows, I could be interrupted and I want to write it out all at once, probably tonight.

Today was an important day. I was officially put in charge of Harling Gardens to be the "principal" of our new school. We'll be starting up a whole new life here and from now on we will be in charge of everything, making our own decisions. Well, not *all* our own decisions, since we'll be getting help and there will be other staff and teachers, but now we'll be able to make our lives better and better. I'm so excited to have this chance after all that's happened. I'm sure there will be a lot of work and times of trouble, but already it feels better to me, much better.

As soon as my official "appointment" was completed, Swift and Cobweb left for Galhea. I imagine Swift's consort Seel has been missing him, as he was away for almost a week. And I know that Swift and Cobweb both miss their harlings, Azriel and Tyson. I'm sure they're already home and busy moving on to all the other business of the Parasiel. Or maybe they're taking a break to enjoy *Forever.* I keep imagining what that house must be like. Swift and Cobweb both told me so much about it and it sounds beautiful, something very special. Swift says that probably I'll be traveling to Galhea in a few months and he invited me to stay with him. Of course Cobweb put out an invitation as well.

As I was saying, though, today was an important day. One thing that happened was that I had a long talk with Paran and Edrei. I'd talked lots with them already, but there were still a few details to work out. Anyway, what Paran wanted to talk to me about had to do with what he called "crimes against Wraeththu." He said they used to call this "crimes against humanity" but of course in this case, that wasn't appropriate. He explained to me that General Aldebaran has already sent out directives among the Gelaming and Parasiel armies to hunt for the administrators, teachers and even some of the hostlings, not to bring them back here, but so that the "war crimes" tribunals can hold a trial and "hold them accountable."

I asked Paran exactly what he meant by that and he said that depending on what could be proved of their guilt, the administrators would be punished. I asked him about the teachers, and whether they'd be punished too, and he said that would depend on their guilt, whether or not they did things willingly or whether they were forced. Then I asked why they would want to find the hostlings and he said it was so they could give evidence. I told him I didn't think any of the hostlings would be willing to speak out. Most of them, if they survived, are probably hiding or don't want to talk about what we went through. Paran agreed that this was true but he said they'll try anyway. He doesn't know if they'll find any of them. For me, it's too early to know exactly what I think of this. I know I hate what they did to us, but according to what Swift told me about Varrs like Ponclast, I think maybe they didn't have much choice. I suppose that's something to be decided in the trial, if it ever happens.

There was one other unhappy matter I discussed with him, and that was the fact of the other facilities, where they had sent the harlings to be trained for the military. Edrei told me he knows I don't want to even think about this, but he said he needed to know if I had any more information. On their very first day here, they'd sent out an alert throughout Megalithica for hara to pay attention to any clues about where this facility might be located so that the harlings could be rescued, he said.

I told him I didn't know anything at all about it and didn't want to. The idea of those harlings makes me frightened and sad, the way I used to be, only worse because now I know more and it's horrible. I know most of those harlings probably didn't have good lives. Probably they didn't even make it into the military, which means they weren't killed in battle, but I know they probably weren't much cared for or loved. I told Edrei I hoped they could find something and maybe do some good, but I don't think I have much hope. And then Edrei mentioned something that I hadn't thought of — he said that if those harlings are found, there's a good chance that Swift will send them here to be cared for by me. He warned me not to count on that, since there's no way of knowing whether the harlings will ever be found, but I am so hopeful about the prospect that one day I might have all the harlings back here together.

After some more discussion, they said they were ready to leave, along with the rest of Gelaming troops. From now on, everyhar here will be Parasiel or part of the Harling Gardens staff. But before they left, I had another little surprise. Paran had gone out, presumably on some last errand, while Edrei and I were talking about the other harlings, but when he came back he had a box that was all wrapped up in pretty paper. It was a gift for me! I opened it slowly, not wanting to ruin the pretty paper, and inside the box was one of those wonderful lamps just like I'd had in my room in Immanion! I was so shocked, as I'd never expected Paran to want to give me anything, especially something so wonderful. I thanked him over and over, but Paran just shrugged it all off. "You kept raving about the lamp in your room when we were in Immanion. We've got plenty of them and I figure it would do you more good, since I expect you're going to be working late into the night on a regular basis."

I just smiled then, and I said that I hoped one day I could do something good for them in return. Edrei said that would be nice but he doubted we'd ever see each other again. I just kind of laughed then I said, "You never know, maybe you'll decide to come back — like once I open my pearl school for couples."

Edrei's mouth dropped open a bit and Paran looked like he was going to be absolutely ill at the thought! I was actually sad to see them go in a way, since I'd seen them change so much, until finally they had real sympathy for me. It's part of the learning I need to do. Hara aren't always the way you think they will be.

That's actually the last thing I want to write about. After everything that's happened since the Gelaming arrived, I can tell that I have a lot of learning to do. In the past, there was so much I didn't know that I made decisions that were wrong, especially when it came to other hara. I had come to really hate the Gelaming and so when they arrived, I blamed them and I fought so much with Ashmael and Paran, but it was only because we didn't understand one another. Fortunately, now things won't be hidden from me anymore and I'll get the kind of honesty I need.

Finally the day is over and I'm alone in my room. All the harlings and everyhar else are in bed. I won't be interrupted. I won't be rushed. Instead I will think about what I was doing just twenty-four hours ago. Or maybe I should go back even further than that, to show how it happened exactly.

We spent most of yesterday getting things organized. Swift was coordinating with his soldiers and we were working out things with the local hara, some of whom have decided to stay here long-term. There was so much to be done and although I managed it, I was in a daze the entire time, once again overwhelmed by how everything has turned out.

Maybe it's because I was in such a daze that things happened the way they did. All afternoon, I'd been taking care of various things all over, and was so wrapped up in everything I was surprised to hear the third bell ringing for dinner. I went into the dining hall expecting to find Swift and Cobweb, perhaps with Edrei and Paran, waiting at a table for me. Instead there was only Cobweb.

He was wearing that beautiful silk blouse of his, along with some light green pants I hadn't seen before. Wondering why he'd decided to change his clothes, I walked up to him and said hello. He smiled at me and I noticed his manner was different than it had been before. He was friendly, which he had been all along (except for when we first met), but now he was also alluring. Beautiful. I felt like I had never seen beauty before and for a moment, I thought "I'm bewitched."

I smiled at him briefly before I went over to the front to pick up my dinner. I came back to the table as quickly as I could because — well, I don't know why really, except I felt like he expected me to. The whole time I was getting my food and coming back to the table and then finally sitting down, Cobweb was looking at me. Then he started talking — telling me that Swift had eaten earlier and that we'd be dining alone. I nodded and started to eat, said something or other, keeping on eating, but then I started feeling uneasy with the way Cobweb was still looking at me. He hadn't touched his food at all, even though it had been on the table since I arrived. Finally I asked, "Aren't you hungry?"

I'll never forget his reply: "Yes. Aren't you?" He wasn't talking about food.

As soon as he said that, I knew that something unbelievable was happening. Cobweb, the most famous Varr consort who we used to always hear stories about, quite incredibly, was trying to seduce me! My mind went into a whirl. He's so beautiful and yet how could he possibly be serious? Why would he be interested in me? I'm not anything special. I don't even have a caste level. Then I started wondering what he wanted with me. If he wanted aruna with me, would he be soume? Or was he going to be ouana?

Quite fortunately, I never actually had to ask any of these questions. Cobweb is very gifted when it comes to reading minds. He told me I will need to learn how to guard my thoughts, but since right now I don't know how, he was able to hear all my confusion and questions and using that, he said just the right things.

He spoke to me softly as I ate and told me he had been thinking about me. He wanted to do something for me. He said a lot of things then. He said he knew I didn't think I was beautiful, but I really was. I was also the most soume har he'd ever met, although he was convinced being soume isn't something that's come to me completely naturally. Every har is ouana at least once, he said. In comparison to me, Cobweb said he felt almost ouana himself, although he's very far from it. What he wanted to do, he told me, was not only have aruna with me, which he wanted to anyway, but give me a gift by letting me do what I'd never done.

I was stunned, of course. I just couldn't believe what he was saying. Was I dreaming? I could taste the food as I chewed it and looked at Cobweb, who seemed solid enough. It was real. "Are you interested?" he asked me. He actually asked me that! And I actually said yes.

Soon we were going up to my room. Cobweb admitted he'd really eaten earlier and had only been in the dining hall to meet with me. He's a sly one, just like the stories we used to hear.

On the walk up the stairs, my heart was pounding in my chest like a hammer and my head was spinning. I felt so intimidated by the idea of what I was going to be doing and who I was going to be doing it with. I didn't know if I'd be able to do it, no matter how seductive he was or all the nice things he said.

Finally, though, we got to the lounge and then suddenly, the spell was broken.

All at once, I felt I was back in the old routine. Aruna. It wasn't something alien to me. It would be with Cobweb, but how different could it really be? I've had lots of aruna with lots of different hara. It was a routine. If anything, this would be like my training right after my feybraiha. I wasn't so intimidated by any of it. This was just something I had to do, like I said, the old routine.

I led us to my room and ushered him inside. "Just make yourself comfortable," I told him, gesturing over to the bed. How many times had I delivered that line? It was part of the routine.

Cobweb went over to the bed, while I went to the mirror to have a look at myself. I've lost so much weight, I really don't look half as good as I used to, but I couldn't change that, only time could change that. So I took the barrettes out of my hair, brushed it out, and straightened out the collar on my blouse, smoothed my skirt. It would have to do, even though for somehar like Cobweb, I really would have liked to look nicer.

Finally I turned back to Cobweb, thinking he'd either be sitting on the bed or already lying down waiting for me. He wasn't. He was standing there looking at me. He had a strange look in his eyes, so I asked him if he was comfortable. He didn't answer me, but instead came up to me and took my hands in his. "Lisia," he said to me, "this is not going to be the routine."

He knew exactly what I'd been thinking! I was so surprised, I backed up, bumping into the dresser. "What do you mean?" I asked him.

He frowned a little and gestured around. "This room, Lisia. It's where you conceived all your pearls, isn't it?"

I stared at him. I didn't want to think about that. Still, I told him that yes, it was the same room, same bed.

Then he said, "I thought so."

I didn't know what to say, so I waited for him to continue.

Finally he said, "Well, that won't do, now will it? I want this to be special."

That did it. Suddenly I knew why I'd become so uneasy. It was the word "special" that did it. That was what Vlaric had always called our aruna: special. And that's what I'd believed — until I'd found out I wasn't special at all. To Cobweb's surprise, I said, "Oh, special, you say? Well I used to have 'special' aruna in the potting shed too, with one of my teachers. We used to do it while I was hosting, so I wouldn't conceive by accident."

"You sound bitter," Cobweb said, frowning in a way that was very sympathetic and understanding. "What happened, Lis?"

I broke away from him and went over to the window, where I looked out into the dark night. "I thought I was something 'special' and it felt so different — not like anything else I'd ever had before." I don't know why I decided to talk about Vlaric, other than that I really do trust Cobweb. Except in this diary I had never told anyhar about it before. "He... told me he loved me and I thought out of all the hostlings and everyhar else he had picked just me and it made me feel so wonderful. I didn't care anymore about anything and I was so happy. Then I found out he had lied to me." I looked back to where Cobweb was still standing. "He was sharing this 'special' aruna with other hostlings too, even though he acted like it was just me. And I can't stand to be lied to, played with!"

This was when Cobweb said something that changed everything. With a calm voice he said, "I know you have little reason to trust me or anyhar else, but please try to believe that I'm not playing with you. All I want to do tonight is have a night of pleasure and possibly some learning. Nothing more, nothing less. I'm not trying to hurt you or get something from you. I want to do something good for you. I want to love you. Just tonight."

The way he said it made me tingle all over and then I felt like I was melting. Cobweb put his arm around me and sat me down on the bed before going on. "Now, Lisia, you just wait here. We don't need to go so fast, so first I'm going to my own room to get ready. I think my room would be better anyway. I'll call you when I want you over." Then he leaned forward and for the briefest moment he pressed his lips to mine in the sharing of breath. In that moment I knew that what he'd told me was true and that he wasn't lying. It was a magic moment. As soon as he drew back my heart started pounding all over again. Before I could even say anything he went out the door and down the hall.

I felt so strange and mixed up. It seemed like Cobweb was really making a fuss over me. What had I done to deserve it? Nohar had ever told me I had to wait while they got ready. The soldiers would talk, but mostly we decided to share aruna and then just did it. That was the routine — the routine Cobweb was apparently trying to break.

I went back to the mirror. Since I now had more time to prepare myself, I decided maybe I should actually dress up, with makeup and jewelry and a change of clothes. I knew right away what I wanted to wear. In fact it was already on top of the dresser, since Tilithia has just given it back to me, freshly washed: my beautiful white feybraiha dress.

I closed the door, which Cobweb had left open, and then I changed. What a lovely dress that is. I hated it for a long time, because it reminded me of how the doctors didn't tell me the truth about deliveries, but despite that I've always really admired it. I decided to go all out and use my silver hairpins and a little makeup. It had been a really long time since I had aruna or made myself beautiful the way I used to. I looked at myself in the mirror. There I was, Lisia, mostly just how I remembered.

My timing was perfect because just as soon as I was ready, I knew it was time to go to Cobweb's room. I say "knew" because suddenly I got a call from Cobweb — in my head! It was just like Chrysm had done at the reception in Immanion. I was surprised, but at the same time, I liked it.

Actually I can't wait to can learn how to do that. It seems like it could be very useful. Imagine if I'd been able to call the doctors when it was time for my pearls! We would never have had to have hara running around for help and we hostlings could even have called one another when it had happened in the middle of the night.

Anyway, I suddenly knew it was time to go, so I opened the door and went out into the hall. I knocked on Cobweb's door and in my head, I received a message: Open. I stepped inside.

I was amazed by what I saw. In only ten minutes, Cobweb had transformed not only himself, but the entire room. He'd lit a long, white candle and beside it smoke curled out from a little dish of incense. It smelled like a mix of cinnamon and some sort of wonderful wood, a sort of magic forest smell.

Then there was Cobweb. He hadn't changed his clothes, but he had changed the way he was wearing them. He had unbuttoned his blouse way down the front and had undone the bottom buttons as well, so that only the two in the middle were holding it closed. His pale skin glowed like the moon, and I caught a glimpse of the lightest sheen of fur running down under the waist of his trousers. He had taken off his shoes and I saw he had silver rings on his toes. He was waiting for me, lying there. On his face was the most sensual expression. His eyes were lined in kohl, his mouth turned up in a lazy, closed-lipped smile.

For a few moments, my heart pounded hard in my chest.

His expression didn't change at all, but he glanced over to the door and gestured for me to shut it behind me. I did. Then he curled his fingers seductively, gesturing for me to come closer.

"You look wonderful," he said to me. "That dress is lovely, most becoming on you, well suited. So pure and innocent."

"It was given to me the day of my feybraiha."

"Ah," he said at once, "then it's perfect for the occasion." Again he gestured for me to come closer. "Come, Lisia, sit." He patted the space next to him on the bed.

I did as he said, using every ounce of grace, sitting down sideways facing him. Cobweb had captured me with his eyes.

"Tonight will be a second feybraiha for you," he said, and when he said that, I knew he was right. That was why I had picked the dress, I think. How did Cobweb know?

At that moment, I felt so young beside him. It would be up to him to guide me.

"Now, Lisia, first, although it's very lovely, I'd like you to take off your dress." This was not an order, but a suggestion. His voice was soft. He was the most beautiful hostling I had ever seen.

I stood up, turning away, and I carefully unbuttoned the buttons and let the dress fall to the floor. Inside me, I was feeling more and more ready for aruna. The air seemed thicker, heavier with smoke and that wonderful forest scent.

"Turn around to face me again," Cobweb said, and so I did.

His expression no longer looked quite so sensual. Instead he looked mildly amused. I didn't know why, not at first.

"Lisia, you should know that our plans aren't going to work that way." His eyes were fixed on a spot below my waist. I looked down and of course I had become soume, just as I always do when I think about aruna. Suddenly, I realized the source of Cobweb's amusement. I was embarrassed and felt my face start to grow hot.

Before it could get too bad, though, Cobweb reached out and put his hand around my forearm. "It's all right, Lisia. I can change that."

I didn't have any idea what he meant. What was he going to do to me? I should have known.

"Look at me," he said staring into my eyes. He needn't have spoken since there was no way I could get away from those bewitching eyes of his — I didn't want to, because inside my head, he was calling me to him and more than that, he was telling me just what he wanted in our aruna. Mind to mind, he told me everything. He wanted to be soume — "water" to my "fire," the images were. "Look at me," he said again, and then as I stared at that beautiful creature, I felt it happen, and it was almost like opening my seal, only it was something else entirely. My ouana-lim came alive!

It was such magic. I'm sure Cobweb has secret powers I never learned about, because at that moment, I wanted him. He was more beautiful even than ever before and inside, I felt like I had to do something about it, to do what he wanted. I was going to give myself to him.

With his mind Cobweb signaled me what to do next and so I got up on my knees and straddled him. His hands came up around my ouana-lim and he began to tease it, stroke it. He knew exactly what he was doing, and I know because I've done it myself, seduced a har, but I swear he was almost better at it than I am. In just a short time, throughout my entire body, I felt the strongest feelings of desire. It was almost like pain to feel what I was feeling, like coming into a warm house after being out in the freezing cold, the flesh hurting from the change as it heats up. I was heating up just like that.

He pulled me to him and we began to share breath. What an immense soul he has, so much bigger than my own. As we mixed together, I felt a spirit different from any I had ever felt before. He wasn't there to father pearls. He wasn't a soldier. In a way, he was a teacher, but he wasn't one of my instructors. He wasn't even like Vlaric, who I thought had loved me. Cobweb was different from all of them. So very powerful and more, he was sharing that power with me, filling me up with strength.

One of his hands massaged the back of my head, while the other continued touching my ouana-lim, so that finally I felt myself signaled and I drew away to look Cobweb in the eyes. *I will be fire,* I thought to him inside my head, hoping he could hear me even without the sharing of breath. I unfastened the last two buttons on his shirt without even looking and then I tugged down his trousers. When they were half way down, he wriggled out of them and wrapped his legs around my waist.

The moment had come and the ice had melted. I was heated through and through with wild desire. I sank into his soume-lam and it was beyond what I could ever have dreamed — far beyond that dream I had those years ago about Calla, the one I thought was so terrible. I felt him all around me, his heat, as we drew closer and closer, and I moved within him as he moved about me. I knew how he must have felt, knew what it was he was doing with his muscles, because I had done it myself and it was strange and wonderful because it was so different, feeling it from the other side.

The sensations were overwhelming and it was difficult for me to concentrate on what I was doing, as I knew I must. I had never done this thing and I know I wasn't doing everything exactly right. I didn't know exactly how to move, although I tried my best, remembering what I enjoyed from a ouana myself and of course sensing what Cobweb wanted, letting him lead me up and up and up. Finally we both reached the point of no return and our souls entwined, our lips and bodies locked together, we spasmed against one another and I felt myself release amidst a furious roar of ecstasy.

Cobweb was replete, and so was I. We held on to one another for minutes, seemingly for hours, still as one body, breathing in unison, energy and happiness washing between us.

Finally I heard him moan, not in pain, but in satisfaction. "Lisia..." he continued, pushing my shoulders gently back, "Lisia, you did it."

I slipped out from inside him and let myself shift over so my weight was off his middle. "Yes, I did," I said softly, proud of myself. "I can hardly believe it."

"Believe it, Lisia," he assured me. "Not bad at all, was it?"

I laughed and shook my head. "No, not at all." I rolled onto my side. "I can't say whether I like it better, since it seemed a lot of work, but it's not bad. All my life I've been taught being ouana is bad for me, but it doesn't seem even a question now. It seems to be a matter more of preferences."

I looked up at Cobweb's face. He was glowing and seemed quite happy. "I'm glad I could help you, Lisia," he said. "I just thought that if anyhar could, I could." He turned onto his side to face me and pulled me to him, wrapping his legs around me again so we were snuggled together, close enough that we ended up sharing breath again. And again.

After that we talked for a long time, quietly, about all sorts of things. He asked me about my aruna training and I explained to him how I had been taught and even about how I could open my seal, the "cauldron of creation," as the Gelaming call it. I was surprised when he asked me about the feeling of conception, but I told him about it. He said he remembered conceiving Swift and how to him it was like he'd been taken to another world. He didn't know what had happened, but it was the most incredible aruna of his life. I told him I knew just what he meant.

I think we must have talked at least another hour before we got back to aruna again. We began by sharing breath and then, without even thinking about it, I began to touch his ouana-lim. As it turned out, he wanted me and I could not resist him so I let him enter into me. There was a worry that flared in me for a moment, that he would open me up and plant a pearl in me, but it was a silly worry, because I knew Cobweb would never do that to me without me wishing it, and I certainly was not going to open my seal. Self-control works both ways, and so I took him inside just as he had taken me and I loved every last second of it, right up until the end when he bloomed inside of me and I saw a thousand colors.

Some things, some hara, I will never forget. That night of aruna is one of them. Cobweb is another. I thanked him over and over, but I want to say it here again: Thank you, Cobweb, for the gift you gave me, my second feybraiha.

I've been so busy with organizing Harling Gardens that I haven't had a chance to write in this diary for weeks. But today I insisted on taking a little time for it again. In fact this is going to be my very last entry in this particular journal ever.

Things have been busy, as I said. We've finally got it to where all the harlings are in classes and not doing any work anymore except a few personal chores now and then. We've got many of our staff but some of the most important teachers and counselors are still being interviewed. That's what I was doing today, in fact. Cobweb sent a group of them here from Galhea today for me to meet. He's been a wonderful help in all of this. It turns out that Cobweb knows how to do a lot more than just be a consort and take care of harlings. He knows how to organize and how judge the best hara. And it was his idea to screen new instructors for me. I'd told him how I was uncomfortable about too many hara finding out that we're here, because I didn't want anyhar coming uninvited and giving my harlings more distractions. Before he left here, he said that he knew a har back home who was good at both teaching and being discreet. He said that together they would quietly find the right hara and then send them to me.

I've been very grateful. And today when the latest teachers arrived, one of them had a package that Cobweb had sent especially for me. Inside was a beautiful book with blank lined pages and bound in a lovely tanned leather. Inside the cover was an inscription from Cobweb. He wrote that he'd seen the book in a shop and its rich color reminded him of me right away and it occurred to him that I should have a journal worthy of my thoughts and experiences. It's fitting I think — a new diary in which to document my new life. And both are beautiful.

Fulfillments of Fate and Desire

The third volume in the original Wraeththu Trilogy, this new expanded edition continues the story begun in 'Enchantments of Flesh and Spirit' and 'Bewitchments of Love and Hate'.

Cal, a pivotal figure from the previous books is lost and wandering in the northern wastes of Almagabra, fears he is being pursued by a dark presence from his past.

After escaping from a brothel with Panthera, a stunning but emotionally scared har, Cal's journey long becomes a rite of passage, as he travels through the land of Jaddayoth. His path leads him always towards Immanion, the mystical city, where his old lover Pellaz rules and the mysterious Thiede waits to pull all the threads of his plan together.

November 2003

ISBN:
0-9545-0362-7

Wendy Darling & Bridgette M Parker

Hermetech

Hermetech or hermetechs n. the science of orgasmic energy potential, esp. within fixed unit (within time, space), adj. of or relating to properties of orgasmic energy [C20, Gk L of Hermes traditionally inventor of magic seal]

A near future Earth is dying due to human interference; Tech-Green is doing its best to repair the damage and is insisting that mankind leaves the planet to give it time to heal.

Ari Famber, is the result of a genetic experiment she knows nothing about. Leila Saatchi, a friend of Ari's dead father, has promised to find her and protect her from others who may seek to use Ari for their own ends.

This stunning mix of Science and Mysticism is once again being published in this new Immanion Press Edition.

March 2004

ISBN 0-9545-0364-3

Wraiths of Will and Pleasure (Revised Special Edition)

The start of a new trilogy, returning once again to the Wraeththu world, the first Book of the Wraeththu Histories is expanded to include extra appendices in this all new UK edition.

As Pellaz fulfills his destiny and Thiede extends his influence over the world, a child is born to the Kakkahaar tribe in the desert of Megalithica. Lileem is different from any who has come before and has a long journey ahead to discover more about what it means to be Wraeththu.

A new future is being carved, old enemies meet once again, uncertain of their past actions. All Wraeththu must come together, but can those supposedly in charge, forgive past grievances and begin again anew?

New extras include appendices on the Wraeththu magical systems and the dehara, the gods of Wraeththu.

Februarry 2004

ISBN 0-9545-0365-1

Wendy Darling & Bridgette M Parker

Wraeththu
From Enchantment to Fulfilment

By Gabriel Strange, Storm Constantine & Lydia Wood

In the future, the world as we know it has changed. Humankind is in decline and a new hermaphrodite race has arisen from the ashes. Insanity, disease and infertility comprise the Achilles' Heel of the doomed human race. Why these problems are on the increase is unknown: all that is known is that humankind has only a few years left to walk the earth.

In this new role-playing game, take on the role of an androgynous Wraeththu 'har' within a world where a dying race is struggling to survive. You can transform humans into hara like yourself through the procedure of Inception. But what will happen when all the humans have gone? There are many myths and legends about how the Wraeththu can reproduce, but are they true or simply folk tales? How will you master your new mystical powers?

Based upon Storm Constantine's internationally selling Wraeththu trilogy, which is soon to be followed by three new books in the series, as well as a multitude of other materials to bolster and expand upon the Wraeththu Mythos, this publication is the first of many books to explore the Wraeththu Mythos in a role-playing format. You are taken inside the world of the story and become one of the hara themselves, thrown into a world in turmoil and despair. The scales have been tipped: the human race knows it is doomed and that the Wraeththu are the heirs of the Earth.

*Whether you're a hardened role-player or beginner this game is for you, many things that have never been explained completely in the 'Wraeththu Mythos' books, comes to life with additional information and descriptions in the first volume of the **Wraeththu RPG**.*

http://www.immanionpress.wox.org/storm/

Printed in the United Kingdom
by Lightning Source UK Ltd.
9683800001B/1-24